THE GREAT AWAKENINGS

1857-1858

PROOF

HOWARD
Fiction

BILL BRIGHT &
JACK CAVANAUGH

Our purpose at Howard Publishing is to:
- *Increase faith* in the hearts of growing Christians
- *Inspire holiness* in the lives of believers
- *Instill hope* in the hearts of struggling people everywhere
Because He's coming again!

Proof © 2005 by Bright Media Foundation and Jack Cavanaugh
All rights reserved. Printed in the United States of America
Published by Howard Publishing Co., Inc.
3117 North 7th Street, West Monroe, Louisiana 71291-2227
www.howardpublishing.com
In association with Steve Laube/The Literary Group

05 06 07 08 09 10 11 12 13 14   10 9 8 7 6 5 4 3 2 1

Edited by Ramona Cramer Tucker
Interior design by Tennille Paden
Cover design by Kirk DouPonce

Library of Congress Cataloging-in Publishing Data

Bright Bill
    Proof / Bill Bright & Jack Cavanaugh.
        p. cm.
    ISBN 1-58229-437-2
    1. Revivals—Fiction. 2. Missionaries—Fiction. 3. Prayer meetings—Fiction. 4. New York
(N. Y.) —Fiction. 5. Holland Reformed Church—Fiction. I. Cavanaugh, Jack. II. Title.

PS3552.R4623P76 2005
813'.6—dc22

2005040213

Scripture quotations are taken from The Holy Bible, Authorized King James Version, public domain.

DEDICATION

To Jeremiah C. Lanphier and the other six believers

who gathered for prayer on September 23, 1857,

believing that God would answer their prayers for revival.

FOREWORD
BY MRS. BILL BRIGHT (VONETTE)

In addition to our Lord Jesus Christ and his loving family, Bill Bright had two great passions in life: (1) helping to fulfill the Great Commission and (2) encouraging spiritual awakening and revival in America and in the world.

Bill fasted and prayed for many years that these two passions would see fulfillment. In each of his last nine years, he fasted for forty days, praying and yearning for the revival he believed to be coming.

The condition of the world and its need for repentance and faith in our Savior gripped his heart. He was burdened by the pervasive sin and people's hurts that he saw. Yet he believed in the power of fervent prayer and that God Himself does, indeed, long to send revival and grant mercy in response to the fervent pleadings of His people.

Beginning in 1994, Bill sponsored annual, nationwide fasting and prayer gatherings, bringing together thousands of Christian leaders and laypeople. In his 1995 book, *The Coming Revival,* Bill wrote, "I invite you to join me in praying that God will continue to use this fasting and prayer gathering as a spark to help set ablaze the Body of Christ in this most urgent and critical moment of history for our beloved nation and for the Church of our Lord Jesus Christ around the world." That would still be his plea today.

Bill promoted fasting and prayer for spiritual awakening and revival for many years. In fact, he immediately donated every dollar of the full one million dollar prize he received with the 1996 Templeton Award in order to promote the movement worldwide. He once remarked that he was "the briefest millionaire in history."

With declining health due to pulmonary fibrosis, which finally took his life in 2003, and knowing that his time was short, Bill teamed up with Jack Cavanaugh to create a series of novels that would be set in American history during times of revival. He knew the books would probably not be published while he was alive.

These novels portray Christians "who were great believers, great hopers, great doers, and great sufferers," using his own words. Those attributes characterized his own life, and he recognized and admired the qualities in others.

Bill prayed every day that revival would sweep across our land, and I choose to believe he intercedes for our nation still. I like to think that his passion for America has not been diminished simply because he now resides in heaven.

It was Bill's fervent desire that this series of novels create a hunger for revival in the hearts of Americans; that the people would call out to God; and that God would hear their prayers and once again bless our great nation with a tremendous outpouring of His grace and power.

ACKNOWLEDGMENTS

Our heartfelt thanks go to Helmut Teichert, for recognizing our mutual passion for national revival and our belief in the power of fiction; if not for Helmut, this book would not have been written, for it is he who brought us together; Tom McKennett and Tim Grissom for sharing with us their historical research on revival in America; your research is not only first-class material, it inspired us as well; Steve Laube, friend and agent, ever faithful and supportive; and Howard Publishing for sharing our vision.

PROLOGUE

"Excuse me, Judge."

"Hmm?"

"Your ten o'clock appointment is here."

Judge Harrison Quincy Shaw glanced at the mantel clock. It was only 9:40. He frowned. "He's early."

"She, sir," the servant clarified.

"She?" Judge Shaw lifted an eyebrow.

"Yes, sir."

"Are you sure?"

The question puzzled the house servant. He stared at the polished wooden floor. "I do believe she's female, sir."

Now the judge was amused. "You're certain, Hendricks?"

"Mostly certain, sir."

Judge Harrison glanced again at the clock. "Tell her to wait."

"Yes sir." The servant stepped back, quietly shutting the door.

Rectangles of morning sun, matching the shape of the window frame, stretched lazily across the floor, warming the room.

Judge Shaw returned to his morning reading of the Scriptures. The Bible in his lap lay open to Galatians. He read a paragraph. It didn't register. He read it again. He still couldn't recall what he'd read. The inspiration was gone.

1

Irritated, he tossed the book onto his desk. The closer he drew to an arm's reach of threescore years, the more routine his life became. Judge Shaw liked routine, and so did most of the men he knew. Routine gave a man's life a semblance of order and peace. Anyone who disturbed a man's routine was as foolish as someone who poked a slumbering grizzly bear with a stick. Men understood this; they respected another man's routine. But women seemed neither to understand nor respect a man's need for routine. Without even thinking about it, they poked the grizzly. And then they seemed startled when he roared. They acted surprised, like they'd done nothing wrong.

"Hendricks!" he shouted.

The house servant reappeared.

"Show her in."

Moments later the study doors opened.

"Miss Nellie Bly," Hendricks announced.

The judge stood, his stiff knees complaining. At six-foot-four, he took longer than most people to unfold. At full height he towered over his female guest. She extended her hand. It was swallowed up by his.

"You're early," the grizzly grumbled.

Miss Bly's hand flew to her chest. "Am I? I sincerely hope I haven't disturbed you."

Judge Shaw said nothing; he simply offered her a seat.

Hendricks stepped out, closing the door behind him.

Miss Bly began to talk even before she was fully seated. "Thank you for your time, Your Honor. As you probably know, I write for the *Pittsburgh Dispatch*. Human-interest stories mostly."

"What makes you think I would know that?" Judge Shaw said as he sat back down in his desk chair.

Since entering the room, Miss Bly's expression had been fixed, as though a sculptor had fashioned a bust titled *Cordiality* and set it on her shoulders. Now the image faltered. What was it about writers that made them assume everybody was familiar with their work?

To her credit, Miss Bly didn't brood over her disappointment.

2

"Anyway," she continued, "two days ago my managing editor approached me—"

He cocked his head. "How old are you?"

"Pardon me?"

"Was the question difficult?"

Miss Bly pursed her lips. She contemplated the blank page of her reporter's pad before replying. "With all respect, Your Honor, it's not polite to ask a woman her—"

"I don't put my manners on until after ten o'clock. You were early. Just answer the question. How old are you?"

"Eighteen, Your Honor."

Judge Shaw stared across the room, his mind flipping through past years. *Same age,* he thought. *Same height.* The similarities were intriguing.

"As I was saying, Your Honor . . ."

He smiled. *Same energy and determination.*

". . . my managing editor thought, and I agreed . . ."

Her features are rounder, but she has the same quick eyes, the sign of a quick mind. And that can be dangerous for a woman, especially if it's attached to an unbridled tongue.

". . . that your wife's story would make a good column for our newspaper. In fact, I'm hoping it will be the first of a series of stories on prominent women in Pittsburgh history. With your permission, I'd like to ask you some questions about her."

"What do you know about my wife?"

Miss Bly smiled. "Your wife is my inspiration. When I first—"

"Your inspiration? How?"

The reporter's eyes flashed annoyance, but she held her tongue.

The judge chuckled to himself. Now *that* wasn't like Tori at all.

"As I was saying, Your Honor, when I first became interested in writing, I read everything I could get my hands on, especially newspapers since I'm interested in journalism. I read every article on every page. Even the obituaries. That's where I saw the notice of your wife's death.

It said she wrote for the *New York Herald*. That intrigued me, given the fact that women weren't allowed to be reporters in those days. I did a little research. Your wife was a remarkable woman, Your Honor."

"How extensively did you research the times?"

"The times?"

"The times, Miss Bly. People don't exist in a vacuum."

She stiffened. "I know that, Your Honor."

"Well, what did you find?"

Nellie Bly swallowed hard. "What I meant, Your Honor, was that I know people don't live in a vacuum. I didn't exactly research the times in which your wife lived."

"Then you know nothing about her, Miss Bly."

The reporter squirmed in her chair like a student who was failing an oral history examination. "Neither did I say I was ignorant of the times."

The judge folded his arms. "Tell me."

"Well, for one thing, I know that the mid-1850s were a time of unrest. That slavery was an extremely divisive issue—"

The judge waved a dismissive hand. "Abolition. Slavery. The war. Yes, yes. What else?"

Miss Bly searched the ceiling as though she were hoping to draw inspiration from on high. She brightened. "The Lincoln-Douglas debates . . . and gold was discovered in California."

He scowled. "Not the whole blessed nation, Miss Bly. The part that pertains to my wife."

"I'm . . . I'm not sure I know what you mean, Your Honor, unless you mean the role of women."

The judge sighed heavily. "Spiritually, Miss Bly. What do you know about the state of the nation's spirituality in the mid-1850s?"

She appeared surprised. "You mean religious history? Preachers and the like?"

"I mean, Miss Bly, what was the spiritual condition of the nation in those days?"

"Good?"

The judge slumped in his chair.

She tried again. "Not good?"

"1857, Miss Bly."

The reporter searched her memory, all the time shaking her head.

"Fulton Street," said the judge.

That was no help either.

"The old North Dutch Church."

Miss Bly had had enough. She repositioned herself in her chair. "Excuse me, Your Honor, but if we could get back to your wife—"

"No wonder our nation is in the state it's in if its citizens are ignorant of the great visitations of God!" the judge proclaimed. "Miss Bly, if you know nothing of the revival of 1857–58, you know nothing of my wife."

For a time neither one of them spoke.

"September 23, 1857," said the judge.

Miss Bly looked at him.

He pointed at her tablet. "You're not writing."

"Sir?"

"September 23, 1857. Write that down."

She wrote it down.

"Fulton Street. 11:58 a.m. The morning dawned like any other morning, with no indication of the momentous events that would soon take place. We were a generation in search of a soul, Miss Bly. The Unitarians sought it through logic and reason; the transcendentalists peered inward. One utopian society after another sprung up, hoping to create the ideal community, while those of us who remained in the church prayed for revival. We hungered for it, Miss Bly. We'd read about former times when God's Spirit revealed Himself in America with might and power—the Great Awakening of the 1730s and '40s, the Yale revivals of the 1790s, and the revival in New York's Burned-Over District in 1825. We prayed that God would do it again. And He did, Miss Bly. He did, beginning September 23, 1857."

As Judge Harrison Shaw settled into a storytelling posture and began to narrate, Nellie Bly recorded his words on her pad. Later, when she wrote up the interview, she used the story as a sidebar.

Two minutes to noon.

A tall, forty-eight-year-old businessman sits alone in an upstairs room of the old North Dutch Church in lower Manhattan. A stack of handbills lies at his feet.

Prayer Meeting

12 — 1 o'clock

Stop 5, 10, or 20 minutes

or the whole hour as your time permits

A weariness washes over him, the kind that goes deeper than tired feet and aching legs.

For three months Jeremiah C. Lanphier had walked the streets surrounding the church, distributing Bibles and tracts, temperance pledges, and handbills as part of a systematic visitation effort. Hired by the trustees of the North Dutch Church, he set out to visit every house, to speak to every person. He wanted to determine the religious condition of the families in the neighborhood. He had no special training for this enterprise. No prior experience. He was a merchant, not a minister. The decision to leave his business to do the Lord's work at a greatly reduced salary was not an easy one for him.

Once he decided, however, Lanphier launched into the task with enthusiasm. One of his more successful ideas was to make arrangements with hotels and boardinghouses for their guests who needed a place to worship. Chambermaids placed in each room small cards that indicated the times of the church services. Then, when guests attended a service, all they had to do was mention which hotel they were staying at, and an usher would seat them in a pew specifically reserved for residents of that hotel or boardinghouse.

The weekday prayer meeting had seemed like a good idea too. But now he isn't so sure.

12:10 p.m.

Lanphier lets out a sigh.

He knows the neighborhood around Fulton and William Streets has changed since the North Dutch Church was built eighty-eight years ago. In those days the streets were populated by families; now one sees mostly businesses. The idea of a prayer meeting for businessmen seemed like a logical one. Why not give merchants, mechanics, clerks, strangers, and other businessmen an opportunity to pause in their busy day and call upon God? They could come and go as needed.

Lanphier had printed invitations and placards. For more than a month, he had visited all the business establishments in the area. The response he had received was encouraging. "That's what this city needs!" everyone told him.

Yet the minutes tick by, and he is still the only person in the room.

12:20 p.m.

Elbows on knees, hands clasped, Lanphier hangs his head.

The idea of a prayer meeting for businessmen had been born out of his personal prayer life. More than once he'd come back to his residence at the church, bone tired and discouraged at the day's lack of progress.

Now, his voice the only sound in the room, Lanphier repeats the words that came to him on the day he surrendered to the Lord's work:

'Tis done, the great transaction's done,
I am the Lord's, and He is mine;
He drew me, and I followed on,
Charmed to confess the voice divine.

12:30 p.m.

He stands up. No one's coming, he tells himself.

He sits back down. No, I'll stay the hour. I announced that the room would be open for prayer for the hour, and so it shall be.

Moments later, the back stairs creak. A man enters the room. He says he's come to pray.

Another man follows.

Then another and another and another, until there are six.

They pray, agreeing to return again the following Wednesday.

Judge Harrison Shaw leaned forward in his chair. He was getting excited. "The following Wednesday twenty to thirty people came to pray. The week after that, thirty to forty. Exciting, but not earthshaking. Then . . ."

He opened a desk drawer. The first item he removed was a lady's pink fan.

Miss Bly smiled when she saw it.

The judge's gaze lingered on the fan. Setting it aside, he dug deeper until he found what he was looking for. A file folder plopped on top of the desk.

"These speak your language." He opened the folder. In it was a collection of newspaper clippings. He selected one of them. "The *New York Times*."

Miss Bly took the article and read with interest.

> During their busiest hours, merchants, clerks, and working men gather day after day for worship. . . . A theater is turned into a chapel, churches of all denominations are open and crowded by day and night.

The judge handed her another. "This one's *Harper's Weekly*."

> The Christian churches of the land are now in the midst of an extraordinary awakening, the greatest, perhaps, which they have ever known. The movement is on so grand a scale that it commands universal attention. . . . The most indifferent and most incredulous lookers-on, even those who profess no belief in Christianity at all, cannot choose but to gaze, if it be only in wonder, to see the heart of almost a whole nation moved by one spiritual impulse.

"Also from *Harper's Weekly*," said the judge, "a regular feature called The Lounger."

"I'm familiar with The Lounger columns." Miss Bly took the article.

> Not even The Lounger can help seeing the universal interest in the great religious movement of the moment. When, at high noon, in the densest business parts of the city, swarms of men are hurrying in various directions, and an observer learns that they are not going to the bank, and that they are not in all this hurry to save their credit but their souls; and when for the first time in his experience, he sees that in a Christian community the Christian churches are not closed for six days in seven but are open; that they are not attended by a few decorous listeners upon one day but thronged with multitudes of eager and excited people several times a day, he will naturally do as

```
this Lounger did—follow the crowds and observe the
scene.
```

"And not just New York," said the judge. He read place names aloud as he picked up one account after another. "Philadelphia. Chicago. Omaha City. Cleveland. St. Louis. Louisville. Baltimore. Hartford. Providence, etc., etc., etc." He handed a fistful of clippings to Miss Bly.

She read one byline aloud. "T. E. Campbell, your wife's pseudonym."

Headline after headline appeared before Nellie Bly as she leafed through the news clippings.

```
New Haven, Connecticut—City's Biggest Church
Packed Twice Daily for Prayer
    Albany, New York—State Legislators Get Down on
Knees
    Schenectady, New York—Ice on the Mohawk Broken
for Baptisms
```

"Your wife had quite an interest in spiritual revival," Miss Bly said. "Something the two of you shared?"

Judge Shaw gave a nod. "I was one of the six who attended that first prayer meeting on Fulton Street."

"Is that where you met? At church?"

The judge leaned back in his chair, his hands interlaced comfortably across his belly. "Miss Bly, have you ever heard of the court case that the newspapers dubbed *The State of New York v. The North Dutch Church*?"

A puzzled expression formed on the reporter's face.

"James Kittredge Jarves prosecuted the case. I was the defense."

Miss Bly's eyebrows arched. "You went up against your wife's father?"

The judge smiled. "She wasn't my wife at the time. The outcome of the trial would determine our future. You see, Miss Bly, I made a promise to her father that if I lost the trial, I wouldn't marry his daughter. And in order to win, I had to prove in a New York court of law that the Holy Spirit not only existed, but that He was behind the extraordinary events of the time."

CHAPTER 1

Harrison Shaw tugged at the sleeves of his dress coat. Actually, it wasn't his coat. It belonged to the Newsboys' Lodge in Brooklyn. All the guys used it for important occasions. Isaac Hirsch wore it to his bar mitzvah. Murry Simon got married in it. Luckily for Murry—or perhaps for Murry's bride—the coat was his size. Isaac wasn't so lucky. When he wore it, the sleeves hung well past his knuckles. He looked like he was playing dress-up with his father's coat. Harrison had the opposite problem. The sleeves didn't begin to cover his bony wrists. He tugged on them again just before reaching for the door knocker.

Hollow brass lion's eyes stared back at him. His coat sleeve rode up his arm as he lifted the lion's jaw to strike the knocker pad. The metal was cold. He shivered—not from the chill of brass in early winter, but from nervous excitement. This was the first time he'd been this far uptown. It had been an intimidating journey as he'd walked past one stately mansion after another. "Millionaire Row," they called it. If the boys at the lodge could only see him now.

Nervously, he shoved a hand into his trousers pocket and fingered a lone coin. An 1831 silver dollar with a nick on the edge. It had been his good-luck piece for as long as he could remember.

The latch sounded. The door opened.

A house servant appeared. She was so short her gaze hit him in the belly and worked its way up, the way it would if she were gazing at a church steeple.

"Deliveries in back," she said, closing the door.

Harrison found himself once again face to face with the brass lion. The lion was smirking at him.

He knocked a second time, this time bending over to speak to the female servant on her level.

The door opened.

"I'm not a delivery boy," he blurted. He spoke the words so quickly—to get them out before she had time to close the door again— that they came out as a single word: "I'mnotadeliveryboy."

His words hit a middle-aged man in the waistcoat.

"Congratulations, sir," said the house servant, looking down at him.

Cringing, Harrison pulled himself up to full height. The servant, distinguished, with gray temples, extended his hand, palm up.

Harrison grabbed the servant's hand and shook it. "Nice to meet you. Name's Harrison Shaw. I'm expected."

The servant stared at Harrison's hand as though it were a three-day old fish. "Your calling card, sir."

"Oh! Calling card!" Harrison retracted his hand sheepishly. He felt his pockets, even though he knew there were no calling cards to be found.

The servant stood motionless. Pigeons could have landed on his arm.

"Um . . . where I live we don't use a lot of calling cards," Harrison said.

"Shocking, sir."

"If you could just check with Mr. Jarves, I'm sure my name's on a list somewhere, or I could run home and get a note from my guardian . . . a letter of introduction . . . that is, if you really need something in writing."

The servant lowered his hand and stepped back. With a heavy sigh, he said, "This way, sir."

Earlier that morning, when Harrison, now in his midtwenties, had climbed out of bed, he knew that the events of this day could very well chart the course of his professional career in New York's dog-eat-dog legal system. He'd worked hard to get this far, and today could very well be the payoff he'd so often dreamed of. Had he known that stepping across the threshold of this Fifth Avenue mansion would launch him down a series of rapids in a boat without an oar, he might not have crossed it so eagerly.

Never in his life had Harrison stood in such an entryway. Four white marble Corinthian columns thrust upward to the heavens. Literally. Overhead cherubs looked down mischievously at him from cotton clouds set against a domed blue sky. Gawking upward, he turned full circle, his feet gliding effortlessly on a floor smooth as glass.

All of a sudden Harrison realized he and the cherubs were alone. The house servant had moved on. He ran to catch up.

Harrison followed his escort at a steady clip through two rooms, both of them larger than the common room at the Newsboys' Lodge, then down a carpeted hallway lined with portraits of well-dressed people who glared at him disapprovingly as he passed.

The servant opened two floor-to-ceiling doors and motioned Harrison into a sitting room. "Wait here. Don't touch anything." The massive doors closed.

Harrison found himself alone in a room that resembled a museum. He wasn't surprised. Jimmy Wessler had warned him that rich people liked to collect a lot of strange and unusual artifacts, not just paintings and statues of ancient Greeks like most people thought. Jimmy knew about this kind of stuff because his uncle was a lawyer for rich people in Albany.

For twenty minutes Harrison remained firmly planted where the house servant had left him, suffering the scratchy constraints of his stiff upturned collar with no complaint as his head swiveled this way and that. Then his curiosity got the better of him, and he inched closer to a polished round table to get a better look at a white porcelain elephant. Just beyond the elephant was an oriental jade chess set; and beyond it, a vase with a painting of a crouching black jaguar. And before Harrison knew it, he had penetrated the room's interior. But he wasn't touching anything.

Floor-to-ceiling windows flanked him on the left, framed by red velvet curtains. Beyond the windows was a small orchard of trees with naked branches. A soft light fell on him and the room's strange assortment of collectibles.

Painfully aware that he didn't have the money to replace anything he broke, Harrison navigated the room's clutter, zigzagging around embroidered footstools, plump sofas and chairs, little tables loaded with trinkets, and cabinets jammed full of porcelain and glass animals.

Oil paintings hung on the walls from long wires that stretched to the ceiling. Pastorals mostly. Metal plates mounted on the frames identified both painting and artist. *The Voyage of Life*, by Thomas Cole, captivated him with its depiction of a young man, tiller firmly in hand, sailing the river of life. The thrust of the young man's chin and his billowing clothes suggested adventure and determination. In the distance a shining castle beckoned him. An angelic being watched over him from the shore. So intent was the youth on his goal, he didn't see the choppy seas and rough water ahead.

Other paintings in the room were interesting but not as dramatic. There were several by Frederick Church depicting scenes of South America and a pastoral landscape by Asher B. Durand that hung in a prominent location. Harrison had never heard of any of these painters before.

Next to the Durand painting hung a scuffed wooden frame that was not displaying a painting. Inside the frame was a piece of paper that showed a crease from being folded over and was now yellowed with age. A letter, penned in French. The signature fascinated him: Marquis de Lafayette. A chill of excitement passed through Harrison at the realization he was inches from a page of correspondence that had been penned by the hand of a true Revolutionary War hero. A relative of Jarves's perhaps?

Something else caught his eye. Something down low on a table. Harrison turned his head to see a stuffed bird beneath a glass bell looking up at him. Its eyes had a murderous glint in them, as though death had come upon it suddenly and it was intent on revenge.

The creature was small and gray with black markings around its eyes so that it appeared to be wearing a mask. Its eyes locked on to him with hypnotic force, and for an instant, Harrison knew the helpless sensation prey feel when they know they're going to die. The moment was beyond unnerving.

Harrison gave the table a wide berth. The bird's eyes seemed to follow him.

Now that he thought about it, the whole house was a bit unnerving—the peeping angels in the entryway, the unsmiling portraits in the hallway, the bird restrained under glass. The unsettled feeling in his gut was more than simply being unaccustomed to the trappings of wealth. There was an underlying dark anxiety about the place. He suddenly found himself craving fresh air—fresh *outside* air.

But he couldn't just leave. Mr. Bowen and the boys back at the lodge were counting on him. What would he tell them—he got scared and ran away before the interview?

He took a deep breath and put some distance between him and the bird, looking for something to distract him. Something that didn't have eyes.

He found what he was looking for beneath another glass bell jar. A pocket watch dangled on a gold chain. It was obviously of sentimental value to Mr. Jarves, because while the watch looked expensive, it was damaged. Its backside was charred; a portion of the crystal was clouded from smoke. The hands of the watch were stilled, frozen at sixteen minutes past one o'clock.

As Harrison bent over to examine it, he noticed something new to the room. Something that hadn't been there when he'd entered. He was certain of it. An odor. What intrigued him was that the odor obviously didn't belong in this museum of musty drapes and old wood and scary stuffed birds beneath bell jars.

The door latch rattled. The massive doors swung open. The house servant who had deposited him in the room eyed Harrison suspiciously. Harrison raised his hands to indicate he hadn't touched anything.

Everything about the house servant said, *Follow me.* Verbalizing it would have been redundant. The servant turned, and Harrison dutifully fell in step behind him.

Their journey was short. They stepped across the hallway, where the house servant opened a second pair of double wooden doors. "Mr. Harrison Quincy Shaw," he announced, stepping aside.

Harrison walked into the largest library he'd ever seen in his life. Three floors of books rimmed the room's perimeter, dwarfing him by their sheer number. Each level was reached by one of three sets of open circular stairways. Harrison recognized the titles closest to him, not that he'd read them. These were books the authors he read quoted.

Just beyond the room's center, four men huddled over a desk. Their backs were to him. They spoke in whispers, giving no indication they were aware he'd been announced. Unsure what to do, Harrison glanced at the house servant, who appeared unconcerned over their lack of response. So Harrison acted equally unconcerned. He tugged at the sleeves of his coat.

From within the huddle came a voice, strong with authority. "Let's get on with it."

The four men turned to face Harrison. They wore identical black suits—all with sleeves long enough to cover their wrists—and identical expressions, which gave the impression their personalities had just been repossessed. Of the four, one was remarkably shorter than the others. Another had white bushy sideburns.

Harrison Shaw's future rested in their hands.

CHAPTER 2

Harrison felt like a specimen under scrutiny. He matched the serious gaze of the four men in black, though not without difficulty. Mr. Bowen had prepared him for this moment. *Always look a man in the eye, Harrison. A man who cannot hold another man's gaze is either weak, ashamed of himself, or has something to hide.*

Or is scared out of his wits, Harrison thought. His gaze moved from man to man. Harrison wondered which of the four was the notorious J. K. Jarves.

Just then the men parted like a curtain—two moving to one side, two to the other—and there, seated at the table behind them, was a fifth man who, by his bearing, was the unmistakable master of everything he surveyed.

J. K. Jarves's clean-shaven face revealed a jaw of granite. His eyes were fixed and hard, harder than those of the brass lion on the front door. His chair scraped the floor as he rose to an impressive height. And when the man spoke, Harrison had a flash of insight of what it would be like to stand before God on the Day of Judgment.

"Step forward," said the voice.

The request was simple. Compliance, however, was not so simple. Intimidation is to memory what an eraser is to a blackboard, and all of a sudden, Harrison forgot the difference between forward and backward.

He was sure he told his feet forward. But somehow they stepped backward, onto the toes of the house servant, who had at some point sneaked up behind him.

Harrison mumbled his apologies and, with a second effort, coaxed his wobbly knees forward.

"You are Harrison Shaw?" said the voice.

It was a ridiculous question. A "huftymagufty"—at least that's what they called them at the lodge. A nonquestion pretending to be a question. A question with an answer so obvious, it never should have been asked. Jimmy Wessler was the master of huftymagufties. He'd ask a person who held a half-eaten roll in his hand what he was chewing. Or a person who was sitting on a newspaper, "Are you reading that?"

Harrison couldn't help being amused. Here he was, in the interview of his life, and the first question asked him was a huftymagufty. He'd arrived at the interview time for Harrison Shaw. He'd been announced as Harrison Shaw. They had Harrison Shaw's papers in front of them on the desk. Who else would he be except Harrison Shaw? If Jimmy Wessler had asked that same question, Harrison would have said, "No, I'm President Buchanan's parrot." However, it wasn't Jimmy Wessler standing in front of him. It was J. K. Jarves, without question the most celebrated lawyer in New York. So Harrison swallowed hard and said, "Yes, sir. I'm Harrison Shaw."

But there are some impulses that master you; you don't master them. And before Harrison could stop himself, he added, "And you are J. K. Jarves?"

The words were greased pigs. They slipped past his lips despite his best effort to hold them back.

He regretted them immediately. The four lawyers, who moments before had served as curtains, frowned at Harrison in unison. The man behind the desk glowered at him with those steely eyes, boring a hole through Harrison large enough to drive a locomotive through. After a seeming eternity of uncomfortable silence, he sat down behind his desk and began examining a sheaf of papers Harrison recognized as his application for the position of J. K. Jarves's legal intern.

For a time nothing was said. Jarves read. The four curtain men watched him read. The house servant, who had put some distance between himself and Harrison, watched Jarves read. Harrison watched him read. The man was the center of the world. All of life radiated out from him in concentric circles.

A minute later the door behind Harrison clicked shut. A backward glance revealed the house servant was gone.

Jarves picked up a pen and used it to guide a systematic review of the document. He launched into a series of questions. "You're twenty-six years old?"

"Yes, sir."

Jarves scratched a note on the application. "You attended Washburn School of Law?"

"Yes, sir."

Jarves looked up. "Where exactly is Washburn?"

"Brooklyn."

"Really? Hmm." Jarves returned to the document. He wrote something. "It says here you graduated top of your class."

"Yes, sir."

"How many matriculated?"

"Fourteen, sir. No, fifteen. Teddy Green made it back from his father's farm upstate in time to take the final exam. None of us thought he would."

Jarves stared at Harrison. "Teddy Green made it back, did he?"

"Yes, sir."

"We didn't get that report here. We can all breathe easy now."

One of the curtain men—the one with the sideburns—sniggered.

With the preliminaries out of the way, Harrison was pelted with questions for over an hour, both personal and pertaining to the law. The four curtain men took turns reading to him from papers he'd written at

Washburn, challenging his logic, his conclusions, sometimes both. Harrison defended his positions.

"You realize, don't you," said one of the curtain men, "that being selected for this internship would be an unparalleled honor."

"It's an honor if only to be considered," Harrison replied.

"Is it now?" Sideburns approached Harrison. The man had a snooty air about him. He made no effort to conceal his feelings for Harrison. "Do you realize how much of an honor it is just for you to be standing here? To be standing in the same place as candidates from Princeton and Harvard and Yale? To be considered with men who graduated with honors, at the top of their class, from the best law schools in America?"

For all Harrison knew, Sideburns was a state supreme-court judge. Despite Harrison's earlier lapses, he decided self-control and discretion were the order of the day.

"A man can do no more than make the most of the opportunities presented to him," Harrison stated. "While I was not given the chance to attend the schools you mentioned, I was, through the sacrifice of a dear friend, granted the privilege to attend Washburn where, I'm confident, we studied the same law that is studied at Princeton and Harvard and Yale. Sir, I believe I can hold my own against any of the other applicants in a court of law."

"Well said," Jarves cried from behind the desk.

Harrison felt a rush of satisfaction, the kind he'd imagined he'd feel in a courtroom when the judge ruled in his favor.

"There's only one thing left to say," Jarves added. He eyed the curtain lawyers, then Harrison's sleeves. "Nice coat."

The house servant was summoned, and Harrison was led back through the house the same way he'd entered. He had no illusions regarding the outcome of the interview. He consoled himself with the thought that the experience had equipped him with a couple of good stories to tell the boys at the lodge, not the least of which was the stuffed bird under the bell jar.

Just as they reached the entryway, a feminine shout came from the back of the house. Not a frightened scream, but an alarm.

The house servant's hand froze on the door latch.

The next thing Harrison knew, he was surrounded by a mob of house servants, every one of them staring angrily at him.

A female servant stepped forward. "The master's pocket watch is missing!"

The four curtain attorneys came running.

"The master's pocket watch is missing!" she told them.

J. K. Jarves himself arrived.

"Your pocket watch, sir," she reported a third time, "the one in the sitting room under the glass jar. It's missing!"

All eyes shifted to Harrison.

The house servant who had been his guide stood between him and the door. On the other side of Harrison was a choir of scowls, two rows deep.

Harrison knew he hadn't lifted the watch, yet he felt guilty. They were staring at him, waiting for some kind of response. He had an overwhelming urge to confess.

What should he say? To deny taking the watch is exactly what a guilty person would do.

He fidgeted under their gaze. His hands went to his pockets. Should he turn them out and show them he didn't have the watch? But then, why should he? Why had they assumed he was the one who took the watch?

Just then Harrison felt an unfamiliar bulge in his coat pocket. His fingers traced a thick, circular shape. And at that moment, he knew exactly how the stuffed bird felt. He was being fitted for a glass bell display.

"Do you know anything about the missing watch, Mr. Shaw?" Jarves asked.

"Search his pockets!" Sideburns shouted.

The male house servant took a step toward him.

Their actions came a little too quickly, as though they'd been rehearsed.

"That won't be necessary," Harrison said. He reached into his pocket and produced the watch.

A housemaid gasped. The curtain attorneys voiced their dismay in unison. Everyone talked at once. In the midst of it all, Harrison was certain he heard someone giggle.

"Summon the police," J. K. Jarves demanded.

No one moved. They seemed to be awaiting Harrison's reaction.

"Yes," Harrison replied. "Yes, by all means, summon the police. And quickly."

Everyone fell silent. They stared at him. Obviously, this wasn't the response they were expecting.

Harrison turned to the house servant. "Didn't you hear Mr. Jarves? Be on your way, man! Summon the police!"

The house servant balked, uncertain as to what to do. He looked to Jarves for instructions.

J. K. Jarves approached Harrison. "An interesting reaction. Why would you be eager to be arrested?"

"Eager to be arrested?" Harrison cried. "Certainly not. What do you take me for, a fool?"

"Then why summon the police?"

"To prevent an injustice."

"An injustice?"

"Certainly, an injustice. It's not likely that I'm going to get a fair hearing in this venue, hence the injustice. I prefer presenting my case to an objective authority."

The senior attorney grinned wryly. A superior grin. The grin of a chess master sizing up his next victim. "Case?" Jarves said. "You have no case, Mr. Shaw. Look around you. All these witnesses saw you pull the watch from your pocket."

"True enough," Harrison conceded. "However, I believe at least one person can testify that I wasn't the one who put the watch into my pocket."

Jarves was intrigued. "And who would that be, Mr. Shaw?"

Harrison took a deep breath to brace himself, very much aware that his reputation, and possibly his freedom, rested on what he said next. "Well, there's me," he began. "I know I didn't put the watch in my pocket."

"A thief declaring his own innocence is hardly a defense, Mr. Shaw."

"Then there's the person who did put the watch in my pocket. That person knows I didn't steal the watch."

"You can produce such a person, Mr. Shaw? Someone who will admit the crime?"

"I believe so, yes. But before I expose the true criminal, there's a witness I wish to question."

"A witness?" Jarves's eyes narrowed appreciably. "You're trying my patience, Mr. Shaw."

"A single witness, one that could prevent a miscarriage of justice. Surely that's not too much to ask, is it?"

Jarves folded his arms. "Very well, Mr. Shaw. Call your witness."

"I can't," Harrison said, sheepishly. "Don't get me wrong, I can produce her. It's just that I can't call her, because . . . well, I don't know her name. But she's"—he pointed across the crowded entryway—"she's hiding behind that marble column over there."

The servants who stood between Harrison and the marble column parted, as though his finger was a loaded pistol. The pillar came into plain view. No one appeared from behind it.

"She must be shy," Harrison said.

"If you're there, come out," Jarves ordered.

For a long moment, no one came out. Then, with a swish of petticoats, a young woman appeared. She was dressed elegantly, all in white. Her head was tilted proudly upward. She walked with practiced dignity.

"Victoria?" Jarves said.

"Another house servant?" Harrison quipped.

The young woman shot Harrison a withering glance.

"My daughter," Jarves said quickly.

"Oh."

Jarves spoke to her. "Victoria, dear, Mr. Shaw claims you are a witness to the theft of my watch from under the glass bell in the sitting room."

"He is mistaken," Victoria said.

Harrison raised an objecting finger. "If you'll pardon me, sir, I never used the word *theft*. In point of fact, I do not believe a theft actually occurred. It is my contention that your watch was, shall we say, pressed into service. And furthermore, begging your pardon, I believe this is my witness. If you have no objections, I believe it is my right to question her first."

Jarves raised a threatening finger. "Do not forget that you are talking to my daughter."

The warning was unnecessary. It wasn't a woman Harrison saw step from behind the marble column, but a goddess descending from her heavenly throne. As befitting her position, Victoria Jarves made Harrison come to her. They stood beneath a canopy of angels looking down at them.

Harrison's nervousness registered on two levels. First, regardless of the attitude of gamesmanship he was projecting, he was fully aware that he was on trial. And second, because Miss Jarves's beauty was so formidable, it struck him dumb whenever he looked at her.

"Miss Jarves," he said, with lowered gaze so he could think, "early today, when you were in the room where the watch is on display—"

"You're mistaken, sir," Victoria replied. "I was not in the sitting room earlier today."

"You weren't?"

"I haven't stepped foot in that room for weeks."

"For weeks? You're certain?"

Victoria Jarves nodded, pleased to refute his assumption.

Harrison scratched his cheek and glanced at Jarves. The senior attorney wore an amused smile. Behind him was a backdrop of smirking attorneys and servants.

"Let me ask you this then, Miss Jarves," Harrison said. "Tell me, when was the last time you looked into the room?"

"The hallway door to that room is normally closed," she explained. "While I may have passed by the room, I would not have been able to see inside it without entering it."

"Unable to see without entering it. That's not exactly true, is it, Miss Jarves? Perhaps I can clarify the question. Miss Jarves, when was the last time you looked into that room from a place other than the hallway?"

Victoria Jarves didn't answer immediately. She cocked her head and looked at him as though she were attempting to read his mind. Harrison prayed she had no mind-reading abilities, for if she did, she'd see 10 percent of his mind attempting to phrase the next question, and 90 percent of his mind totally agog to be standing this close to her.

"I'm not sure I understand what you're asking," Miss Jarves said.

"What perfume are you wearing?"

"I beg your pardon?"

"Your perfume. It has a name?"

She looked at her father.

He shrugged.

"Desire du Paris," she answered.

"Desire du Paris? Really? Hmm. All right. Desire du Paris it is. Tell me, Miss Jarves, how many other people in this household wear Desire du Paris perfume?"

"I don't see how that is any of your—"

"You're wasting our time, Mr. Shaw," Jarves said.

Harrison persisted. "Miss Jarves, do any of the house servants wear Desire du Paris perfume?"

"They couldn't afford it."

"Do any of these fine gentlemen attorneys, all neatly dressed in black, wear Desire du Paris perfume?"

"Mr. Shaw!" Jarves warned.

"Mr. Jarves, I'm simply trying to establish the fact that only one person in this house wears Desire du Paris perfume, an important fact considering that I distinctly remember smelling that fragrance while waiting in the sitting room."

Victoria started to say something.

Harrison cut her off. "Miss Jarves, please don't attempt to deny it. It was your fragrance that alerted me that you were lurking behind the marble column a few moments ago."

"I don't lurk!" Victoria Jarves protested.

"But you do spy, don't you, Miss Jarves? If I were to inspect that room, or ask the police to inspect that room, I would discover that there is a secret passageway behind the walls, wouldn't I? One that allows a person to see into the room without being seen by anyone in the room. Were you spying on me, Miss Jarves?"

"I certainly was not!" Miss Jarves sputtered.

Harrison pointed to the heavenly dome. "Under God, Miss Jarves. Remember, your testimony is under God."

Victoria looked up. Cherubs looked down.

Before she could reply, Harrison turned to Jarves: "And while I believe that Miss Jarves witnessed the person removing the watch from beneath the glass bell, that still doesn't explain how it got into my pocket, does it?"

"You had an accomplice," Jarves suggested.

"So it would appear. However, what kind of thief would I be to steal a watch and, at the same time, have something of mine stolen from me?"

Jarves snapped, "What the devil are you talking about, Shaw?"

Harrison turned his trousers pockets inside out to reveal nothing was in them. The house servants, the curtain attorneys, Victoria, and even Jarves himself stared at the two white tongues protruding from the sides of Harrison's trousers.

"When I entered this house for my interview, I had in my possession a silver dollar, dated 1831. It has a nick just above the eagle's left wing. It's an heirloom of sorts. I carry it for good luck. And why wouldn't I? Today of all days, when I had such an important interview. I distinctly remember rubbing it between my thumb and forefinger just before one of your house servants mistook me for a delivery boy. And now it's gone." He flapped both trousers pockets. "Not there."

Harrison felt ridiculous standing in the entryway of a million-dollar mansion on Fifth Avenue with his pockets turned out. It wasn't exactly how he'd envisioned his interview would go.

"So, by all means, summon the police," Harrison pressed, "because once they question Miss Jarves, I believe they'll learn that she concealed herself in a secret hiding place and that she can identify the person who removed the watch from the sitting room. I further believe that when they search the pockets of the house servants, they will find my 1831 silver dollar. I believe they will conclude, as I have, that the person who stole the coin is the same person who lifted the watch, for reasons of his own."

The house servant, the one who had served as Harrison's escort, felt his vest pocket. His eyes grew wide with alarm. Reaching into the pocket, he withdrew a coin. A silver dollar. It had a nick on the edge.

"Sir!" he cried, his eyes imploring, "I didn't . . . I wouldn't! I have served this family honorably, with pride, doing everything you've instructed me to do, without question . . . you know I wouldn't—"

"Summon the police!" Harrison cried.

"No!" the house servant pleaded. "Tell him. Tell him, sir. I was only doing as I was instructed!"

Jarves calmly approached the servant. He held out his hand. The man handed him the coin. Jarves turned and handed it to Harrison. "Mr. Shaw, you will be notified of the results of your interview at an appropriate time."

Harrison was shown the door.

After the door was shut, Harrison stood outside, on the steps, his heart racing. He fortified himself with deep breaths of crisp air. As his pulse returned to normal, disappointment set in.

Well, he thought to himself, *your first trip uptown is your last.*

He'd be a fool to think otherwise. He consoled himself with the thought that he'd made it this far in the interview process. That said something, didn't it? If nothing else, it would look good on his résumé.

Tugging on the sleeves of his coat, he took another deep breath and sauntered down the steps, fully intending to ogle the line of mansions with their stately columns, empire windows, and impressive lots. The boys back at the lodge wouldn't believe some of the things he'd seen.

Yet, despite his ogling intentions, as he turned homeward, images of Victoria Jarves dominated his thoughts—her flawless, pale skin, the feminine rustle of her dress, the feisty glint in her eyes.

He found himself smiling at the realization that when he got back to the lodge, he would tell Isaac and Jimmy about the mansions and all the things he saw in the sitting room and the entryway cherubs, but the memories of Victoria Jarves he would keep to himself. Some treasures were best left uncirculated to preserve their value.

The sound of an upper window opening and the flutter of curtains pulled him from his reverie, followed by an explosion of glass at his feet. Startled, Harrison jumped back. The concentrated scent of Desire du Paris engulfed him, so strong it made his eyes water.

Harrison looked up at the open window. No one was there.

CHAPTER 3

With his wrists still uncovered by a coat too small, Harrison Quincy Shaw stood at the X-shaped convergence of Worth, Baxter, and Park Streets, the multicornered intersection that gave Five Points its name. He wasn't concerned about how he looked here. Five Points wasn't Fifth Avenue. What he was wearing wasn't an issue. Staying alive was.

In the distance the bell of a departing ferry sounded. There would be only one more crossing tonight, and if Stick didn't show up soon, Harrison would miss it.

He leaned against a street lamp, its gas jet quiet for the moment. The late-afternoon sun was still holding its own against the shadows, slicing them into orderly blue gray parcels with shafts of light that cut between the buildings. It wouldn't be long before the shadows combined their strength and tossed the sun out of the neighborhood for the night.

Anxious to make it to the river in time to catch the last ferry, Harrison considered navigating the notorious neighborhood on his own. Fortunately God had cursed him with good sense, and he decided he'd better wait for his escort.

There were certain neighborhoods in New York a sane person didn't enter uninvited. Five Points was on the top of that list. Harrison had once heard a politician say he'd rather risk an Indian fight than venture among the creatures of Five Points. Even the police avoided the area.

For the tenth time, Harrison scanned the street traffic. Stick was supposed to meet him here over thirty minutes ago. He'd only met the man once before. First impressions were powerful. Harrison remembered thinking he'd never want to run into this guy on the street at night. Now here he was, waiting for that same guy, and night was falling fast.

He was looking for a short, bandy-legged Irishman with a receding red hairline. The man's mouth was set in a perpetual sneer, and he carried a black club that he stuffed in his waistband. At the time Murph—the leader of the Plug Uglies and the one who introduced them—joked that the black club was the same stick Saint Patrick used to drive the snakes from Ireland. He prophesied that Stick would use it to drive the Fly Boys from Five Points.

Harrison laughed at the joke because he was afraid not to. He had to admit, though, that there was humor in placing Stick in the same company as Saint Patrick. He wondered what Saint Patrick would think of the pairing.

Murph was Harrison's usual escort. For reasons unexplained he was unavailable tonight. He informed Harrison that Stick would cover for him. Harrison tried to back out, but Murph insisted he'd be safe with Stick. Harrison decided not to press the point. It would make him appear less than manly.

Of Stick, Murph had said, "He's not much to look at. But 'tis grand to have him on your side when he's in a rage."

Harrison didn't know about that. He questioned his own sanity for paying a thug to keep him safe from thugs, consoling himself with the thought that danger was inherent in missionary work. He discovered that at the outset, but it was work that needed to be done. He viewed Five Points as a great moral enterprise of no less importance than Adonirum Judson's work in Burma.

The heroic faith of Judson, that great missionary from Andover Seminary, inspired him—his thirty-eight-year labor to translate the Bible into the language of the natives; his dogged persistence despite being jailed and tortured; his heartrending bouts with discouragement and depression; and how he pressed on despite the deaths of successive wives and several children.

Five Points was Harrison's Burma.

Even now, standing at the corners, he saw himself as a self-commissioned missionary, chin set determinedly toward the slum. He made a silent vow that the bag of food at his feet would be delivered, regardless of the danger.

A voice interrupted his grand dream. "Ah, the bull looks anxious to be let loose in the field today, from the look on your face. Got a woman waitin' for you, have ya?"

Even though Harrison had been looking for him, Stick had managed to sneak up on him. The man's colorless clothes blended perfectly into the colorless buildings. As the escort drew near, Harrison wondered if Adonirum Judson ever had a guide as frightening or as foul as this Plug Ugly.

"It's about time you got here," Harrison said. "It's nearly dark."

"Whatcha grousin' at? I'm here, ain't I?"

Harrison stooped to pick up the bag of food. "Let's go. I want to get back in time to make the last ferry to Brooklyn."

Stick sniffed the air. "Ooooweee! Get a whiff o' that!"

"What?"

"That girlie smell."

Harrison's faced burned. Desire du Paris. His pant cuffs reeked of it.

"It's nothing," he said quickly. "Something was spilled on me. Let's go."

Stick grinned wickedly, showing blackened teeth. "You already been with a woman, have ya? You reek of her. And now you're goin' for more?" Stick was impressed.

"It's not what you're implying," Harrison snapped.

"I ain't plyin' nothin'. I knows a girlie smell when I smells it."

"It's getting late." Harrison stepped into the street.

Stick grabbed his arm. "You know us goin' in there is sendin' the goose on a errand into the fox's den."

"I know." Again Harrison started out.

Again Stick stopped him. He cleared his throat and stuck out an open palm. "I'm without a penny, if you know what I mean."

Shifting the bag into one arm, Harrison fished in his pocket. He handed Stick a silver dollar. His lucky piece. It was painful to part with it, but it was all he had. He'd spent the last of his money on foodstuffs. In a way, the silver dollar was still serving as his good-luck piece. By giving it to Stick, with any luck, he'd get out of Five Points alive.

"Hey! Whaddya tryin' ta pull here?" Stick cried. "Dis one's broke." He held the coin up to the fading light, running his finger along the edge.

"It's a nick, that's all. It spends just as well as any other silver dollar."

"God's truth?"

While Stick scrutinized the coin, Harrison set off down Baxter Street.

He didn't get far when another traveler fell in step with him, matching his stride. Harrison glanced down at a solitary swine rambling along casually. He was an ugly brute, tan with unsightly black splotches and an offensive odor.

"Friend o' yours?" Stick snorted as he caught up. "He's partial to that girlie smell, ya know."

The swine was the snooty sort. He refused to acknowledge he was walking beside two men of inferior social status. Early that day Harrison had been shunned in similar fashion while walking down Fifth Avenue. After a couple of blocks, the swine left them without the courtesy of a farewell.

As they penetrated the heart of Five Points, the buildings began to close in upon them. The streets became narrower, at times no more than walkways. The darkening sky became a lid pressed upon the rooftops. The air grew heavy with the odors of human waste and rotting wood. Poverty and desperation lived here.

The area was saturated with humanity, yet more boatloads of immigrants continued to arrive with hope for a piece of the American dream.

Overburdened houses slumped against each other like drunken men. Roofs sagged. Gaps between ceilings and walls provided ready access to the sun in the summer and wind and snow in the winter. In a futile effort to keep warm, tenants stuffed newspapers and crumpled posters in the cracks.

Harrison's introduction to the neighborhood came by way of English novelist Charles Dickens, who wrote of Five Points following a tour of New York City. Dickens lamented: "Where dogs would howl to lie, women, men, and boys slink off to sleep, forcing the dislodged rats to move away in quest for better lodgings."

The streets were worse. Even with a club-toting Plug Ugly beside him, Harrison walked warily. They passed two street brawls in as many minutes, shrugged off a loud drunk, and stepped over three men who had passed out in the middle of the street. Toughs glared at them from doorways as they made their way. Prostitutes called to them.

On one street corner, Harrison saw two ragged girls rummaging through a trash barrel. They were collecting snippets of human hair.

"They sell it ta wig makers," Stick explained. He sniffed. "They do all right by themselves. Sixteen hours a day, six dollars a week. Not a bad livin'."

A young boy with a tattered bowler hat and blackened eye appeared from nowhere. He accosted Harrison.

"Penny for matches, mister? Penny for matches?"

Harrison knew something about this profession. One of the newsboys at the lodge had got his start this way. He would buy seventy-two boxes of matches for twenty-four cents. Then he'd take the matches out of the boxes and bundle them with string. That way he could make an additional twenty-five bundles, which he'd sell door-to-door for a penny apiece. Harrison wanted to help the match boy, but he already had matches and no money.

"Go on with ya," Stick growled, "or I'll break your head."

The boy ran away.

"That was uncalled for," Harrison said.

"What's it to ya?"

They turned down an alley that narrowed to barely three feet wide. The stench made Harrison recoil. To take the edge off the odor, he pressed a forearm against his nose. The residue of Victoria Jarves's perfume on his coat sleeve brought a slight grin to his face.

"Whatcha doin' there?" Stick asked. "Thinking o' your colleen?"

"Trying to keep from getting sick."

"Sick? Sick o' what?" Stick looked offended.

"Just keep walking."

The ground was squishy with mud and refuse.

"What's wi' the fancy coat?"

"What do you mean?"

"It's different from the one ya wore last time."

In Stick's world people only had one coat.

"It's not mine."

"Ya lift it?"

"No, I didn't steal it. It's a community coat. Several guys share it."

"Figures."

"What do you mean by that?"

"Looks like you're wearin' your little brudder's coat."

Harrison sighed. When the fashionable Mr. Stick of Five Points noticed the short sleeves, it was definitely time to stop wearing the coat.

"This here's 87 Baxter," Stick announced.

"Wait for me."

"I figured you as a man who could last a little longer with the ladies."

"I'm dropping off a package."

"I coulda done that for ya."

Harrison had tried the Plug Uglies' delivery service twice before. They had a perfect record of nondelivery.

"Thanks. I like to do it myself."

"Don' take too long." Stick glanced over his shoulder in a way that made Harrison nervous.

"Why? Is something wrong?"

"Les jus' say the streets ain't too friendly tonight."

For a Plug Ugly to say the streets weren't friendly was like a Roman soldier telling a Christian the lions in the coliseum were looking a might peckish.

Harrison squished his way toward an enclosed flight of stairs, the entryway to a four-story brick tenement. A wave of filthy air tumbled down the passageway, worse than what was in the alley. Harrison lowered his head as he would against a stiff wind and began to climb.

Behind him, Stick ambled about, hands in his pockets, singing:

More's the pity one so pretty
As I should live alone.

Harrison reached the first landing. It was so dark he couldn't see anything. He lit a match. The air was so foul, the halo around the flame was brown. Two more flights, two more matches.

With one arm carrying the package and a hand holding the match, he could no longer cover his nose. He breathed through his mouth, which made his stomach twist like a rag being wrung.

On every level, noise—as foul as the air—surrounded him. Men and women yelling at each other. Babies wailing. Doors slamming. Children shouting. All manner of cursing.

Having reached the third floor, Harrison followed his lit match down the hallway. Overhead the ceiling was covered with yellow drops, like the early formation of stalactites. The walls were green and slick. To think that people lived here was overwhelming. This was a level of hell worse than anything Dante had imagined.

Harrison found the door he was looking for and hesitated. It surprised him that he hadn't thought this through before now. Should he knock or leave the package on the doorstep? He started to knock, then heard yelling. A woman cursed her son for spilling his drink on her sewing. Harrison pulled his hand back. It wasn't exactly a good time for a social call. Kneeling, he set the package against the door. As an afterthought—the match went out; he lit another—he rummaged for a pencil and wrote a note on the bag:

This food is for Mouser and Katie and their family.

He started to put the pencil into his pocket, then thought to add one more word.

Hosanna

Unable to stomach his surroundings any longer, he hurried back down the hallway, his feet sticking to the floor with every step. He bounded down the three flights of stairs. By the time he bolted into the alley, his head was swimming. He gagged once, twice—gulping fetid alley air between gags. He bent over, pressing his sleeve against his nose and mouth.

Expecting a snide remark from Stick but hearing none, he looked up. Stick wasn't there.

Harrison glanced around. He was alone in the alley, shadows his only company.

On shaky knees Harrison made his way toward the street with a single thought: *get out of Five Points as quickly as you can.*

He encountered his first problem. Actually, there were five problems, all of them blocking the alley entrance with weapons in their hands. One stood in front, backed by the other four. The leader wore a dirt-smeared black top hat. His thumb was hooked in his waistband; his free hand held a piece of timber.

"It's all right, fellows," Harrison said, trying to clear his head and sound calm. "I'm with Stick."

Top Hat took a swaggering step toward him. "You with Stick, are ya?"

Harrison scouted the street. It was eerily empty. No more than a handful of people—all of them hurrying away.

"Yeah. He was supposed to wait for me. I'm sure he'll be back momentarily."

"Here dat?" Top Hat laughed. "Stick'll be back *momentarily.*"

The other four laughed.

Top Hat took another step forward. "We'll keep ya company 'til he returns."

While the stomach-wrenching effects of the stench had not worn off, it was the least of Harrison's concerns now. He took stock of his situation. He was pretty well blocked in. Even if he managed to get past the five men who blocked the alley, he doubted he'd get far. Footing was treacherous, and he'd never been much of a runner. Retreating to the stairway was a possibility. Not a good one, but a possibility.

What else was there besides fighting or fleeing? He could go with his strength. After all, he was a lawyer. Trained in argument. Words were his weapons, and in that battle, the five standing before him were woefully outmatched. Maybe now was the time to see how good he really was.

Harrison stepped forward confidently. "Let me speak to you on terms I'm sure you'll understand. This is your territory, right? Well, I respect that. I paid good money for passage. I made the arrangement with Murph, and he appointed Stick as my escort. While nothing was signed, it was a contract nonetheless, one the Plug Uglies are bound to honor. Should you violate that contract, you will not only disrespect yourselves, but you will disrespect Murph and all Plug Uglies."

Top Hat grinned viciously. "We kill Plug Uglies! Ain't dat right, boys?"

Laughs and animal grunts backed him up.

It was a tactical error, one that Harrison would remember for a long time.

"And if ya should live so long ta see Stick again?" Top Hat said. "You might want ta ask for ya money back, 'cause I think your contract's about ta get broke."

Harrison was backing up.

In the distance the bell for the last ferry to Brooklyn tolled. It didn't look like Harrison was going to make it on time.

"I'm . . . I'm no threat to you," he said. "I'm just here trying to help out."

"Does it look like we're da ones here dat needs help?"

Top Hat had a point.

The five circled him, cutting off Harrison's retreat to the building.

"Dis here's Fly Boys' turf," Top Hat said. "And you made a mistake comin' here widdout first gettin' our say-so. I want you ta know that, jus' so you'd know who it was dat killed ya."

Harrison didn't see the blow that knocked him to the ground, nor did he remember going down. The next thing he knew, he was lying cheek in the mud while a thousand elephants danced on his back and legs and head. Then, just as he was losing consciousness, he heard what sounded like an Indian war cry, while all around him feet stomped and slipped and splattered in the Five Points dance of death.

CHAPTER 4

The Shaw interview created a stir among the curtain-attorney consultants. Actually, only two of the consultants were practicing attorneys. One was a banker. One was a judge.

"The boy's got a lot of nerve. Too much for someone his age," the judge said.

J. K. Jarves sat comfortably behind his desk as the four men took turns approaching him and pleading their cases. Each had his favorite candidate, selected before the interviews began. Jarves was not so foolish as to believe otherwise.

"Shaw used our own tactic against us. Shows resourcefulness."

Judge Edwin Walsh blustered, "Shows a lack of respect, if you ask me."

"At least he didn't bawl like a baby, like that Finley fellow," said attorney Aaron Sedgwick, the youngest of the consultants and a former finalist in the intern-selection process.

Gustave Lieber laughed. "Didn't he wet his pants?"

"Gustave," Jarves said, "you're the only one among us who's made a living outside the legal profession. What's your impression of Mr. Shaw?"

Sedgwick leaned close to Walsh. "Notice he said 'outside the legal profession,' not 'outside the law.'"

That got a laugh.

Lieber laughed with them. For the most part, they were a genial bunch, preferring to relish in their role as Jarves's consultants rather than to do any serious infighting. But that didn't keep the discussion from at times becoming lively.

"In the banking profession," Lieber replied, "I judge applicants according to their ancestry. I want a man who has banking in his blood. His schooling is secondary."

"Coincidentally," said Eli Hodge, who was a good twenty years older than the rest of them, "my candidate has a father who's a judge and a grandfather who's a retired judge."

"And who attended a second-rate school," Walsh said.

"Yale is not a second-rate school!" Sedgwick objected.

"Regardless, academics are no substitute for blood!" Lieber cried.

Jarves said, "All right, Eli, who do you recommend?"

"My money's on Whitney Stuart. Harvard. Top of his class. Excellent references. *And* he has blood—third-generation attorney."

"*And* you are indebted to his father," Lieber added.

"That's confidential!" Hodge shouted. "I'm offended you said that. For the record, my personal business dealings have no influence on my recommendation."

"In a pig's eye!" Sedgwick scoffed.

As his consultants debated—shouted at each other—the merits of each of their candidates, Jarves scrutinized them.

Sedgwick had the sharpest mind. Ambitious, he'd spent the last three years trying to prove Jarves had made a mistake not selecting him for the intern position. His weakness was that he overreacted. Push him into a corner, and he'd do something impulsive and stupid.

Lieber was a respected banker with enormous gambling debts. He thought nobody of consequence knew it—Jarves knew it.

Eli Hodge was a broken man, having recently suffered financial reversals so severe that he was forced to file bankruptcy. At the same time his wife was involved in a public scandal, caught in an act of moral indiscretion. A woman of her age, of all things.

Judge Walsh drank heavily. This was no secret. But because of this, he was vulnerable, and he knew it, which made him amiable to court-room deals.

As for their opinions? Jarves didn't care what they thought. It was all a show. He never took the advice of his annual team of consultants. He never took anyone's advice. He'd made his reputation and money by observation and shrewd deduction. He chose his consultants accordingly. These men weren't here to consult. They were here to be observed.

Upstairs, Victoria Jarves was neck deep in water and bubbles. The level of her bath peaked like a storm on the high seas as she scrubbed her arms and legs furiously. She used an ordinary bar of soap she'd obtained from one of the house servants, not one of the perfumed soaps that were in her cabinet. She paused occasionally and then only long enough to sniff her arms for any lingering evidence of Desire du Paris. Then she was back at it again, scrubbing with renewed determination.

As his consultants' behavior became boringly redundant—Sedgwick attacking, Lieber blustering, Hodge pleading, and Walsh posturing—Jarves withdrew to his own thoughts.

He shuffled the applications on his desk, reading comments he'd written in the margins:

As indecisive as a two-headed goat.
How could Sam and Maude produce
an offspring so painfully ugly?
What is this fellow's fascination with his nose?

Beneath the last application there was a newspaper article clipped from the *New York Herald*. It was Horace Conant's weekly column.

```
The annual lawyers' cotillion begins this week
at the home of New York's most prominent attorney,
```

J. K. Jarves. For those not familiar with the event, a bevy of hopefuls is put on the block, each one competing to be selected as this year's Cinderella apprentice. For seven years Jarves has hosted this pageant of stiff-collars. Previous winners all have become successful attorneys, with Lenox Beckwith (1853) going on to be elected governor of New Hampshire, and Roger Dorr (1851) elected to the U.S. House of Representatives. Each year the competition grows increasingly competitive, attracting dozens of applications from the best schools in the nation, which makes this reporter question Jarves's motives, if not his abilities.

Maybe I'm missing the point, but what skill is required to win a race if one has his choice of horseflesh from the best stables in the country? If the inimitable J. K. Jarves is truly the shrewd judge of character he makes himself out to be, let him pick a local nag and turn him into a thoroughbred. But alas, it is far easier to rest on one's laurels, which is not only unsightly, but results in little to show for the effort, other than squashed laurels.

Jarves thumped the article with his forefinger. The debate was louder now than when he left it.

"Academics, gentlemen! He has the academic credentials!"

"Blood! Blood! Blood!"

"Three generations! Grandfather, father, son!"

Jarves stood and by doing so closed the debate. "Thank you, gentlemen. I'll take your opinions under advisement."

From the looks on their faces, they had just begun to argue. Nevertheless, each, in his own way, composed himself in preparation for leaving.

"You've made your decision?" Lieber asked.

"Gustave," Jarves said, "you know I never reveal my choice before the formal announcement."

Sedgwick spied Conant's column on the desk. It was he who had clipped it out and brought it to Jarves. "I certainly hope you're not going to let that broken-down journalist goad you into doing something foolish."

Jarves replied only with a smile.

Sedgwick grew concerned. "J. K., please tell me you're not considering that Brooklyn bumpkin?"

"I like his coat," Jarves said.

He walked them to the door, thanking each man for his investment of time.

Eli Hodge was the last to leave. Jarves shook the man's hand.

Hodge clung to him. Making sure the others were out of earshot, he whispered, "J. K., I want to thank you for standing with me these last few months when all others have forsaken me. You're a true friend, and I'm eternally in your debt. I just wanted you to know that." There were tears in his eyes.

"You'll see better days soon, my friend," Jarves said.

But he wouldn't. And Jarves knew it.

CHAPTER 5

Harrison's climb to consciousness began with the awareness of light. It was bright. For a moment he thought he was eleven years old again and sitting at his window desk at the schoolhouse squinting against the spring sun. Only he didn't remember being in this much pain at the schoolhouse or chewing foul-smelling mud that had a hint of what? Whatever it was, it made him think of girls.

He groaned. His cheek squished against something cold and wet, as though his head were in a bowl of pudding. A blink and another groan. The sun, sharp as a stick, poked his eyes.

The next thing he knew, a floodgate was raised. A tide of pain sloshed through him from head to foot. With the pain came images of a top hat and sadistic sneers. Harrison tried to lift his head. Big mistake. The effort set off a series of explosions in his neck. He went limp. The pain eased, but not by much.

Someone nudged him in the ribs. He winced. Why couldn't they leave him alone?

"No more," he moaned. "Please, don't hurt me anymore."

Another nudge. More pain. *The sadistic pigs!*

He heard a snort. Another nudge and another snort. It was a pig!

Next, he heard sloshing footsteps.

"Shoo! Shoo! Shoo, pig! Shoo!"

44

Harrison shielded his eyes with a sleeve heavy with mud. He saw a boy chasing away a swine, tan with black splotches. It looked like the same animal that had accompanied him into Five Points. When? Last night? Good Lord, had he been lying in this alley all night?

"Harrison? Dat you?"

A familiar voice—and the reason Harrison had entered Five Points in the first place. He'd delivered a sack of food to the boy's front door.

"Whatcha doin' in the mud?"

"Mouser? Help me up."

Even with assistance it was all Harrison could do to roll over and sit up. After that he needed a rest before testing his legs.

The boy helping him was slight for his age and fair of skin. Harrison guessed him to be in his midteens. He always wore the same ragged clothes and a newsboy's cap. There was intelligence behind the boy's eyes, and he was plucky, which explained how he could survive in Five Points.

"Boy, dey got you good." Mouser shook his head. "Dey got Stick even worse."

Not until Mouser pointed it out did Harrison realize he was lying next to someone. The twisted body of Stick was sprawled within touching range. His eyes were half-open.

"Is he?"

"Deader than pork on the plate," Mouser said.

Harrison stared at the body beside him. It was trampled so deep in the mud, it looked as though the earth was reclaiming one of its own. Dust to dust.

He couldn't help but admire Stick. He'd come back, probably with reinforcements. That would explain why this morning Harrison could sit up and breathe and do the things living people do.

"Was it the Fly Boys what got to you?" Mouser asked. "It was the Fly Boys, wasn't it? Boy, I'll tell you what. We're gonna git dem stinkin' Fly Boys, and dey're gonna wish dey never thunk o' crossin' Canal Street. You jus' wait and see."

A queasy wave passed over Harrison. He put a hand in the mud to steady himself and felt something hard. It was smaller than his hand. Flat. Round. He picked it up. His lucky silver dollar. The one he'd used to pay Stick for his protection.

"What's dat?" Mouser asked.

Harrison slipped the coin into his pocket. "Nothing. Help me up."

"Yeah boy. We better get you outta here."

Mouser slipped and slid as he assisted the taller Harrison out of what could have been a muddy grave.

Voices from the street interrupted them. Two chattering girls. Both in maids' uniforms. One look at Harrison and they stopped talking. They hurried past the alley.

On his feet now, Harrison's head was swirling. He had to pause to blink back a rising tide of nausea. The last time he felt like this, he had spent three days in bed with the flu. Mouser, his flesh-and-blood cane, attended him patiently. Harrison took a step. Then another. Everything seemed to be working. Not well, and not without complaint, but working.

"What about Stick?" Harrison asked.

"Somebody'll come for 'im. Dats da way o' things in Five Points. Stick know'd dat. 'Spect he know'd he'd die someday fightin' dem stinkin' Fly Boys."

"I thought he ran out on me last night."

"Stick? He ain't never runned out on nobody in his life."

"He died protecting me."

The realization hit Harrison like another punch in the gut, a double blow. A quick one-two. Anger and nausea. Anger for the senseless cruelty of the death; nausea because it could have been him.

"And I missed it too!" Mouser cried. The boy sounded genuinely disappointed and unaffected by the death.

Harrison peered down at his helper. What kind of a world was this that a boy like Mouser had to grow up with violence and death, where filth and stench and disease were everyday facts of life? Mouser would be lucky if he lived long enough to see his twentieth birthday.

"I left something at your door last night," Harrison said. "Did you get it?"

Mouser stared up at him with a blank expression.

"You didn't get it?"

"Get what?"

"I left it on your doorstep. A bag."

Mouser wiped his nose with the back of his hand. "Someone musta lifted it." He didn't seem all that concerned about it.

Harrison kicked himself. "I knew I should have knocked."

Mouser didn't look up, didn't say anything.

"Wait a minute," Harrison said. "Was the bag missing, or did you just not see it?"

Mouser avoided looking at him. "You best get outta here, Harrison boy. Dem Fly Boys could show up any minute."

Harrison glanced around. There was no immediate danger. Traffic on the street consisted of people going to work—beggars, drunks, and prostitutes. It was a typical Five Points morning. True, danger could be found around any corner, but all the same, Mouser was avoiding the question.

"You didn't go home last night, did you?" Harrison asked.

Mouser sniffed.

"Where were you? Crown's Grocery running bets?"

"Hey! Don't give me lip! Dats how I makes money."

"Mouser! I've warned you about that place! It's not safe for you there."

"Look, I can makes foldin' money runnin' bets. So leave me alone, all right? I's can take care of myself."

Harrison didn't like it, but what could he do? Of the two, he was in no shape to give lectures on how to avoid danger. They trudged the muddy street in silence. Harrison's legs slowly regained their strength.

"At least promise me you'll go home and check on your mother and sister," Harrison said. He couldn't leave it alone.

"I's busy helpin' you!"

"Just to Park Street. After that, go straight home. Promise me. See if they got the bag of food I left on the doorstep."

"You shouldn'ta left it in the hallway. Someone'll lifted it for sure."

"Well, go home and check for me, all right? Promise?"

Reluctantly, Mouser agreed.

"And tell your sister I said hello."

"She's at work."

"Then tell her when she gets home."

Mouser kept walking.

"You'll tell her?"

Exasperated, Mouser said, "I'll tell her! I'll tell her! All right?"

"Thank you."

They were nearing Park Street, and there was no sign of Fly Boys or Plug Uglies.

Mouser narrowed his eyes. "Why are you so interested in my sister anyway?"

Harrison shrugged self-consciously. "I'm not especially interested in her. It's just that I've grown fond of her, that's all."

"Fond. Is dat some kinda love?"

"Something like it."

Mouser stopped. He stepped away and squared his shoulders. "You're sweet on my sister, ain't you?"

"I'm concerned. Is that a crime?"

"You're sweet on her!"

Harrison continued walking on his own. It was more of a hobble. "Forget I asked."

Mouser blocked his way. "You keep your hands off my sister, Harrison boy. You got dat?"

The boy's outrage was genuine, if not comic. Harrison suppressed a grin.

"I mean it, Harrison! You keep your hands off Katie."

"I'm not going to touch your sister," Harrison said.

"I better not hear that you put your hands on her, or you'll be worse off than ol' Stick."

They had reached Park Street.

"Thanks for your help, Mouser."

"You jus' remember what I said about my sister!"

He meant it. Harrison could see it in the boy's eyes.

"I will. And thanks again. Now go home."

But Mouser didn't go home. He stood on the edge of Five Points and watched Harrison limp toward the ferry landing.

CHAPTER 6

Had any of the other residents at the Newsboys' Lodge stayed out all night, then returned bruised and battered, they would have been reprimanded. If it was a repeat offense, they'd have been thrown out. Carousing was frequently cited in dismissals.

When Harrison straggled into the lodge bloodied, muddied, and bruised, no such actions were taken for two reasons:

First, because the idea of Harrison Quincy Shaw carousing was itself laughable. His stand against all the physical vices was well documented in lodge folklore, which Isaac Hirsch kept as the unofficial lodge storyteller. Since the lodge saw its share of sailors and men who lived on the streets, the introduction of one vice or another occurred rather frequently, even though there were rules posted in every room expressly prohibiting them. Whenever the opportunity arose to break the rules, Harrison never had to decline the offer. Hirsch did it for him. Usually in litany form:

"Shaw doesn't smoke."

"Shaw doesn't chew."

"Shaw doesn't drink."

"Shaw doesn't swear."

"Shaw doesn't frequent those kinds of places."

Which inevitably prompted a question as to whether or not Harrison Shaw was human.

For Harrison it wasn't so much a moral decision—though his personal beliefs figured into it—as a practical one. He'd tried smoking once. It made him sick. He'd tried chewing tobacco. It made him sick. He'd tried a sip of gin. It made him sick. He viewed cursing as the sign of a weak mind and saw too many men suffering the effects of social diseases to find the risk worth taking.

The second reason no action was taken against Harrison for fighting at Five Points was because director George Bowen believed Harrison's story. Bowen didn't approve of Harrison's venturing into Five Points, but he couldn't fault Harrison's missionary motives. Harrison hadn't told him about his burgeoning feelings for Katie.

Harrison Shaw was Bowen's favorite. Everyone knew that. It wasn't a problem, because Harrison never took advantage of it. He pulled his weight and kept his nose clean.

Originally founded by George Bowen to provide temporary inexpensive housing for the growing number of newsboys who slept in doorways and alleys, the Newsboys' Lodge had expanded over the years to a home for a select number of orphans and cheap lodging for sailors who just stayed a night or two. Having lived there for as long as he could remember, Harrison was the senior resident. George Bowen was the closest thing to a father he had.

However, Harrison's all-night excursion into Five Points was not completely without its consequences. Isaac Hirsch wasn't talking to him. Isaac had planned on using the community coat to do a little courting. The time and place had been arranged, and the girl—according to Isaac—was eager. But now he didn't have anything suitable to wear.

Harrison sat on the edge of his bed in the nearly empty dormitory, having just endured another verbal assault from Isaac, who accused Harrison of being more concerned with establishing his own sainthood than with the love life of a fellow lodger.

Isaac stormed past George Bowen who was walking in.

"Let me take a look at that eye," Bowen said.

He stepped in front of Harrison and bent over to get a look. He didn't have to bend far. Bowen was a small man, round and genial in manner. But it was a mistake to interpret his friendly nature for weakness, as anyone who crossed him soon found out to their detriment. Only twice could Harrison remember the police being summoned to handle an unruly guest.

"It's still swollen. Can you see out of it?"

"It's a little blurry and like looking through a crack in a fence," Harrison replied.

Bowen poked the swollen part. Harrison flinched.

"Your eye's red in the corner. Looks like a burst of fireworks." Bowen stepped back, still studying the eye.

Harrison's earliest memories were of Bowen caring for him. Sending him off to bed. Bandaging a scraped knee. Listening to his woes.

"Oh! Before I forget. This was delivered for you a little while ago." Bowen extracted an envelope from his back pocket. It was addressed to Harrison. Name only, in large, beautifully penned letters. Harrison opened it, read the note, then tossed it onto the bed beside him.

"Well? A man in a fancy black carriage delivered it."

Harrison sighed. "It's an invitation to a masquerade ball."

Bowen's bushy eyebrows raised. As the man aged, the hair on his head thinned, but his eyebrows and mustache grew bushier. "Climbing the social ladder, are we?"

"It's the internship. The winner is announced at the ball."

Bowen picked up the invitation and read it. "Says here you're a finalist."

Harrison shrugged. "Makes no difference. I'm not going."

Bowen didn't comment. He let Harrison's words hang in the air unchallenged, like laundry on a line. That was his way. He'd let them hang there for all the world to see until Harrison defended them or reeled them in.

Finally Harrison said, "It's laughable to think Mr. Jarves would choose me."

"He sent you an invitation."

"A courtesy. All finalists get invitations."

"How many finalists are there?"

"Five."

"And how many applications were there?"

It was obvious where Bowen was going with this.

"The other finalists all have someone to champion them," Harrison complained. "They matriculated at Yale, William and Mary, and Harvard. They come from a long line of lawyers, judges, congressmen. The fact is, they bring to the table things I can't pretend to offer."

Bowen thought about this. "Maybe you bring to the table something they don't have. Besides, how certain are you that you don't have someone championing you?"

Harrison looked up. It was hard to argue with a person who believed in you.

"There's another reason I can't go. I don't have a costume."

"We have a month to find one."

"I'm not going."

Again Bowen appeared thoughtful. "We could keep it simple. Considering how that eye looks, you could go as a bruised banana."

Harrison laughed, but there was no way he was going to put himself in a position to be humiliated and ridiculed in front of New York's wealthiest and most influential citizens.

Harrison adjusted his pirate's cutlass and, taking a final two-eyed look at the brightly lit mansion across the street, pulled a black patch over his bruised eye. The eye patch was Bowen's idea, and it was a good one. While the swelling had gone down, there was still a prominent black-and-blue crescent under his eye.

Harrison was in no hurry to cross the street. He was playing it cautious. He'd checked and double-checked the invitation, each time expecting the word *masquerade* to have mysteriously disappeared. He held the invitation up to the street lamp and checked again, just to be sure. With memories of a coat too short, he had nightmares of walking into a Fifth Avenue ballroom as the only one wearing a costume.

His plan was simple. He'd watch from a distance while other guests arrived. If they arrived in costumes, his fears would be dispelled. However, if they arrived in anything remotely modern, it was back to the ferry and home.

He pulled his bandanna from his pocket.

His costume had become a lodge project. With a half dozen sailors in residence, ready access to nautical wear provided the theme. Harrison borrowed a pair of baggy canvas breeches that came up two inches above his ankle—they were supposed to—and a black-striped pullover shirt from one man, and a red handkerchief bandanna from another. Bowen fashioned the eye patch from a piece of black cloth and string. Harrison had had second thoughts and had almost backed out until Jimmy Wessler walked in with the pirate cutlass. He said the guy he borrowed it from picked it up in Barbados. He bought it from another sailor who swore it once belonged to a real pirate.

It wasn't every day Harrison got the chance to wear a real pirate sword.

A carriage pulled up in front of the mansion. The moment of truth was at hand.

The night was cold. The sky clear. Servants appeared from the mansion to open the carriage door for the guests.

While this was J. K. Jarves's announcement ball, for reasons unknown to Harrison, it was held at someone else's mansion, a huge Victorian-Gothic structure, gaily lit for the occasion.

"Here it comes," Harrison muttered to himself, eagerly waiting for a glimpse of the guest's attire. He shivered.

"Ah!"

Three people emerged from the carriage. From the looks of them, a middle-aged couple and their son, who was old enough to be one of the finalists. To Harrison's relief all three were dressed in eighteenth-century costumes, complete with powdered wigs and silk breeches.

Harrison sighed in relief. He'd worried needlessly. He still didn't want to attend. He'd do it for Bowen. He'd make an appearance. Jarves would make his announcement. Bowen would commiserate with him when he didn't get it. And Harrison could get on with his life.

One night. Was that too much to ask, considering all that George Bowen had done for him?

Harrison crossed the street, the pirate cutlass slapping his leg. He took the steps two at a time. Inside, a harpsichord was playing. A minuet, if he wasn't mistaken.

Harrison readied his invitation. He knocked on the door.

A doorman answered.

Took one look at him.

And laughed.

Drink in hand, Harrison stood with his back to the wall, his face redder than the punch. His heels kicked the baseboard for the hundredth time. As much as he wanted to, he couldn't back away any farther.

It would all be over at midnight when J. K. Jarves revealed his selection. Meanwhile, the room was filled with music and gaiety and forced laughter, the nervous kind that usually precedes an announcement of any magnitude.

"*Dear* boy . . ."

A woman appeared before him. Her face was heavily powdered. Sagging skin gave her the appearance of a dripping candle. She wore a towering powdered wig and fluttered a fan as she spoke. "Dear, *dear* boy, didn't you get the word?"

The fan did little to conceal her amused expression. She had a black beauty mark on her cheek that did a little hula dance when she talked.

"Word, ma'am?"

"The party theme, dear boy!" She half turned and waved the fan at the other guests. "The Revolutionary War, don't you know?"

The beauty mark did a little jig when she said "Revolutionary."

"Um . . . no ma'am. There was nothing about a theme on my invitation."

She laughed and slapped his forearm with her fan. "Oh, dear boy, don't be silly. Of course it wouldn't be on the invitation!" She walked away laughing.

"Don't mind her."

Harrison turned toward the voice beside him.

It was a young man dressed in a minuteman costume. Beneath his tricornered hat, he wore a powdered wig tied in the back with a red ribbon. "She enjoys embarrassing people," he said.

Harrison grinned. "She's good at it."

They stood shoulder to shoulder, watching half a dozen uncoordinated dancers murder the minuet.

"You do look ridiculous though," said the minuteman.

There was something about the way he said it that prevented Harrison from taking offense—good-natured teasing, the kind he'd expect back at the lodge.

"My name's John Blayne." He offered an effeminate hand that fit his undersized frame.

Harrison shook it.

"Are you one of the finalists?" Blayne asked.

"Supposedly. You?"

He looked too young to be a finalist, but Harrison asked anyway.

Blayne laughed at the thought. "I'm here with family."

The minuet droned on. Harrison raised his cup to take a sip. It was empty. It had been empty the last two times he'd raised it too.

"Have you met the other finalists?" Blayne asked.

"Haven't had the pleasure."

Blayne scanned the room. "Over there." He directed Harrison's gaze to the far corner of the room. "That's Whitney Stu . . . wait . . ." His attention was diverted. "Oh, you're going to love this."

To a harpsichord fanfare, a large woman emerged from behind a curtained doorway. She was wearing a full-length toga that looked like it had been made from an American flag. Holding high a white hanky in her left hand, she sashayed across the floor and took up a position beside the keyboard instrument.

The room stilled, whether from the fanfare or the shock of this woman's attire, Harrison couldn't tell.

Lady Liberty, smiling broadly, accepted the room's attention obligingly and held it for several beats. Then, placing a hand on the instrument, she nodded solemnly to the accompanist.

"Who is she?" Harrison whispered.

"Our hostess. Mrs. Pierre Jerome Belmont," Blayne said with a mischievous grin.

Following an introductory stanza, Mrs. Belmont launched into a very loud, very off-key version of the national anthem. She warbled like a three-hundred-pound canary.

Everywhere Harrison looked guests raised hands and hankies to their mouths to conceal their amusement. Blayne was more obvious. He chortled unhindered, blinking back tears, which earned him a number of disapproving glares.

Lady Liberty girded herself for the crescendo— *"land of the free."* She grasped the side of the harpsichord and held on to the high note with the desperation of a drowning man. Atop her head a harp-shaped crown ignited in an array of tiny flames.

There was a collective gasp.

Blayne burst into laughter.

Harrison learned later that Mrs. Belmont's rendition was something of an annual tradition. The fiery display was achieved by hiding little gas containers in her hair. One year the flames ignited a pair of draperies.

The song and pyrotechnics sputtered to an end. The room erupted with applause. Harrison clapped for the soloist without pretense. Being the only pirate in a room of George and Martha Washingtons, he was freshly aware of what it was like to be the object of ridicule.

Blayne was laughing so hard he could barely stand, prompting a second round of disapproving stares.

"Show a little restraint," Harrison whispered.

"Can't help it." Blayne laughed more. "That woman has more bats in her belfry than Boston's Old North Church."

"She may be eccentric, but that doesn't mean she's crazy."

Blayne sobered somewhat. "Oh, she's crazy, all right."

"She's our hostess."

Wiping his eyes, Blayne took a long look at Harrison. "You're an odd duck, aren't you?"

By now Lady Liberty had departed, and a general buzz of conversation resumed.

"Would a sane person walk the halls, bowing and chatting to imaginary guests?" Blayne asked.

"You're making that up."

"Her noodle hit the wall shortly after her husband died. Doctors said it was from the stress of building this house for her. But if he died to get some rest, he didn't get to rest for very long."

"I'm not following you."

Blayne's eyes came alive. He clearly enjoyed knowing and telling secrets. "Body snatchers. Dug the old boy up. Held 'im for ransom. Twenty-thousand dollars."

"That's horrible! And Mrs. Belmont couldn't come up with the money."

"Are you kidding?" Blayne scoffed. "She's got millions. The problem was, whom does she pay? Or better yet, how many times does she pay?"

"Again, I'm not following."

Blayne grinned like an imp with a secret he couldn't wait to tell. "For weeks, bits and pieces were delivered to the front door! Gift wrapped!"

"That's disgusting! You're making this up!"

Blayne was laughing so hard, he could barely speak. "The truth! I swear it!"

"Poor woman!" Harrison said, looking at Lady Liberty with sympathy. "No one should have to go through something like that."

Blayne dried his eyes with the palms of his hands. He shook his head at Harrison, surprised that he wasn't joining in on the fun. "You *are* an odd duck, aren't you?"

The astonishment went both ways. Harrison couldn't believe that a boy so young could be that callous over suffering and tragedy. He never would have thought it of the wealthy. Stodgy, yes; but not cruel. The way these people amused themselves with Mrs. Belmont's suffering, the way Blayne joked at her tragedy . . . Put a soiled hat on them and stick their thumbs in their waistbands, and they were Fly Boys and Plug Uglies.

In the front of the room, Mrs. Pierre Jerome Belmont made an encore appearance. Stepping from behind the curtain, she did a jig, turned, and kicked up her heels, revealing little red boots with bells on them.

Her antics sent Blayne into a fresh round of guffaws.

"I'm going to go get some punch," Harrison said.

"Wait . . . wait," the boy cried, holding on to Harrison's arm. He tried to speak through his laughter. "I . . . I . . . haven't yet . . . pointed out . . . your compe . . . tition."

People were staring at them. Blayne was drying his cheeks, sniffing a couple of times, trying to control himself.

Harrison endured the stares. He didn't want to stay, but then he didn't want to leave either. A pirate cutting a swath through an assembly of colonials was too inviting of a target.

"I . . . can do this," Blayne said, pulling himself up. "All right. Now then." He cleared his throat. "Cast your good eye in that direction."

Harrison frowned down at Blayne.

"Sorry, couldn't help myself," Blayne apologized. "Far corner. See the dandy? The one in the white silk who looks like Lafayette?"

Harrison nodded.

"Whitney Stuart III. Odds-on favorite. Got it all. Harvard. Top of his class. Three generations of lawyers. When word got out he was applying, a number of well-qualified chaps didn't even bother to submit applications."

"Nobody could match his qualifications?"

"His father and Jarves are close friends."

"Oh."

Blayne directed Harrison's attention to the punch bowl. "William Reid. The short, dashing fellow. The one talking to those two trollops . . ."

"Blayne!"

"What? My, you are a strange one, aren't you? Trust me, they are. Anyway, Reid's a Yale man."

And on it went. Four finalists and Harrison. Each of them with impeccable credentials, established family backgrounds, and letters of recommendation from governors, congressmen, and senators.

"Why did I even bother?" Harrison mumbled.

"Why did you bother?" Blayne asked.

Harrison studied the boy. He wondered if Blayne knew as much about him as he seemed to know about the other finalists.

"I had my reasons."

"Did you really think you had a chance?"

Harrison lifted his cup to take a drink, only to be reminded it was empty. "No. I never thought I had a chance."

At the stroke of midnight, J. K. Jarves, dressed as General George Washington, took center stage to make the anticipated announcement. It was obvious he thrived on the attention. He paced back and forth in front of the gala, looking very much like a commander addressing his troops.

"Each year the decision of selecting an intern becomes increasingly difficult. Each year there are more applicants. Better qualified men."

Harrison surveyed the room. He and Blayne were the only ones who hadn't moved forward to hear the announcement. The four curtain attorneys—Sideburns and the others—entered from a side room, looking very judicial. Harrison hadn't seen them tonight until now. Without exception they looked ridiculous in powdered wigs.

He thought now would be a good time to leave.

"Where are you going?" Blayne asked.

"Back where I belong."

"To your ship?" Blayne grinned. "Sorry, couldn't help myself." Then, more seriously, he added, "But what if you're the chosen one?"

Interesting choice of words. Harrison had been called "the chosen one" at the Lodge. Often in derision, but only because there was an element of truth to it since he was clearly George Bowen's favorite.

"You said it yourself," Harrison replied. "What are the chances? But I am glad I got to meet you, John. Thanks for talking to me."

He meant it. John Blayne was the only person in the room who had made an effort to talk to him tonight—not counting the woman with the beauty mark. All the other guests sniggered at him behind glasses of punch from the safety of their circle of friends. Blayne made the evening endurable, despite his occasional bout of bad manners.

For his part, Harrison was certain he'd given the boy an ample amount of story grist for future parties. Besides, there was something about the boy he liked. John Blayne reminded him of a cleaned-up version of Mouser.

In the front of the room, at the same spot where Lady Liberty sang the national anthem, J. K. Jarves continued with his announcement. "In the process of reviewing this year's crop of applicants—and I'm certain my advisors will agree with me on this point—I must say I was impressed. America's future is in good hands."

Applause resounded throughout the room.

"Leaders all! Mark my words. From among these men will come senators, statesmen, ambassadors, and possibly even a president or two."

More applause.

Harrison shook Blayne's hand.

"Aren't you the slightest bit curious?" Blayne asked.

Harrison glanced at Jarves. There was nothing for him here. He'd applied for the intern position at George Bowen's urging. Then, as the process progressed, Harrison thought some good might come of it. He'd hoped it might give him an opportunity to talk to Jarves about Five Points. If a powerful man like J. K. Jarves knew the conditions there, maybe something could be done to improve them. But the opportunity never arose, and now it never would.

"I'll read about the winner in tomorrow's newspaper," Harrison said to Blayne.

From the front of the room: "And so the time has come for me to announce my selection," Jarves said. The celebrated attorney paused dramatically. It was a practiced move, one he'd honed in courtrooms before dozens of juries. His reputation was legendary. He'd been known to move jurors to tears, to make them laugh, to wring their emotions, and shepherd their thoughts until they had no choice but to make the decision he wanted them to make. Now he had his audience, in all their colonial finery, exactly where he wanted them—leaning forward in anticipation, begging him with their eyes not to keep them in suspense any longer, but to lift the veil and reveal to them his choice for intern.

"Whitney Stuart III . . ."

The room erupted with applause and cheers.

Walking toward the door, Harrison turned and met John Blayne's gaze. They exchanged knowing shrugs.

Actually, Harrison was glad he'd stayed long enough to hear the announcement. At least when George Bowen asked, he'd be able to tell him.

Jarves's voice could be heard from the front of the room. "Whitney, I have no doubt you are destined for greatness. When American school-children of the twentieth century study the history of this great country, they'll memorize your name."

Applause.

Whitney was beaming. So were his parents. So was the oldest of the four curtain attorneys, Whitney's champion.

"It is for that reason," J. K. Jarves said, "that I did not select you."

The room was stunned to silence. Had the hand of God ripped off the roof and the face of the Almighty peered down upon them, the assembled colonials would not have been any less dumbfounded.

At the door Harrison stopped. He turned back into the room.

The shocked assembly tittered nervously. They searched Jarves's eyes for a glimmer of humor, his mouth for the slightest twitch, anything that might indicate he was jesting.

For his part, Jarves fed off their surprise. He grinned at their shock, giddy that he'd succeeded in dangling them over a chasm of disbelief, thrilled that he'd knocked their world cockeyed, delighted in the knowledge that they desperately wanted him to balance their lives again and give it order.

But he wouldn't. Recklessness danced in his eyes.

Jarves approached the frontrunner. Whitney's face was Christmas red. His eyes were lit with fury. His jaw bit back his humiliation.

"Whitney," Jarves said, soothingly, "you don't need me to become a great statesman. Neither do you need this internship to propel you down the path to greatness. Your course is set, your victory sure."

Whitney wasn't buying it. Jarves didn't care.

"And that is why this year I have selected a dark-horse candidate. This year it will be my task to make an unknown great, possibly even in spite of himself. This year for my intern I have selected Harrison Quincy Shaw of the Washburn School of Law."

CHAPTER 7

Following the announcement, the only congratulatory handshake Harrison received came from John Blayne, and then it was just a quick pump, accompanied by a lopsided grin of surprise and amusement.

From the front of the room, J. K. Jarves called to him. "Come on up here, Harrison. Let the people see you."

Frankly, given his costume, Harrison didn't think being seen by everyone was a particularly good idea. But what recourse did he have? Jarves was leading the others in a round of applause, a solo effort.

Harrison made his way to the front of the room. A sea of angry colonials parted in front of him, creating a path large enough to sail a ship through. The expressions he saw along the way were historically familiar to pirates—as they walked to the gallows.

Jarves greeted him with a crushing handshake and a smile so large it was frightening. Gripping him by the shoulders, he turned Harrison to face the hostile room of well-wishers.

"He's not much to look at, is he?" Jarves joked. He surveyed Harrison. "But he's quick on his feet, and he's an independent thinker—two traits that earned him this internship. Who else among us, having learned it would be a colonial theme, would think of coming as a colonial pirate?"

Harrison could hear Blayne laughing in the back of the room. Nobody else seemed to be in a jovial mood.

"A little rough around the edges," Jarves continued, "but mark my words, you're going to hear impressive things regarding this young man. I'll make a lawyer out of him or die in the attempt!" To Harrison: "That's my promise to you, son."

Something about Harrison's eye patch caught Jarves's attention.

"Why don't you take off your eye patch and bandanna, and let everybody get a good look at you?"

Harrison winced, remembering what was beneath the eye patch. He leaned toward Jarves and whispered, "That might not be advisable, sir."

Jarves laughed. To the crowd he said: "The boy's shy! Well, we'll change that, won't we?"

J. K. Jarves was giving every impression of having a good time, though it seemed to Harrison that the man was selling an oddity, not unlike the barkers at P. T. Barnum's museum of the weird and unusual. In this case Harrison himself was the weird and unusual oddity.

"Lesson number one, son," Jarves said loud enough for everyone to hear his words of wisdom, "never be ashamed of who you are. Now take off that silly eye patch."

His options reduced to taking off the eye patch or sprouting wings and flying away, Harrison removed the patch and bandanna with a single motion.

Maybe it was his imagination, but the gasp from the crowd seemed louder than it was for Mrs. Pierre Jerome Belmont's flaming headdress.

Beside him J. K. Jarves took a step back, stared at the bruised eye, then shouted, "He's a fighter! I'll give him that!"

Harrison remained where Jarves had planted him.

"People will want to congratulate you," Jarves had said.

He was wrong. Nobody congratulated him. The kinder colonials made a wide path around him as they departed. Others turned their backs, turned up their noses, muttered unkind things to each other loud enough for him to hear, or laughed behind his back or to his face.

Meanwhile, Jarves flitted from one disappointed contestant to another, salving egos, slapping shoulders, and generally trying to minimize the damage done by his controversial announcement. From the looks of it, the man would be repairing relationships for years.

As the room emptied, Harrison searched for a friendly face, but John Blayne was nowhere to be found. Not surprising, really. It was late, and he'd undoubtedly gone home with his parents, though Harrison had no idea who his parents were.

So he stood there. Alone. At the height of his young, professional career.

Soon, the only persons in the room with him were the cleaning staff and servants. Even they eyed him with amusement.

Jarves was nowhere to be seen. The last time Harrison saw the great attorney, he was walking someone to the door, his arm around the man's shoulders, and laughing a little too loudly at something the man said. Harrison stayed, thinking that Jarvis would want to talk to him before he left.

He waited ten minutes. Then fifteen. He assumed Jarves wanted him to stay so that he could be told where and when the internship would begin.

The servants began dousing the lights. Harrison found himself standing in the dark, which was ridiculous, so he made his way to the front door. He tarried in the entryway. How long should he wait? Had Jarves forgotten him, or was he merely detained?

Ten minutes passed. Then ten more. The house was quiet. He imagined himself still standing here in the morning like an obedient dog. Mrs. Belmont would come down and find him. She'd laugh at him for taking Jarves's instructions so seriously. Or possibly she'd think he was one of the imaginary people she talked to in the hallways.

Just when he decided to leave, Harrison heard an unseen door open. There were voices. Then shouting. A moment later John Blayne appeared, crossing in front of Harrison, but at a distance. He didn't see Harrison. J. K. Jarves followed him. He didn't see Harrison either.

They disappeared into a side room.

At least Harrison knew Jarves was still here. He could hear everything they were saying.

Jarves: "Of all the brainless stunts! What were you thinking?"

Blayne: "I didn't do anything wrong! I was just observing, that's all."

Only it didn't sound like Blayne. Well, it did, and it didn't.

"What if someone recognized you?"

"Nobody recognized me."

"Is that right? Our hostess did."

"Lady Belmont? I don't believe you."

"She told me she thought your costume was amusing, but inappropriate for the occasion. Tomorrow, everyone will know."

"She's nuts. Who's going to believe her?"

Harrison felt uncomfortable listening in on the conversation, but it wasn't as though he could help it. Maybe he should wait outside. But what if he did and Jarves left by another door?

"Don't get impudent with me," Jarves shouted. "You still haven't explained yourself."

"There's nothing to explain."

"You told me you weren't going to attend."

"I said I wasn't going to dress up like Betsy Ross."

A new thought struck Harrison. If he was still standing here when they came out, they'd know he'd overheard their conversation. He'd better wait outside.

"And take off that silly wig," Jarves said. "I saw you talking to Harrison Shaw."

"He doesn't know anything."

"How can you be sure?"

"I tell you he doesn't know. He shook my hand."

The voices were getting louder. They were coming out of the room. Harrison stepped toward the front door. No. If they heard it shut, it would appear even more suspicious than if they found him standing here. Still, he felt guilty standing here and not letting them know he could hear them. Maybe he could make it back to the ballroom.

The next instant the decision was made for him.

Wig and hat in hand, Victoria Jarves emerged from the room wearing John Blayne's clothes. She was followed by her father.

They both saw him.

"Well, he knows now," Victoria said.

Horace Conant's Monday morning column in the *New York Herald* read:

> Fifth Avenue received a one-two, red, white, and blue knockout punch Saturday night when noted attorney J. K. Jarves announced that his coveted internship was being awarded to a pirate.
>
> But I said there were two blows, didn't I? The first blow had nothing to do with Jarves's announcement and everything to do with questionable taste as Mrs. Pierre Jerome Belmont gave a less than inspiring and more than amusing rendition of "The Star Spangled Banner," complete with flaming head-dress. It's been reported by federal authorities that at the exact hour of her song, the body of Francis Scott Key climbed out of his grave and tried to hang himself.
>
> The second red, white, and blue blow was the announcement itself. Red were the faces of the celebrants when they heard the news. White were their powdered wigs (it being a costume ball with a Revolutionary War theme). And blue (and black) was

the new intern's eye when he received the honor. At Jarves's insistence the unassuming recipient lifted his eye patch to reveal a ruffian's badge from an undisclosed pummeling.

Did I mention the candidate was wearing a pirate costume at the time in a room filled with Martha Washingtons and Samuel Adamses? And did I mention that his name is Harrison Quincy Shaw, a resident of Brooklyn's Newsboys' Lodge? (Yes, you read that correctly.) As it turned out, Mr. Shaw's eye wasn't the only thing bruised that night. So, too, were the considerable egos of Misters Whitney Stuart III of Harvard and William Reid of Yale, who were considered preannouncement front-runners in this annual running of the blowhards.

On a personal note, it warms this old reporter's heart that the inimitable J. K. Jarves would take up my challenge. Now we'll see if he can indeed make a silk purse out of a sow's ear. And best wishes to Mr. Shaw, who won't be the first pirate to be thrown to the sharks.

CHAPTER 8

"What do you think of my choice?"

Victoria looked up from the breakfast table as her father entered the room. Carrying a cup of coffee, he took the seat opposite her.

She raised an eyebrow. He never joined her for breakfast. "I think you ought to put milk in it," she said.

Jarves sipped his coffee. "Don't play dumb with me."

"Then don't ask me dumb questions."

He wanted something. He never asked her opinion about business matters. Women weren't to concern themselves about such things. Their minds were to be occupied with the running of the household. So what did he want from her? The fact that he was speaking to her at all meant he'd finally decided to forget her little escapade a week ago at the announcement ball.

"I want to know," Jarves insisted. "What do you think of him?"

Victoria put down her spoon. She sat back, touching a napkin to her lips. A servant was instantly at her elbow, whisking away the empty cereal bowl. Another servant took his place, bringing her a cup of tea. She said nothing as he added sugar and milk, stirred, then stepped back, making himself invisible.

Leisurely, Victoria took a sip of tea. "I think he's deliciously low."

Jarves grinned. "He is, isn't he?"

The early morning wind whipped across the deck with staggering force. Harrison gathered the lapels of his coat closed with a fist. It was the first real winter storm of the season. In such weather, ferry crossings were brutal.

His thoughts were on what awaited him at the Jarves mansion. The first week had been mostly researching nonsense topics that had nothing to do with law, or being handed over to this clerk or that associate to acquaint him with the layout of the land, which operated under one simple maxim: Jarves is king. From comments made, Harrison had been led to believe that today the real work would start.

The vessel's steam engine chugged dutifully, belching black smoke from its stacks as the craft approached the Manhattan side of the river. They were close enough that Harrison could see patches of white on the docks from last night's snowfall. They wouldn't last the day.

A stream of immigrants debarked from a ship that had recently docked. Forty such ships arrived every day, some with as many as seven hundred men, women, and children crammed into dank, reeking cargo holds. So many of them died during the thirty-day crossing that the vessels were dubbed "coffin ships."

They wore European clothing. They carried luggage, bags, babies, and held children's hands, eager to take their first steps on American soil. As they descended the gangplank, they looked up at the New York buildings with great weariness, but also hope. Always with hope.

Another ship just like it was entering the harbor.

Harrison leaned against the railing and watched the new arrivals. He knew what was awaiting them. Within a week they'd be sleeping in stinking hovels in Five Points. All of them would look for work, few would find a job that paid enough to meet a family's needs. Their children and women would live among thugs and thieves. The men would daily be propositioned by half-dressed women, yelling at them with words that would make a sailor blush. To survive, their sons would be forced to join a street gang that would teach them about turfs and how to fight with sticks and clubs.

They'd be lucky to survive the winter. For the next couple of months, they'd huddle together in corners to keep from freezing, watching their children's ribs grow more pronounced. The little ones would play in mud and filth, the kind that not only dirtied the flesh but soiled the soul.

Give them one winter, then ask them what they think of America, Harrison thought sadly.

A heavily bundled man joined Harrison at the railing. Leaning forward with gloved hands clasped, he puffed industriously on a cigar. It seemed a little imitation of the ferry's smokestack. He watched the immigrants disembark for a few minutes, then said, "Know what I'd do if I had my way? I'd erect a gallows at every landing in New York and hang every cursed one of 'em the moment they stepped foot on shore."

Harrison assumed the man expected him to voice his agreement. There were plenty of people in New York who would.

"They just want what everyone wants," Harrison said, keeping his voice even. "To be healthy and happy. Can't fault them for that."

The man bit down hard on his cigar. "I can, when they're the ones bringing disease and ruining the economy for the rest of us." Disgusted, he tossed his cigar into the river and walked away. He didn't go far before turning back. "You know," he shouted, "it's addleheaded morons like you who are going to ruin this country! If we don't protect what we have, we're going to lose it."

The man started to say more, evidently wanted to say more, but his anger got in the way of his words. After sputtering a few disjointed phrases, he threw up his hands and stomped away.

"Out of the question."

A clink of teacup against saucer punctuated Victoria's decision. Subject closed. She turned her head and stared out the window.

But J. K. Jarves hadn't risen to prominence by being put off easily. "I'm told you spy on him whenever he's in the house."

"Spy on him? Ridiculous!" Victoria snapped.

Jarves grinned, having gotten the response he was after.

"Yes, I may have spied on him that one time, in the sitting room, the day you were interviewing applicants," she admitted, "but not since then. And it wasn't only him I spied on, if that's what you're alluding to. I spied on the others as well. Men can be so disgustingly amusing when they think they're alone in a room. But for you to sit there and imply that I've ogled Mr. Shaw when he's in residence, why it's preposterous. And I demand you identify who is telling you otherwise."

Her father took a long sip of tea.

She knew what he was doing. He'd gained the upper hand and wasn't about to relinquish it.

After several more sips, he said, "You spent a great deal of time conversing with him the night of the ball."

Victoria paused before answering. She wasn't going to let him rile her. "I was amusing myself. For you to infer otherwise is insulting."

"It's just one afternoon. That's all I'm asking."

"My afternoon is planned. Besides, it would take more than an afternoon to teach that Brooklyn barbarian proper manners."

"Rearrange your schedule."

"My schedule is not mine to arrange. I'm shopping at A. T. Stewart's with Mrs. Aspinwall and her daughters this morning. In the afternoon I'm playing cards with Lady Gallatins. I'm afraid I couldn't possibly accommodate you."

"You despise the Aspinwall girls."

Victoria sniffed. "Until the day comes when a single woman can appear alone in public and not create a scandal, one is sometimes forced to consort with undesirables."

Jarves pushed back his chair and stood. "Harrison Shaw will be here within the hour."

"I won't be."

"Teach him the proper way to enter a parlor." He turned to leave.

Victoria spoke to his back. "The only thing Mr. Harrison will learn today is disappointment when there is no one here to receive him."

The rumble of heavy wagons at the docks gave way to the more lively whirl of carriages as Harrison headed uptown. His calves ached from walking too fast. A disputed right of way on the river had delayed the ferry and made him late.

He hurried past the Astor Library on Lafayette Place. Since starting his internship, he'd spent a number of hours here. The last four days, he never once stepped foot in the mansion. The house servant met him at the door with a research assignment that would be due the next day. When he returned the completed assignment, he'd be handed a new assignment, along with hastily scribbled comments in the margins of the previous day's work.

> *You call this research? Dig deeper.*
> *Flawed reasoning.*
> *Are you making this stuff up?*
> *Proof! Proof! PROOF! Cite your source!*
> *I expected more from you.*

Harrison was no stranger to research or critical comments. Both were inherent in studying law. He'd studied under some professors who wouldn't be satisfied if you handed in your assignment on two stone tablets written by the finger of God. So it wasn't Jarves's demands that were unusual; it was the topics of research. The renowned litigator J. K. Jarves had Harrison doing research on birds, insects, and animals.

He figured that's why he was directed to the Astor Library. Jarves's legal library was probably a little thin on topics like blue herons and alligators. The Astor Library, on the other hand, was a treasure trove with its eighty thousand volumes. With none of the volumes able to leave the premises, Harrison would spend the entire day researching, and at night he'd write the report while Hirsch and Wessler horsed around. Just like law school. More than once Harrison turned in a paper that had been mangled during good-natured roughhousing.

With his research report on alligators in hand, Harrison bounded up the steps to the Jarves's mansion. Would he start doing legal work today, or another research paper, possibly on monarch butterflies?

The winter sun bounced brightly off the front of the house. Harrison had to squint as he reached for the lion's head knocker and then blink to adjust his eyes after stepping inside.

As usual, Charles, the house servant, was waiting for him. Charles had been the one who had planted the watch on Harrison for an internship test and who, in return, had had Harrison's silver dollar planted on him. All was forgiven now. Neither held anything against the other.

Like every other morning, the cherubs looked down on them in anticipation of the exchange of assignments. This morning, however, they would be disappointed.

"You've kept a lady waiting," Charles said.

Harrison had already offered the alligator report. It wavered between them. "Pardon me? Lady?"

"She's waiting for you in the parlor."

Harrison didn't know anything about a lady. While he tried to make sense of the news, he wiggled the report in front of Charles like a worm. The house servant didn't take the bait. Harrison hadn't realized it before, but Charles looked a little like a salmon—pink complexion, large mouth . . .

"This way, sir," Charles said, turning to swim upstream.

"Aren't you going to take this report?" Harrison asked.

Turning, Charles accepted the report as though it were a major inconvenience. "This way, sir," he said again.

A puzzled Harrison followed close on the house servant's heels to an adjoining room.

Stepping to one side, Charles announced him: "Mr. Harrison Shaw."

Harrison stepped into an ornate room with Chinese décor—red and gold wallpaper, towering bamboo plants in pots, pagoda-style frames around the doors, Chinese letters spelling who knew what on long banners. In the center of the room—looking nothing like a Chinese woman—stood Victoria Jarves. Every inch of her bespoke wealth and femininity.

"It's rude to keep a lady waiting," she said, chin raised in arrogance.

Victoria Jarves suppressed a grin. The expression on Harrison Shaw's face when Charles announced him was priceless. This was going to be fun. So much more fun than what she had planned for the day, which wasn't shopping with the Aspinwalls or playing cards with Lady Gallatins. She'd just made that up. If Father knew what she really did with her days, he'd lock her up in her room.

"My apologies," Harrison said, appearing a bit white in the face. "Had I known a lovely young lady was waiting for me I would have—"

She interrupted. "Lesson number one, Mr. Shaw: always arrive at the stroke of the hour. A second later, and your reputation is ruined."

"Lesson?" Harrison said.

"My father has enlisted me to teach you proper social etiquette. Surely he informed you."

"As a matter of fact, he did not. I was expecting another research assignment. That's all I've been doing since—"

"Since the night you mistook me for a boy, Mr. Shaw?"

That seemed to knock the breath from him.

"You were dressed . . . I mean, in my defense, you were dressed in a minuteman costume."

"Mr. Shaw, do you contend that simply because I wasn't wearing a dress, you were unable to determine my gender? Do I look like a boy to you, Mr. Shaw?"

"Certainly not, Miss Jarves!" he stammered, his gaze ranging from the hem of her dress, to her corseted waist, to her face and hair. His previously white face was now turning red.

"It's impolite to stare at a woman's figure, Mr. Shaw."

Victoria wouldn't have thought it possible, but his color turned an even deeper red as he muttered an apology.

"Would it help if I spoke like this?" She thrust out a hip and used the voice she used the night of the ball. "Blayne. Just call me John Blayne."

"That's it!" Harrison cried. "Yes! Put that voice in a minuteman's costume, and you have a boy. Anyone would have made the same mistake."

Victoria reassumed the posture of a lady of wealth. She glided over to him, touched his arm, and spoke demurely. "Really, Mr. Shaw. Do you persist in this impossible defense of yours that I could ever be mistaken for a man?"

Harrison gaped delightfully. Despite his searching for the boy, every evidence of John Blayne had disappeared.

This will indeed be fun, Victoria thought.

"Now, Mr. Shaw, wealth and grace should be synonymous." She launched directly into the lesson, hoping to keep him off balance. "There is nothing more repulsive in this world than undignified wealth. You may have heard of a certain millionaire who would spew tobacco on the rug while sitting at the dinner table, and who wiped his mouth on his hostess's sleeve." She shuddered for emphasis. "Tell me, Mr. Shaw, is it your desire to live with similar brutish manners?"

"Of course not, Miss Jarves."

"Then it is imperative you learn how to behave in a refined manner."

"If you'll excuse me, Miss Jarves," Harrison said, "while it's true I do not wish to appear a brute, it is also true that I am not a person of wealth."

Victoria lowered her head and shot him a disapproving glare that knocked him back a step.

"It's just that you were speaking of the expectations of wealth, Miss

Jarves," he explained, "and while I appreciate your showing me the ropes, so to speak, I just wanted you to know that I'm not wealthy, and probably never will be."

She said nothing, only glared.

"By that," Harrison stammered, "I mean to say, while it's good that I learn how to act with high society, I doubt I will ever *be* high society . . . if that makes any difference, that is."

She continued glaring.

"With the lessons. And all."

More glaring.

"I just thought you should know."

She waited until certain he was finished. Just to be sure, she asked. "Are you quite finished, Mr. Shaw?"

"Yes."

A pause. She had learned well her father's tactics.

"As long as you understand," he added. Then, seeing the look on her face, he finished rather weakly, "What I'm trying to say . . . about the wealth . . . and all."

A pause.

This time he kept silent.

"Mr. Shaw, you are without doubt the rudest person I have ever met."

He started to say something.

She stopped him with a hand abruptly raised. "Your business and your bank account, now and in the future, are entirely of no concern to me. I have agreed, as a favor to my father, to attempt to do the impossible—to instill in a man of obvious inferior breeding, a semblance of decorum. If you persist in this boorish behavior, we will cease this moment, and I will report to my father that there is absolutely no hope for you. Is that what you wish?"

"Certainly not, Miss Jarves. Believe me when I say, it was not my intention—"

Her hand cut him off again. "Mr. Shaw. Will you, or will you not, cooperate?"

"I place myself in your capable hands, Miss Jarves, and do so with a silent tongue."

"That would be heaven, Mr. Shaw."

Charles, the house servant, was still in position at the doorway. It was not proper to leave two single young people of opposite sex alone in a room. Until now, he was a statue, giving no evidence that he heard anything. That is, until this last exchange. He fought a grin. Victoria frowned at him.

She paced the room, leisurely, giving the appearance of being in thought. "You will do everything I say?"

"Yes, Miss Jarves."

"Without question?"

"Without question, Miss Jarves."

As disciplined as she was, she couldn't stop a smile from forming. She had to turn her back on Harrison to keep him from seeing it. Humbling him was easier than she thought it would be. Now the fun would begin.

CHAPTER 9

The prospect of spending a morning with a beautiful young woman appeared far superior to the thought of burrowing in dusty library stacks, researching the migratory patterns of North American birds or some such nonsense. But after twenty minutes with Victoria Jarves, Harrison would have gladly exchanged his life for that of Elwood Thomason, the eighty-year-old research librarian.

"Are you listening to me?" Victoria snapped.

"Of course I am."

"You had a faraway look in your eyes."

"I heard every word."

"Really?" She'd been pacing as she lectured. Now she took a seat and folded her hands on her lap. "Then repeat to me what I just said."

Harrison matched her gaze. Truth be told, he had done more staring than listening. Of course, he did it when she wasn't looking. What struck him most was the way the dark green material of her dress caused the pale skin of her neck and cheeks to shimmer. After that, how the rustle of her dress made an unmistakably feminine sound, a sound you just don't hear often growing up in a boys' lodge. And he was fascinated by the way her hands played as she talked, sometimes in tent fashion, fingertip to fingertip; other times entwining themselves so delicately, so expressively.

80

"Well, Mr. Shaw? I'm waiting." She folded her arms, anticipating his failure.

Harrison cleared his throat and concentrated as best he could. It just occurred to him that she didn't smell of Desire du Paris. In fact, there was no perfume scent at all.

"Well?"

"Yes, of course," Harrison said. "You were going on and on—a might too tediously in my estimation."

Victoria narrowed her eyes.

Why did I say that? he wondered. *I hadn't meant to say it. It just popped out.*

He continued, "That a gentleman must act in a refined manner at all times. That he must display grace, be a polished conversationalist, and carry himself with a self-assured bearing. Furthermore, you said he must master the art of paying visits and receiving visitors properly; that he must display a delicacy of feeling, a capacity to handle embarrassment, and rigorous self-control—all the while acting as though these things came naturally to him." He gave a grin to signify that he had concluded.

Victoria stared up at him. There was surprise in her eyes. "Yes, well, a suitable rendition." She stood. "The next thing you need to know—"

"Suitable?" Harrison asked. "Only suitable? It was word for word, minus of course, that comment about its tedious nature."

She took exception to this. "I have rendered my judgment, Mr. Shaw. Now let's approach the matter of your attire."

"You just can't bring yourself to admit it, can you?"

"I don't know what you're talking about, Mr. Shaw."

"My rendition. It was perfect. Word for word. You just can't bring yourself to admit that I did good."

"Well, Mr. Shaw. That you did well."

"Thank you. Now was that so difficult?"

Victoria flustered. "I was not praising you. I was correcting you."

"And you did it well."

"Are we quite ready to proceed, Mr. Shaw?" she huffed. "Or do you wish to persist in this nonsensical banter?"

Harrison indicated he was ready to proceed with raised eyebrows and silent lips.

"Now then . . ." Approaching him, she waved an appraising hand up and down to introduce the topic of how he was dressed. Harrison followed the hand up and down. He was wearing his best pair of trousers and his Sunday shoes. "We'll discuss how to dine . . ."

Had he been eating wrong all these years?

"How to walk . . ."

Now that was something he knew how to do. His feet had gotten him here from Brooklyn, hadn't they?

"How to bathe . . ."

"Will that be a personal demonstration, Miss Jarves?"

Unlike the tedious comment that just popped out, this one was pushed out by a rising level of frustration.

Victoria paused. Her hand halted midair. He thought she'd blush. She didn't.

"How *often* to bathe, Mr. Shaw," she clarified and without humor.

"We each get a turn twice a week."

She glared at him.

"Just stating a fact. We have a schedule where I live. Twice a week."

At the door, Charles chuckled, then attempted to cover it with a cough.

Victoria was not amused. "Today," she said, emphasizing the word, "we'll start with something simple. How to enter a parlor properly."

Harrison glanced at the doorway. Had he done it incorrectly? How many ways were there to enter a parlor? Either you were in or you were out.

"First and foremost," Victoria continued, "you must always arrive at the top of the hour, the stroke of the clock."

"A moment later and your reputation is ruined," Harrison repeated.

"Yes, well, I believe you've already established your ability to regurgitate words, Mr. Shaw. The question remains as to whether or not they will be sufficient to make up for a lack of natural breeding."

Harrison took exception. "That's the second time today you've spoken ill of my lineage, Miss Jarves. Do you have any idea who my parents are?"

"Immigrant day laborers according to your attire and lack of manners—especially your inability to keep a promise."

"Now you're calling me a liar."

"Mr. Shaw, did you, or did you not, promise to place yourself in my capable hands with a silent tongue?"

Harrison tried to think of an objection, but she had him, and she knew it.

"Continuing on," she said haughtily. "When you arrive at the door, present your calling card. Then, after you have been . . . yes, Mr. Shaw?"

Not wanting to interrupt but needing to say something, Harrison raised his hand like a shy schoolboy. "I don't have a calling card."

She looked at him as though people were born with calling cards, and being without one was like walking around without a head.

"We don't have much use for them at the Newsboys' Lodge," Harrison explained.

Victoria didn't laugh. Neither did she smile, which made Harrison wonder what it was about women that made them lose their sense of humor whenever they were teaching something.

With an impatient sigh, Victoria crossed the room, opened a drawer from a lampstand that had curled-under toes and curvy legs, and removed from it a pink fan. Returning to Harrison, she slapped it against his chest. The perfume or powder scent from the fan made him sneeze.

"Until you have calling cards printed," Victoria said, "use this."

"A woman's fan?"

"Carry it with you at all times."

"I'm not going to carry around a woman's fan!"

"Then our lesson is ended. Good day, Mr. Shaw." She turned to leave.

Harrison stared at the fan, then at her retreating figure.

"I'll have cards printed."

Victoria continued walking.

Harrison watched her go. He called after her, "I didn't mean to offend you."

She didn't return.

"I apologize!"

Charles stood at the doorway looking at him.

"I'll carry the fan!" Harrison shouted.

He waited.

Nothing at first. Then she reappeared. "It's not a fan. It's your calling card."

She stepped into the parlor with the stride of the victorious. To Charles, she said, "Show Mr. Shaw out. Use the rear entrance." To Harrison, "Let's see if your performance is as good as your memory."

With the house servant leading the way, Harrison followed down a long hallway, through the kitchen, through the pantry, and out the back door. The door closed behind him and latched shut.

It was chilly outside. Harrison stepped into the sun and warmth. Here he was, standing outside a mansion on Millionaire Row without a coat and holding a woman's pink fan. It made as much sense as researching alligators. No matter. He was here. Now what to do?

He reviewed what he'd been taught: "Always arrive at the stroke of the hour. A second later and your reputation is ruined."

Clutching his calling-card fan in one hand, he dug for his watch with the other, flipping open the cover.

"Why that little minx."

The minute hand was nearly straight up. The second hand was just completing a downward sweep. In a little more than thirty seconds, it would be the top of the hour.

"A second later and your reputation is ruined," Harrison muttered.

He took off running.

Rounding the back corner of the house, he pulled up short. A six-foot hedge rose up to block his way. It was too tall to leap, and there was no getting around it. Should he have gone the other way around the house? How did he know there wasn't an identical hedge on that side? What if he presented himself at the back door? No, that was a servant entrance, surely not suitable for guests. But what then?

He spied a gap at the base of the hedge. It was low, but with effort . . . Running to it, he dropped to his knees and examined the gap. It was smaller than he thought. Was it possible? He dove in headfirst. Branches clawed his hair, his clothing, holding him back, trying to prevent him from getting through. All the while, time was ticking.

Harrison reached back to snap the twigs that snagged him. Emerging on the other side, he got to his feet, stumbled after two steps, managed to maintain his footing, and ran for the front door.

But without the fan!

He looked back. It was on the ground on the other side of the hedge.

Racing back, he fell to his knees, reached through the opening, snatched the fan, then ran for the front door, cutting a jagged path through a patch of rosebushes. Leaping up the steps, he lunged for the lion's head door knocker while simultaneously pulling out his watch.

Ha! Two seconds to spare!

He grinned. She didn't think he could do it!

The door opened. "Yes?" From the expression on his face, Charles didn't fully appreciate Harrison's victory.

"My card." Harrison wheezed, out of breath. He handed Charles the pink fan.

Charles stared at the fan. Didn't take it.

"My card," Harrison said again. "You were there. I'm to use this until I get cards printed."

Charles still made no effort to take the fan. He did, however, step aside to let Harrison pass.

While Charles moved like molasses, Harrison bolted like lightning, not bothering with an escort. He knew the way. Bounding into the parlor, his breathing labored, he spread his hands wide—one still holding the pink fan—to indicate his arrival.

"At the stroke of the hour and with my calling card!" he said triumphantly.

"Looking like something the cat dragged in!" Victoria cried.

Scowling, she stared at his knees, which had damp circles from crawling under the hedge. She picked at twigs and leaves sticking to his coat and hair. She recoiled at the lines of perspiration streaming down the sides of his face.

"Gentlemen never, NEVER stumble into a parlor, unannounced and unkempt. Nor do they enter huffing and puffing. A gentleman's entrance should command elegance and dignity. That is why we have staging rooms, so that he can compose himself and"—she wrinkled her forehead in disbelief—"let his knees dry and pluck the twigs from his coat."

"What did you expect? You gave me only thirty seconds! And you knew there was a hedge out there!"

She took in his appearance with mild reproach. "There's a gate on the other side. And I gave you an hour to reflect on what you've learned and to present yourself in a suitable manner. Do you think for a moment I expected you to charge around the house like a wild man when it has been my stated purpose from the start to teach you how to act in a refined manner?"

Harrison stood speechless.

Victoria Jarves sighed with forced patience. "Let's try it again, shall we, Mr. Shaw? Same instructions. Charles, please show Mr. Shaw out."

With that, she left the room.

Seconds later Harrison found himself on the back steps again, holding a pink fan, with fifty-eight minutes separating him from the top of the hour.

As soon as she was certain Harrison was outside, Victoria Jarves let out a laugh. She could contain it no longer.

What a sight he was, standing there covered with twigs and leaves, with two oval spots on his knees. She never imagined he'd crawl under the hedge. However, she did expect him to run. That was her plan from the beginning. She'd timed his dismissal with a table clock in the room. She expected him to arrive out of breath, but not looking like he'd journeyed for a week in the forest!

Her heart light—she hadn't had this much fun in years—she walked to the conservatory, where a servant brought her a cup of tea and a scone. She ate and drank leisurely while leafing through a book. Her eyes passed over the words, but her mind was elsewhere, devising new ways to torture Harrison Shaw.

For the first thirty minutes, Harrison sat on the back steps of the Jarves's mansion, aiming his knees at the sun, trying to get them to dry. They were still damp after a half hour, this being winter. Harrison stood and brushed them off, then walked to the side of the house—the side he had yet to explore. Sure enough, there was a gate. A pull on the latch string and within thirty seconds, he was in front of the house. Without running. And he still had twenty-nine minutes before the top of the hour. However, now that he knew there was a room in the house where gentlemen go to prepare themselves to enter parlors, he knocked on the front door.

Charles opened the door. He refused a second time to take Harrison's calling card/fan. This time, however, instead of charging ahead, Harrison waited for Charles and was shown to a room that was not lacking for mirrors. So for the next twenty-eight minutes, he paced while frequently checking the knees of his pants to see if the dark patches had disappeared.

While he waited, it struck him that this was oddly reminiscent of the first time he was in this house. The day of the interview. He thought of the stuffed birds under glass and of the watch. He also remembered . . .

Stepping to the center of the room, he examined the perimeter, looking for any place that might conceal a peephole. He sniffed, half expecting to get a whiff of Desire du Paris. But he wouldn't, would he? Victoria Jarves wasn't wearing any perfume. Was she not wearing perfume for a reason? The thought disturbed him. If she had a reason, it couldn't be good.

At the top of the hour, Charles came for him. Harrison had a lot of experience following Charles and felt rather comfortable doing it. Though he never did find a peephole, he couldn't get rid of the feeling that someone had been watching him. Maybe it was all the mirrors.

Having reached the parlor, Charles introduced him.

Victoria nodded her approval, but he also caught her stealing a glance at his knees.

"Now let's see how you do *receiving* guests," Victoria said.

She left the room without another word.

Harrison positioned himself where she'd been standing, thinking that if she was standing there it must be the right place to stand. *That is, unless it's the right place to stand if you're a woman receiving guests, and the wrong place if you're a man receiving guests.* He looked down at the spot where he was standing and took one step to the right.

He waited for her entrance.

She didn't return.

Five minutes passed. Then ten.

Harrison stood alone in the parlor.

Fifteen minutes.

That's when it came to him. Top of the hour. She wouldn't return for another forty-five minutes.

Shoving his hands in his pockets, Harrison strolled around the room and examined the collected artifacts that adorned the tables and shelves. He also scanned for peepholes.

After thirty minutes of walking in circles, he sat down.

At the top of the hour, Charles announced the arrival of Victoria Jarves. Harrison, having retaken his calculated receiving position, crossed the room to greet his guest.

He bowed slightly.

She offered her hand.

He took it.

"Now, offer me a seat," she said.

He led her to a seat. "If you please."

She sat.

The next instant she shot out of the chair as though she'd sat on a pine cone. Her eyes were wide with horror. Her cheeks cherry red.

"What? What's wrong?" Harrison cried, scrutinizing the offending chair, expecting to find an exposed nail or something equally hideous that hadn't been there when he sat on it.

"Mr. Shaw!" Victoria screamed, facing him.

"What? What did I do wrong?"

There was nothing he could have done wrong, he was certain of it. Still she had jumped up, and it had to be his fault.

Unable to find the words to express her indignation, Victoria shook her head and headed out of the room.

"Tell me what I did wrong!" Harrison cried.

She whirled around, thought better of it, turned to leave, then whirled back around, charging. She pointed an accusing finger at the chair. "How dare you!"

"How dare I what?"

Harrison looked at the chair again. He saw no protruding nail, no broken leg, no pine cone—nothing but the seat of the chair.

"That chair is warm!" Victoria cried.

"It's what?"

"Warm! The seat is warm! You were sitting in it prior to my arrival, weren't you?"

"You're angry because the seat is warm?"

"Admit it! You were sitting in it!"

"Yes, I was sitting in it, but I didn't—"

"Oh! How revolting!" Victoria cried. "How utterly disgusting!"

Harrison was shaking his head. "I still don't understand."

Victoria took a deep breath to compose herself. Then another. "When a lady enters the room," she said with difficulty, "a gentleman never, NEVER offers her his chair. Why?"

Harrison was hoping the question was rhetorical, because he didn't have a clue he'd done anything wrong.

"Why?" she asked again for emphasis. "Because it is still warm from his body. Mr. Shaw, don't tell me you're unaware that body warmth is offensive to refined sensibilities? It's disgusting. What kind of world do you live in that you're not aware of this?"

Harrison was glad she asked, because he'd had his fill of all these utterly nonsensical society rules. "I don't think you really want to know. And I don't think you should ask if you really don't want to know."

It was evident she was taken aback by his tone. She thought she was supposed to be the offended person in the room.

"But I'm going to tell you anyway, even if it offends your refined sensibilities!" He advanced on her, getting angrier by the second. "You want to know about the world I live in? I live in a world where ten of us share a dress coat because none of us can afford one by ourselves. I live in a world where two, sometimes three guys share a bed at night and count themselves lucky because that means they don't have to sleep curled up against some brick building on the street. I live in a world where Arney Arkwilder takes the socks off his feet and loans them to Sylvester Gray because Sylvester got a job shoveling snow and his socks have huge holes in them. And you know what? Arney doesn't wash them before loaning them. And you know what else? Sylvester doesn't care! He counts himself lucky to have a friend like Arney who will share his socks!"

He was so angry that he was nearly ranting now.

"I know you won't understand this, but we all count ourselves lucky because it could be worse. We could be living in Five Points. You may not believe this, but people there aren't offended by body warmth either. You know why? Because they count on it to survive the night! Men and women huddle together in corners because their rooms are drafty and have no heat! They pull their children close against them, sharing body heat just so they won't freeze to death. So you'll excuse me, Miss Jarves, if I offended you by offering you a chair I sat in while you kept me waiting for an hour. I'm leaving now." He strode past her.

To Charles at the door, he said, "I know my way out."

"We're not finished," Victoria shouted.

Harrison turned back. "We are for now. I have an appointment."

"Does my father know about this?"

"I haven't had two seconds with your father since the ball."

"He won't approve."

"That's between him and me."

"What about our lesson?"

"We can finish it when I return."

"I won't be here when you return."

"It really doesn't matter, does it? I think you've taught me all I care to learn about warm chairs."

"Don't be insolent. It's not gentlemanly."

"I thought you'd figured that out by now. I'm not a gentleman!"

"At least have the courtesy of informing my father where you'll be."

"At the old North Dutch Church on Fulton Street."

"Church? But it's not Sunday."

"Good day, Miss Jarves."

Harrison walked out, leaving Victoria Jarves standing beside the warm chair.

CHAPTER 10

It was a few minutes past noon by Harrison's watch. He quickened his step as he waded upstream against Broadway traffic. The singing would have already begun. He wove his way through a clattering of hackney cabs, coaches, private carriages, and foot traffic, eager to get as far away from Victoria Jarves as possible.

When he returned, he would face the consequences for his sudden departure, of that he was certain. But he hadn't known he would be taking lessons at the mansion today. He thought he'd be researching at the Astor Library where nobody cared if he slipped out for a while. As for informing Jarves of this weekly commitment, he had intended to all along. But he hadn't had a single meeting with the man yet. At the mansion, while pacing outside waiting for time to pass, he'd considered missing today's prayer meeting. He didn't want to, but he felt he had an obligation to stay. Then, all of a sudden, that feeling of obligation dissipated more quickly than body warmth on a chair seat.

Harrison quickened his pace. Jeremiah Lanphier always began the prayer meetings on time. People knew this and would begin arriving at twenty minutes before the hour. By two minutes to noon, the room was usually full, with people standing one and two deep along the walls. He'd be lucky to find a place to stand.

Lanphier began the meeting the same way every time, by reminding everyone of the five-minute rule. For those who arrived late, it was posted at the entrance and several places around the room.

BRETHREN ARE EARNESTLY REQUESTED
TO ADHERE TO THE FIVE-MINUTE RULE.
PRAYERS AND EXHORTATIONS NOT TO
EXCEED FIVE MINUTES,
IN ORDER TO GIVE ALL AN OPPORTUNITY.

Following the reminder, Lanphier usually read a verse or two from a hymn aloud. Then they sang it. They were singing as Harrison vaulted up the back steps of the Ann Street entrance.

Salvation, Oh the joyful sound,
'Tis pleasure to our ears.

The room was tightly packed. Just inside the door was a portly man wearing a three-piece black suit with a gold pocket-watch chain draped across his midriff. He shared a hymn book with a dockworker standing next to him who had a bailing hook hanging from his belt. They both looked at Harrison as he entered.

A sovereign balm for every wound,
A cordial for our fears.

The banker's singing was more like rhythmic grunting. His bare upper lip was moist with perspiration, his face red. He'd evidently hurried to get here too.

It still amazed Harrison at how many people from different backgrounds and interests all wanted to be here. They all felt the same way he did. They knew something was going to happen, something exciting, something from God, and they didn't want to miss it.

As odd as it sounded, the only time Harrison had felt like this was the first time he went to P. T. Barnum's American Museum. Before going he'd heard so many things about the place from Jimmy, Isaac, and Simon, things to astound and amuse—a woman 160 years old, Japanese mermaids, a white whale Barnum insisted was Moby Dick, wild animals, circus acts. That's exactly how everyone felt about the recent outbreak of prayer meetings, but without the freakish factor. People couldn't wait to see what God was going to do next.

The song ended. Closing the hymn book, the dockworker—who brought the fishy odor of the docks in with him—glanced curiously at Harrison's waist.

Harrison looked down. The pink fan was sticking out of his waistband. His face warmed as he covered it with an arm.

In the front, Lanphier caught Harrison's eye. They exchanged nods. There was an electric excitement in the leader's eyes. He shared the feeling of expectation too.

"Let us pray that God will move unhinderably among us today," Lanphier said as he led them into prayer.

Unhinderably. Harrison smiled. It was one of Jeremiah Lanphier's favorite words. They'd found it together in the early days while studying the Acts of the Apostles, last chapter, last verse, the last phrase. The passage described the ministry of the apostle Paul—how he preached the kingdom of God with confidence. The Authorized Version concluded with the phrase, "no one forbidding him." Having studied Greek and Latin and German, Harrison knew enough to look up the word. An adverb, meaning freely, in an unhindered manner. *Unhinderably.*

The word became something of a watchword for them. It expressed their desire for New York, and for all of America. God's Spirit was moving—that much was evident—but not unhinderably. Harrison prayed that before he died, he could witness the Spirit of God moving through the nation unhinderably.

Witness. No, more than that. Participate. All he'd done to this point was witness the answered prayers and amazing events in the lives of others. It was like standing outside the house, looking in through a window. Someday he wanted to be inside. To be a part of something great. Not only to see the Spirit in action, but to feel it. At present he watched as the wind of the Spirit swayed the high branches of trees; he wanted to feel the wind on his cheek.

"Amen." His prayer concluded, Lanphier moved to a table piled high with prayer requests. It was ten minutes past the hour.

Sealed envelopes, each one containing a prayer request or praise report from somewhere in the nation, were mailed to the Fulton Street prayer meeting in surprising numbers as word spread across the country of the kinds of things that were happening at the prayer meeting. Gut-wrenching letters. Human sorrow with punctuation. Desperation stuffed and stamped.

But it wasn't all misery. Buried in the pile, like streaks of gold in the side of a hill, were letters of answered prayer. A drunken, abusive husband now working and loving. A rebellious runaway found. An immoral life abandoned. And while the stories were unique, the credit was always the same—someone prayed, God heard, the Spirit acted.

The reading of the letters was a trumpet sound that echoed down the streets of Manhattan and sounded across hills and plains, calling people to holy prayer. The rustle of the first page of the day brought a hushed anticipation to the room.

Lanphier's arm did a trombone slide until the writing came into focus.

"This one's from Ohio," he said. "A fourteen-year-old boy requests prayer for his mother. Says she used to read him Bible stories when he was young, but now they've fallen on hard times. Oh my. Says here his father ran off. Now it's just him and her. He says she never smiles anymore." Lanphier lowered the page. "Let's pray that this boy's mother will smile again."

A man stood. A common worker by the looks of him. Unruly salt-and-pepper hair. He turned a hat in his hands as he spoke. "I'll pray for her. I have a son and daughter who prayed for me. If not for them, I'd be lying face against the wall in some alley right now, sleeping off last night's bottle."

He barely got out those last words before being overtaken by sobs. He gripped the chair in front of him and prayed aloud. Many of his words were emotion-garbled, but the intent of his heart came through clearly enough.

Lanphier opened another letter. "This one's from Boston. A sailor. He requests prayer for his shipmates. Seems he's the only believer on board his ship, and they're about to set sail."

"I'll pray for 'em," said the dockworker close to Harrison, "if you'll all pray for my brother. He's a jack-tar too. A common tar. We was on the same ship until my accident."

Not until this moment did Harrison notice the man's right leg was as stiff as a board.

"If you've never been a sailor, you don't know how hard it is to be spiritual on board—it gets in the way of all the sinning. My brother's name's Jim. He's sailin' for the West Indies next week."

A man in the second row stood. "Aboard the *Haswell*?"

"That'd be the one."

"I jus' signed up aboard the *Haswell*!" he cried. "I come here to pray 'cause I thought I was the only Christian on board! You talkin' 'bout Jim Barrows?"

"That'd be him!" cried the dockworker.

"Well, praise God!" said the man in the second row. "I'd been prayin' God would send me someone!"

The dockworker crossed the room, his limp not slowing him down. The two men embraced like they were lifelong friends.

The banker standing next to Harrison blinked back tears. He stepped forward. "I'd like to request prayer for my two sons." He had to fight back a wave of emotion before he could speak again. "They're grown. They've scrapped like dogs all their lives. They're godless. Ruthless. And it's my fault. I haven't been a good father." He was weeping openly now. "Will someone pray for them? They don't know better. They think this is how life's supposed to be."

Harrison put his hand on the man's shoulder. "I'll pray for them. And for you."

Glassy eyes blinked gratefully at him.

Ninety minutes after he'd left, Harrison was back at the Jarves's mansion. He stood in front of the house waiting for the top of the hour.

At his knock, Charles opened the door.

"Please inform Miss Jarves I have returned." Harrison presented the pink fan.

At the sight of the fan, the corners of the house servant's mouth turned up, but only slightly and only for an instant. His practiced expressionlessness quickly reasserted itself. "Miss Jarves is not in. Would you like to leave your"—he glanced at the fan—"your calling card, sir?"

Victoria's unavailability came as no surprise. Even if she were home, she had probably told Charles to say she wasn't in.

Harrison pulled back the pink fan. It was the only valid calling card he had. "Thank you, no. Is Mr. Jarves in residence?"

"I'm afraid not, sir," Charles said. "Would you like to leave him your calling card?"

The house servant's eyes twinkled as he said it. Harrison grinned. He was beginning to like Charles. Given different circumstances, he would have liked to sit down with the man and get to know him. Did he have a wife? Children? Musical interests? As long as the man was in the employ of J. K. Jarves, Harrison would never know.

"Did Mr. Jarves leave any instructions for me?" Harrison asked.

"No, sir. Will that be all, sir?"

"Yeah. That'll be all."

The door closed in his face. Harrison ambled down the steps. All of a sudden he had a free afternoon. He'd probably pay for it tomorrow, but for the moment, it was free.

Only reluctantly had he returned to Fifth Avenue. The feeling that he didn't belong here was stronger than ever. There were only two places in the world where Harrison felt he was vitally connected—the lodge where he grew up and the Fulton Street prayer meeting. Despite the fact he knew only about half the people there on any given day, there was a common spirit among them. A family spirit. A loving spirit. A willing spirit. A spirit that was totally alien to what he felt at the Jarves's mansion.

Grateful in a way that he didn't have to deal with it or Miss Jarves this afternoon, Harrison stuffed the pink fan in his waistband and set his feet toward Broadway. First stop? A calling-card print shop.

CHAPTER 11

The days were growing shorter. By the time Harrison placed the order for his calling cards and ran a few errands, the cold shadows of New York businesses had already blanketed the streets interspersed with streaks of soft blue light. Harrison had one more stop to make before taking the ferry back to Brooklyn.

As he set off toward Five Points, a fist-size lump of nervous excitement radiated in his chest. He could think of no other way to describe it. It was a unique sensation. He got it only when he was about to see a girl he liked.

Mouser said his sister returned home shortly before five o'clock. Harrison was hoping to catch her in front of the opera house before she crossed Park Street into Five Points. He stood beneath a street lamp just north of Chatham, his hands thrust deep into his pockets because once it got dark it got cold quickly. Every so often the wind would whip around a building and blindside him with enough punch to take his breath away. After a time he took to hopping on one foot, then the other, in an attempt to stay warm. People stared at him warily as they passed. He didn't care. He was cold.

Then he spotted her. On the opposite side of the street, bent over as she walked into the wind. Her servant's uniform poked from beneath a threadbare, brown coat with a hood and muffler to keep her head and hands warm. Covered as she was, still he recognized her.

"Katie!"

She kept walking. Either she didn't hear him, or she didn't recognize him.

Victoria Jarves's voice sounded in his head. *"Mr. Shaw, it's rude to hail a lady from across the street."* Even when she wasn't here, she was hounding him!

"Katie!" he called again, going after her.

This time she heard him. She slowed to take a half glance over her shoulder, then began walking again. Faster.

"Katie! Wait!"

He'd seen her less than a dozen times, spoken to her only twice. The first time, nearly a year ago, she was carrying a bundle of newspapers. When she dropped them, he helped her pick them up. She was so shy, she wouldn't look him in the eyes. But there was a sweetness about her that was striking. The second time he saw her, she was with Murph, the leader of the Plug Uglies. It was Murph who told him she was Mouser's sister. Harrison could see it—they were about the same height, and there was a family resemblance in their faces. During this second encounter, she had dared to look at him, if only a glance. Her innocent brown eyes captured his soul in an instant. For Harrison it was a magical moment he'd relived a hundred times.

"Katie! It's me. Harrison." He touched her shoulder.

She flinched. A brunette curl slipped from beneath her cap, dangling attractively against her pale cheek.

"Katie, I just want to talk. It's me. Harrison. Remember? I helped you with those newspapers that one time."

She slowed and risked a glance.

"Remember?" Harrison stepped in front of her so she could see him. The glance was fleeting. It fell quickly to her heavily scuffed and worn shoes.

From beneath layers of clothing that covered her nose and

mouth, a muffled voice said, "Is there something I can do for you, Master Shaw?"

Harrison bent down, trying to catch her gaze. "You can call me Harrison."

"No sir, Master Shaw. That would be improper, you being a gentleman and all."

"But I'm not a gentleman!" Harrison cried.

Katie stiffened and took a half step back. He'd frightened her.

"I mean, I'm not a gentleman in the titled sense. In every other sense, I am gentle . . . and I'm a man. So I guess, in the truest sense, I am a gentle man." He was rambling. "But I'd never hurt you, Katie. I hope you know that."

"I must get home." She navigated around him.

He fell in beside her.

"I was hoping we could talk for a while."

"It's cold."

"Yes, it is, isn't it? I wish there was someplace we could go."

Had it been summer, they could have walked in the park or down to the docks. As cold as it was, the only places they could go were noisy taverns and clubs, hardly the places you'd take a lady.

"I need to get home." She kept walking.

"Did you get the bag I left at your doorstep? With the food? Hopefully nobody stole it. You got it, didn't you? Did you like it?"

Katie halted. She looked at him fearfully. "I'm sorry, sir. Please don't be angry with us."

"Wait. Sorry? I'm not angry. Sorry for what?" Harrison was confused.

"You're angry with us because we didn't thank you properly."

"Angry? No! I just wanted to make sure you got it. But you did. Get it, I mean. By what you just said. You got it. That's good. I thought maybe it had been stolen." He was rambling again.

She blinked at him several times, trying to follow. "You're not angry? But you came here to be thanked."

"No. That's not why I came."

Harrison was in a quandary. What to tell her? If he told her he came just to see her, he might scare her away.

"Did you like the jam?"

Dumb question. Dumb. But it worked. Her eyes smiled.

"We likes it very much, sir. Thank you."

She stood in front of him, like a servant before her master, head bowed, responding only when spoken to and then briefly and courteously. Harrison hated the world for frightening an innocent girl into this kind of fear and servitude. He wondered what she'd been like before Five Points, imagining that she'd been a happy, carefree sprite of a girl, instead of a young woman so terrified of men she couldn't carry on a casual conversation. He hadn't worked this hard to sustain a conversation since Humphrey Albertson got stung on his tongue by a bee.

"Is there someplace we can go to sit down? Someplace quiet, where there's no gambling or drinking or dancing or loud music or prostitutes or . . ."

"This is Five Points, sir," she replied.

"Of course. You're right." He looked around. "At least let's move over here, out of the way, beside this streetlight."

The lamplighter had just passed by and lit the gas jet. Harrison escorted Katie to the pole. With the darkness thickening around them, the light from the lamp formed a pocket of light for them to stand in.

As the girl moved into the light, Harrison could see she was wearing two scarves, both of them threadbare. Her cheeks and nose were red from the cold. But her brown eyes—the ones that melted him every time they looked at him—were bright and full of spirit. That was encouraging. So many of the people in Five Points had lost the spark in their eyes. They walked around like the living dead.

"Tell me about your day," he said.

"I scrubs."

"Yes, I know. But how was it? Good? Bad?"

She shrugged. "I scrubs yesterday. I scrubs today. I scrubs tomorrow."

They fell silent. Two men on horses passed. Not until the *clop, clop, clop* of the hooves died out did Harrison speak again. "My day was interesting. Unusual, to say the least."

He chuckled and started to tell her about the prayer meeting, but then thought she might find the events at the Jarves's mansion amusing, so he told her about that first.

He told her about the calling-card fan and the running and the hedge and warm chair. She listened in silence, never once looking up at him or responding in any way.

"This is the fan," he said, with a grin, pulling it from his waistband as proof that what he'd told her was true. In this colorless world of mud and gray and rotting timber, the bright pink lace of the fan made it appear almost gaudy.

Katie glanced at it, looked down, then glanced again. After that, she couldn't seem to take her eyes off of it. While her mouth was hidden behind scarves, Harrison was certain she was smiling. Her eyes danced with delight, and Harrison's heart soared.

"Do you want to hold it?" he asked.

Her arms remained folded. She made no effort to take the fan, but he could tell she wanted to touch it.

"Go ahead, it's all right." Harrison offered it to her.

"I couldn't," Katie said. But she couldn't take her eyes off of it.

"It's all right, really!" Harrison insisted.

"I couldn't," she said again, this time looking away.

When she turned her head, Harrison wanted her to take the fan more than ever. He was desperate for her to take the fan. "Please, Katie, take it. It's my gift to you."

Her eyes gravitated back to the fan, with a look of disbelief.

"Of course, it's not going to do you any good for a while," Harrison said. "It's six months or more until spring, but you can look at it. It is pretty, don't you think? Please, Katie, allow me the pleasure of giving it to you. What am I going to do with a pink fan?"

For a moment he thought she'd take it. Then the moment passed. She looked away.

"I must get home." She buried her arms deeper within the folds of her coat.

Harrison didn't know why he did what he did next, but something inside him made him believe that giving Katie this pink fan was his sole purpose in life; that if he didn't give her the fan, all was lost. He grasped the crook of her arm and, smiling, pulled gently, trying to goad her into taking the fan.

She resisted, shrugging him off. It wasn't until later, thinking back on the incident, that he remembered the time when he'd helped her pick up the newspapers. Then, as now, she'd worn a coat with sleeves that covered her hands. He remembered piling newspapers on her handless arms. But he remembered it too late. Now he was on a mission to get her to accept the fan.

"I want you to have it, Katie."

She shook her head.

"Please. It's a gift. I'm not expecting anything in return."

"Leave me alone. I must get home." She walked away.

"Katie!" he pleaded, grabbing her arm.

She pulled away.

The only way Harrison could describe what happened next was that his innate maleness kicked in, the same maleness that drove men to boast and wrestle and launch countries into war for no other reason than they were men. He grabbed her arm, intending on forcing her to take the fan.

Katie tried to pull away but wasn't strong enough. Her eyes showed fear. Her voice became frantic. She twisted her shoulders hysterically, desperate to get away, shouting, "No! No! No! No!"

Frightened himself—by what he was doing and by her reaction—Harrison let go. He stepped back, his hands held up in an attempt to convince her he meant her no harm.

Katie sniffed and buried her hands even deeper in the folds of her coat.

And suddenly Harrison understood.

Her hands. She didn't want him to see her hands. If accepting the fan meant showing him her hands, she wanted nothing to do with it.

Harrison stood awkwardly, holding a woman's pink fan. Two women passed by. They eyed Katie, then him, and scowled.

An early moon, full and bright, peeked over a rooftop, slowly making its way toward the center of the street. Their breaths were visible now.

"Why don't you want me to see your hands?" Harrison asked softly.

Katie sniffed. "I scrubs."

"I . . . I didn't mean to frighten you." He looked at the fan. "I still want you to have this. How about if I . . ."

He took a step toward her. She backed away. He held up his hands again to show her he meant no harm, then made a second attempt. This time she stood her ground.

Gently he set the collapsed fan on the shelf of her folded arms, then backed away. She stared at the fan, not at him. She made no effort to take it or to refuse it.

"I'd best be on my way." He stepped back.

Katie didn't move—not a step, not a gesture, not a glance.

"I didn't mean to frighten you," he said. "Once you get to know me, I think you'll understand that. I'd never hurt you. Please believe me."

A couple more steps. He turned to leave. Then turned back.

"I hope we can be friends."

Just as he was about to turn to leave, she looked up, and there they were—those eyes. Peering at him like a rabbit from the back of its hovel. Innocent. Vulnerable. Igniting a radiating feeling in his chest that surged with life and love and hope. He fed on it, like a summer bloom seeking the sun, drawing life from its rays.

How he ached for the future, when they could commune openly, without fear. How he ached to convince her that all he wanted to do was protect and make her happy. To take her places where the sun was warm, the grass was green, the lakes were blue, and the birds sang happily. Where they could walk and talk of nothing, or everything. He wanted to know everything about her. He wanted to share his heart, his life, his hopes, his dreams with her.

But for now, all they had was a muddy, filthy street, the hiss of a dim gas lamp, and a pink fan. She'd go back to a stinking tenement, and he'd go to a crowded boys' lodge that smelled of dirty socks.

Harrison's hands flopped at his sides. There was nothing left to do but to say good-bye. So he did. "Good-bye."

At the corner of Baxter and Chatham, he looked back. She was standing where he'd left her, but she'd turned and was gazing at him. Rounding the corner, he leaped, punched the air happily, and let out a whoop.

During the ferry ride back to Brooklyn, he thought of all manner of ways he could help Katie and her family. Most of his ideas required money he didn't have. But now he had contacts with money. Harrison renewed his determination to speak to Jarves about Five Points. Somehow he had to convince the man of the need of the people in the tenements.

But first he had some fences to mend. He hadn't left the mansion under the best of circumstances. He had his work cut out for him in the morning.

First he had to explain his prayer meeting attendance to Jarves and hope he could convince his new mentor of its importance and gain his permission to continue attending weekly. Then he had to apologize to Victoria. He'd have to swallow a little pride. In her own spoiled way, she was just trying to help her father. He realized now that he'd been too hard on her. She'd been raised to believe that parlor entrances and the like were important. Having never been to places like the Newsboys' Lodge or Five Points, how could she know any different?

Harrison resigned himself to submitting to her instruction, as distasteful as it would be for him. He would go to any measure to help Katie and further his career in hopes of helping hundreds of Katies and Mousers.

PROOF

With that settled, his thoughts turned again to Katie. He couldn't help but think how unkind the world was to adorn a woman like stubborn, self-centered Victoria Jarves with comfort and wealth while consigning someone as sweet and innocent as Katie to a life of squalor. Victoria had done nothing to deserve a life of ease and luxury. She hadn't earned it. It had been handed to her. As a result she was smug, demanding, and pretentious—a spoiled brat with a rock for a heart that no quantity of Desire du Paris could make attractive.

Katie, on the other hand, had done nothing to deserve the life she lived. She had committed no crime, no sin that would warrant hunger and hardship. Yet, despite it all, she was kind and sweet and unassuming. No amount of dirt or tattered clothing could hide her beauty. Harrison would take a woman who smelled of soap like Katie over a perfumed Victoria Jarves any day.

"*I scrubs,*" she had said.

"Well, not for long, my dear," Harrison mumbled to himself. "Not for long."

He remembered fondly how she'd gazed at . . .

The pink fan!

What was he going to do tomorrow for a calling card?

CHAPTER 12

The next morning Harrison presented himself at the top of the hour at the Jarves's mansion on Fifth Avenue. As usual, Charles opened the door. As feared, he asked for Harrison's card.

"Please extend my apologies," Harrison said. "They're being printed as we speak."

Charles appeared puzzled. "For certain individuals, sir, a fan is as good as a calling card."

"Well, that presents a different problem," Harrison explained. "Unfortunately, I don't have the fan with me. Please extend to Mr. Jarves or Miss Jarves my humble apologies."

Charles's eyebrows raised. He shook his head sympathetically.

This isn't good, Harrison thought.

"Very good, sir," Charles said. "I'll relay your message."

The door closed.

With all the time Harrison had spent with the brass lion on the door of the Jarves's mansion, he wondered if he should give the animal a name.

Charles reappeared. "I'm afraid Miss Jarves is unavailable. However, she wishes for me to inform you that should you retrieve your calling card and present yourself again, she would be most happy to receive you."

"If you will kindly relay to Miss Jarves," Harrison said, "that I would be ever so grateful if she would receive me this once without the calling card, I'm certain I can explain everything to her satisfaction."

He wasn't certain of anything of the kind. At the moment, though, his goal was to get inside and at least gain a hearing.

The house servant shook his head at the futility of Harrison's request. Dutifully he excused himself to deliver it.

The door closed.

"Leo is too common a name for a lion, isn't it?" Harrison said to the door knocker.

Moments later the door opened. "Miss Jarves has asked me to convey to you her deepest regrets," Charles informed him, "but that receiving a gentleman without a calling card would be a betrayal of everything a woman of breeding believes in. And that a true gentleman would never think of putting a lady in the position of forcing her to make such a decision."

Harrison's hands flopped. "What now?"

"Are you asking me, sir?"

"Yeah," Harrison said, surprised by the house servant's offer.

"I wouldn't presume, sir."

Harrison turned away, frustrated by this new world with its societal laws and passwords and gracious-sounding words that revered a caste system over humanity.

"Come on, Charles," Harrison cried, making one last attempt. "Help me out this once."

The house servant's expression of practiced indifference never cracked. But Harrison thought he saw a glimmer of empathy in the man's eyes.

"It might be best," Charles said, "to retrieve one's calling card."

Harrison cringed. "That's not possible."

"I see, sir," Charles said. "Please wait here."

The door closed.

"What do you think of Richard?" Harrison said to the door

knocker. "You know, Richard the Lion. 'Hearted' is sort of understood, but you got that, didn't you?"

The door opened.

Charles handed Harrison a familiar flat package.

"It's the best I could do, sir," Charles said.

"Thank you, Charles."

Another research assignment. On the envelope Harrison recognized the handwriting of J. K. Jarves.

Research
the Mantis religiosa.
Have report on my desk
by tomorrow a.m.

Setting a course for the Astor Library and feeling like he'd been banished, Harrison wondered what a praying mantis had to do with the study of law.

After a day of researching the praying mantis and feeling that all manner of creepy-crawlies were on his neck and arms and hands, Harrison ventured into Five Points, hoping to see Katie. No matter what, he would not ask her for the fan. He was emphatic about that. He'd given it to her as a gift. Somehow he'd come up with a way to work things out with Miss Jarves.

He didn't find Katie, but he did find her brother, Mouser, walking the streets. He looked the same as always with his cap and a coat that was too big for him. He had his sister's eyes. His face was smudged, and he always wore gloves that were worn at the tips so that his fingers poked through.

The boy asked Harrison if he helped other people the way he helped his family. He said he knew a man who was in need of a cap and scarf. His had been stolen when he laid them across a fence while he unloaded a wagon. He also knew of a little girl who was sick with a cough and needed medicine.

"She coughs somethin' awful," Mouser said. "And her mama's real worried."

"A friend of yours, Mouser?"

Mouser didn't take kindly to the question. "I jus' hear things."

A ferry trip later, Harrison explained the situation to George Bowen. With Bowen's help Harrison was able to come up with all three items. The cap and scarf came from the lodge's lost-and-found box, the medicine from lodge supplies. Harrison promised Bowen he'd replace the items.

"When you're a famous lawyer," Bowen said with a grin. "Until then, don't concern yourself about it. My investment in you will pay off someday. Just be careful. A dead lawyer is no use to anyone."

Another crossing and Harrison was back in Five Points, eager to deliver the items as quickly as possible. He still had a report to write.

He met up with Mouser. The boy led him to the house of the man who had lost his cap and scarf. Harrison had Mouser leave the items on the man's doorstep, knock on the door, then run away. Next Mouser led Harrison to the tenement where the coughing girl lived.

"I don't get you," Mouser said.

They crouched in the shadows of an alley, their backs against a wall, the cold of the bricks penetrating their coats. The night air had a definite bite to it.

They'd hidden here when they'd heard voices. Male. Two, maybe three. Harrison was mindful of the fact he was trespassing through Five Points without an escort. But he hadn't seen Murph since before Stick's death, and the man and little girl needed these items now. Besides, he felt responsible for Stick's death and didn't want to endanger anyone else. As soon as Mouser showed him where the little girl lived, he was going to send the boy home.

"What don't you get?" Harrison said.

"Why all the sneakin' aroun'?"

"Simple. I don't want to end up like Stick."

"Not that. I mean, why don' you want people ta know you're givin' dem things? If I was doin' it, I'd want dem ta know it was me what was givin' it to dem."

"For one thing, I'm not rich," Harrison said.

"You're richer than anyone I knows."

The lad has a good point.

"That may be, but I'm not rich enough to meet the needs of everyone in Five Points. But even though I don't have a lot, I think it's our responsibility to share some of what we have with those less fortunate."

"Plenty of dem here."

The voices in the street were fading. They sounded more like drunks than troublemakers.

Reaching into his pocket, Harrison pulled out the bottle of medicine. It was in a brown bag. Reaching in another pocket for a pencil, he wrote on it.

"Why do you do dat?" Mouser asked.

"Just something I want to do."

"Why?"

"It's a message of hope."

"You should just write *hope* den. Nobody 'round here knows dat word you're writin'."

Harrison eyed the one-word message he'd printed all in capitals.

HOSANNA

"Sure they do," Harrison said. "It's the word the crowds shouted when Jesus rode into Jerusalem. It means 'Save us now.' You've been to church, haven't you, Mouser? You've heard that Bible story, the one where the crowds wave the palm branches?"

"Been ta church. Hated it."

"Maybe you just haven't been to the right church. I'll have to take you to mine."

"Do they sing songs at your church?"

"Yeah."

"Singin' with a beat or funeral music?"

"It's the words that are important."

"Funeral music. Figures. And at your church everyone acts happy?"

"For the most part."

"And a guy what looks like his best horse just died gets up and yells for two hours?"

"He preaches to us. It's good stuff if you listen."

Mouser pondered this. "Nah. Went there. Hated it."

"There are some pretty wonderful things happening at my church. The Spirit is moving in some amazing and unusual ways. We're living in some pretty exciting times."

Mouser was dancing a little jig to keep warm. "Excitin', huh? As excitin' as writin' foreigner words on a bag while your toes freeze off?"

The street was silent now.

"Oh, before I forget . . ." Harrison reached into his trousers pocket. "Give these to your sister."

He held out a pair of brown knit gloves. They dangled between the two of them like a limp hand.

"For Katie?" Mouser took the gloves, examining them.

"Yeah, I figured, you know, she might need them, as cold as it's getting and all."

Mouser jammed the gloves into his coat pocket. Suspicious, he squinted at Harrison. "You jus' keep your hands off'n my sister, hear?"

"Mouser . . ."

"Don' deny it, Harrison boy. I knows you sweet on her. I jus' better not hear you been tryin' ta get at her, you know what I mean?"

"I know what you mean. And you should know me better than that by now. I'd never do anything to hurt your sister."

"Yeah? Well, I knows guys. And guys have needs. And all I's sayin' is . . . well, you knows what I's sayin'."

Harrison stared at the boy. "How old are you, Mouser?"

The boy sniffed. "Old enough ta know what's what."

And young enough he shouldn't know what's what, Harrison thought. *Grow up fast, die young. The Five Points story.*

"Let's go," he said, stepping from the shadows.

With Mouser leading the way, they traveled two blocks east. They encountered no one else. It wasn't surprising. A person would have to be crazy to be out on a night like this.

The wind whipped off the river with open hands, slapping everything in sight—signs, papers, cheeks. As Harrison and Mouser walked, their footsteps crackled on frozen mud puddles.

Mouser led Harrison past a tavern, its interior light spilling into the street. A fiddle and tambourine could be heard from inside. Hand clapping and shouts urged the musicians on.

Just past the tavern, Mouser pointed to a tenement house with an exterior set of stairs. "Second floor, first door inside."

"Right or left?"

Mouser stared at his hands. "Which one is this one?"

"Got it. Left."

"I'll waits for ya."

"No, your job is done. I can take it from here. Go home."

Mouser looked up and down the street. "I'd better waits for ya."

Harrison shook his head. He was concerned for the boy. They'd been lucky tonight, and he didn't want to press it. The longer either of them remained on the street, the worse their chances.

"Make sure you give the gloves to your sister," Harrison said. "And tell her I said hello."

The boy didn't move.

"What's the matter, Mouser? You afraid? If you're afraid, I can walk you home."

"Afraid?" Mouser shouted, indignant. "Only thing I's afraid of is that you're gonna get yourself seriously killed without me to protect ya!"

"OK. You're right—we'll stick together. Stay here. When I get back, I'll walk you home."

"When you get back, I won't be here. How do you like dem apples?"

"Just give me a minute."

In a crouch, Harrison hurried up the stairs, which turned out to be an adventure in itself. In several places they'd pulled away from the building, shuddering and swaying as he climbed.

Remembering what the interior of the tenements smelled like, at the top of the stairs, he took a deep breath and ducked inside. Placing the bag next to the door with the word *HOSANNA* facing up, he knocked on the door, turned, and ran.

The journey down the stairs was more frightening than the journey up, and Harrison bypassed the last five steps by jumping. He hit the ground hard, slid, and came to a soggy, freezing halt. Jarred and bruised, but not broken, he scrambled to his feet and looked for Mouser.

The boy was gone.

Just as well. Like it or not, the boy inhabited the streets at night regularly. He knew his way around. He was known. If anything, being with Harrison was probably more dangerous than his being alone.

Now if only Harrison could make it out of Five Points without being spotted by any unfriendlies.

Slipping and sliding down the street, his breathing was more anxious than labored. His right leg and arm hurt from the fall and became all the more stiff from the wet and cold. He was feeling vulnerable. Scared. His nerve had left with Mouser.

He made it to Baxter Street. A right turn, a couple of blocks, and he'd be safe. Relatively speaking. Could anyone really be safe on the streets of New York City?

He reached the intersection and looked left.

What he saw stopped him in his tracks.

Mouser. Surrounded by three larger boys. They were bouncing the boy back and forth like he was a pinball. Mouser slipped and fell. His tormentors thought that funny. One of them picked him up, but only so the game could continue.

Harrison didn't think—which was probably a good thing. He turned up the street, toward the heart of Five Points and Mouser. No philosophizing.

No rationalizations. No thought of trying to talk them out of this. Fly Boys and their kind don't reason. They communicate with clubs and fists. And Harrison knew that—like it or not—he was going to have to speak their language.

He quickened his pace, slowing only long enough to pick up anything he could find that was heavy. Stones. Sticks. He saw a horseshoe and grabbed it. When he couldn't carry any more, he started running. They still hadn't spotted him. No matter. He'd get their attention soon enough. With each step closer to his own demise, his anger grew until he was running and snorting like a horse.

Within throwing distance now, Harrison let loose with a scream that could curl hair. He unleashed a barrage of objects, a snorting, hurling machine.

He looked ridiculous.

He felt brave.

For the moment.

The bruise makers and bone breakers were sailing only one direction right now. That was about to change.

His scream, followed by the barrage, achieved its purpose. The three bullies, startled, backed away, throwing up their hands and arms to protect themselves. It gave Mouser the time he needed to get away. The boy scampered into the shadows and was gone.

Surprises are effective, but they don't last long. And when this one dissipated like a puff of smoke, Harrison found himself facing three angry gang members.

From their expressions, Harrison realized that they were quick to size up the situation. Three street toughs versus a now empty-handed, skinny lawyer who attended prayer meetings. Harrison's faith in prayer and miracles was about to be tested, because he was going to need one if he was going to survive the night.

The street toughs started toward Harrison, slipping at first in the mud, but with speed once they found their footing.

A person didn't have to be a student of battlefield strategy to know that now was a good time to retreat. Harrison turned to run. His foot slipped. He caught himself. He slipped again, ramming his knee into the ground. Pain shot in two directions—up to his hip and down to his toes. The murderous shouts and curses of approaching gang members urged him on.

Getting back on his feet, running, hobbling, Harrison joined his voice to theirs, shouting for help.

Not a single door cracked. Not a single curtain lifted. The residents of Five Points either didn't care, or they were too scared to come to his aid. Harrison was on his own.

If he could make it across Chatham and out of Five Points before they caught up with him, he might have a chance. Chatham was the boundary between civilization and chaos. Police patrolled Chatham. While they wouldn't cross over into Five Points, they made certain Five Points didn't cross over into the rest of the city. If he could make it across Chatham . . . if he could hail a policeman . . . if he could keep his knee from giving out on him . . .

It wasn't looking good.

They were closing on him. He could hear them. Not just their shouts. Their labored breathing. Harrison's own breathing grew increasingly painful, rubbed raw by exertion, scratched by the icy air.

One of the toughs yelled for him to stop. Did he look that dumb to them? Did they really expect him to stop and take a pummeling, just to save them the trouble of catching him?

One block to go.

He could see the lights of Chatham Street. They were brighter than the street lamps of Five Points. The bright lights promised safety.

His legs were cramping. Pain hammered his injured kneecap with each step. His breathing grew increasingly labored, each breath shorter. He was getting less air, and air was his fuel. He was slowing.

He wasn't going to make it.

Chatham Street widened before him. The finish line.

He urged himself on, praying for strength, driven by desperation.

He reached the corner untouched. Stepped into the street. Afraid to look behind him, he was now in the middle of the street. There was no traffic. At any moment he expected hands to grab him, to pull him back into Five Points. He vaulted to the far side, the freedom side of Chatham.

He'd made it!

The next instant, he was bowled over. Someone forgot to explain the rules to these guys. Harrison rolled across the ground like a wheel with his three pursuers riding him. A flurry of fists and knees and feet assaulted him. There were too many of them; a single pair of hands and feet weren't enough to block the blows.

His head broke the surface just for an instant, and in that instant he spied hope in the form of a policeman on horseback. It was the strangest thing, really. So many blows hitting him at once, and yet Harrison's mind recorded a perfect portrait of this policeman. Their eyes met, and Harrison saw the man's concern for him. He saw the man's thin face, the furrow on his brow, ruddy cheeks, a thick brown mustache, and even the triangular cleft in the man's shaved chin.

Then everything went black.

The last thing Harrison remembered hearing that night was the shrill police whistle. The last thing he remembered seeing was the full moon looking down on him with pity.

CHAPTER 13

For a second time, Harrison Shaw was featured in Horace Conant's *New York Herald* column:

> Strange things are happening in Five Points. It's come to this reporter's attention that noted attorney J. K. Jarves's prize stud is leading a double life. Nothing seedy, mind you, but amusing nonetheless. And while warm and cuddly isn't my usual fare, this being the Season, consider it my Christmas gift to you.
>
> It seems rough and rugged Five Points has an angel of mercy. His name? Harrison Shaw. While every other New York attorney is in bed dreaming of sugarplum profits from other people's misery, our angelic Mr. Shaw (sans "wings," according to my source) surreptitiously visits the poor and desperate, leaving them gifts on their doorsteps, presumably to bring a smile to their dirty faces and a glimmer of hope to their troubled breasts.
>
> One such visitation was made to the home of Dicey Timrod, a hard-drinking, swearing, and swaggering day laborer. Dicey had his hat and scarf stolen.

He'd removed them and set them on a fence to help a friend unload a wagon, and when he returned, they were gone. Mr. Shaw learned of this and couldn't bear to think of poor Mr. Dicey walking around all winter without a covering for his head and neck. So the saintly Mr. Shaw procured a new scarf and cap and left them on Dicey's doorstep. Anonymously, of course, as any good angel of mercy would do. The only key to the identity of the giver was a single word from heaven.

While this reporter is in favor of kindly acts (heaven knows New York sees too few of them), I can't help but wonder what the good Mr. Shaw's reaction would be if he knew that Dicey's cap and scarf were stolen while he was helping unload an illegal shipment of booze destined for the notorious Crown's Grocery, where all manner of gambling, drunken vermin are known to congregate.

That same night Saint Shaw delivered cough medicine to an eight-year-old girl (the daughter of a prostitute), and rescued a boy (a known scallywag) from a beating by the nefarious Fly Boys, and gave a scrub girl a pair of gloves. Unselfish acts all, with the possible exception of the gloves. According to my source, Shaw may have less than saintly motives toward the scrub girl. But in this writer's opinion, a slightly tarnished angel is a good fit for New Yorkers who wouldn't know what to do with a perfect angel. Even when it comes to heavenly beings, we prefer their halos to be a bit cockeyed.

As for Saint Shaw's heavenly message? HOSANNA. It means, "Save us now." A suitable sentiment, especially during the Christmas season. And God

only knows we can use a little old-fashioned salvation (but not too much, mind you). So maybe the good
Mr. Shaw is onto something. But I can't help but
think if New Yorkers merely exercised a little more
wisdom and discretion in the coming year, our world
would be a better place on its own. I wonder what
the Hebrew word is for "Save us from ourselves"?

The next morning, when the column appeared, a battered and bruised Harrison Shaw awoke at the Newsboys' Lodge to find his clothes pinned to the wall. Shirt. Trousers. Socks. All in place as though he himself had been pinned to the wall and stepped out of them. While this was odd, it was the extra touches that puzzled him. Sprouting from the shirt's shoulders were a pair of paper wings. And there was a metal hoop where the top of his head would be.

Practical jokes were common at the lodge. Harrison had master-minded his fair share of them. He had once helped tie Isaac Hirsch to his bed while he was sleeping, then yelled "Fire!" and watched as Isaac squirmed like a bug on his back. And then there was the time he hid Murry Simon's clothes an hour before his wedding. Poor Murry thought he was going to have to get married in his altogether.

When Harrison saw his clothes on the wall, he understood that it was a joke but didn't understand the inspiration behind it until George Bowen showed him Horace Conant's column. Harrison joined in the humor of the article and the joke. Waking up to find himself unexpect-edly alive had put him in a good mood.

He wasn't laughing a few hours later when J. K. Jarves showed him the article.

"You have thirty seconds to convince me not to dismiss you!" Jarves shouted, slamming the newspaper on his desk.

It was just the two of them. Jarves stood behind his desk, pacing from corner to corner like a caged tiger. Ferocious eyes fixed on Harrison.

Harrison sat in front of the desk like a schoolboy caught pulling a prank.

Having been trained to think while speaking, Harrison thought now would be a good time to apply his education. Jarves had given him thirty seconds to defend himself. Harrison hoped Jarves's watch didn't run fast.

Where to begin? With the story itself? This was the second time Horace Conant used Harrison as the subject of his column. Why? Harrison had never met the man. As for the story's source? Harrison had his suspicions. Mouser. Who else had detailed information about the gifts and the Hosanna message? But what was Mouser's connection to Conant? The only thing Harrison could figure was that Conant plied the boy with a few coins.

With his grace period ticking away, Harrison cleared his throat and began, "I was as surprised as anyone—"

"Do you realize how this reflects on me?" Jarves thundered.

So much for Harrison's thirty seconds.

Jarves picked up the newspaper. "Illegal trafficking in alcohol! Street gangs! And you slumming with a Five Points wench!"

"She's not a wench!" Harrison cried, coming out of his chair. "And we're not—"

"Sit down!"

Harrison sat.

"Do you know the humiliation this will bring me?" Jarves paced. "You work hard all your life to cultivate the proper image. To keep yourself from scandal. Then along comes a backwater bumpkin who can't control his lustful impulses and blows you out of the water!"

"I'll find Horace Conant and talk to him."

Jarves stopped pacing.

Harrison wished he would start again. The attorney looked angrier when he wasn't pacing.

Jarves leveled a stern finger at Harrison. "You will *not* talk to Horace Conant!" he shouted. "You will not reason with him. You will threaten him with a lawsuit. You will threaten him with physical violence, if necessary. But you will, you *will* put the fear of God in him. And you will get him to clear my name of all improprieties."

"Yes sir."

Harrison stood, eager to have done with it, and with this. However, now that he finally had J. K. Jarves's ear . . .

"As for my business at Five Points—"

"You have no business at Five Points!" Jarves shouted, punctuating his loud message with an air-jabbing finger. "You will stay out of Five Points. If I hear that you've come within a block of Five Points, I'll terminate you on the spot. Do you understand me?"

Harrison hoped Jarves meant he'd terminate the *internship* on the spot.

"DO YOU UNDERSTAND ME?"

"Yes sir," Harrison said.

Risking termination of his internship and in direct violation of Jarves's order, Harrison returned to Five Points, but not without first tracking down *New York Herald* columnist Horace Conant.

The *Herald's* offices were located across from city hall on a five-block stretch called Printing House Row. There were twenty dailies in all, including William Cullen Bryant's *Evening Post* and Horace Greeley's *Tribune*. In addition to the dailies, there were dozens of weeklies. The *Tribune* was the most influential of the newspapers; the *Herald* was the most popular. It gave the news the masses wanted, rather than the news they needed.

Upon reaching the *Herald* offices, Harrison was passed to five different people before learning that Conant hadn't put in an appearance at the paper for nearly a year. His articles were submitted to his editor by courier.

"Which courier?"

They wouldn't give him that information.

Understandable. He imagined there were any number of people who had a score to settle with Conant over his columns.

Harrison had no choice but to do a little investigative work himself. He hung around the outside of the *Herald*, talking to every boy entering who looked like he might be a courier. One turned out to be a youthful junior accountant. He didn't take kindly to Harrison's mistaking him for a courier.

After several toe-freezing hours, Harrison found a boy who said he knew Conant's courier. Harrison was about to purchase Conant's address with his lucky silver dollar when Whitey Turner showed up and gave him the information for free. Whitey had roomed at the lodge the previous summer. He had always been a real sharp dresser. Harrison had tutored him in math to help him get a position in a bank. While that hadn't worked out, Whitey was grateful to Harrison all the same.

Conant's address was in a low-class neighborhood, which surprised Harrison. It wasn't Five Points, but it was run-down and shabby nonetheless. Harrison had always assumed reporters made a good living.

Standing at Conant's apartment door, Harrison rehearsed his opening lines one final time. He would state his case firmly and with conviction, and he wouldn't leave until he had Horace Conant's word that a retraction would be immediately forthcoming.

Harrison took a deep breath and knocked.

No one answered.

He knocked again.

Just his luck. Conant was probably out bribing some starving kid for information.

He knocked again, just to make sure. Still no answer. Harrison leaned against the wall, arms folded. He got comfortable. He could spend weeks trying to catch Conant. His best chance was to wait. Conant had to come home sometime.

After a couple of hours of musty odors and phantom sounds, an elderly woman appeared. She toddled down the hallway lugging a bag of groceries. Harrison greeted her. She stared at him with wary eyes. After passing him she muttered something under her breath in a language Harrison didn't understand.

Unlocking the door of the apartment next to Conant's, she scowled at Harrison and disappeared inside. Several locks engaged.

Harrison settled back into a waiting posture.

Fifteen minutes later the woman's locks sounded again. She poked her head out, looked at Harrison, scowled, muttered something incomprehensible, then locked her door again.

Her second appearance suggested that she might be the nosy sort, the kind of person who might keep tabs on a neighbor.

Harrison walked to her door. It was worth a chance. If she spit in his eye, he wouldn't be any worse off than he was now. Except for a soggy eye.

He knocked.

No answer.

Doesn't anyone answer their doors in this building?

He knocked a second time.

Still no response.

"Excuse me," he shouted at the door. "Ma'am? I know you're in there. I just want to ask you a question."

His words bounced back in his face.

"It's about Mr. Conant, your neighbor," Harrison shouted. "Do you read his columns? He wrote about me. I'm the one he called the angel of Five Points."

Still, the door and nothing but the door.

"I just want to talk to him. Do you know when he might return?"

Nothing.

Harrison sighed. It was worth a try. He turned to take up sentry position again.

"He's there." The voice was so weak, Harrison almost didn't hear it.

"I'm sorry. Did you say he was there?"

"Go away," she said.

She'd said he was there, hadn't she?

"Are you sure?" Harrison asked. "I knocked and—"

From the other side of the door came that other language again. From the woman's tone, they weren't nice words. Then, "You asked. I told you. Now go away!"

"All right," Harrison told the door. "Thank you."

Returning to Conant's door, he knocked again.

No response.

"Conant? I know you're in there."

He pounded this time.

"It's Harrison Shaw. You wrote about me in your column. I want to talk to you. Open the door."

Silence.

Harrison tried the knob. The latch sounded. The door opened a crack.

"Conant?"

Harrison pushed the door open a little more.

"Horace Conant?"

He stepped inside the columnist's apartment. The place reeked of unwashed clothes, sweat, spoiled food, and whiskey. It was worse than anything he'd ever smelled at the lodge, and that was saying something. Bottles and clothes were strewn everywhere. Against one wall was a chest of drawers. Every drawer was open. And every drawer looked as though it were regurgitating clothes. There was a dirty window in the wall directly in front of him, providing muted light for a table that served as a desk with a chair. The desk was as cluttered as the rest of the room.

The columnist himself was on the bed in the corner. He may have been "in" technically; consciously, he was out. One arm was draped over the edge of the bed. On the floor, at his fingertips, was an empty bottle of whiskey.

The man was an unkempt mess. Unshaved. Half-dressed. Pungent. He snored softly. From his appearance he'd been in this condition for some time. It was difficult to think that such a man could write his name, let alone a newspaper column. It was equally difficult to believe that if Harrison did manage to rouse him, he would be capable of human thought or speech. Anytime soon anyway.

Harrison walked over to the desk. Papers covered the entire top, several sheets deep. There was an inkwell. Several pens. The papers were works in progress, or possibly practice sheets. Some pages had sideways writing in the margins with arrows pointed to where they should be inserted in the text.

The strange part about the writing was that it was in a legible hand. It even had a certain flair to it. Harrison was pretty certain the flowery pen strokes on the page didn't come from the plump, hairy, lifeless hand whose knuckles were scraping the floor. Conant undoubtedly had a secretary. He probably dictated his columns.

One of the pages caught his eye. Harrison spied his name. In the margins Conant had tried several ways to describe him—stringless puppet, dress-up doll, and stud *du jour*. In the end he settled for "prize stud."

The man on the bed was Conant, all right. This was a rough draft of Harrison's column.

Leaving the *Herald's* star columnist passed out on his bed, Harrison crossed Chatham Street into Five Points, fully aware of the danger to his personal safety from Fly Boys and his career if Jarves found out.

He went in anyway.

Sometimes a man is guided by his mind, sometimes his heart. And sometimes he doesn't know which is guiding him; all he knows is it's something he has to do. Harrison knew he had to do this. He had to find Mouser and Katie. Mouser, to warn him against the likes of men like Horace Conant who use money to get what they want without concern for whom they hurt. Harrison didn't blame Mouser. The boy was desperate for money. He didn't know that by profiting off an innocent exchange of information, he would be getting Harrison in trouble. The boy trafficked in far worse things. And Katie, because he wanted to see her again. He wanted to arrange to meet her somewhere outside of Five Points. There was a bridge in the park not too far distant, so possibly there. The thought of conspiring to meet her at a rendezvous gave the encounter an added element of romance. His breathing quickened just thinking about it. And if she refused to meet him? He didn't want to think about that. He'd already imagined her lifting her head slightly, smiling, and signaling her affirmation with her eyes—with eyes like hers, words were mundane.

Harrison made his way down familiar streets toward Mouser and Katie's tenement. As he walked he scanned the streets, hoping to catch a glimpse of either of them, hoping to spot any Fly Boys in the vicinity before they spotted him. He reached the tenement and was in the process of bracing himself for the odious journey upward when he caught sight of Mouser coming toward him.

"Mouser!"

Mouser looked up. He ran.

"Mouser! It's me!"

The boy kept running. Harrison gave it a good effort, but after three blocks, his legs and lungs gave out. Mouser had disappeared around a corner and was gone. Panting, doubled over, Harrison made his way back to the tenement building.

Out of breath, his legs heavy, Harrison faced the repugnant darkness of the stairway. He really didn't want to make that journey again. Nevertheless, he began climbing.

The hallway of the third floor was even more disgusting than he'd remembered. He fought the demon stench with one lit match after another. Reaching the door to Katie and Mouser's apartment, he knocked.

The sensation of error flashed in his mind.

It wasn't the top of the hour! He had no calling card!

He chuckled. Wrong neighborhood.

A woman opened the door. She was young in years but cruelly aged by tenement life. Two infants in soiled nightshirts clung to her legs. She held another in her arms. All three of them were crying.

"Excuse me," Harrison said over the bellowing. He tried talking without breathing too deeply. "My name is Harrison Shaw, and I've come calling on Katie."

Was this woman Katie's sister? She was too young to be her mother.

"Katie?" the woman said. She had tired eyes. "No Katie. Don't live here. Are you a lodger?"

Behind the woman, stretched out with their faces to the wall, were two fully clothed men sleeping on straw covered with a blanket. It was common for tenants to defray their expenses by renting out space. Boarders paid for sleeping space and food. Lodgers paid for sleeping space only.

"I'm not a lodger," Harrison said. "I'm looking for Katie. Your sister?"

The woman appeared disappointed Harrison wasn't a lodger. Her children, all three of them, were in constant motion. The two on the ground were crawling up her legs, the one in her arms grabbed fistfuls of hair.

"No sister. No Katie," she said.

He had the right door; he was certain of it. "What about Mouser?"

"You waste my time. You want mouse or rat, try alley!" She slammed the door.

There are recurring themes in life. For Harrison, one theme seemed to be a closed door in the face.

It was twilight. He sloshed down the street, dodging stray pigs, ignoring the obscene calls of painted women, avoiding eye contact with men loitering on corners, and stepping over drunks. He was confused. So far today he'd faced a tongue-lashing and two mysteries.

Reaching the edge of Five Points, he stopped long enough to scrape the mud from the bottom of his shoes with a stick. Five Points mud was unique in its grittiness and foul odor.

He took the ferry back to Brooklyn.

CHAPTER 14

Charles opened the door even before Harrison knocked.

"Master Jarves is waiting for you in the library," the servant said, stone-faced.

Harrison's heart froze.

No calling cards. No obstacles. Something was wrong.

Had Jarves somehow learned he'd been to Five Points? Possibly he wanted a report on Conant. What was there to tell him?

I went to his apartment. He was drunk.

What else could he say?

But men like J. K. Jarves don't listen to excuses.

And if Jarves wanted to see him about Five Points, Harrison was finished.

He followed Charles from the domed-heaven entryway to the library.

He'd know soon enough what this was all about.

J. K. Jarves was waiting for him. As always, Jarves was impeccably dressed in a tailored black suit. Every inch of him portrayed a man of confidence, wealth, and power.

"Ah! Right on time," Jarves said cheerily.

Harrison saw no indication of impending doom.

Maybe he's just waiting for the doors to close before unleashing the storm.

PROOF

The house servant shut Harrison in. He was alone with J. K. Jarves. "Take a seat!"

Jarves offered Harrison one of two chairs in front of the desk. The desk itself was curiously covered by a red silk cloth. Beneath the cloth were round objects of various sizes, creating a landscape of rolling red hills.

Jarves joined Harrison on the visitor's side of the desk, taking the seat opposite him. The esteemed lawyer crossed one leg over the other. There was nothing in his demeanor that suggested wrath. But then Jarves struck Harrison as the kind of man who fired employees and dismissed interns calmly and with a smile.

"Coffee?" Jarves asked.

"Thank you, I'm fine."

"I'd like some coffee," Jarves said. He called for a servant and ordered himself some coffee, then turned his attention back to Harrison. "I think it's time for me to become directly involved in your internship."

Harrison breathed easier.

"I assume at this point you're wondering what all those research papers have been about."

Endless hours in the Astor Library researching birds and bugs. Why would he think that?

"You assume correctly," Harrison said.

Jarves looked at him expectantly. An eyebrow raised. He seemed impressed that Harrison didn't say more, which made Harrison wonder what the previous interns' reactions were to the bug assignments.

There was a soft knock at the door. A tray of coffee was wheeled in.

Jarves excused himself and poured himself a cup. Three cubes of sugar, the clanking of a spoon, and he was back in his chair, handling saucer and cup with the smooth movements of a well-bred man.

"Tell me," he said after taking a sip, "at what point is a jury trial most likely won or lost?"

Finally! A question that had to do with the law!

"The selection of the jury," Harrison said.

"Explain."

While Jarves peered at him intently over the rim of a coffee cup, Harrison said, "The jury decides the outcome of the trial. A good lawyer is one who has the ability to select men with a capacity for clear thought and reasoning, men who are not biased against his client. If he's successful, he can be reasonably confident they will arrive at a just verdict."

A soft *clink* and the cup was back on the saucer, the saucer resting comfortably on Jarves's knee. "Textbook answer. What other factors figure into ensuring a favorable verdict?"

Harrison was ready for him. "Preparation and presentation. A good lawyer does his homework. For each trial he must become an expert on all facts, legal and otherwise, pertaining to the case. Not only must he know the facts, he must be able to present them in a lucid and persuasive argument."

"Textbook. Textbook. Textbook." Jarves sounded bored. He set his cup and saucer on the desk, on a corner of the red cloth. "With thinking like that, you get good grades in school." He paused. "You also lose a record number of cases." He took a breath, giving his comment time to sink in. "Mr. Shaw, your real legal training begins now. It starts with your learning how to think beyond the textbook."

Jarves didn't look at Harrison as he spoke. He stared into the distance with unfocused eyes, as though he'd given this same teaching a hundred times to a hundred different interns.

"Law schools are factories," he said, "cranking out lawyers year after year who can do little more than quote from a textbook. A good parrot can do what they do. What separates a brilliant lawyer from a mediocre lawyer is his ability to observe and adapt."

Harrison listened intently, though the red lumps on the desk were something of a distraction.

"Who teaches at law schools?" Jarves asked. "Topnotch lawyers?" He scoffed. "They're too busy practicing law and making money. Law professors are men who couldn't make it as lawyers. They are left with a choice: teach the concepts they themselves couldn't master, or return to Uncle Abner's farm and pick turnips."

Jarves reached for his cup and seemed surprised to find it empty. He rose to get a second cup of coffee and returned with two cups. He handed one to Harrison.

"Thank you," Harrison said.

"Listen to me." Jarves sat down. "Here's the real secret to selecting a jury. It takes two. You want to find two men with strong personalities. Leaders. Why two? A lone juror can become a demagogue; three strong jurors choose sides. But two men with a single point of view are a force to be reckoned with."

Harrison was doing his best to listen, but his saucer and full cup were an even greater distraction than the lumpy desk. He set the saucer on his leg as Jarves had done. Coffee spilled over the rim, and now the cup sat in a caramel-colored pool.

"Once you have two strong jurors, you load the rest of the jury with sheep—ten men who couldn't form an intelligent thought between them. Now your task is simplified. Win the two strong men over, and they will convince the others and deliver a favorable verdict."

Jarves sipped his coffee. Even though Harrison hadn't asked for coffee, it had been offered, and he would be a poor guest if he didn't take at least one sip. Balancing the saucer on his knee, Harrison pinched the delicate handle of the cup between his thumb and forefinger. He raised the coffee to his lips and sipped. Drops from the bottom of the cup stained his shirt and trousers.

Sitting straight backed, poised, and stain free, Jarves studied him.

It didn't take a genius to deduce that Harrison's next etiquette lesson would have something to do with drinking.

"Why do you want to be a lawyer?" Jarves snapped.

Hurriedly placing cup on saucer, Harrison said, "I want to change things."

"What about money? Prestige?"

"I'd be less than honest if I didn't admit that money holds a certain attraction."

Jarves smiled knowingly.

"But only because money gets things done. People listen to men who have money."

An eyebrow raised. "Power, Mr. Shaw? I wouldn't have thought it of you."

Harrison was taken aback by the implication. But then, it *was* power he was seeking, wasn't it? Power to change things, like the conditions at Five Points. Power to help people who have been rendered powerless by their position in society.

"We have that in common, Mr. Shaw."

Jarves took a perfect sip of coffee effortlessly, his eyes fixed on Harrison.

"The law is a marvelous tool, Mr. Shaw. A flexible tool. That's the beauty of it. The law can be changed. Those who understand this are the truly powerful and wealthy. Consider, Mr. Shaw. Our nation is built on laws, laws that determine what is right and what is wrong, simply because we say it is so."

Harrison squirmed, and not from his inept handling of a coffee cup.

"Boundaries, Mr. Shaw—property, political, legal, moral, ethical— all are determined by law. Change the law, you change the boundary. Change the law, and suddenly you have the votes to get elected. Change the law, and the mineral rights are yours. Change the law, and what is scandalous today is not only accepted tomorrow, it's protected."

Clearing his throat, Harrison straightened himself in his chair. "Excuse me, sir, are you saying . . . ?"

His hand hit the edge of the saucer.

Like a medieval catapult, the saucer launched the coffee cup toward Jarves, spewing coffee everywhere as it tumbled on its trajectory.

The lesson came to an abrupt halt as both men dabbed at coffee stains on their clothes. Jarves bellowed for assistance. In no time an army of house servants appeared, mopping and dabbing at Harrison's mess.

Without so much as a glance at Harrison, Jarves excused himself and left the library.

There was no mention of the coffee mishap when Jarves returned in a fresh set of clothes. The coffee cart had been removed, and all evidence of Harrison's blunder had been expunged. If anyone were to walk into the room right now, it would appear that Harrison had spilled only on himself.

"You undoubtedly have questions," Jarves said.

An understatement. Where to start? The ethics of what Jarves was proposing? The self-serving morality? Or was now a good time to bring up the desperate situation at Five Points? Yes, it was a touchy subject, but maybe he could use Jarves's comments about the law to . . .

"Questions concerning the assignments I've given you," Jarves prompted.

That limited the discussion.

"Certainly you have questions about your course of study since becoming my intern?" He smiled the smile of a man who was about to solve a mystery.

Walking to the business side of the desk, Jarves clutched the corners of the red silk cloth that covered it. With a magician's flourish, he swept the cloth aside.

What had moments before been red bumps were bell jars of various sizes, each one encasing a bird or insect.

"Recognize these?" Jarves asked.

The subjects under the glass bells were all subjects of the research studies. Not all the studies were represented on the table. The blue heron, the alligator, and a couple of African cats were too large. But all the others were there.

Harrison stood. Jarves gave him time to acquaint himself with the display.

"I told you I wanted you to think beyond the textbook."

Jarves took his seat, pressing his hands together at the fingertips, then touching them to his lips. He studied Harrison as Harrison studied the specimens.

One of the bell jars Harrison had seen before. From beneath the glass, a masked bird stared at him with bulgy, fixed eyes.

"Pick it up," Jarves said.

Harrison did as he was instructed.

"Tell me what you know of him."

A test? A good lawyer must be able to marshal all manner of data and information at a moment's notice in a courtroom. Is this what Jarves was trying to teach him?

"Family name, Laniidae," Harrison said, from his research. "One of sixty-four species of medium-size birds. They hunt large insects, lizards, mice, and other small birds for food."

"Their nature?"

"Predatory."

Jarves stood. He took the jar from Harrison and gazed at the imprisoned bird. Unless Harrison was mistaken, Jarves seemed to look at the bird lovingly.

"Also known as the strangler, Jackie hangman, the butcher bird."

Harrison gulped.

"See his hooked bill? He uses it to attack other birds and mammals, breaks their necks, then impales them on some sharp object, like a thorn."

Like a meat hook, Harrison thought.

"After skewering his prey, he tears it apart." Jarves smiled. "This one's a male. He'll often build a cache of victims to attract the females. A northern shrike, his call is shrill. But I'm told there are other species of shrikes that, after killing, sing a sweet song of victory."

Harrison was stunned. Immobile, hypnotized in disbelief.

Still looking at the shrike, Jarves said, "Do you prey, Harrison?"

"Pray?" The sudden change of topic caught Harrison by surprise. "Well, yes . . . every day."

"Another thing we have in common." Jarves sounded pleased. He set the shrike back on the table and picked up another bell jar. "I've learned a great deal from this one," he said, showing the same tenderness and respect as he had for the shrike. "*Mantis religiosa.*"

"Praying mantis," Harrison said.

The specimen beneath the glass was mounted on a tree branch. Its back was arched, its saw-edged forelegs held high with pride.

"In parts of Europe, it's believed the mantis is imbued with magical powers," Jarves explained. "Some Italian peasants believe that when they become ill, it's because a mantis has looked at them. The residents of Provence believe it can direct a lost child home with a gesture of its foreleg. The Sardinians believe that harming a mantis in any way brings bad luck."

Jarves stroked the glass. Had it not separated him from the insect, he would have stroked its back.

"Mantises prey on bees, wasps, butterflies, moths, crickets, and grasshoppers. They've been known to eat each other—their mates, their siblings, even their own offspring. Do you find that strange, Harrison?"

A few days ago, Harrison had thought scrambling under a hedge with a pink fan was strange. This was downright creepy.

"To the Chinese, the mantis is a symbol of bravery and ferocity. They print its image on scrolls and household wares. Look at those forearms, Harrison. Did you know they can strike in one-twentieth of a second?"

"It's in the paper I submitted . . ."

Jarves wasn't listening. His attention was devoted to the mantis.

"A couple of years ago, I read a story about a woman, a bird lover who set out a feeder for hummingbirds. One day she noticed a mantis sitting on it, snatching honeybees that were attracted to the syrup. Along came a hummingbird. The bird inspected the mantis, determined it wasn't a threat, and began feeding. The mantis struck. Both tumbled to the ground. Horrified, the woman ran outside to see what had happened."

Jarves shook his head in wonder and awe.

"What did she find? The mantis, tearing away at the hummingbird's feathers. Stunned, the bird offered no resistance." His face turned sad. "The woman killed the mantis and rescued the bird. Sad, isn't it? Of the two, she killed the nobler one."

Harrison didn't answer.

Suddenly J. K. Jarves's demeanor changed. He was a lawyer again. The insect lover was gone. "Listen carefully, my boy. There are three hunting strategies associated with predators."

Harrison kicked himself for not seeing it sooner. All his research subjects had one thing in common. They were all predators!

"Three strategies," Jarves repeated. "There are those who chase their prey, like the hawk. There are those who ambush their prey, like the alligator. And there are those who stalk their prey, like the heron. Chasing one's prey is an energy-consuming proposition. Ambushing one's prey is a time-consuming proposition. I prefer stalking, like the heron, but with an additional element common to many predators—aggressive mimicry."

Harrison's eyebrows shot up. *Had he heard correctly? Did Jarves say he preferred stalkers? Surely he meant as an observer, didn't he?*

"Do you prey, Mr. Shaw?"

All of a sudden Harrison understood the question.

"Take the mantis, for example," Jarves continued. "They can adapt to a variety of habitats—twiglike, antlike, barklike, leaflike. A mantis can sit inches from a katydid and not be noticed. Death is one-twentieth of a second away, and the katydid suspects nothing! And when it strikes"— Jarves's clawlike hand shot out in demonstration—"it strikes suddenly, and the last conscious thought of its victim is surprise."

Harrison didn't move; he didn't breathe; he didn't so much as twitch.

"While I've never seen one," Jarves said, taking his seat, "I've been told that there's a two-headed snake that lives in Central Africa. Its tail resembles the head of a snake, while its poisonous head resembles a tail. He even moves his tail to imitate the movement of a snake head, tricking his prey. The attack comes from the least likely of places."

Jarves chuckled. "It was this specimen that inspired me in a recent business transaction, the result of which destroyed another man financially. He has no idea it was me who ruined him. And here's the best part: the other day he put an arm around me and thanked me for being the only friend to stand by him during this trying time in his life. It was priceless!"

Harrison was speechless.

"You've met him," Jarves said. "Eli Hodge. He was one of the advisors in this year's interviews."

Jarves leaned forward. His tone changed to that of a father advising his son. "So now do you understand why I was so angry with you over that blasted newspaper column? And why it is important to develop your social graces? Mimicry. It allows us to move unnoticed among our prey."

The library door opened. Charles appeared. "The time, sir."

Jarves produced his pocket watch. He stood with a sense of urgency.

"Think beyond your legal studies, my boy. These friends"—he waved a hand over the bell jars—"have taught me more practical lessons than I ever learned in law school. And now they are your teachers. Stay an hour. Look them in the eyes. Study their posture. Speak to them. Listen to them. We'll meet again tomorrow."

With a few long strides, Jarves was gone.

Harrison stood alone in the room under the gaze of more than a dozen predators.

CHAPTER 15

Harrison stayed the hour as instructed. But he didn't talk to the predators on the desk; he didn't listen to them or seek their counsel. Instead he dragged his chair to the far side of the room, as far away from the bulgy-eyed butcher bird as possible, set his back to the rogues' gallery, and turned his thoughts heavenward.

"Do you prey, Mr. Shaw?"

"Why, yes sir, Mr. Jarves, sir. I pray."

He felt like an idiot.

It took a while for the shock of this morning's lesson to wear off enough for Harrison to be able to think. For nearly half an hour, all he could do was stare and slap at imaginary insects crawling on him. Then, when lucid thought returned, he got really scared.

The man's extremely weird fascination with nature's killers aside—had Jarves actually confessed to him that he deliberately ruined a man's life? Boasted of it, in fact? But what really shook him, shook him to his bone marrow, was that Jarves saw fit to confide these things to him.

The decision to do that came this morning. Of course the whole internship selection process was part of it, but there was a moment this morning when Jarves had studied him and made the final decision to proceed.

What was it that tipped the scales that way? What did Jarves see in him, or think he saw in him, that would make him think Harrison would be receptive to such vicious theories? What did Jarves see that made him think Harrison would cheer the ruination of another man?

It would be like one of the Fly Boys vouching for him to the other gang members. *He's all right, boys. He bashes heads with the best of them.*

What made Jarves think Harrison Shaw was anything like him?

Christlike. That's how Harrison wanted others to see him. If Jesus Christ had been in the room this morning, would Jarves have given his predator presentation? Would he have boasted of how he destroyed a man?

All of a sudden Harrison felt like one of Jarves's moths, perfectly camouflaged and invisible in a wicked world.

In the solitude of J. K. Jarves's law library, Harrison's thoughts turned from preying to praying. Suddenly everything became clear to him. Two rooms characterized his world: the upstairs room in a church, where men humbled themselves and prayed and there was healing and reconciliation; and a mansion library, where men plotted and schemed to build personal empires at the expense of other men. Given what he'd witnessed and heard this morning, he couldn't possibly continue as Jarves's intern. He had to resign, and the thought scared him to death.

Grateful to have Fifth Avenue at his back, Harrison felt an incredible need to be with someone. Katie was the first person who came to mind. He walked to Five Points. The neighborhood almost felt clean after being shut up in a room with all those predators, and Katie, despite her ragged clothes, looked like an angel.

Maybe it was his imagination, but when she caught sight of him, she slowed her step to let him catch up. Real, or imagined, it sparked a warm feeling in his chest.

"I was hoping to find you," he said, catching up with her.

Katie hid her hands away like she always did, but not before Harrison caught a glimpse. Mouser had come through. She was wearing the gloves. You never knew with Mouser. Harrison wouldn't have been surprised if the boy had sold them.

As if the gloves weren't enough, Harrison saw something else that gave him pleasure. Poking out of her purse, which was little more than a brown cloth bag with a drawstring, was the butt of the pink fan. He couldn't help but wonder if, when she was alone, she unfolded it and looked at it and thought of him.

"Well, you founds me," she said, keeping her eyes lowered. "What do you want?"

"Let's step around the corner," Harrison suggested, "and get out of the wind."

The sky had been slate gray overcast all day, one of those days when you couldn't tell if it was morning or afternoon without looking at a clock. The wind had picked up within the last half hour, a howling northeaster.

Eying him suspiciously, she edged around the corner. Just being off the main street somehow made their encounter more intimate.

"I see you got the gloves," Harrison said.

"You fishin' for another compliment, Master Shaw?"

"No!" He really wasn't.

"I likes them fine, thank you very much."

"I'm glad you like them."

"Is that all, Master Shaw?" Katie asked. "I's cold."

"I just wanted to see you, that's all."

"What for?"

"Does there have to be a reason? I just wanted to be with you. Talk to you."

"When one person stops another person in the street, there's usu'ly a reason for it."

Why was she making this so difficult? Hadn't he made his affections known? Was she just shy, or was this her way of telling him she wasn't interested?

Isaac Hirsch had taught him about women. It was one of those lazy summer nights following a full day—splashing in the river, running, fishing, getting yelled at for horsing around inside the general store. When the sun went down, talk turned to girls.

"They like to hear you say you like their dress or their hair or their shoes," Isaac explained. "A punch in the arm or a good joke ain't good enuf for them."

At the time Harrison thought Isaac was just spouting off. He was known to speak with authority on a whole range of topics he knew nothing about.

He was right about girls though.

"I just wanted to see you," Harrison said. "I think you're pretty."

"Now you jus' pokin' fun at me!" She turned to leave.

"I'm not! Katie, I'm serious! I think you're pretty!"

She whirled around. "Look at me, Master Shaw! Take a good look. What could you possibly see that's pretty about me?"

"Your eyes."

The quickness and conviction of his response stunned her.

Conscious now of her eyes, Katie didn't look up for the longest time. When she did, her gaze weakened his knees.

"Thank you, Master Shaw," she said. "You's very kind." She turned away.

"Can I see you again?" Harrison called after her.

Katie looked back over her shoulder. "I'd like that."

Had they been edible, Harrison could have lived a month on those three words.

Not until he'd left Five Points did he remember he had meant to ask her about the woman in the tenement who knew nothing of her or Mouser.

"Resign the internship?" George Bowen cried. "Don't you think you're overreacting?"

Maybe Harrison hadn't explained it well enough. He told the resident director about the butcher bird and the mantis—including the story with the woman and the hummingbird—and the backward African snake. If Bowen could see the shrike, the way those eyes bulged . . .

"Men of wealth are often eccentric," Bowen said. "You have to allow for that."

"This goes beyond eccentricity. Who knows how many men Jarvis has ruined? He only told me of the one."

"Sit down," Bowen ordered.

Harrison settled into the straight-backed chair next to George Bowen's desk. He had grown up in this chair. He had sat here when Bowen told him he'd been accepted to college and after that to law school. It was here that he'd heard counsel about how to walk away from trouble, about integrity and finances, about the importance of giving back so other boys could be helped. He was sitting in this chair when Bowen showed him the handbill advertising a midweek prayer meeting at a church on Fulton Street.

As it always was, the desk next to this chair of education was covered with stacks of bills and paperwork. George Bowen did all his own accounting.

"Let me explain to you about wealthy people," George said, moving a stack of papers between them from one side of the desk to the other. "Often they develop odd philosophies because they're so far removed from life. They have no daily worries like most men. They don't have to worry if they have enough food to last the month or whether or not they'll have a roof over their head. They don't have to work to survive. Consequently, they have too much time to think. And a man with too much time on his hands can come up with all sorts of outlandish ideas about life.

"Nature fascinates them," he explained. "Possibly because they've insulated themselves from it. What does a man like J. K. Jarves know of life in the wild? The forest is a place of sport for him. Naturally, his fanciful theories are no more valid than the belief that the world rests on the backs of an infinite number of tortoises. Believe me, Harrison, as bizarre as his presentation must have been to you, I doubt as you continue you'll find any substantial correlation between it and the way the man practices law."

Sitting in this familiar comfort, listening to objective counsel, Harrison wondered if he had overreacted. Had he let a couple of bugs and stuffed birds scare him off? His shock at Jarves's presentation now seemed overblown, almost silly.

"What of Eli Hodge, the man Jarves ruined?" he asked.

"Mr. Jarves is a competitive man with an inflated ego. Such men often exaggerate their conquests."

Harrison nodded. That was true. He'd seen it often enough, most recently at law school.

"Give your decision some thought," Bowen urged. "It would be a shame to throw away an opportunity like this. It's your future we're talking about."

"Maybe you're right," Harrison said.

George Bowen wasn't right. Harrison found that out quickly enough. His lessons at the mansion went from bizarre to beyond bizarre.

The lecture series continued the next morning.

"Survival, Harrison. That is life's singular goal," Jarves expounded. "To remain alive while all others die around you."

Jarves paced as he taught, addressing his comments at times to Harrison, at other times to his gallery of killers who were still arrayed on the desk.

"And to this end, we commit every resource. Wealth. Power. Laws. Education. Social standing. If there is a physical resource we need, we obtain it at any cost. To put it simply, Harrison, imagine you're a cave man. Times are hard. You and your mate and offspring are starving. You've gone hunting, but game is scarce, and you've come home empty-handed.

However, your neighbor has happened upon a kill. What do you do? Let your family die while his family eats and lives? No. Not when survival is within your grasp. You do what you need to do to survive." Jarves snatched at the air, imitating the preying mantis. "Either his family dies, or your family dies. Which will it be?"

"You could ask him to share the meat," Harrison suggested.

Jarves's disappointment registered on two levels. First, for being interrupted. Apparently the question was rhetorical. And second, for the answer itself.

Harrison defended his response. "You said by any means. It seems to me one possibility would be to work out some kind of deal with him—maybe offer him a portion of your next kill, or something he wants in exchange for food. If he agreed, you could avoid a fight, get what you need, and maybe even gain a friend."

To his credit, Jarves weighed Harrison's words. "I suppose. Of course, he'd be a fool to surrender a portion of his food, but then there is no shortage of fools in this world, is there? So . . . good answer . . . swindling him out of his meat is a valid approach."

Swindle? Harrison started to object.

Jarves cut him off. The interactive part of the lesson was over. "However, the problem with your approach is that you're assuming he doesn't understand that survival is life's goal. It's the natural order, son. You may argue that we live in a civilized society. That we're no longer cave men. But that's convoluted reasoning. At what point has mankind ceased being part of the natural order?" His forefinger became an exclamation point. "Ah! You see? We haven't! Down through history all the laws, all the rules, morals, ethics, have been established by those in power for one reason, and one reason only—to give them the resources to survive over the weaker species."

He picked up the bell jar encasing the shrike.

"Do you think this fellow, after impaling his prey on a thorn, lies awake at night and wonders what others think of him? Or this one . . ."

He picked up the mantis.

"Does this fellow spend his days worrying whether or not his friends like him? Of course not! They understand! There is but one goal in life—survival!"

He wasn't finished.

"You may ask, 'Why do we even have a society and laws then? Why not go back to the days of the cave dwellers, where it's every man for himself?' I'll tell you. We have never left those days. It's still every man for himself. Life is ruthless, son. Society was created by thinking men to be a ruse. It's the perfect camouflage, whereby we are able to live among our prey, to smile, to laugh, to dance, to lead unthinking men to believe that we are a civilized people. The man who understands nature knows differently."

He paused to let that thought sink in.

"Do you know what my greatest challenge is with you?" he asked.

"No sir."

"To teach you the error of the teachings of your guardian, George Bowen. He doesn't understand. He's a bleating sheep among bleating sheep. He teaches boys to think like sheep, to act like sheep, which is just what the wolves want him to do."

Before Harrison could object, Jarves launched into a series of examples of a shrike-inspired legal philosophy. Tales of bullied jurors, bribed judges, kickbacks, and political favors all exchanged for favorable verdicts. Of double- and triple-crosses. Moves and countermoves. Ambushes, legal and literal. All under a cloak of respectability.

The afternoons were no better. While mornings were lectures, after-noons were social lessons taught by Victoria. It came as no surprise to Harrison when he was handed over to Victoria for "tea lessons"—how to handle a cup and saucer.

Dressed in a pale yellow dress that rustled as she walked, the always prim and proper Miss Jarves stood as Harrison sat in a chair in the middle of the parlor. Harrison couldn't decide which was sharper—her gaze, her temper, or her tongue.

"Any baboon can drink tea at a table," she began, "but a gentleman can balance both cup and saucer while at the same time being amusing and entertaining." She balanced a book on top of Harrison's head. "For posture. Your back should be straight, your head regal and steady."

On his hands she placed a pair of heavy workers' gloves. Harrison felt ridiculous.

With a clap of her hands, Victoria summoned a servant bearing tea on a silver tray.

"You will be asked if you would like some tea," she said. "The correct response is to smile and nod slightly."

"Nod? While balancing a book on my head?"

"Must you always be so obstinate?" Victoria cried. Taking the book from his head, she placed it on her own head. She nodded, as much with her eyes as with her head, but it was a nod nonetheless.

"After nodding," she said, placing the book back on Harrison's head, "you are to pour yourself a cup of tea, place two cubes of sugar in the cup, stir the tea with a spoon, then lift both cup and saucer, setting it on your lap without spilling."

"While wearing these gloves?"

Victoria ignored the question. "Oh, one thing more. You are to do this while amusing me with a witty anecdote."

"An anecdote?"

"A *witty* anecdote. You did bring your wit with you, didn't you, Mr. Shaw? Or did you leave it back at the lodge?"

"What if I don't want tea?"

"You do not insult your hostess, Mr. Shaw. You always take tea. If you do not wish to imbibe, then you pretend to sip it."

"Seems like a lot of fuss over nothing."

"Are you ready, Mr. Shaw?"

Harrison sighed. "Ready, Miss Jarves."

She picked up a rider's crop.

"What's that for?"

"Discipline, should you fail, Mr. Shaw. Allow me to demonstrate."

WHACK! She rapped him on the forearm.

"Ow!" Harrison cried. The book fell into his lap.

"Place the book on your head, Mr. Shaw, and let us begin." She summoned the servant to her side. "Mr. Shaw, would you care for some tea?"

Harrison nodded with his eyes.

"What was that?"

"A nod. Just like you did."

"That's certainly not how I did it. That was a blink, not a nod. Your head didn't move. Now try again."

She asked the question again.

This time Harrison's head moved. He knew it did because the book slid from it and crashed down onto the tea set, knocking it from the servant's hands. Tea exploded from the pot, and sugar cubes rolled like dice across the floor.

WHACK!

"Ow!"

Victoria stalked out of the room. It took the servants a good ten minutes to clean the chair and floor before they could begin again. The cuffs of Harrison's trousers were splattered with tea.

On the second attempt, Harrison managed to keep the book on top of his head, but pouring the tea wearing gloves proved more awkward than he'd anticipated. His aim was off, and a stream of tea overshot the rim of the cup.

WHACK!

"Ow!"

The third attempt was like the second.

WHACK!

"Ow!"

On the fourth attempt, Harrison managed to hit the cup, but when gripping the sugar with a pair of tongs, he pressed too hard and the cubes went flying.

WHACK!

"Ow!"

As difficult as pouring the tea proved to be, coming up with a suitable anecdote was even harder. Miss Jarves was not amused with his story about the time he and Isaac and Murry were swimming in the river and stole Albert Decker's trousers, leaving him a dress in its place, forcing Decker to run through the streets of Brooklyn wearing frills and bows.

Nor was she amused by the story of Francis White, who kept falling asleep during school. One day Isaac, who sat next to him, leaned over, nudged him, and whispered, "The teacher just asked you to pray!" He hadn't. In fact, the teacher had his back to the class, parsing a sentence on the blackboard. So, in the middle of class, White jumped to his feet and started praying.

Two stories. Two whacks.

For a week Harrison attempted to salvage the internship. After that he couldn't take any more. Jarves's horror stories of legal chicanery gave him nightmares, and his arms were red with welts, courtesy of Victoria Jarves. For Harrison the decision to resign couldn't have been clearer had the hand of God scribbled it on J. K. Jarves's wallpaper. God had numbered Harrison's days in this house, and they had come to an end.

He would tell Jarves in the morning.

"Oh, Mr. Shaw," Victoria said as he was leaving for the day, "I believe you still have my fan. The pink one."

Harrison had hoped she'd forgotten about it. "The fan."

"Yes. The one you used as a calling card. I assume you have printed cards now?"

"Soon. They should be ready in a few days."

"Then you'll no longer be needing the fan."

"If it's all the same to you, Miss Jarves, if I could purchase it from you . . ."

She gave him the strangest look.

"I've grown fond of it. You understand, don't you? It's something of a reminder of our time together."

"I'm sorry, Mr. Shaw, but that particular fan is a family keepsake. It belonged to my mother."

"A keepsake? You never told me it was a keepsake." A shiver of horror passed through him.

"Mr. Shaw, you still have my fan, don't you?" Her eyes glazed with tears.

"I can replace it!" Harrison said lamely.

Victoria began to cry. "A keepsake, Mr. Shaw? And will you also replace the memories of a departed loved one that are attached to it?"

Harrison felt like a scoundrel.

"My grandmother brought that fan with her from Southampton. Grandpa gave it to her on the night he proposed marriage. As the story goes, she didn't take him seriously at first and slapped him on the arm with it."

That was easy to believe. Whacking seemed to be a family trait.

Sniffing, Victoria continued. "So Grandpa took the fan from her, set it to one side, took her hands in his, and proposed a second time."

Harrison didn't feel like a dog. No, a dog was too noble. Harrison felt like a worm. *Bring on the bell jar.*

"I don't know what to say."

"What exactly happened to it? When did you see it last?" She looked up at him hopefully, as though she might help him recover it.

Maybe he could buy another fan and swap with Katie.

His hesitation raised her suspicions.

"You sold it for money, didn't you, Mr. Shaw?"

"No! I didn't! Miss Jarves, believe me, I would never—"

Victoria gasped. A dainty white hand flew to her mouth. "You gave it to another woman!"

Harrison hadn't thought he could feel any lower. He was wrong.

"Miss Jarves, had I known—"

"You did! You gave it to another woman." She became indignant. "Was it for services rendered, Mr. Shaw?"

"Miss Jarves!" Harrison cried.

"Well? Was it?" In the absence of a fan, Victoria fluttered a hand. "I can't believe you would use my grandmother's fan to pay for carnal pleasures!"

"Miss Jarves, I did not use your grandmother's fan for anything of the kind. I'll try to get it back. That's the best I can promise."

Victoria turned away, hand fluttering. "See that you do, Mr. Shaw. See that you do."

She started to leave. At the doorway she turned back. "Considering this current state of affairs, Mr. Shaw, I don't think it will be possible for me to continue our tea lessons."

"Perfectly understandable," Harrison said meekly, considering he'd already come to the same conclusion.

CHAPTER 16

After a fitful night's sleep, Harrison returned to Fifth Avenue, mindful that it would probably be the last time he walked down Millionaire Row. It had snowed the night before. The street, the houses, the bare limbs of the trees were all heavy with a pristine white layer that shimmered in the morning sun. His were the first tracks in the snow. Like fairy-tale breadcrumbs, they would show him the way home.

His gloves were five winters old. He'd worn a hole in the tip of his right forefinger.

Isn't there some kind of proverb that says, "If one finger is freezing, the whole hand loses feeling"? If not, there should be.

He shoved his exposed finger into his trousers pocket. His fingers wiggled in search of warmth and found a nicked coin instead. As it turned out, the coin had more of a history than he knew until last night.

"Do you still carry your lucky coin?" George Bowen had asked him.

This was in response to Harrison's news that, after careful thought, he'd decided to resign the internship. Puzzled by the request, Harrison had fished the coin from his pocket and handed it to Bowen. Like everyone else who touched the coin, the tip of Bowen's finger went straight to the nick.

"Do you remember when I gave this to you?" he asked.

"My fifth birthday."

"Fourth."

"Fifth. Same year the dorm was built."

Bowen did some mental calculations. "You're right. Fifth." He examined the coin. "I haven't seen it in years. There's something you need to know about the coin that may influence your decision."

Harrison had prepared himself for this talk. He was determined Bowen wouldn't talk him out of resigning a second time.

"This coin belonged to J. K. Jarves," Bowen said. "He gave it to you."

He paused to allow time for the news to register. A good idea, since Harrison was stunned by it.

"What . . . I don't . . . how . . . is that possible?" Harrison stammered.

Bowen grinned playfully. "I hope you form your questions better than that in a courtroom." He inhaled deeply, an indicator that the explanation was not going to be any easier for Harrison to digest than the initial news.

"The night of the fire," he began. "The night your mother died . . . as I told you before, moments before the floor gave way beneath her, she handed you to a rescuer. What I didn't tell you is that his name was J. K. Jarves."

Harrison squinted, trying to assimilate the news. "You're certain of this? How can you know?"

"There's more."

"More? You're not going to tell me that Jarves is my father, are you?"

Bowen laughed. "That would make a good story, wouldn't it?"

Not after what I've seen, Harrison thought.

Bowen held up the coin. "No. Jarves isn't your father. He gave this coin to me the night he rescued you, knowing that you had just become an orphan. He told me to give it to you as a good-luck piece when you were old enough to appreciate it."

"That doesn't sound like the J. K. Jarves I know."

"People change." Bowen handed the coin back to Harrison.

"We were strapped for funds in those days," Bowen said.

"Aren't we always?"

Bowen grinned. "There was no money for a birthday present, so I gave you the coin. You were going through a rough time. Your best friend had just left the lodge."

"Gary Richmond." Harrison hadn't thought of Gary for years. An image of a gap-toothed, big-eared, round face that wasn't nearly big enough for all the freckles that were on it came to mind. Gary was an infectious giggler. Those were happy times.

"You missed him terribly," Bowen recalled. "You'd take that coin to bed with you at night and tell me that when you were old enough, you'd use it to buy a train ticket to go visit Gary."

Harrison hefted the coin.

"There's more," Bowen said.

"More? How can there be more?"

"Jarves paid your college tuition."

"But I thought you—"

"I told you I'd take care of it, and I did. What I didn't tell you was that I already had. Along with the coin, Jarves gave me a small sum of money. He was touched that you had lost both of your parents within three months. It wasn't a fortune, mind you. Harold Fielding helped me invest it."

Harrison knew Mr. Fielding. He was the president of Fidelity Bank and a member of the lodge's board of directors.

"That money became your college fund."

Harrison fidgeted. "Does Jarves know he—"

"I don't know. I've puzzled over that myself. I've not had any direct contact with him since the night of the fire."

"He never inquired after me?"

"Remember when you said all the other intern candidates had someone championing them, all but you?"

"And you told me not to be so sure."

"Who knows?"

"That's why you pushed me into applying for the internship in the first place!" Harrison cried.

"There was always a chance he'd remember you."

"So you think that's why he chose me?"

"You'll have to ask him."

"The coin."

"What about it?"

"Jarves saw the coin," Harrison said. "The day of the interview. He saw the coin. Held it, in fact."

Bowen threw up his hands. "Well, there you have it."

But what did he have? That's what Harrison had wrestled with all night long. Did Jarves know he was Harrison's benefactor? Is that why he selected Harrison over the other candidates? And if so, why hadn't he said anything?

It was difficult to think this was the same man. Giving money to an orphan wasn't exactly something a shrike or a mantis would do.

While Bowen's revelation hadn't changed Harrison's mind, it made it more difficult to do what he had to do.

His boots crunched the snow leading to the front door of the mansion. With his right hand finally getting warm in the pocket with the coin, he reached for the door knocker with his left.

Had he ever settled on a name for the brass lion?

How was he going to tell the man who had saved his life and paid for his education that he no longer wanted to have anything to do with him for moral and ethical reasons?

J. K. Jarves was in a good mood. The first clue was that the servants were in good moods. Charles greeted Harrison at the door with a hint of a smile. Moments after being escorted to the library, Jarves burst through the door with a pleasant, "Good morning, Mr. Shaw. And how are you today?"

Harrison couldn't help but wonder who Jarves had destroyed overnight to put him in such a mood.

To say that Jarves had a spring in his step would be a gross exaggeration. However, his rocky facial lines appeared almost fleshy, and his stony demeanor was mildly carefree.

"Ready to get to work?" Jarves said. "Ah! But first . . ."

He called for Charles and ordered coffee.

Certainly he hadn't forgotten last time he ordered coffee, had he?

"And some of those French cakes. The chocolate ones with the—" He made a squiggly motion with his finger.

Whatever it was, Charles knew what he was talking about. "Very good, sir."

So J. K. Jarves had a sweet tooth.

"Discovered those little cakes in France," he said to Harrison. "Liked them so much, I brought the pastry chef back with me for occasions such as this."

Harrison wondered if he'd be staying long enough to try one of the cakes.

"Now, to business," Jarves said. "Join me."

Jarves walked to the desk. Harrison stood beside him. In front of them were the dead predators, arranged so that every eye was looking up at them.

Jarves fished in his pocket. "Here it is." He pulled out a ring and set it on the table between him and the other predators. It was gold with an amber stone that was large but tasteful. The ring was identical to one Jarves wore.

"I deplore fanfare," Jarves said, "unless, of course, it suits my purpose in a trial." He laughed at his own joke. "Take it. It's yours."

An array of dead eyes watched as Harrison picked up the ring. Harrison felt their gaze keenly.

"You are now part of a society of elite men," Jarves said. "The men who wear this ring are bound by a common philosophy of life that is as ancient as nature itself. To name a few—"

Harrison tried to interrupt.

Jarves wouldn't let him. "Judge Harold Rutherford. Judge Edwin

Walsh. Judge Horace Mayhew. Congressman Roger Dorr. New Hampshire Governor Lenox Beckwith. And now, Harrison Shaw. We have no formal organization but are a loose confederation of like-minded men. On occasion we have been known to join forces for our mutual benefit."

Given their survival philosophy, Harrison wondered how close their fellowship could be. But then, even jackals banded together until time to divide the kill.

He didn't know what to say. Jarves obviously meant this to be a distinct honor.

"I don't deserve this," he said.

Jarves slapped him on the shoulder. "No, you don't. But you will."

Harrison couldn't put it off any longer. He had to say something. All night long he'd practiced an opening line.

"Mr. Jarves," he said. "Do you recognize this?" He produced his lucky silver dollar.

Jarves glanced at the coin. Didn't take it. "A common silver piece."

"Look closer."

"What is this, Mr. Shaw?"

"Please, sir."

Jarves took the coin. He fingered the nick. He grinned. "This is the coin you planted on Charles. Well done, by the way. Edwin Walsh was irate you'd turned the tables on us. I was impressed. Your quick thinking got you this internship."

"Then you don't recognize the coin?"

Jarves's eyes narrowed. "What are you getting at?"

"You don't know who I am."

It was becoming apparent Jarves didn't much care for mysteries. His tone became agitated. "If you have a point to make, Shaw, make it."

George Bowen was wrong. Jarves hadn't been championing him.

Harrison said, "You gave this coin to me. A long time ago."

Jarves examined the coin again, shaking his head. "I don't recall ever giving you this coin."

"I was an infant. There was a tenement fire."

Jarves took a step back. The memory of that night was returning. "Your mother died."

"You rescued me."

Jarves was back there now in his mind. "The flooring gave way," he said with a distant voice. "She handed me her baby. There was a man on the ladder behind me. I told her to hold on. Then I turned, handed the baby down. When I turned back, she was gone."

"I'm that baby."

Nodding, Jarves said, "There was another young man. He fought tirelessly that night. It was his first week on the job at the YMCA, if I remember correctly."

"George Bowen."

"That was George Bowen? Well, I'll be. That young man was George Bowen."

"A year later he founded the Newsboys' Lodge."

Jarves chuckled. "I never would have put the two of them together. He's gotten fat."

"You gave him money."

"Yes! Yes, I did. So he used that money to launch out on his own, did he? It was supposed to go to you."

"He invested it. I attended college on that money. You sent me to college."

"Well, I'll be—," Jarves said.

The library doors swung open. A young female servant pushed a tray with coffee and cakes into the room. With one last look at it, Jarves returned the coin to Harrison.

"Well, this is turning into something of a celebration, isn't it?" Jarves boomed, crossing the room to the cart. "How do you like your coffee, Shaw?"

"Sugar. No milk."

"Come here, Son."

J. K. Jarves called him son!

Harrison joined him at the coffee cart.

"Try these." Jarves offered him a bite-size chocolate cake. "A taste of heaven."

Harrison was in no mood for cake and coffee. There was still unfinished business between them. "Mr. Jarves—"

Jarves bellowed for Charles. The house servant appeared immediately. Jarves whispered something in his ear. Charles nodded and left the room.

"Mr. Jarves—" Harrison tried again.

"Let me tell you about that night," Jarves said cheerfully, picking up one of the cakes and stuffing it into his mouth.

What would Victoria say if she saw her father eating like that?

"I haven't thought about that night in years. It goes without saying, it changed the course of your life, but what you might not know is that it changed my life too." Jarves licked icing from his fingers, reached for another cake, and balanced it on the edge of his saucer. "Let's sit over here."

He led Harrison to a pair of stuffed chairs, angled intimately toward each other, with a small table and lamp between them. Jarves sat in one, putting coffee cup and saucer on the table. He attacked his second cake while Harrison caught up with him.

Harrison managed to spill some of his coffee into the saucer as he sat down. He flinched instinctively at the error, expecting to be whacked on the arm.

Jarves finished his second cake with relish, brushing crumbs from his hands. "I remember the night of the fire with clarity but for different reasons. That was my tenement that burned."

"Your tenement?"

"My first property investment. And nearly my undoing. That fire nearly ruined me."

There was a soft knock at the door.

"Come," Jarves said.

Charles entered. He handed Jarves a pocket watch.

Harrison recognized the watch. It was the one kept under the bell jar. The one he'd been accused of stealing.

Harrison and Charles exchanged glances.

"It seems destiny has decreed that we are to cross paths several times in this life," Jarves said. He held up the watch for Harrison to see. "I was wearing it that night. Thought my time was up at one-sixteen that morning. I was battling the blaze. My coat caught fire, and I went down. Was almost overcome by smoke. I've kept this watch to remind myself that death is a predator too. It nearly had me that night. Nearly had both of us. Ironic that we'd be reunited this way, don't you think?"

Jarves set the watch on the table between them. "Come to find out, it was my best friend who started that fire."

"Your best friend? Why would he do that?"

"Jealousy. There is nothing harder on a man than to see a friend prosper. We attended law school together. Had similar backgrounds. Came up the hard way. Poor families. No connections. We spent many a late night neck deep in law books."

His mind drifted back. "I'd just won my first major court case and used the money to buy that property. Went out on a limb to do it. Borrowed heavily. We shared a room at the time and walked past the building every day on the way to the courthouse. The building got to him, passing it every day like that. It reminded him that I was on the way up. He was still doing minor clerking jobs. He really didn't have the mind for law. I was talking of moving out on my own. So he put a torch to the building to keep me from going."

Harrison looked away to hide his emotion. Rivalry and jealousy. His mother had been killed because of rivalry and jealousy between two men.

"How did you find out?" Harrison muttered.

"He told me. Guilt got the better of him."

Harrison looked Jarves in the eyes.

"Did you forgive him?"

A shadow of disappointment crossed Jarves's face, with a touch of sadness.

"Had him arrested." Jarves rose abruptly and refilled his coffee cup. Even in the simple act of crossing the room the man exuded confidence, power, and unflinching strength. "Tell me, Harrison. What are the predatory characteristics of the blue heron?"

"Mr. Jarves, I need to—"

"The predatory characteristics of the blue heron, Mr. Shaw."

Harrison sighed. His heart wasn't in this. He answered anyway. "The blue heron stands motionless, then strikes its prey quickly when it wanders within range."

Jarves turned to face him. "Magnificent creatures. Their stiletto-like bill darts forward with amazing speed. Their prey never see it coming. I studied the heron on Black Swamp Creek, where it feeds into the Chesapeake. Impressive. Each bird has its own territory. Just as each of us who wears this ring has his own territory."

He chuckled. "Once I saw a heron spear a fish. Another heron tried to snatch it away. Both birds fell into the water. You never heard such a racket." Jarves strolled back to his chair and sat. "That heron taught me how to handle James—my Judas friend, and all others who would cross me, including those who wear the ring. I waited until he was released from prison. I took him in. Befriended him. Waited, waited, waited, like the heron, until just the right moment." Jarves sipped his coffee. "James never saw it coming."

"You killed him?"

A wry smile. "I ruined him. Destroyed any chance he had of having a meaningful life. Consigned him to a living hell so that every day he wished he were dead."

Another sip of coffee.

"It was the tenement fire that started me on my lifelong study of nature's predators. I'd thought along those lines before then, but it was James who gave purpose to my thoughts."

Harrison could take no more of this. This had to end, and it had to end now.

"I can't accept this ring," he said, placing it on the table.

Jarves stared at the ring, then at Harrison.

"If this is an act of humility, Shaw, I'm not impressed. Pick up that ring."

Swallowing hard, Harrison stood. "After a great deal of thought, I've come to the conclusion that I must resign as your intern."

There. He'd said it.

Steely eyes stared at him, eyes as hard and unblinking as those of the brass lion on the front door. Only there was a presence behind these eyes. A menacing presence.

"Don't get me wrong," Harrison said, "I'm grateful for all you've done for me."

Jarves didn't move. He didn't blink. His chest rose and fell, each time with a greater swell as though a deadly storm were brewing inside.

"It's just that . . ." Harrison cleared his throat. "It's become obvious that we have . . . well, I guess the best way to put it is that we have philosophical differences."

Still no movement. Just the stare.

"I . . . I don't want to be a disappointment to you, sir. That's why I think it best for me to resign now before we go any further."

With a suddenness that was frightening, the storm passed. Jarves appeared calm. He sipped his coffee. "I don't find your humor amusing, Mr. Shaw." Jarves casually set down his saucer and picked up the ring. He examined the amber stone.

"Mr. Jarves, this decision hasn't come easily. However, after due reflection—"

Jarves hurled the ring at him with sudden ferocity. The ring cut him off, and cut his cheek. It impacted just below his right eye and spun halfway across the room.

Jarves was on his feet. "Just who do you think you are?" he thundered. His eyes were alive, wild with rage. His jaw and neck muscles were taut and crimson red. "You're nothing! Nobody! You're pond scum! Who do you think you are, coming into my house and telling me this? Other men would kill for this position. You don't choose! *I* choose!"

Harrison touched his cheek where the ring had hit. It stung and was wet. There was blood.

The door opened. Charles stuck his head in, saw what was happening, and backed out.

Jarves advanced on Harrison, backing him into the chair, forcing him to sit. Jarves towered over him.

"I don't belong in your world," Harrison cried. "We both know that. I know you had your reasons for selecting me, but it's obvious that I'm right, isn't it?"

"I pull you out of the sludge, and this is how you repay me?"

Harrison lifted his hips over the side of the chair. An awkward maneuver but one that got him on his feet. "Mr. Jarves, I appreciate all you've done—"

"You appreciate nothing! You're an ingrate. A dupe. A buffoon. I told you things in confidence. Names. I trusted you."

"And I'll keep your confidence, Mr. Jarves. You can trust me."

"You're right about that. You will keep your mouth shut." Jarves walked to the desk to be with his own kind. "Because you know what will happen to you if you utter a single word you've heard in this house."

Jarves picked up the bell-jar shrike, the bird that impaled its victims on thorns, then sang a happy song.

"Mr. Jarves—"

"Get out."

"If I can just say one thing more—"

"I went against my instincts to select you for this position. I knew you were dirt. I selected you anyway. I have few regrets in life, Mr. Shaw. My greatest regret is that I didn't let you burn to death in that fire with your mother."

A shiver of horror chilled Harrison's flesh.

"Get out."

Harrison didn't want it to end this way. He knew there was nothing else he could say. But he felt he had to try. "Mr. Jarves—"

"Get out!"

"Maybe someday—"

"Get out! GET OUT! GET OUT OF MY HOUSE!"

The shrike came flying at him. Hurled by Jarves, the jar and bird separated. It was free, flying at Harrison, its killer eyes bulging.

Harrison ducked.

The jar smashed against the door. The bird tumbled after it, falling to the floor, lying face up. Harrison had to step over the shrike to leave the room. Harrison knew it was dead and stuffed, but he could have sworn the bird snapped at him as he fled the room.

CHAPTER 17

Two days after Harrison resigned the internship, J. K. Jarves struck. The police raided the Newsboys' Lodge and shut it down.

The raid made all the newspapers. The list of crimes was long. Stolen property. Guns. Explosives. Lewd drawings, the descriptions of which shocked the public. George Bowen was arrested. The building was padlocked. The residents were thrown into the street.

The strike on the lodge was as overwhelming as it was sudden. Bowen professed his innocence. The residents cried foul. They'd seen none of the items that were confiscated. Well, maybe a knife or two. Nobody listened to them. Nobody cared. If anything, it confirmed the public's opinion of such places—nothing but thieves and hooligans, transients and undesirables.

An oddity of the raid was that George Bowen was the only arrest. Not so odd to Harrison. Jarves had targeted Bowen to get to him, knowing that the destruction of Bowen would hurt Harrison more than any personal attack. He was right.

"Remember I told you someday my investment in you would pay off?" Bowen said, trying to keep the mood light when Harrison visited him in jail.

"I'll try not to let you down."

Harrison Shaw's first trial case couldn't have had any greater personal implications. He'd been in the courtroom before, filing motions and assisting other defense attorneys. But not until now had he been the attorney of record. So much was on the line. If he lost the case, George Bowen would go to jail. He had to win. It was that simple.

Bowen's mood was optimistic as the trial opened. His faith in Harrison was obvious. Bowen did what he'd always done—encouraged, supported, believed in his young charge. For his part, Harrison felt the support. He entered the courtroom confident.

His confidence died a quick death thirty seconds into the trial.

The judge called both attorneys to the bench. He wanted to lay down some ground rules, or so he said. His real agenda was to flash his ring. A gold band with an amber stone. Just like the one Jarves had offered Harrison. The prosecuting attorney sported an identical ring, which he worked with his thumb every time he was near Harrison.

The trial was a travesty. The entire thing was scripted by J. K. Jarves and performed without improvisation by the judge and prosecuting attorney. Harrison didn't have a chance. Every ruling went against him, while the prosecuting attorney piled physical evidence and eyewitness testimony on top of expert testimony.

George Bowen was portrayed as a sleazy criminal mastermind who used the lodge as cover for his nefarious deals. The prosecution charged that he used innocent boys to support a network of gambling, prostitution, and illegal weapon sales.

Frustrated and sensing the inevitable, Harrison fought a valiant fight. But he had no weapons. He was an infantryman against an army with cavalry and cannons. But the most painful blow in his defeat didn't come from the opposition. It came from George Bowen.

"You just had to throw the internship in Jarves's face, didn't you?"

Bowen had resigned himself to his fate. As the trial wound down and George Bowen's life's work and good name were systematically destroyed, he became sullen. There were no words of encouragement on his lips, no upbeat assessments, no hope of a bright future. He was discouraged. Broken.

Following the sentencing, Bowen was led from the courtroom. His last words to Harrison were: "How cold do you think it's going to get tonight on the streets?"

Bowen was thinking of Isaac Hirsch and Jimmy Wessler and all the others who no longer had a place to live.

In the days following the trial, Harrison attempted to visit George Bowen. The place in which he was jailed was called the Tombs, a dismal building with Egyptian-style architecture. There were four levels with a prison yard in the center. A bridge spanned the yard for ease in getting from one side of the building to the other.

The cells were small and bare with an open slit to let in the light. The cell doors were thick iron, like furnace doors. The prisoners Harrison saw were sallow of skin and filthy. The odors reminded him of Five Points.

A guard escorted Harrison to George Bowen's cell. The door was opened.

George was crouched in the corner. The guard shouted at him that he had a guest. Harrison spoke to him. George Bowen turned his back on Harrison. He refused to speak to him.

Harrison never saw George Bowen again. Years later he heard George had been released and had gone to Philadelphia where he worked for his brother, a butcher.

CHAPTER 18

It was spring 1858. Neither Harrison nor the city had fully thawed from winter. He wasn't going to do it here on the docks. The shadows from the buildings and the briny wind that leapt off the East River combined to make the wait a chilling experience, despite the clear skies overhead.

Harrison clamped shut his coat. Standing on the wharf, he used people as a windbreak, choosing his conversations by position in relationship to the wind rather than by people he knew.

It seemed half the city was here. Like him, they came to hear if the reports were true.

But more than personal interest brought Harrison to the docks. He was working. Following George Bowen's trial, Harrison applied for positions at every legal office in the city. No one would hire him. While they didn't tell him to his face, he suspected they were afraid of Jarves. He heard the whispers behind his back. His legal career was dead.

He felt the sting of Jarves's vendetta in his personal life too. Gone was the lodge. His friends were scattered. He ran into Isaac occasionally in Five Points, but their conversations were strained. Harrison fought bouts of depression.

One of the strangest changes for Harrison, completely unrelated to his other problems, was the disappearance of Katie and Mouser. It was as though the muddy streets of Five Points had swallowed them. He returned to the tenement to search for them. The woman with her three babies was still there, looking exactly like she had on his previous visit. For weeks he waited for Katie nearly every night on the route she used after work. She never showed.

The only part of his life that remained unaffected was the old North Dutch Church on Fulton Street. It proved to be his salvation. Jeremiah Lanphier, bless his heart, spoke to the church authorities and was granted permission for Harrison to room in the church basement temporarily. In return, Harrison would document some of the more extraordinary stories of the revival—which was showing no signs of slowing down. Attendance at the prayer meetings was increasing. Churches, theaters, and meeting houses throughout the city were opening their doors at noon for prayer. In cities throughout the country, similar attendance figures at prayer meetings were reported.

It was the report of an extraordinary spiritual phenomenon that brought Harrison to the docks. Reporters, ministers, curious bystanders, all huddled against the cold and peering toward the entrance of the harbor, anxiously awaiting the return of the *Levant*, a square-rigger.

They saw it in the distance. It had just entered the harbor. And the closer it came, the louder the buzz of anticipation.

According to the report, something phenomenal had happened aboard the ship. While the ship was still a good distance from land, the captain signaled an emergency. Two words followed: "Send minister."

An hour earlier a smaller frigate had docked. They'd passed the *Levant* coming in. The story they were telling—if it was true—was amazing. Word spread through the streets like a three-alarm fire.

Harrison watched the approaching ship as it docked. He wasn't a sailor. The only time he'd spent on the water was on the ferry between Manhattan and Brooklyn. But he'd seen enough ships dock to know something was amiss. Just a handful of men manned the ropes. A skeleton crew. Where were the rest?

Those sailors that were manning the rigging had the queerest expressions. They were somber. Some were crying.

The captain appeared on deck.

"A minister!" he shouted at the docks. "Is there a minister here?"

There were many. Four were let on board.

Thirty minutes passed. Forty. An hour.

A sense of fearful dread settled over the crowd.

Then the first of the sailors came ashore. The captain was among them. They were smiling. Some were crying, their arms around each other.

The crowd on the docks rushed them, everyone speaking at once. Harrison shoved with the rest until he was within earshot of the captain.

The man was a weathered salt, in his late thirties. Thin. His skin was brown and leathery from a lifetime at sea. He tried to speak. His voice broke. Clearing his throat, he tried again. "Ain't seen nothin' like it in all my days. I once seen a whale swallow a boat off the Antilles. I seen Saint Elmo's fire light up a mast so bright it turned night to day. But I ain't never seen nothin' like this."

A dozen questions came at him all at once.

He waved them off. "If you'll jus' listen, I'll tell ya! And remember, I ain't no preacher. Can't say I understand what I saw, nor can I make sense of it. All I know is that it happened."

His lower lip trembled with emotion. It was disturbing to watch this old salt blink back tears.

Finally he said, "Jensen was the first. We was about a mile off shore, headin' into port. Jensen was on a starboard line, when all of sudden he lets go and grabs his chest, like he was havin' some kind of attack."

The captain looked over his shoulder at the ship. "Jensen ought to be tellin' ya this hisself. It's his story."

An uproar from the crowd convinced the captain to continue.

"All right, all right! Simmer down!" he cried. "Like I said, he grabbed his chest. A fearful weight was pressin' down on him. Buckled his knees, it did. And the next thing we know'd, he was cryin' somethin' awful, sayin' what a sinner he is, and that he's doomed and there's no hope for him.

"Well, the fact that he was a sinner came as no surprise to any of us." He chuckled. "We've lived with the man for three years. Yes sir, he's a down and dirty scoundrel, all right. Drinkin', cheatin', gamblin', swearin', carousin'. We did 'em all, too, but Jensen did 'em better than the rest o' us. So there he was, flat on the deck, screamin' that the devil had 'im by the heel and was draggin' 'im down to hell."

The captain sniffed and gruffly wiped a tear from his cheek with his sleeve. "Next thing you know, we all feels it."

"Felt what?" someone shouted.

"Why, the fear of the Almighty God! If ya felt it, you'd know. We all knew. The Spirit o' God swooped down upon us. Not a man among us escaped. Covered the whole ship, it did. And I don't mind tellin' ya, it was somethin' powerful strong. More powerful than anything any of us had seen or felt before, and that's sayin' somethin'! Knocked everyone to their knees, it did. And all we could think about was how rotten the bunch of us was, and how none o' us had any good in 'im. Not a lick."

A stone-cold, sober expression came over the captain. "I tell ya, it's a awful thing to see yourself the way God sees ya. Ain't no worse, unde-servin' feelin' in the world. Makes you wonder why He don't jus'—" The captain's eyes glazed. His chin quivered.

"Maybe it was something in the food or water," a reporter sug-gested.

The captain spat. "Don't be daft, man!" His ire rose. "I'm tellin' ya what we seen and felt. All of us! I been sailin' since I was eleven. Don't you think I'd know if it was a bellyache?"

"Why did you send for a minister?"

"Why?" the captain thundered. "If a man is ill, ya send for a doctor! If a man's stricken in his soul and close to dying, ya send for a minister."

"Didn't you have a Bible on board?"

"On a ship? What for?"

"Weren't any of your crew members already churchgoers?"

The captain reacted to this as if he was going to say something, then changed his mind. "Up 'til now, if I knowed a man was a Bible-totin' fellow, I wouldn't sign any of 'em up aboard one of my ships. They can be a confounded nuisance among a bunch o' cussin', drinkin', whorin' sailors. But now look at 'em. I got a whole shipload o' men prayin' and singin' and praisin' God!"

After a time, the captain went back on board to check on his men. Notepad in hand, Harrison made his way around the wharf, listening to one sailor after another tell much the same story. They had been about a mile from shore when, suddenly and unexpectedly, the Spirit of God had fallen upon the ship.

The thing that excited Harrison most about this incident—and the revival in general—was the pureness of it. Like a wind, the Spirit of God was blowing through the city, across the nation, and now out to sea, without human instrument of any kind. No preaching. No organization. Only time set aside for prayer.

Harrison invited three of the sailors to come to the Fulton Street prayer meeting to tell their story. As he was giving them directions, he spotted Mouser.

The boy was no more than fifty feet away, standing with a sailor and what appeared to be the sailor's wife and infant child. Mouser's newsboy cap was pulled down so that it nearly covered his eyes, like it always did. The sailor was pointing at the ship. Mouser's attention was concentrated on the ship.

Harrison made his way toward the boy, hoping to get close before Mouser saw him coming.

When Harrison was within a dozen feet, Mouser saw him and ran. "Mouser! Wait! I just want to talk!"

The boy didn't look back. He kept running.

Mouser had a good head start. Within just a few strides, he was out in the open, his legs a blur. Harrison had to dodge several groups of people before breaking into the open.

At the corner of Beekman Street, Mouser looked over his shoulder. He was heading toward Five Points. If the boy crossed Chatham before Harrison caught up with him, it was over.

Harrison made it to the corner of Beekman just in time to see Mouser disappear onto Water Street. Harrison had gained no ground. If anything, Mouser had increased the distance between them. At Water Street, Harrison took the turn wide. He slowed. Then stopped, standing in the middle of the street, bent over, his hands on his knees, his lungs fighting for air.

Mouser was nowhere in sight. Dogged determination set Harrison in motion again. On to Five Points? Maybe he'd get lucky.

It just didn't make sense. Why was Mouser running from him? The boy had avoided him ever since Conant's column came out. Did Mouser really think he'd still be angry over that? The boy was smart. Couldn't he figure it out that Harrison's beef was with Conant, not him?

Harrison pulled up. It was either that, or collapse.

Gulping air, he scanned the street. A thought came to him.

Maybe he's not heading back to Five Points, he thought. *Maybe he's . . .*

It was a hunch, but one worth following.

At the next corner, Harrison turned in the direction of Horace Conant's apartment.

The hardwood floor was gritty under his shoes. Harrison scuffed his feet to get some of the grime off before continuing down the familiar hallway. It took a moment for his eyes to adjust. While the walls were water-stained and he had to kick a path through the trash, the place was a palace compared to the tenements in Five Points.

Had Mouser come this way? He couldn't tell.

He passed a door that separated him from a marital spat. A loud one. It sounded like the couple were maybe two feet distant. A thin wooden door panel separated him from them.

"I'm your wife, not your mistress!"

"You're whatever I say you are!"

"How do you expect me to feel romantic when you smell like a sewer? Look at you! You're filthy!"

"Yeah? Well look at you! What's to wash up for?"

There was a loud thud against the door.

"Don't push me!"

"I'll push you if I want to!"

Harrison hurried down the hallway, not wanting to be standing there should the door open. There were other sounds as he made his way to Conant's apartment—a fussy baby, the clank of metal pots, a woman complaining loudly that her employer had no consideration for her, that all he was concerned about was his quota.

At Conant's door Harrison lifted a hand to knock. He stopped.

What if Mouser was in there? If he knew it was Harrison, would he run? Climb out the window?

Harrison put his hand to the doorknob. He hesitated. A lifetime of politeness and timidity stood between him and such a brash action. What if Conant was undressed? or occupied?

Knock or barge?

Harrison decided. All his life he'd knocked. This time he was going to barge.

Taking a deep breath, Harrison charged into Horace Conant's apartment.

He pulled up short.

"What are you doing here?" he cried.

Seated at Conant's desk, startled by the intrusion, was Victoria Jarves.

"Don't you knock?" she cried.

Stunned didn't begin to describe Harrison's reaction. Flabbergasted came close.

It was the oddest sight. Victoria Jarves's head on Mouser's body. It was her head, all right. No doubting that, though her hair was in disarray. And it was Mouser's body. No doubt about that. His body. His clothing.

Flustered, she grabbed the newsboy cap from atop the desk and flopped it onto her head, shoving raven curls up into it. She looked silly. After a moment she realized this and stopped fighting the curls. She threw the cap onto the table.

"What are you gawking at?" she cried.

In the corner of the room, Horace Conant lay in his usual position. Facedown on a mattress. Snoring.

"What are you doing here?" Victoria shouted.

Instinctively, Harrison reached into his pocket and pulled out his calling card.

"I suppose you think that's funny."

That was the thing. Harrison wasn't thinking at all. His brain had seized. He'd never expected to see Victoria Jarves again, especially here. Yet here she was. He had been chasing Mouser, and he'd caught him. He thought. Maybe not.

"Well? Aren't you going to say anything?"

She was angry. Why was she angry? And what had she done to Mouser? Harrison tried to say something. His mouth opened, but there was no coherent thought to express.

"Mouser—" was all he could manage.

"You want Mouser?" Victoria snatched up the newsboy's cap and, this time, deftly shoved her hair under it. With the cap pulled down over her eyes, she moved from behind the desk.

"Here I am, Mister Harrison," Mouser said.

The transformation was sudden. Complete. Real.

"You wants I should take yous to Worth Street? Maybe Crown's Grocery for a bet or a drink? Oh, I forgots. You don' like me goin' to Crown's Grocery, do you? Not wid dem prostitutes and gamblers and drunks. Not a good influence on a 'pressionable boy like me."

Suddenly the hat was off. Mouser was gone.

"Or do you prefer John Blayne?" She thrust out a hip. "Hey, Harrison. What say you and me go over to Lady Belmont's and have us some fun with her?"

PROOF

It was Blayne's voice.

Victoria's head.

Mouser's clothes.

Harrison's head hurt.

His mouth chugged along until finally it managed to put together a couple of intelligible words. "You're Mouser—"

Victoria smiled. It was her smile, all right. Attractive, but derisive. "Very good. A little thickheaded, but you get there eventually."

"Does . . . does Katie know?"

"Katie?"

"About Mouser. Does she know that you're . . . but then, she'd have to, wouldn't she, know that Mouser's a girl, I mean you, but how—"

Victoria bent over and rummaged through a bag.

A sickening feeling clutched Harrison's insides. It was icy, with tentacles.

The next thing he knew, Katie was standing behind Horace Conant's desk. In her gloved hand, she held a pink fan—*the* pink fan. It fluttered demurely.

"I scrubs," Katie said.

CHAPTER 19

On the New York wharf, an impromptu prayer meeting had broken out as some of *Levant*'s sailors and their families gathered in a circle to talk and pray. In Five Points, Isaac Hirsch was kicked in the ribs for trying to homestead in someone else's corner in Bottle Alley. At the *Herald*, the editors and production staff were finalizing tomorrow's edition. And in Horace Conant's apartment, Harrison Shaw was feeling sick.

The shock was wearing off.

"Close your mouth before a bug flies in it," Katie said.

She'd never spoken to him this way before. She'd never looked at him this way before. It wasn't Katie's skittish-as-a-fawn gaze; it was Victoria Jarves's do-it-until-you-get-it-right gaze.

Katie's wrap came off her head, and she was Victoria again.

Emotions swarmed all over Harrison. Dark. Heavy. Like an anchor threatening to pull him under.

"Well, say something!" Victoria shouted.

But he couldn't. He tried. Couldn't.

His mind had descended to a lower level of existence that had no vocabulary, only swirling confusion that could no more be pinned down than an ocean current.

He turned and walked out of the room.

Harrison Shaw walked the streets, though he couldn't tell you the names of any of them. His eyes weren't registering such pedestrian thoughts. Conscious sight was turned inward as he ambled aimlessly.

He was counting his losses, beginning with George Bowen, who had been both father and mother to him as well as friend. Harrison couldn't remember a time when Mr. Bowen wasn't part of his life. Now the man wouldn't talk to him, didn't want to see him.

Then there was the lodge. More than just a place to live. A home. George Bowen's life's work. Isaac and Jimmy's refuge from the streets, along with countless others who dwelt there for a time. His lifelong friends had dispersed. They were homeless. He was one of the lucky ones. At least he still had a roof over his head; he had an entire building over his head. And as grateful as he was for it, the church basement was damp. He slept surrounded by junk, not friends. *Unless you counted the rats.*

He'd lost his career as a lawyer. Years of study for nothing. A coveted internship tossed aside. He'd had grand dreams of helping others. Now he was the one who needed help.

He'd lost Mouser. And Katie.

He shut his eyes and moaned.

Oh, Katie. Though he didn't really know her, he'd fallen in love with the dream of loving her. And now to think she was gone. That he'd never see her again.

How could he hurt so badly for someone who had never existed?

But the pain in his gut was real. The gnawing sense of loss was real. It was as though she died. But she wasn't dead, was she? She was alive in Victoria Jarves. It was her eyes that had so captivated him.

No, impossible! Victoria Jarves and Katie were two completely different people. To think that there was any of Katie in Victoria was . . . was—he winced—was reality.

Harrison squeezed his head with his hands.

He still couldn't make sense of it. He couldn't—wouldn't—allow himself to admit that all those times he was with Mouser and Katie, he was actually with Victoria Jarves!

"And what about the fan?" he shouted to the sky, startling an elderly man who was walking behind him.

The man crossed the street, keeping a suspicious eye on Harrison.

What about the fan? Harrison muttered to himself this time. *Victoria gave it to me. I gave it to Katie, who accepted it, all the while knowing that it belonged to Victoria. Then, Victoria, knowing I'd given it to Katie, asked for it back! When she had it all the time!*

He'd been played. From the very beginning, he'd been played. Did Victoria Jarves know who he was the day of the interview? She had to. He knew Katie and Mouser before then. She must have recognized him.

"All this time . . . all this time . . . ALL THIS TIME!" he shouted.

He pivoted back in the direction of Horace Conant's apartment.

There was a question he wanted answered.

"Why?"

Horace Conant's door slammed open. Harrison breathed heavily from a combination of exertion and anger that had fueled his return journey.

Victoria Jarves sat at the desk. She was reading. Light from the window was sufficient. He could see through the paper enough to recognize handwriting.

In the corner, Horace Conant hadn't moved.

Victoria looked up. "I knew I should have locked that door."

"Just answer me," Harrison shouted.

"Why what?"

"Why did you do it?"

"Do what?"

Katie's shawl was draped across the corner of the desk. Harrison picked it up, offering it to her as evidence. "This. Why this? Why Katie?"

"If you've come back to play prosecuting attorney, I don't have the time. Good day, Mr. Shaw." She turned her attention to the paper.

Shawl still in hand, he moved around to her side of the desk. "I want an answer!" he shouted with a voice that startled them both.

She took the shawl from him and draped it over her head. "I scrubs," she said, averting her eyes.

"Don't—," he warned her.

Her voice took on a deeper, masculine quality. "Miss Katie, I think you're pretty."

Now she was Katie again. "Master Shaw, now you jus' pokin' fun at me."

Harrison had known anger, but never like this. It was a beast of such enormous size that it eclipsed all reason, all thought, and it knew only one emotion—rage.

His fist slammed on the table. "WHY?" he roared.

"Because I'm a woman!" she roared back.

Gone were Katie's eyes, Katie's demeanor. Gone was all pretense. All playfulness. Neither was there any derision. All that remained was Victoria Jarves in a way he'd never seen before.

"I need more than that," Harrison said.

"There are a lot of things you need that you're not going to get." Victoria threw the shawl into the open bag on the floor. "Now leave me alone."

"I'm not leaving without answers."

She picked up the paper and looked at it. She pretended to be reading it, but Harrison knew she wasn't. There was no way.

"It's obvious what you're doing." Harrison stepped back.

"You're right. It's obvious. Now get out."

"You dress up in all these costumes. Sneak around like you did at the ball dressed as a minuteman. Listening. Eavesdropping. Gathering stories. Then you run back here and sell the information to Conant."

"Congratulations," she said flatly. "You have it all figured out. Now go."

He pulled the paper from her hands. "And from the looks of it, you take his dictation too. Really, Miss Jarves. Dictation? Isn't that a bit beneath you?"

She reached for the paper just as he saw what was printed on it. He pulled it out of her reach and read it aloud.

"SPIRITUAL REVIVAL—SO CALLED"

It was a story about the *Levant*.

"What does Conant mean, 'So Called'? He wasn't there." Harrison moved closer. "But you were. At least you'd think you'd tell the story right!"

She snatched the paper back. "I did get it right."

Harrison shook his head. "Conant won't print that. It's not the truth. He's a newsman."

"I'd appreciate it if you would just leave!" She was close to tears.

"When does he get up?" Harrison walked to the side of the bed, which from the odors accumulating in the corner was a big mistake. He turned to Victoria. "Wake him up. I'll tell him what really happened."

"Please leave."

"I'm not leaving until I speak to Mr. Conant. When does he wake up?"

She stared at him.

He stared at her and folded his arms.

"Fine," she said. "Just leave me alone while I work."

"Fine. And I'll just wake up Mr. Conant and have a chat with him."

Harrison approached the bed.

"Leave him alone," Victoria said.

Bending down, Harrison poked Conant with a finger.

"Leave him alone!" she repeated.

"Mr. Conant, I'd like to speak with you, sir," Harrison said, still poking.

For some reason Harrison's poking Horace Conant greatly irritated Victoria, which was probably why he kept doing it.

"Mr. Conant, sir? Mr. Conant?"

Harrison noticed that Victoria closed her eyes, as if attempting to control herself.

"Mr. Conant?"

She bit her lip.

"Mr. Conant, sir?"

"I'm Horace Conant!" Victoria shouted.

The drunk in the corner stirred.

Harrison stood up.

Victoria glared at him from behind the desk. She moved to the front of the desk. "That man in the corner hasn't written a word in over a year."

"But his columns."

"*My* columns."

Harrison shook his head. "He tells you what to write."

"Why do you say that?" Victoria cried. "Why? Because I'm a woman? You think I can't write because I'm a woman?"

A different person stood in front of him than the one who lived on Fifth Avenue and spent her afternoons whacking interns on the arms. This woman was assertive, driven. The Fifth Avenue Victoria was spoiled and mean. Another act?

"Conant was on the verge of being dismissed," she said. "I met him at a social function. He was drunk."

"And who were you when you met him?"

"John Blayne," she said with a wry smile. "I've always wanted to be a reporter, and this was my chance to talk to an award-winning writer."

"Only he was less impressive than you expected."

"He passed out in his chocolate mousse."

Harrison glanced at Conant. Unconscious seemed his natural condition.

"That week I came over here . . ." She paused in thought. "I don't know exactly why I came here. Maybe I was thinking as you were. That if I could just work with him, maybe I could work myself into some sort of writing position."

"A job? Victoria Jarves employed?"

She was deadly serious when she said, "You don't know what writing means to me."

Serious enough to wipe the grin off Harrison's face.

"While I was here, a courier came for his column. Horace was as he is now, and I couldn't find a scrap of an article on his desk. The courier was prepared for this possibility. He conveyed a message from the editor. If Horace didn't have a column by five in the afternoon, he no longer had a job with the paper."

"And you couldn't help yourself."

"It was an opportunity to see if my writing was any good."

"Did they publish it?"

"Since I've been writing Horace Conant's column, circulation has increased. And Horace, I mean, *I* have won two journalism awards. I have a letter from the editor saying the column has never been better. Of course, it's addressed to Conant and usually accompanied by—"

"A bottle of whiskey."

"Which Horace drinks," she said.

For a moment Harrison forgot to be angry. "Surely you've proved yourself. Why not just reveal what you've been doing? If the paper has any brains, they'll give you Horace Conant's column."

Victoria stiffened. "They don't let women write columns or be reporters. And even if they did, my father would never allow me to be a reporter."

"So the disguises."

"The disguises," Victoria echoed.

"But why so many?"

"Each one protects me and gains me access to places in different ways. Now I have a question for you."

Harrison folded his arms. He still didn't like her.

"What are you going to do?"

"Go back home."

"I mean, about all this? You know. Nobody else knows. If word were to get out, it would be over. I'd never write again."

She was vulnerable. Harrison took pleasure in that.

"I'll have to think about it."

"What's to think about?"

"I'm leaving." He walked to the door.

"What's to think about?"

"Good-bye, Miss Jarves, or whoever you really are."

"Wait. Give me your word that you'll keep my secret. I'll believe you."

"Which secret, Miss Jarves? There are so many of them."

"Promise you won't tell anyone about Horace Conant."

"Good-bye, Miss Jarves."

CHAPTER 20

⟆⟊⟋

Revenge wasn't what Harrison had in mind. However, knowing Victoria Jarves's secret gave him a satisfying feeling of control, something he'd never felt around her before. He just couldn't understand why he hadn't seen it before. It was so obvious to him now.

Following the incident in Horace Conant's room, he'd see her two, maybe three times a week, which didn't come as any surprise. Both he and Victoria were doing the same job, looking for good copy. She, for the *Herald*. He, for the old North Dutch Church. So it just stood to reason that they'd run into each other occasionally.

A week after the incident, he spotted her just outside Matt Brennan's saloon on Pearl Street. Word on the street was that men were going into the saloon expecting to down some spirits, only to be filled with the Spirit instead. The owner wanted the police to do something about it. While his saloon was packed every night, he was going broke. Men were praying, not drinking. He was demanding they do something, but what could the police do? Arrest the Holy Spirit?

When Harrison arrived, he saw Victoria interviewing a couple of men who appeared at first to be drunk. Victoria was having difficulty getting them to slow down and take turns so she could get their story.

She was dressed as a boy, a combination between a newsboy and a courier. It wasn't a disguise Harrison had seen before. But now that he knew, all he saw was Victoria Jarves dressed in boys' clothes, talking to a couple of men who were convinced she was one of them.

Although Harrison knew the truth, everyone else was fooled. Harrison watched as she interviewed several men in succession. None of them appeared to have the slightest clue she was female.

He approached her from a blind side. Standing behind her, slightly to one side, he listened as she conducted the interview. She was good. Her questions were insightful, if not a little biased. She was skeptical that what they were telling her was true.

The interview over, she stood alone, transferring the last of the quotes to a pad of paper.

Harrison leaned close to her ear. "Hello, Victoria."

He startled her. She spun around. Surprised. Then, when she saw who it was, angry.

"Keep your voice down!"

"Does your father know where you are?"

"I don't see how that's any of your business."

She walked away. He followed.

She spun around a second time and was startled again to see him still behind her.

"How did you know?" she whispered. She felt the back of her head, checking to see if there were any wayward curls.

"You don't believe those men you interviewed, do you?"

"No, I don't. How did you know it was me?"

"Why don't you believe them?" He made a gesture at the excitement that was spilling out of the saloon. Brennan's saloon hadn't heard so many "Amens" and "Hallelujahs" in its existence. It was a curious sight.

"I don't believe them, because it doesn't make sense. There's an explanation, and I'm going to find it."

"I'll explain it to you. It's called *revival.*"

Victoria scoffed. "How did you know it was me?"

She was deadly earnest. His ability to recognize her disturbed her on a deep level, like it did the day of his interview, when he smelled Desire du Paris.

Harrison relented. "I just knew. I looked up and knew, that's all."

"Something had to give me away."

"It could have been your hands."

She called the suspected traitors forward and examined them. They were ungloved.

"Katie always hid them from me."

"Because they weren't a scrubwoman's hands," she said, still examining them. Having found them suspect, she reached into a pocket and pulled out a pair of gloves. The gloves Harrison had given to Mouser to give to Katie. Or, more correctly, the gloves he'd given to Victoria, to give to Victoria, that were now being worn by Victoria.

The sight of the gloves pained his heart.

"Stop following me." She took a few steps, then turned back. "It didn't take long for Father to replace you," she said with a wicked smile. "One day."

"Whitney Stuart III?"

"The two of them are hitting it off famously."

Victoria turned and disappeared into the night.

The next time he saw her, she was wearing a different disguise with gloves. She'd even managed some facial hair. A small mustache.

It took Harrison several minutes to control his laughing before he could approach her. He did it the same way as he did the night outside Brennan's saloon, from behind.

"Hello, Victoria," he whispered in her ear.

This time she was equally surprised but angrier. She grabbed him by the sleeve and pulled him aside. "Stop doing that!"

His newfound control over her couldn't make up for the loss of Katie, but still it was oddly satisfying.

"Get any good quotes?" he asked.

They stood in front of a sawmill. The owner and his son had been vicious competitors for years and had furnished the *Herald* with many stories of suspected arson, sabotage, price undercuts, and brawls. It was just a matter of time before one of them killed the other. Now here they were, arm in arm, announcing that they were merging their businesses. They credited the Holy Spirit with healing their stormy relationship.

"I'm wearing gloves. How did you know it was me?"

"How do you explain this one?" he replied, referring to the father-and-son announcement.

"Tigers don't change their stripes. One of them is up to something. My guess is, the son is playing along. He'll kill the old man in his sleep. How did you know it was me?"

Harrison was shaking his head. "How can you ignore what's happening all around you?"

"I don't believe in ghost stories," she replied. "People do things for reasons that benefit them in the long run. All these niceties are masks to get away with murder—in this case, literally. Now, how did you know?"

"I don't know how I know. I just know."

"Is it the mustache?"

"The mustache looks fine."

Though it did cause him to chuckle.

"If it's not the mustache, then what?"

"I don't know! I can just tell. Maybe it's your scent."

She glared at him, making the connection to Desire du Paris. "I'm not wearing any."

"Not perfume. Your scent. You know how animals recognize the scent of other animals?"

Of course, she knew. She was J. K. Jarves's daughter.

"Well, maybe I can detect your scent. I mean, I was able to smell the perfume through a wall."

She stared at him for a long moment, then walked off in a huff.

He spied her again a couple of weeks later at the Fulton Street Market, an outdoor affair where farmers sold produce, and fishermen, their daily catch. It was a raucous gathering of buyers and sellers who bartered and occasionally stepped aside for cattle to be driven down the street or to sidestep hogs that fed on yesterday's vegetables that had been thrown into the gutters.

Harrison wasn't there for a revival story. He was there for corn that he'd been craving for the better part of a week. He caught sight of her from a distance. She was disguised in a variation of John Blayne, meaning she wasn't dressed in a minuteman costume. She didn't see him.

He felt a tap on his shoulder.

"You're Harrison Shaw, aren't you?"

Turning toward the question, he came face-to-face with a man roughly his own age and height. Thin nose and lips to match a long face that ended with a pointy chin.

"Name's Roger Curtis, reporter for the *Chicago Tribune*. I've seen you around. You're the one collecting stories for that church, right?"

"That's right."

"I'd like to talk to you. Ask you some questions."

Harrison nodded assent.

Curtis pulled out a pad and pencil. "What kinda stories you got so far?"

"About the revival?"

"Sure, about the revival. Any good ones?"

"You want to print these in the *Tribune*?"

"Hey, I'm the one asking the questions, all right? Otherwise, this is gonna take all day."

Roger Curtis of the *Tribune* clearly had no interest in the events of the revival. He was probably given the assignment by an editor. But what did that matter to Harrison? If the revival stories were printed in the *Tribune*, that was good, right?

"Do you want to hear about how it all started?" he asked. "I attended the first prayer meeting."

"Sure. Why not?"

The man had all the enthusiasm of a boy who had to work while his friends went swimming in the river.

"It was last September, the twenty-third," he began. He knew the date because he'd written it up recently for his own project. "The meeting was scheduled to start at noon, but no one showed up on time. Jeremiah Lan—"

Already, he'd lost the reporter's attention. The man was looking over Harrison's shoulder at something behind him.

The reporter cursed.

Harrison turned to see what he was looking at. It was Victoria.

"That's one of Horace Conant's boys," Curtis said. "There's a story over there, I know it."

"There are a lot of stories here," Harrison said.

"No, you don't get it," Curtis said, without taking his eyes off Victoria. "Horace Conant has a nose for the good stuff. If he sent one of his boys to talk to that fisherman, something's up."

He folded his pad and began moving in the direction of Victoria and the fisherman, stopping first at a vegetable stand, pretending to examine a potato. He glanced back at Harrison. "Wait for me."

Had it not been the *Chicago Tribune*, Harrison wouldn't have waited. He watched with mild amusement as the reporter stalked Victoria Jarves, inching within earshot. Not until the reporter was in range did Harrison think he should probably do something to warn Victoria. He didn't know why; it just seemed the right thing to do. However, it was unnecessary. Victoria concluded the interview and was soon lost in the market traffic.

"Didn't get anything," Curtis groused when he returned, though his mind was still on the incident. "I could go back and talk to the fisherman. Ask him what he was telling Horace Conant's boy."

Harrison laughed. Victoria was fooling everyone, except him. Roger Curtis of the *Tribune* had not the slightest suspicion he was obsessed over a woman reporter.

"Things aren't always as they seem, Mr. Curtis."

Curtis looked at him suspiciously. "What do you mean?"

"Horace Conant's boy. Things aren't always as they seem."

"Why would you say that?"

"It's nothing. Do you want to hear the revival stories, or don't you?"

Curtis studied Harrison with a suspicious squint. Then he eyed the fisherman again. "Maybe later." Turning his back on Harrison, he left. Harrison was disappointed the stories didn't get told. Maybe he'd wander over to the *Tribune* and talk to one of the editors later this week.

Carrying a couple cobs of corn, Harrison left Fulton Street Market for his basement home. There was something disturbing about the way that reporter looked at him. Harrison couldn't shake the feeling that he'd said too much.

Three days later, at noon, Harrison attended the prayer meeting in the upper room of the old North Dutch Church. As usual it was crowded. Jeremiah Lanphier had asked him to relate some of the revival stories he'd collected.

When Jeremiah introduced Harrison to the assembly, Harrison stood. He was struck again by the diversity of people who attended these meetings—clerks sat next to common laborers, farmers sat next to bankers, dockworkers sat next to city officials. The one thing they had in common was a thirst for the spiritual. You could see it in their eyes, in their longing expressions.

He thought he'd begin with the Brennan's saloon story. He set the stage with a description of an average night at the saloon, telling them about Wilbur Hunt, a worker at the Novelty Iron Works on the river at Twelfth Street. Just as he was describing, in Wilbur's words, "the first wave of the Spirit as it washed over him," there was a pounding on the wooden steps leading up to the room. Someone was in a hurry.

A moment later that someone burst into the room.

Victoria.

Red-faced. Out of breath. Dressed like a woman. Clutching a newspaper. She scanned the room. There was fury in her eyes. It was obvious she was looking for someone. For Harrison, the object of her search was no mystery.

Her eyes wandered up one row, down another.

Should he say something?

He didn't need to. She found him.

"Harrison Shaw!" she shouted. "You snake!"

Heads swung back toward Harrison.

"You just had to do it, didn't you?" she shouted.

Heads swung back to her.

Jeremiah Lanphier approached Harrison from behind. He said confidentially, "Do you know this woman, Harrison?"

If there was ever a time in Harrison's life when he was tempted to lie, it was now. But in this room, truth was king, no matter how ugly or painful.

"I know her," he said.

"Maybe you should take this outside," Jeremiah suggested.

Excusing himself, Harrison worked his way to the door down a narrow path between the chairs and the feet of men standing against the wall.

Victoria was shouting, "Did you derive some sort of pleasure from this?" She was shaking a rolled-up newspaper at him.

As he made his way toward her, Harrison felt the weight of everyone's gaze on him. Halfway to the doorway, a hand grabbed his arm. He turned to see a heavily whiskered man.

"When the missus has murder in her eyes like that," advised the man, "don't waste time trying to explain. Just beg for mercy, boy. Beg for mercy."

CHAPTER 21

"You embarrassed me back there," Harrison said.

They stood in the shadow of the old North Dutch Church edifice. The tree-lined street was quiet, except for Victoria's yelling.

"You just had to do it, didn't you?" she shouted. "This is revenge against my father, isn't it?"

She whacked him on the shoulder with the newspaper.

"What are you talking about?"

"This!" She whacked him again. "As if you didn't know!"

"What?"

Another whack.

Harrison took a step back to get out of arm's reach.

"You had to go to him, didn't you? Well, you got what you wanted. I'm ruined. You got your revenge."

Victoria's jaw set in a strangely vulnerable way as she fought back tears. Real tears, different from the theatrical waterworks she'd produced at the mansion. She appeared genuinely wounded. Still . . . Harrison couldn't help wondering if this was another one of her acts.

With a hesitant hand, he reached out to her. "Victoria, I honestly—"

She threw the paper against his chest. He caught it and unrolled it. It was the *Tribune*. Front page. Below the fold there was this story:

PROOF

CELEBRATED HERALD COLUMNIST A FRAUD

by Roger Curtis

It has been learned by this newspaper that the award-winning New York Herald columnist Horace Conant no longer writes the column that bears his byline. Once known for its witty and at times scathing review of New York society, the column's readership declined following several well-publicized scandals surrounding Conant's drinking. With his career teetering on destruction, it was believed at the time that the venerable writer isolated himself, sobered up, and took to writing earnestly once again. In what appeared a miraculous turnabout, his columns once again displayed the wit that made him famous. It was all an illusion.

Horace Conant lies in a drunken stupor in his apartment. What of his revived column? Credit a young woman. For the past year, Victoria Jarves, daughter of attorney J. K. Jarves, has been writing Horace Conant's columns for him. New York Herald editor, Thomas Mayfair, denies any knowledge of this subterfuge, but given the Herald's penchant for sensationalism . . .

"You went to him, didn't you?" Victoria threw up her hands. "And the *Tribune*! Why couldn't you have chosen another paper?"

"I didn't choose any paper!" Harrison cried.

He tried to hand the article back to her. Then he realized he was handing back the weapon she used to beat him. Luckily for him, she didn't take it.

"How can you stand there and lie like that?" Victoria screamed. "You are the only possible source for that story. Nobody else knew."

"But I didn't—"

"You didn't what? You didn't give Roger Curtis the story? You've never even met Roger Curtis? You expect me to believe that?"

Harrison shuffled his feet. "I have met him."

"Ah! There! Now you're admitting it."

"But I didn't give him the story."

"You must have said something!"

Harrison winced. "Well, I did say something. But it was nothing."

"Nothing. You said nothing, and the next thing I know I catch Roger Curtis of the *Tribune* rummaging around Horace Conant's apartment."

"You caught him in the apartment?"

"What did you expect he'd do after you tipped him off?"

"I didn't tip him off. Not exactly."

"What exactly did you do?"

"I may have said something."

"You said something. What exactly did you say?"

She was dragging it out of him.

"I told him things aren't always as they seem."

Victoria stood with hands on hips, waiting for all of it.

"We were at the market on Fulton Street. He saw you. Called you one of Conant's boys. And I said something about things aren't always as they seem."

She stared at him incredulously. "You told him that?"

"It was an innocent comment."

"Innocent?" Victoria cried. "A statement like that to a reporter is like a meat bone to a bulldog."

So he was responsible. Harrison felt lousy. "What did they—" he began.

"They're taking the column out. I'll never get published again."

"But . . . but, it was good. What you wrote. It was good. Just as good, if not better—even Curtis admits that—than Horace Conant. Why don't they just let you continue writing the column? You've proven to them you can do it."

"I deceived them."

"All right. Then what about another newspaper? One that needs a—"

"I'm a woman! Can't you get that through your head? They're not going to let a woman write for them!"

"Even though—"

"They're not going to let a woman write for them."

Harrison's shoulders slumped.

Victoria was out of steam too.

"How did your father react?" Harrison asked.

"At first he was furious. He doesn't like the attention it's brought."

Predators don't like bright lights, Harrison thought.

"But after a while, he settled down. He scolded me. Then he told me he was proud of me."

"Victoria, I never—"

But she was done with him. She'd turned and disappeared around the corner of the church.

"Wait!"

Harrison couldn't let her leave like that. He caught up with her, the rustle of her dress very determined in its pace.

"Victoria."

She pretended not to hear him. His mind flashed back to calling to Katie on the streets of Five Points. When she swung around, he saw the resemblance between the two. Same height. She swung around the same way Katie did.

"I have nothing more to say to you," Victoria said.

"Then just listen."

She set herself in a resistant stance. The edge of her anger had dulled, but that didn't mean it was gone altogether.

"I can't leave it like this," he said. "There has to be something I can do to help."

"You don't want to help."

He should have known she couldn't just listen.

"Of course I want to help."

"You want to feel better, that's what you want. You feel bad the way things have worked out, and you want to feel better."

"I do feel badly—"

Her face showed mock sympathy. "And it hurts, doesn't it, Harrison? And you want the hurt to go away, don't you?"

"I feel responsible," Harrison said, "and I want to help put things right."

She folded her arms and studied him. Not the way he looked—which was undoubtedly pathetic—but deeper. She looked at him as though she were peering into his soul.

"Why do you think that is, Harrison? Have you ever asked yourself that? Why do you help people?"

"I don't understand—"

"You're always doing it. That's why you venture into Five Points, isn't it? To help people? Dicey Timrod's scarf and hat. Laura Hamblin's cough medicine. Leaving food at the door for Katie and Mouser. Katie's gloves. Why do you do things like that, Harrison? Have you ever asked yourself why?"

He'd never given the matter a thought. That's what good people did. They helped others. "I've always been taught to help those less fortunate than myself."

"You do it because you like thinking of yourself as the savior of the world. That's why you do it," she stated emphatically.

He frowned. "No, that's where you're wrong."

"You do it so that people will thank you. You do it so that people will look up to you. You do it for the praise, Harrison. You love the adoration, the attention that comes from being good, from helping others. When you asked Katie about the food. The gloves. When you gave her the pink fan. I saw it in your eyes."

She assumed Katie's posture. Head down. Glancing up fleetingly from the tops of her eyes. "You fishin' for a compliment, Master Shaw?"

She became Victoria again. "You wanted to hear her say it, because it made you feel good. Tell me you didn't dream of riding into Five

Points on a white charger and carrying Katie far away from there. And she'd put her arms around your neck and kiss you, but mostly, she'd be eternally grateful that you saved her from Five Points. Even when you dreamed that dream, your chest swelled with pleasure, didn't it, Harrison?"

The truth? Of course it did. Until this moment Harrison hadn't realized how much pleasure that dream had given him. But not only that. Every time George Bowen looked on him with pride, every time Bowen complimented him for a job well done, Harrison ate it up. He'd do anything to make George Bowen proud of him. And Five Points? While he'd left the scarf and hat and medicine anonymously, if he were being honest with himself, he hoped that one day they'd learn the identity of the secret Samaritan. And that would bring him pleasure.

"Well, Harrison, I don't want any part of your crusade. Go save someone else." Victoria turned and left him standing there. Her words, like venom, paralyzed him.

"Wait!"

He fought the paralysis, shaking his head to clear it. He caught up with her again.

"What were *you* doing in Five Points? All those disguises. Deceiving people. Leading them on. Exploiting them."

He succeeded in stopping her again.

"Just let it go, Harrison."

"No. I want to know. You had great fun deceiving me. Laughing at me behind my back. Leading me on."

"I never led you on," she snapped.

"Yeah? Well, you put me at risk. I rescued you from a beating, and ended up getting beat up for the effort. I think that earns me the right to some answers."

She thought on that a moment. "All right. I was searching for news stories."

"For Horace Conant's column."

"Yes, and for other stories."

"And you had to use deception to get them?"

She gave him one of those "Did you just step off the boat?" looks. "Of course, I used deception! Do you think anyone would talk to me in Five Points if I walked in dressed like this? How far do you think I'd get? Forget Five Points. Tell me one place in the city where I could ask questions for a news story dressed like Victoria Jarves and be taken seriously? And even if I did get a story, who would print it?"

"Be truthful now," Harrison said. "You derive pleasure from fooling everyone, making them believe you're someone you're not. I saw it in your eyes at the announcement ball when you were John Blayne. You had fun deceiving people."

Victoria covered a grin with her hand. "I certainly had fun with you. Especially when you were making a fool of yourself with Katie."

Harrison felt his face color.

"But that's not why I was there," she added quickly. "I was looking for stories that the *Herald* would print. Gripping stories. Stories of life and death and drama and danger. Those are the kinds of stories I want to write." She'd become deadly earnest. "Do you recall the story of Helen Jewett?"

Harrison shook his head.

"No, of course you wouldn't."

Harrison started to take offense.

She cut him off. "All I mean is that it happened a good number of years ago. The only reason I know it is because I've read through past issues of the *Herald*. It was a sensational story. Helen Jewett was a beautiful young woman, a prostitute. One day she was found dead in her room on Thomas Street. Her head had been split open with an ax, and her bed set on fire."

Harrison grimaced.

"The reporter covering the story found a bundle of love letters she'd received from a well-educated Connecticut jewelry-store clerk that led to his arrest. It was a gripping story of a spurned lover—tragedy and drama. Everybody in New York followed it. The *Herald*'s circulation tripled. I'm looking for my own Helen Jewett story. Or, should I say, *was* looking. Even if I were to find the story, how would I get it published? Forget that I'm a woman. The *Herald* would never print anything I wrote now."

"There are other newspapers. There's the *Tribune*."

"The stuffy old *Tribune*. They'd never print the stories I want to write. The *Tribune* prints stories the people need. The *Herald* prints stories the people want. Suicides. Murders. Fires. They once printed an eyewitness account of a guillotine execution in France."

"And these are the kinds of stories you want to write? Why?"

Victoria cocked her head. "What's the matter, Harrison? Are you afraid Katie wouldn't approve?"

"But you couldn't write those kinds of stories under Horace Conant's name, could you?"

"No. I knew I couldn't write Horace's columns forever. It's just that by the time I was ready to make a switch, I thought I'd have it figured out."

Harrison grew thoughtful. "Why not write under another male pseudonym? Submit your articles using a courier like Conant did—like you did pretending to be Conant—you know what I mean."

Victoria shrugged. "I've given that some thought. It might work. For a time. Problem is, the couriers aren't always reliable. If one of them knew it was me writing the articles, they'd snitch on me sooner or later."

Harrison grinned. "How about if the articles were submitted to the publisher by a legal representative?"

Victoria's head tilted back as she thought. "And that legal representative would be?"

Harrison spread wide his arms.

"Out of the question," she said.

"Of course, the articles would have to stand on their own. There would be no hiding behind Horace Conant's reputation anymore. So if the writing wasn't good, then you couldn't blame it on me."

"I'm a good writer!" Victoria insisted. "People have said that the articles I wrote for Horace were some of his best work."

"Yes, but they thought *he* had written them. If they were to get an article from an unknown, they'd be skeptical. The writing would have to be so good, they couldn't pass it up. But if you don't think you can write to that level—"

"Don't get smart with me, Harrison. You're not good at it."

"Then you'll try it? You write an article. I'll take it to the editor and negotiate its publication."

Victoria was shaking her head. "I don't like it."

"What's not to like?"

"It places you in the role of savior again."

Harrison smiled. "Maybe that's just something you'll have to live with."

Victoria sighed. "All right, I'll do it—under one condition."

"What's that?"

"That you get something out of it other than getting to play the role of the great crusader again."

It was Harrison's turn to be earnest. "I'll get to be a lawyer again."

CHAPTER 22

———————— ❧◦❧ ————————

Twice they met at an appointed time in front of the big iron gate at City Hall. Twice Victoria showed up empty-handed.

"I just haven't found the right story," she said.

"Are you having trouble getting out of the house since the whole Horace Conant affair?" Harrison asked.

"That's not the problem. I hardly see Father. And he's too busy with business and making Whitney Stuart's life miserable to check up on me. Things haven't changed in that regard. I pretty much come and go as I please."

Whitney Stuart III. Jarves's new intern. Harrison wondered if Whitney had been introduced to the predator collection yet. Or was he still doing research that made no sense?

"Are you giving Whitney lessons on how to enter a parlor?" Harrison hoped the answer was negative.

Victoria smiled. It was a nice smile. A smile between friends. Harrison reveled in it.

"Whitney Stuart III needs no lessons in etiquette. Those were specially designed for Brooklyn bumpkins," she said.

"Do you think you'll have something by next week?"

"Who can say? I've come up with nothing."

"Nothing is happening in Five Points?"

"Just the usual. Muggings. Gang fights. Corruption. Nothing exciting. Nothing out of the ordinary. Nothing sensational. This first story has to be unique."

"I have some stories," Harrison said. "They're unique. Sensational, to say the least. Nothing like them has happened in New York before."

Victoria wrinkled her nose. "Not those Holy Spirit stories."

"Roger Curtis of the *Tribune* wanted them."

"Curtis wanted them?"

"He came to me."

Victoria thought on this, then added: "No, I just don't buy it. The stories are phony. Made-up."

"They are not!" Harrison protested. "Some amazing things are happening all across the United States—things that can only be explained by an invasion of an all-powerful spiritual presence in our world."

He'd struck a chord of interest. He could see it on her face. "I'll tell you what. Let me take you around. Introduce you to people. Listen to them tell their stories. Investigate them. Challenge them. Do everything you can to discredit their stories. And if you prove them false, then you have a great story—hundreds of New Yorkers banding together to pull the biggest hoax the city has ever seen."

Victoria was listening.

"But if you can't disprove the stories, then you have a story there too. You'll have proved that the Almighty God has invaded our city in strange but powerful ways. Either way, you've got a story."

"A hoax, huh?"

"That's something you would know about!" Harrison grinned. Then he said more seriously. "But you have to tell the truth."

"A citywide hoax."

"Involving hundreds of people."

"It might be worth looking into," Victoria said.

"So you'll do it?"

"I would have to spend a lot of time with you. Guess it's the price I'll pay for the story."

"And I'm looking forward to spending the time with you too." Harrison said it in jest, but there was an element of truth to it.

"When do we begin?" Victoria asked.

"Whenever you're ready."

"Very well. I have two hours before I have to be back at the house. Can we do anything in two hours?"

"I can take you to Matt Brennan's saloon on Pearl Street. There are a couple of men you'll want to talk to there."

"I can't go there dressed like this," Victoria said.

Harrison had forgotten that part. "Who will you go as?"

"Not Katie."

"No, not Katie. Definitely not Katie."

"I could go as Mouser."

"Why not go as Victoria, only in a dress that wouldn't make you stand out so much?"

"The men wouldn't talk to me as a woman."

"They will if I'm with you. I know these men."

"Go as myself?"

"Is that a problem?"

She gave it some thought. "All right. I'll meet you here, same time tomorrow."

"Fine. I'll be here."

"And Harrison?"

"Yeah?"

"Do me a favor. When you introduce me, call me Tori. I hate the name Victoria."

"The center desk. The man who's yelling."

Harrison thanked the receptionist. It took Tori less than a day to write the story after they were at Brennan's saloon. It was good. Now it was up to Harrison to sell it.

He wove his way through a checkerboard of desks, most of them unoccupied. In the middle of the board, a squat man was yelling something at a boy about a press run. The boy sprinted off, showing no sign that he took the yelling personally.

The man behind the desk saw Harrison coming. "What do you want?" he barked.

"Thomas Mayfair?"

Mayfair looked him up and down disdainfully. "Tell the mayor, for the last time, he's not getting a retraction. Now get outta my newsroom." He dropped into his seat and attacked a stack of papers.

"I'm not representing the mayor," Harrison said.

Disgust puckered Mayfair's face. "Good Lord, you're a lawyer."

Mayfair was a compact man with a barrel chest. His sleeves were rolled up, exposing thick, hairy black arms that had evidently done more than just push pens around. Exasperated, he raked a hand from forehead to crown across his smooth skin.

Harrison retrieved papers from his satchel. He extended them to Mayfair, who glanced at them but gave no indication he would take them.

"I represent T. E. Campbell, a talented young writer. On behalf of my client, I submit this article for your consideration. I believe you'll find it in keeping with the *New York Herald*'s editorial slant."

An amused grin formed on Mayfair's face. "You're a little old to be a courier, aren't you, boy?"

"I'm prepared to wait while you read it," Harrison said.

Mayfair shook his head. "I don't publish writers I haven't met. Tell Campbell to make an appointment. If he impresses me, I'll give him a shot."

"I'm afraid that won't be possible," Harrison said. "My client prefers to keep a low profile."

"Then tell your client to keep his low profile at someone else's newspaper." Mayfair returned to work.

Harrison kept the article extended. "Thirty seconds, that's all I ask. Give the article thirty seconds. If it doesn't interest you, I'll leave.

However, I'd be willing to bet that in thirty seconds, not only will you want this article, but you'll want to sign my client to an exclusive contract."

Mayfair rolled his eyes. Had Harrison overplayed his hand? He was gambling that Tori's writing was strong enough to command Mayfair's immediate attention. It certainly had done that for Harrison when he first read it.

"I'll give you ten seconds," Mayfair said.

"Agreed." Harrison pushed the paper closer to him.

The editor leaned forward. At first he read without taking the paper from Harrison.

Ten seconds passed.

Mayfair took the article from Harrison, still reading, and sat back in his chair.

MURDER STOPPED BY HOLY STALKER

by T. E. Campbell

On April 9, 1858, Jesse Kirkland walked into Brennan's saloon on Pearl Street with murder on his mind. He was edgy not so much about the murder—he'd resolved himself to that—but because he was being followed.

That night the saloon was louder than usual. Kirkland went in anyway to get off the streets and to get drunk for the last time, because after he killed his wife and daughter, he would kill himself. He picked a seat facing the door and ordered a drink. He didn't know that his stalker was already inside the saloon.

Kirkland was familiar with the saloon and the neighborhood. He'd spent his entire life associated with thieves and murderers. Stuffed in his waistband was an eight-inch blade he'd just purchased for the murders. He wanted something silent.

The Kirklands had seen happier days in their three years of marriage. Jesse Kirkland had married his school sweetheart. They'd planned to have children and move out of the city. Kirkland invested heavily to make their dream a reality. Then came the financial crash. He lost everything. His wife had a difficult delivery. The baby was sick a lot. Medical bills mounted. Kirkland was heavily in debt. And his wife battled daily depression. The couple fought constantly. Their lives weren't supposed to be like this, he thought. With no hope of relief, Kirkland had decided that the only way they'd ever find peace was through death.

Just then someone bumped him, spilling his drink. It was a raucous night. There were too many drunks, and it was too loud. Kirkland decided to leave. Perhaps his stalker had given up on him.

Just as he stood up, a hand gripped his shoulder from behind. In one swift motion, Kirkland grabbed his knife with one hand, the man's hand with the other, swung around, and put his blade to the man's throat. "You want something, buddy?" he shouted.

"I didn't mean anything by it, mister!" the man cried. "I only wanted to ask you: do you have the Holy Spirit?"

Kirkland froze.

The man continued, "I came here for a couple of drinks with my buddies . . . only tonight, something was different. I walked in and they were singin', and I mean singin' loud! I'd never seen them like that. Only they weren't drunk. They were filled with the Spirit. And, well, we prayed and, guess what? The Spirit filled me too! So I just wanted to know, mister, do you have the Holy Spirit?"

Kirkland began to tremble. He sank to his knees. Weeping. "Where I come from," Kirkland told this reporter, "a person who puts a hand on your shoulder is going to proposition you or put a knife in you, but this man said, 'Mister, do you have the Holy Spirit?' My stalker took dead aim and shot me through the heart. Then the Spirit reached down and made me alive again!"

He explained: "I know now that the One stalking me was the Holy Spirit. And that night, in Brennan's saloon, I got myself right with God."

When Jesse Kirkland went home that night, he was armed. Not with a knife, as he'd planned, but with a Bible and prayer.

Kirkland's story is just one of the amazing accounts of a mysterious movement that is sweeping New York City and hundreds of surrounding cities and towns. Not just in churches, but in theaters and—of all unlikely places—Brennan's saloon.

"I'm the last person you'd ever think would get religion," he claimed. "Not after all the disgusting things I see every day on the job."

You see, the would-be murderer is a policeman. A criminal investigator. Jesse Kirkland is head of New York City's homicide division.

"What do you think?" Harrison prompted. "Can you use it?"

Mayfair sniffed, reread a section, then tossed it onto his desk. *A good sign*, Harrison thought. He didn't hand it back and tell Harrison his time was up.

"Well?

"Good writing," Mayfair admitted. "Story's questionable. It would've been better had Kirkland murdered his wife and kid, then found God. More blood that way. Our readers like blood."

"My client is willing to sell it for—"

"Not so fast."

"But you said you liked it."

Mayfair took a hard look at him. "What's going on here?"

"What do you mean?"

"I mean, what's going on? I've been editing for four decades. I've read a lot of authors, enough to be able to tell one writer from another. I know this style."

Harrison fidgeted.

"What did you say your name was?" Mayfair asked.

"Harrison Shaw."

Mayfair was nodding vigorously. "Yep, yep. J. K. Jarves's golden boy."

"I'm no longer associated with Mr. Jarves."

"That so? But you're associated with his daughter, aren't you, pal?" Mayfair picked up the article and tossed it across the desk. "Can't use it."

"You said you liked it."

"That was before I knew it was written by a woman."

Harrison shuffled his feet. If he was going to go down, he was going to go down swinging.

"Who's going to know? Nobody reads bylines anyway."

"Sorry, pal."

Harrison picked up the article. "I'll take it to the *Tribune*."

"They won't want it. Too racy for their taste."

"*Tribune* reporter Roger Curtis came to me recently, looking for stories like this one."

Mayfair sat up. Harrison had struck a nerve. Competition between newspapers was fierce.

"I could notify them that T. E. Campbell is a woman," Mayfair said.

"You could. But what good would that do? This is a good story.

People all over New York are hearing about the spiritual revival that's going on. Interest is high. Why squash a good story?"

Mayfair considered this. "Can she get more?"

"My client is in a position to get as many stories as you're willing to print."

"Ah," Mayfair grunted. He reached for the article. "Who reads bylines anyway?"

CHAPTER 23

Harrison was elated to find himself in this position. He never expected to be here. In fact, had someone told him a couple of weeks ago he'd be in this position, he might have shuddered. But now it was nice. More than nice. If anything, the spontaneity heightened the moment. Victoria Jarves had a lock on his neck with her arms. Her cheek pressed against his ear.

"Really? They're going to publish it?" she squealed.

In fact, had anyone told Harrison a couple of weeks ago that Victoria Jarves could squeal with delight, he probably wouldn't have believed it.

"Not only that," he said. "They want more. As much as you can give them."

She pulled back, clasping her hands with joy. "More? But where am I going to find more stories?"

"I can give you plenty of leads."

She eyed him and sobered just a bit. "I can't write more stories like that one."

"Mr. Mayfair said that's what he wants."

"But I want to do—"

"I know. Murders. Mystery. Scandal. Blood. And I'm sure Mr. Mayfair will want those stories too. But until you find your perfect murder, you can do revival stories."

"And he doesn't suspect a thing about—"

"Oh, he knows. He recognized your writing."

"He knows?"

"It troubled him at first. Of course, I never confirmed you were the client. He wants to publish you anyway. You're that good."

"But revival stories—"

"You're going to expose them, remember?"

Doubt shadowed her eyes. Harrison couldn't believe what he was seeing. Was she beginning to suspect that what she was hearing was true? But then, why not? She'd grilled Jesse Kirkland; Matt Brennan, the saloon owner; and more than a few of the men who were there that night. Everything had happened just as they described it. And apparently it was enough to put doubt in Tori's eyes.

The second *Herald* article attributed to T. E. Campbell had the following headline:

A TRASHY STORY

by T. E. Campbell

Cleanup is the bane of workers following any public gathering. Wherever two or more are gathered, there will be trash. Revival prayer meetings are no exception. At the conclusion of every meeting, volunteer workers pass among the chairs picking up trash and miscellaneous items left behind. Therein lies the story.

Such trash you have never seen. Workers have picked up guns, knives, vials of poison, and sacks filled with large sums of cash. At the Mercer Street Presbyterian Church, workers found a Revolutionary-era sword.

"It's not unusual for us to find guns and such," Harold Beecher said. "Each one has a story." Harold ought to know. He cleans up after hundreds of worshipers a week.

One can only speculate as to why people would bring such items to a prayer meeting. However, two things are clear: First, these items have been left behind deliberately. These aren't the kinds of items a person absent-mindedly forgets. And secondly, because they have been left behind, a tragedy has been averted.

"Even our trash gives testimony to the power of the Holy Spirit to change lives," Beecher claimed.

"T. E. Campbell," Harrison mused. "How did you come up with that name?"

Tori looked up from her writing. She was seated at the desk in the prayer-meeting room at the old North Dutch Church. The last person from the afternoon prayer session had just descended the steps, leaving Harrison and Tori alone. Tori was writing notes from the meeting. Harrison was picking up trash.

"T is for Tori," she explained. "I always thought when I published under my own name, I'd use Tori Jarves. E is for Ellen, that's my middle name. And Campbell is my mother's maiden name."

She resumed writing.

Harrison went from chair to chair, bending over and picking up handbills that announced the meeting, wrappers, pencils, a handkerchief, and—

"Hey, look at this." He straightened, holding up a pair of brass knuckles. He tried them on, flexing his fingers. "I wonder who these were intended for."

Tori was only half listening. Her mind was on what she was writing.

"It's the scope of this thing that's boggling me." She consulted her notepad. "Just today we have men here from Maine, North Carolina . . . here's one from Tennessee, and another from Ohio. And the letters . . ." She flipped a page. "New Hampshire. Kansas. Even one from England. There may be a story in that one."

"The wind bloweth where it listeth," Harrison quoted.

"What does that mean?"

"It's a passage from the Bible. 'The wind bloweth where it listeth, and thou hearest the sound thereof, but canst not tell whence it cometh, and whither it goeth.' It describes the Holy Spirit. He goes wherever He wants. We can't see Him, but we know when He's around, just like we know there's wind when the leaves rustle."

"So you're saying we know God is near because all these strange things are happening," Tori said.

"Yeah. That's one way we know God is near."

"Have your leaves ever rustled?"

Harrison removed the brass knuckles. "Are you asking me if I've ever experienced God?"

Tori nodded. She looked earnest enough.

"I had a conversion experience when I was younger."

"What was that like?"

"Well, it happened here. Downstairs in the sanctuary. The preacher was preaching on sin. I felt convicted. Guilty. And when the preacher said that all my sins could be forgiven, I thought that sounded like a good idea."

"How old were you?"

"Ten."

Tori smiled. She sat back and folded her arms. "What kind of horrible sin could you be guilty of at ten years old?"

"It's not the degree of sin. Sin is sin."

"So what sins had you committed?"

Harrison blushed. "I don't want to tell you."

"Oh, come on! I want to know if little Harrison Shaw was a bad boy."

"There was the usual, I guess. I'd lie occasionally to get out of trouble. I once stole a lucky rock from Tommy Morris."

"How about since?"

"You want to know if I've sinned recently?"

Tori laughed. "That's not what I meant, but yeah. Tell me your sins, Mr. Shaw."

Harrison grinned with her. "What did you mean?"

"Have you experienced any personal rustling since all this spiritual stuff started happening?"

Harrison lowered his head. Her question poked him in a tender place. While he was thrilled to see the Spirit moving so freely and dramatically, there had been no personal rustling, as Tori put it. More than once he'd felt like a boy standing outside a house, his nose pressed against a windowpane, watching a party inside.

"No," he said.

"How do you go about getting your leaves rustled?"

Harrison went back to work. "The wind bloweth where it listeth. It's not up to us."

They worked in silence for a time. She on her notebook. He on the last two rows of chairs.

After finishing the trash detail, Harrison began straightening the chairs for tomorrow's prayer meeting. "Look at us. Who would have figured you and I would be together like this?"

"Are you fishin' for a compliment, Mr. Shaw?"

"I was just . . . no. It just seemed to me . . . forget it."

He concentrated on getting the row straight. Straighter than it had ever been before. Straighter than it had any right to be. Straighter than . . .

"I'm sorry," Tori said. "That was uncalled for."

She knew how to jab where it hurt, didn't she? Ever since she accused him of being addicted to personal praise, he'd thought about it often. Wrestled with it. He wanted to do good for good's sake, yet he knew he loved the attention and the praise. It was a weakness.

"That's all right," he said, though it would take awhile longer to cool his simmering anger.

"Possibly you were referring to something else altogether, Mr. Shaw?" she asked lightly.

He looked at her questioningly.

"Possibly you were referring to the fact that we're alone in this room, you and I—alone, without a chaperone?"

Harrison knew she was teasing. Yet her eyes were wide, her voice flirtatious, and the combination was nearly fatal to Harrison. First it stopped his heart cold, then whipped it into a gallop.

He wanted to reply with something light, airy, witty. But he couldn't think of anything. In fact, he couldn't think of *anything*. Some kind of remark was needed, but all he gave her was silence, which was growing larger by the instant.

Say something, he told himself. *Anything.*

"Um . . . ah." He cleared his throat. "Um . . . the next." Throat cleared again. "Um, the next interview we have is with five women a short ride out of town."

She raised an eyebrow. "Five women?"

"A short ride out of town." Harrison gulped and began breathing again.

"Women," she said. "I like that idea. Maybe I can get to the truth about all of this. What's their story?"

"The five women?"

Tori nodded, with a hint of a grin.

"Ah, they . . . they made a pact to pray for their husbands, who have never been saved. They prayed for one until he came to the Lord. Then they prayed for another until he came to the Lord. Last week the last of the men was baptized."

"Good. I'll have some questions for them. Can I ask you one thing more?"

Having straightened the last row of chairs, Harrison stood to the side and folded his arms to indicate he was ready for the question.

"Join me," Tori said.

Join her? Thoughts of the hug were fresh in Harrison's mind. But he didn't think that was what she had in mind now . . . or was it? Why was she asking him to join her?

Pondering all these things in his heart, Harrison walked as casually as he could to the table. Tori had reached for a chair and pulled it to the table for him. Did she know that sitting this close to her would be a distraction of such magnitude that he might not even hear the question?

He sat.

She paused.

Was she having second thoughts? No matter—the longer she paused the more time he had to look at her without fear of getting caught.

Maybe it was the change in settings, but he thought she'd changed. She was softer than at the mansion. It showed in her manner. Her appearance. Her voice.

Tori took a breath. "Why are you doing this, Harrison?" she blurted out. "Why are you helping me?"

He started to answer, even though he didn't yet know what he was going to say.

She spoke again before he could. "You've never spoken ill of Father, though the two of you parted on bad terms. And you've never spoken ill to me about all the mean things I did to you."

"You weren't just trying to teach me?"

"Are you kidding? I was downright abusive to you!"

"Making me run around to the front of the house."

Tori nodded. She wore an impish smile.

"The garden gloves."

"Whacking you on the arms," she added.

"That hurt! And the silly fan."

"You did give that away to another girl; you just didn't know it was me."

"And the warm chair? How outrageous was that?"

"I was serious about that," she said. "That's just disgusting."

"Well, I did catch you spying on me the day of the interview."

"I spent all afternoon scrubbing that horrid perfume off my skin." Tori laughed.

"I wore it on my cuffs into Five Points. It got me all sorts of unwanted comments."

Tori laughed harder. "Why, then? Had the same happened to Whitney Stuart III, both Father and I would be his sworn enemies for life."

"'The life of a righteous man is a stout tree. Generations will find comfort beneath its branches.'"

"Again from the Bible?" she asked.

"No, that's from the Gospel According to George Bowen, my guardian and mentor. He was always making up sayings like that. Some made sense. Others we laughed at."

"He's the man who owned the lodge?"

Harrison nodded. A cloud passed over his face.

"I'm sorry," Tori said. "Father is a very vindictive man. It's one of his uglier traits."

Harrison looked at J. K. Jarves's daughter. He wondered how much she knew of her father. Did she know his whole philosophy surrounding the shrike, or was that just a bird under a jar to her? Someday he'd ask her.

"I miss Mr. Bowen," he said. "It's as though an entire part of my life has suddenly vanished. And the more time that passes, the harder it is to believe it was real. I fear that in time it will be little more to me than a dream."

"What were some of his other sayings? Do you recall any more?"

"Ah, one of his favorites whenever any of us was downcast over something was, 'Don't stare at your feet, gaze at the stars.'"

"Not bad for a Brooklyn philosopher."

"Let's see . . . another one was, 'Idleness is the drink of fools.' He used that one when we wanted to go to the river and he wanted us to clean the dorm."

Tori was enjoying this.

"One more," Harrison said. "This one always made us laugh. He'd say, 'There are moments in life when everything is perfect. Don't worry, it won't last.'"

She was smiling at him. Harrison wished he had a hundred more Bowenisms to keep her smiling this way forever.

"He evidently did a good job raising you."

She was looking into his eyes. He was hypnotized. What was more, he was looking back, and she didn't turn away. She was enjoying it as much as he was.

How often had he fantasized about moments like this one, where the room, the city, the world was nonexistent. It was just him and her communing, mind to mind, soul to soul. The ball of emotion in his chest was fully charged and functioning. He was lost in her. He had no control over his mind, his limbs, his breathing, his mouth, which is why it shouldn't have come as a surprise when he said, "Katie . . ."

"What?" Tori snapped back.

Harrison was barely aware he'd said anything, yet his ears heard a name. Surely, he didn't—

"What did you say?" Tori asked. It was her mansion teaching voice.

"I said—"

"You said *Katie!*"

Harrison tried to make light of it. "You are Katie, and John Blayne, and a whole host of others—"

"You're still in love with her, aren't you?"

Harrison scoffed. "No, of course I'm not in love with her. I never was in love with her."

"Even though she's an illusion. A part I played. A wardrobe. I can't believe this." Tori was angry and getting angrier. She began to gather her things. "I'm trying to be decent to you, and all the time you're sitting there bedding a nonexistent Katie in your mind."

"I was not!" Harrison protested.

Tori swung around to face him. "I know that look in your eyes!" she shouted. "I've seen it before. When you looked at *her!*"

Harrison was on his feet, backing away.

"I have to get home." Tori stormed out the door and down the steps, leaving a bewildered and embarrassed Harrison standing in the room at old North Dutch Church by himself.

CHAPTER 24

The carriage bounced happily past Fourteenth Street and into the countryside with Harrison holding the reins.

"This is my first time out of the city," he said. "You?"

Tori looked at him. She was adorable with the wind in her hair. "I've been out this way three or four times for a Sunday afternoon ride."

"With your father?"

"Suitors."

Harrison glanced at her again. He wondered if the guys who took her for carriage rides knew what they were up against. The news that Victoria Jarves had suitors came as no surprise. Harrison just didn't like to think about it. He wondered if Whitney Stuart III was one of them.

The day was glorious. Sparkling sky. Fresh spring air. Warm enough that you didn't need a coat. It was the kind of day that defied the blues. Anyone who was downhearted in this weather had serious problems.

The horse felt it too. Breaking out into the open country, he got frisky, challenging Harrison's control. With a shudder the carriage picked up speed. Harrison reined him in.

"Are you sure you know how to drive a carriage?" Tori asked.

"I've driven the lodge wagon plenty of times. It's a lot heavier than this, and it was all street traffic. I'll adjust."

One of the church elders had offered to let Harrison use the carriage for the day when he heard the purpose. The elder was an outspoken supporter of using the newspapers to get word out about the revival.

For Harrison it was a day alone with Tori.

The spring day was a distraction Tori allowed herself at intervals. Harrison was a distraction she tolerated, knowing he'd prefer to be taking the trip with Katie. But if she thought about that, she'd get angry. She chose instead to think about the upcoming interview. She was looking forward to talking to women about these revival stories. Perhaps now she'd get the truth.

Tori prided herself on knowing women. Her observation of them was the inspiration behind her disguises. She'd observed that women play roles to get what they want. These roles fit in one of two categories: domineering or manipulative.

For example, an outwardly genteel matron was the preferred mask of the domineering type. However, behind the closed mansion door, the domineering type ruled everything and everyone, barking orders, never satisfied. To the public her husband was a figure of manhood, a captain of industry. Behind closed doors he was a kowtowing toady who did as he was instructed, if he knew what was good for him.

Women who had stronger-willed husbands resorted to manipulation. Tori's mother had been this type of woman. Headaches. Moaning. Simulated fainting spells. Brooding. Flattery. Attention given and withheld. These were the preferred weapons of the manipulative woman.

In public men boasted openly about their romantic conquests and battles won at home. It was a way of salving their wounded male egos. Harmless enough. Their women permitted it, as long as they didn't start believing their own boasts.

Meanwhile, women compared notes frequently. How they got their husbands or their children or some merchant to do what they wanted them to do. They loved swapping strategies. That was why Tori was confident she'd be able to get to the truth behind the so-called miracle of the five praying wives. All she had to do was get the women alone.

Polly Denison was nothing like Tori expected. She'd heard stories of religious women who lived on farms. They wore severely plain clothing. Bonnets. Long black dresses with capes over their shoulders, shawls, black shoes, and stockings. They never wore jewelry, and their personalities were as drab as their wardrobes.

But the woman who emerged from the farmhouse was very feminine in a simple blue-and-white-checked dress. The brunette hair that fell to her shoulders needed attention. She had cheeks kissed by the sun and an easy smile. She waddled a little when she walked, being great with child.

The house from which she stepped was modest. The roof needed repair, and the whitewashed exterior was peeling in places. A barn rose up behind it in the back.

Polly greeted them.

Harrison leaned close to Tori and whispered, "I brought my calling card, but it's not the top of the hour. Should we wait?"

"Stop acting juvenile," she said.

"You're early," Polly called to them. "The other women will be here shortly. Ethan is in the barn. He could use some help."

"Anything a city boy can do?" Harrison asked.

"Most farm work is hands and muscles."

"I think I brought both of those." Harrison bid the women farewell and headed for the barn.

That was easy, Tori thought. She'd wanted to be alone with the women. Now she could talk to Polly alone. Woman to woman.

"If you don't mind," Polly said, "let's sit on the porch. That way I can keep an eye on Emma and Todd. Besides, the house is a mess."

Two children played a short distance away at the edge of a patch of woods—Tori guessed them to be five and three. They sounded happy.

Polly eased herself into a rocking chair and offered Tori another one next to her. As Tori passed the front door, she was able to catch a glimpse of the interior of the house. The furnishings were modest. Neat. Not a mess at all.

After an exchange of comments about the spring weather and the ride out to the farm, Tori said, "The story of how you and your friends prayed for your husbands has sparked a lot of interest in the city."

"Don't you want to wait for Mr. Shaw to join us? And the other women?" Polly said.

It was common for people to assume Harrison was the reporter and Tori was the—well, she never knew for sure what they thought she was. And frankly, she didn't want to know.

Tori dismissed the comment with a wave of her hand. "We work closely together. This way, I can talk to you woman to woman. I'll fill him in later. We've found that sometimes it's easier for a woman to speak more candidly to another woman, if you know what I mean."

"I suppose," Polly said.

"Tell me what happened," Tori urged.

"Not a whole lot to tell. God did the hard part. All we did was love our husbands and believe in God."

Polly began with what Tori considered the public version of the story. That was to be expected. After they warmed up to each other, the woman would feel more comfortable telling her the real story.

"We're all churchgoin' families," Polly said. "Though the men, more often than not, found excuses to miss church. A fence would need mendin'. A cow was about to give birth. A roof needed patchin'."

"Aren't those things important?"

"Important, yes. But you can run a farm without neglectin' worship. They were excuses."

Tori nodded. It was as she expected. The women wanted their men to do something the men didn't want to do. The trick was to figure out how to get them to do it. Polly didn't strike Tori as the domineering type. That meant manipulation.

Polly continued, "We'd heard about the wonderful things the Spirit of God has been doin' in the city and all across the country. Then one Sunday it came to me. We weren't takin' prayer seriously. I mean, if God is God, and He's told us to bring our problems to Him, we should do it. Right?"

Tori nodded. It was a continue-on nod, not an "I agree with you" nod.

"So I talked it over with the other women. We have a quiltin' Saturday once a month, just the five of us. We all agreed we should start prayin' for our husbands in earnest." She reached over and touched Tori's hand. "You understand, we'd been prayin' for them, of course—"

"Of course."

"But we hadn't been prayin' *earnestly*. So—I think it was Harriet who came up with this approach—we decided to pray for one husband at a time. All of us together. Five against one, so to speak." She smiled at this. "Well, five plus God against one. Ethan never had a chance."

"So you used your quilting time."

"Gave it over to prayer," Polly said. "But we didn't tell our husbands. We wanted them to think we were still quiltin'."

"Why keep it a secret?"

"These are proud men, Miss Jarves. If word got out that we were gangin' up on our husbands with prayer, well, it's sort of like callin' them infidels, don't you think?"

"Infidels. Interesting word."

Polly laughed. "Abigail came up with that word. She's the reader of the group."

Tori took note of Polly Denison's unassuming manner. She spoke plainly and was generous to her friends.

"We also decided to send a letter to the Fulton Street prayer meetin' in the city," Polly said. "We figured changin' the lives of five grown men was no small task. We didn't know if anybody would really join us in prayer; I hear there are so many requests. Have you seen the letter?"

"That one, and a second one informing the meeting of your success."

"Of *God's* success, Miss Jarves." Polly sat back and smiled as though there was nothing left to say.

For Tori the discussion was just getting started. "You got what you wanted—all five men began attending church."

"Oh, more than that, Miss Jarves. Church attendance is but a symptom of the soul's condition. All five men were saved by the power of the Holy Spirit."

Tori leaned forward. It was time to get this woman to open up. Her hunch was that word of their prayer efforts was deliberately leaked. The men found out about it. Felt ashamed. And began attending church to keep from appearing as infidels. It was that word that probably did the trick.

Tori asked softly, "Would you recommend this tactic to other women?"

Polly didn't answer right away. She gazed at Tori, sizing her up, probably wondering if she could be trusted. "You're not saved, are you, Miss Jarves?"

Tori was taken aback. "I don't see what that has to do—"

"It's apparent you don't understand what happened here," Polly continued. "It wasn't a matter of our getting' our way. Our husbands weren't happy. They were restless. Angry at life, at themselves. Ethan worked impossible hours, which wasn't difficult for him to do. On a farm there's always somethin' that needs to be done. He thought if he could just get caught up. If he could just increase the yield of the crops or get to the place where he was able to set some money aside. He kept himself busy all the time, Miss Jarves, because if he slowed down long enough to think, he'd be forced to take stock of himself. He didn't want to do that, because he knew he wouldn't like what he saw, because he didn't like who he was."

Men's voices came from the side of the house. Harrison and a man Tori assumed was Ethan appeared. They were acting like they'd known each other for years. The men corralled a couple of chairs and joined the women on the porch.

Ethan removed his straw hat and rubbed the back of his neck. It was a sizable hand and neck; both were weathered. Harrison looked like a skinny kid next to him.

When Ethan stepped onto the porch, the first thing he did was walk over to his wife and kiss her and ask how she was feeling. He placed a hand on her swollen belly and rubbed it gently. Tori had never seen this kind of affection between a husband and wife.

Never. Her parents shared a house and lived in two different worlds. His and hers. Tori couldn't remember them touching each other, let alone showing affection. Their conversations were business discussions about house matters and scheduling.

At his wife's prompting, Ethan launched into a narrative of what happened as a result of the women's prayers. "I was out in the cornfield," he began. "Of course there was no corn growin'. It was late winter. I was sizin' up a new growin' season. Thinkin' of expandin' the field."

"Tell her what day of the week it was," his wife said.

"Oh, it was Saturday. Polly and the ladies were at Harriet Gardner's quiltin'. At least, at the time that's what I thought they were doin'."

"You didn't know they were praying for you?" Tori asked. "Word hadn't somehow gotten to you, maybe in a roundabout way?"

Polly smiled at her.

Ethan shook his head. "Nope. They said they was quiltin'. Had no cause to think otherwise. Anyway, I was toein' the soil. The snow was gone, and the ground was just beginnin' to thaw. All of a sudden I felt an incredible heaviness press down on me. Now I'm a big man, Miss Jarves. It would take a couple of hefty fellows to force me to my knees. But that's what happened, and no one was around. It was like an invisible winepress was pushin' me to the ground." He used the flat of his hand to illustrate. "At first I thought I was havin' apoplexy, or somethin' of that sort. The pressure was bad, but what was worse was an incredible sense of guilt that came over me."

"Guilt? What had you done to feel guilty about?"

"Life, Miss Jarves. About a hundred little things a day when I'd do or say somethin' that wasn't right, that wasn't kind. There were some big things too. In my past. I don't reckon I know you well enough to tell you about them. Believe me when I say, there was plenty for me to feel guilty about.

"Anyway, all these things started to come to mind, and I didn't like what I saw. Didn't like it one bit. And I knew that if I died at that moment—and I thought that's exactly what was happening—well, let's just say that I knew I would deserve whatever punishment I got. And the next thing I know, I was cryin' out to God, because He was the only one I could think of that could save me."

He paused, reliving the moment. "You see, Miss Jarves, the way I figure it, God let me see myself the way He sees me. And neither one of us liked what we saw."

Two wagons approached the house, stirring up a lot of dust. Each wagon carried two women.

Tori and Harrison were introduced to the other members of the Saturday quilting bee.

Harriet Gardner was the eldest of them by a dozen or so years. She was a mother hen, especially to Polly because of her condition. Anna King was a petite woman with a flat face and thin smile. Grace Adams was large in a round way, and cheerful. And Abigail McIntyre appeared bookish with her wire-rimmed glasses.

For the second time in a matter of minutes, Tori was struck by the display of affection. These women cared for one another, even though they didn't always get along. There were two squabbles between Anna King and Harriet Gardner during the time Tori and Harrison were there. One was over how much work Polly should do. Harriet kept telling the pregnant woman to get off her feet. Anna kept saying, "I plowed in the mornin' and had my babies in the afternoon. A little work ain't gonna hurt nothin'." Still, the women were close-knit.

After a while they all settled down, and each of the women narrated her version of what happened. It was basically the way Polly had described it, with minor variations. Each included an account of her husband's story, which was similar to what Ethan experienced.

Tori listened and took notes. She didn't ask questions.

As Tori and Harrison were leaving, Polly pulled Tori aside and whispered, "I just want you to know, I'll be prayin' for you."

Tori wasn't sure how to respond. She'd never been prayed for before, and none of the etiquette books she'd read covered the topic.

"And I think you and Harrison will make a wonderful couple," Polly added.

Before Tori could object, Anna King pulled Polly away to settle another dispute between herself and Harriet Gardner.

CHAPTER 25

The Fulton Street prayer meeting started on time. The room was full. Every chair taken. The line of those standing extended out the door and down the steps.

Jeremiah Lanphier, tireless as always, read the words to the hymn and then led the singing:

> *All glory, laud, and honor,*
> *To thee, Redeemer, King,*
> *To whom the lips of children,*
> *Made sweet hosannas ring.*

Before prayer requests were taken, Harrison was asked to relate one or two narratives of the current revival. He'd been admonished to keep this report brief, since the purpose of the meeting was prayer.

Harrison addressed the gathering, which was composed of half regulars and half newcomers. It was the usual assortment of the New York population, from the out-of-work to wealthy businessmen. Harrison told them about one report he'd received: there were five prayer meetings in Washington D.C., all of them continuing around the clock. He was just about to tell them about "Awful Gardiner," a prizefighter who was saved and now visiting his old friends at Sing Sing Penitentiary, giving them his testimony, when a general shuffling at the door caught his attention.

Men were stepping aside, with difficulty, to let a lady in. Her head down, at first all Harrison saw of her was the top of her mobcap and a shawl-covered shoulder as she squeezed between two portly men. Having made it into the room, she straightened her shoulders.

It was Katie.

By now most everyone had turned to see what the interruption was and what Harrison was staring at. A sailor stood and offered her his seat. Then, when she took it, he realized he had no place to stand. A little shuffling along the wall, and he was afforded a tight spot.

Harrison couldn't remember finishing his report. But he must have, because the next thing he knew, he had exchanged places with Jeremiah, who was opening the first letter and reading the prayer request.

Men prayed. One man requested prayer for his estranged brother. An inheritance dispute of twenty years ago had separated them. Another man requested prayer for himself. "Vile wretch that I am. I abandoned my wife and children six months ago. When I returned home, they had moved. I have no idea where they are."

There were more requests. Salvation. Healing. Forgiveness.

But Harrison heard none of the requests or praises. His eyes were on Katie.

That's how he thought of her, because that's what he saw, though he knew it was Victoria beneath the mobcap. Had she come dressed like that to torment him? If she did, it was working.

She hardly moved. She sat with her head bowed. Listening. At times she would rock back and forth in subtle rhythm. Before, when she'd come to the meetings, she'd taken notes. Looked for stories she could write up. But she'd always informed Harrison she'd be there. He got the impression she was afraid to attend the meetings by herself. She'd given him no indication she'd be attending today.

The hour passed slowly. By the last fifteen minutes, Harrison had figured out his strategy to get to her following the final prayer. He wanted to make sure he reached her before she slipped out. A part of him had to know why Victoria had come dressed as Katie. Another part of him wanted to see Katie.

The meeting ended. Harrison bolted to his feet to get to the side aisle before it clogged. His goal was to get at least within reaching distance, should she try to leave.

He was cut off. Worse, he lost sight of her.

Though he was taller than most of the men, Harrison jumped up and down as the crowd inched toward the doorway. He looked for the mobcap.

Nothing. No mobcap. No shawl. Had she managed to get out already? Or was she in front of that broad-shouldered gent? Harrison was already planning the route he'd take once he hit the bottom of the stairs, anticipating Katie's most likely route, when he saw her out of the corner of his eye.

She was still seated. She hadn't moved from her place.

Harrison shuffled in line until he reached her row, then stepped sideways and sat next to her. She didn't look up; neither did she acknowledge his presence. He sat silently next to her as the room emptied. Jeremiah was the last to leave. The two men exchanged glances. Harrison nodded to indicate he had things under control.

Which he didn't, of course. He didn't even know how to address her. *Katie? Tori?*

Without lifting her head, she cleared her throat to speak. "I think Polly is praying for me." She began to weep. "I can feel it. What Ethan felt. I can feel it. I'm scared, Harrison. I'm scared."

It was Victoria's voice, so that's who Harrison addressed. "Why are you dressed like that?" he asked.

She looked up. Her eyes were watery. Her hands shook. "I don't know how to come before God. You like Katie. So I thought maybe God would too."

Harrison grasped her hands in his. "You don't have to put on a disguise to come to God. He loves you for who you are."

"How can that be?" Tori said, tears shining in her eyes. "*I don't love me. I don't even like me. I never have.* Do you want to know what the real Victoria Jarves is like? She's a petty, selfish, weak, unimaginative nothing. Without my disguises, I'm my mother. A manipulative outcast. Miserable to the day she died."

He squeezed her hands.

"And you make it worse," she said.

"Me?"

"Until we met Ethan and Polly, I thought you were the only one of your kind. An aberration. A freak of nature. But there are others like you. A whole lot of them."

"It's not anything we've done," Harrison tried to explain. "It's what God has done inside of us. It's what these prayer meetings, this revival, is all about—God changing lives. There's a song we sing:

Amazing grace! how sweet the sound—
That saved a wretch like me!
I once was lost, but now am found,
Was blind, but now I see.
'Twas grace that taught my heart to fear,
And grace my fears relieved;
How precious did that grace appear
The hour I first believed."

"Believed?"

"That God loves us, but that our sins have separated us from Him. And that His Son died on the cross to take our sin away and to lift the weight of our guilt."

"I don't know if I can do that."

Harrison reached up, slowly. He removed Katie's mobcap. For the first time, he wanted to be with Victoria, not Katie. "You have to come to God without pretense."

"Will you help me?"

"Yes."

"Harrison? Do you like me?" Her question was real; her longing to know the answer glimmered in her eyes.

"More and more with each passing day."

Victoria Jarves finally got to write a story about death. Her own. It was never published. She read it to the prayer meeting at the old North Dutch Church on Fulton Street.

There once was a scrub girl named Katie.

"I scrubs," she said whenever anyone greeted her.

Katie was a homely girl and sad. She was sad because she knew no one ever fell in love with scrub girls.

One day a prince saw her. He fell in love with her.

"How can this be?" she said. "You reign. I scrubs. Even if it were true, we could never live together. The muddy alleys where I live are too filthy for a prince. And I'm too filthy for your spotless palace."

"That's true," he said.

So Katie, the scrub girl, walked away, sad of heart. Cursing her life. Cursing herself.

Then the prince did the strangest, most wonderful thing. He took Katie's mobcap and put it on his head. And he took her shawl and threw it around his shoulders. At first she thought he looked silly in them. But then they had the most awful effect on him. The prince's skin grew pale and gray. His cheeks sunk. He became sick, hunched over and weak. He turned and hobbled away in great pain.

Katie cried when she saw what her garments did

to him. She cried harder when she heard that the prince had died.

She cried so hard, she fell facedown in the mud of the alley where she lived.

Then a hand touched her shoulder. And a voice said, "Katie, your days of scrubbing are over."

She looked, and it was the prince! He was healthy and radiant.

He lifted her out of the mud. And from his head, he took the mobcap, only it wasn't a mobcap any more—it was a crown! He placed it on Katie's head. He took her shawl from his shoulders, only it wasn't a shawl anymore—it was a regal robe. And he placed it on her shoulders.

"But these are too fine for a scrub girl to wear," she said.

"Yes, they are," he replied. "But not for a princess."

He led her to a mirror. And she saw herself as he saw her. There was no trace of scrub girl in her.

"Katie the scrub girl is dead," he told her. "Now she is Katie the princess."

He was right. She was beautiful. Much more beautiful than she ever thought she could be. She was fit to be the bride of a prince.

And the prince took his bride to the palace, where they lived their days in happiness.

CHAPTER 26

Two days after her conversion, Tori disappeared. She and Harrison were going to meet an hour before the prayer meeting. She didn't show. Harrison was concerned, not worried. She knew how to find him.

She didn't show up on the third day. Or the fourth. On the fifth, Harrison journeyed uptown to Millionaire Row, where he found himself face-to-face once again with the brass lion door knocker.

"Thought you'd seen the last of me, didn't you?" he muttered to the steely eyed lion.

Charles answered his knock. A slight flash of alarm in the house servant's eyes was the extent of Harrison's homecoming.

"It's the top of the hour, and here's my card. I wish to see Tori . . . Miss Jarves. Please announce my presence."

Charles handed the card back to Harrison. "Miss Jarves is not entertaining guests."

"But she's here," Harrison said. "And well?"

Charles fidgeted. Harrison had known the man to fidget only once before, when he was caught with Harrison's silver dollar in his pocket. "Please leave, sir."

Something wasn't right.

"Can you deliver a message to Miss Jarves for me?" Harrison asked.

"That wouldn't be wise, sir." The man's eyes were warning Harrison away.

"Charles, tell me what's going on."

The house servant heard something in the interior of the house. Without another word he stepped back and closed the door.

What now? Harrison wondered. *Knock again? Come back tomorrow?*

The door opened, but only partway. Charles thrust a scrap of paper at Harrison, then quickly shut the door.

> *Leave immediately!*
> *Meet tomorrow.*
> *City hall. 1 p.m.*

Harrison stewed over the note all night long, even in his sleep. The note wasn't in Tori's handwriting. He'd seen enough samples to recognize her hand, and this wasn't it. So who wrote it? Charles? Was Charles representing Tori in this matter, or Jarves? Exactly who was going to show up tomorrow in front of city hall, and for what purpose? Why city hall?

Too many questions. And too many hours separating Harrison from the answers.

The morning hours dragged unmercifully. Nothing Harrison did could urge them to pass more quickly. He couldn't read because he couldn't concentrate. Writing proved equally frustrating, so he paced. Thinking a half hour had passed, he checked his watch.

It had only been five minutes since he last looked.

He went outside, telling himself he'd walk the streets and, when it was time, make his way to city hall. By 11:00 a.m. he was in front of city hall, and there he stayed until the designated hour.

He paced in front of city hall, running his fingers along the wrought-iron fence that surrounded the building. He watched as a steady stream of people passed in and out of the huge gate that arched between two stone pillars. He recognized none of them.

The top of the hour came and went.

Five minutes past.

Ten.

At twelve minutes and twenty seconds past the hour, he spied Charles, who looked completely out of place outside of the mansion.

"Tori! Is she all right?" Harrison said.

Charles was all business. He was guarded. His eyes darted this way and that, never resting. "Miss Jarves is unharmed."

"When can I see her?"

Charles grabbed Harrison by the arm. "You must never come to the mansion again." The gravity of his voice was a stronger warning than the words themselves.

"Charles, what's happened?"

"Follow me," Charles said.

He turned and walked at a brisk pace. Harrison followed. Past the edge of city hall property, past businesses, street vendors, a boot shop.

Harrison had no idea where Charles was taking him, or for what reason. The more he thought about it, the more he realized Charles had told him nothing other than to warn him away from the mansion. Harrison still didn't know who Charles was representing. For all he knew, Charles was doing Jarves's bidding, just as he'd done the day of the interview.

They came to a large stable. Charles turned in, walking like he owned the place. There was a man working on an anvil, sweating, forearms bulging, his clothes smudged black. Another man stood at the forge, working the bellows. They both looked up when Charles passed by them but then returned to their work and said nothing.

The further they walked inside the structure, the darker it got. The place smelled of old straw and manure. Nearly every stall was occupied by a horse or mule.

"Where are you taking me?" Harrison asked. He was beginning to get worried.

Charles didn't reply. He kept walking, all the way to the back of the structure, the last stall. Once there he took up a position against the wall and showed Harrison into the stall the same way he'd escorted him into the mansion parlor.

There, crouched in a corner, Harrison saw—

"Mouser! I mean, Victoria . . . Tori!"

Harrison started toward her.

Charles stopped him. He looked Harrison in the eye with a fatherly gaze. "I entrust her to your care. See that no harm comes to her."

Then Charles left them.

"Get down!" Tori motioned for Harrison to crouch lower than the side of the stall.

Harrison crouched beside her. "Why are you dressed as Mouser?"

"I told Father what happened at the prayer meeting." Her eyes were teary.

In the dim light, Harrison had to keep reminding himself he was talking to Tori, not Mouser. "He didn't take it well," Harrison said.

Tori rolled her eyes. She began to cry. "I thought that when I got right with God, I'd be happy. Like Polly."

Harrison repositioned himself, sitting with his back against the stall. "Putting things right with God doesn't mean that all your problems disappear. Sometimes the decision creates new problems. The thing you have to remember is that you're not alone anymore. You have the Holy Spirit inside you. He's more than just a comforter. He's a guide. He'll help us through this."

"Had I known it would be like this—"

"What happened?"

Tori wiped away the tears, one eye with one hand, the other eye with the other hand. "I didn't expect he'd be pleased. He's been angry with me before. But never like this." She stared at Harrison. "And he has it in for you. He blames you for 'addling my brain,' as he put it."

Harrison remembered what happened last time J. K. Jarves had it in for him. Would he strike as quickly? And directly this time? Or would he go after someone close to Harrison? Who was left? Jarves had pretty well taken care of everyone the last time when he'd destroyed George Bowen and closed the lodge.

"You still haven't told me why you're dressed as Mouser," he said.

"Father locked me in my room. He threatened that if I ever saw you again he'd—"

"Kill me?"

"Ship me to Europe."

"So you ran away."

"This is the only way I can travel the streets safely. Mouser moves more quickly and has hiding places that Victoria could never use."

"What's Charles's role in all this?"

"He caught me attempting to get out of the house yesterday morning. I tried to talk my way past him, but he wouldn't listen. Then you showed up at the door. He agreed to let me escape, but only on his terms."

"So he brought you here and handed you off to me," Harrison said.

"Charles is old-fashioned. He still thinks I need an escort."

"Well," Harrison said, ready to move on, "let's get you to the church. You can stay in my room in the basement. I'll see if I can make arrangements for other—"

"I'm going to Five Points."

"Five Points!"

"Father will look for me at the church. I know Five Points. Once there, he'll never find me. Even if he did, he'd never catch me."

Harrison could attest to that. Still, he didn't like it. "Where will you stay?"

"Mouser has places."

"Certainly not Crown's Grocery. You stay away from Crown's Grocery."

Mouser moved into a crouch. "You've done your part. I can take care of myself from here."

Harrison thought of her as Mouser because she acted, moved, and spoke like Mouser. Which made what he did next feel extremely strange.

He grabbed her by the shoulders. "I've come to care for you very much," he said, searching for some sign of Tori or Victoria, because otherwise this was really weird. "And I can't just let you run off to Five Points. It's too dangerous."

There! Mouser's eyes became Tori's eyes, but only for a second. Then she was Mouser again, and Mouser was angry.

"Listen, Harrison boy. I was runnin' bets at Five Points long afore you showed up. So stay outta my way. Hear?" Mouser shook himself free.

"Wait! You're right," Harrison conceded, though he didn't mean what he was saying. "Just let me come along. All right? Show me where you're staying, so I know where to find you?"

"You really want to do that, Harrison boy? Every times you walks inta that place, you gets your face pushed in."

That was true enough.

"How should I put it?" Harrison said. "If you really cared for someone, wouldn't you risk getting your face pushed in just to be with her?"

Harrison looked for Tori but saw only Mouser.

"You're an odd duck, Harrison boy. But I likes you."

The blacksmith barely glanced at them when they walked out. Had Tori been dressed as Victoria instead of Mouser, he no doubt would have given her lingering attention.

"This way," Mouser said. "I knows a shortcut."

Tori. It's Tori, not Mouser, Harrison kept reminding himself. He wondered if any other guy in all New York had as much trouble keeping the identity of his girl straight.

His girl. He was thinking of Tori as his girl, wasn't he? Victoria Jarves, no less. Who would have thought?

They cut through an alley and emerged onto busy Broadway. Horse-drawn trolley cars, personal carriages of all sizes, and wagons dominated the center of the street. Some of the wagons had canvas covers with advertisements painted on their sides.

ICE FROM ROCKLAND LAKE

THE BIGGEST ROGUE IN THE WORLD

Harrison wondered what the biggest rogue was all about. Then again, that was what the entrepreneur wanted him to wonder, wasn't it?

Since Tori was smaller and moving in and out of traffic like a boy, Harrison was finding it difficult to keep up with her. Suddenly Tori stopped. Harrison bumped into her—and into a woman in a bonnet. He begged her pardon. She gave him a wrinkled nose of disgust instead.

"Father's men," Tori said ominously.

Two men stood on the street corner, surveying the ebb and flow of Broadway traffic and giving special attention to pedestrians. They wore workers' clothes: the taller one, striped pants and a loose shirt; the other, a vest and newsboy's cap. Even from a distance, they looked unpleasant. It probably came from working for Jarves.

"Stay close to me," Tori whispered. "I have more experience at this than you."

Just what a guy wants to hear from his girl when hiding from street thugs. She was right though. And Harrison did his best to become her shadow.

They needed to cross Broadway and duck into an alley without being spotted. Harrison made a silent determination. He was going to get Tori to Five Points at all costs. As crazy as that sounded, it was her best chance of eluding her father's grasp.

Tori stepped into the street, keeping low, matching the pace of a wagon loaded with vegetables bound for market. A closed carriage was pulling up from behind at a faster clip in the middle of the street, so Tori smoothly fell away from the wagon and picked up the carriage, keeping it between her and the men on the corner who were obviously searching for someone.

Harrison stumbled. His hand slapped the side of the carriage to keep himself from falling. Curses erupted from within.

Tori gave him a warning glance. Her eyes said, *Don't do anything to call attention to yourself!* With his eyes Harrison signaled, *I'm sorry. It wasn't on purpose.*

They strolled in the wake of the carriage for a time.

"Get ready," Tori said. "This one's going to be tricky."

She'd picked her next moving blind. It was a wagon with a canvas cover, similar to the one that delivered ice, only this one had no writing on it. The wagon was moving in the opposite direction of the carriage. As it passed, Tori nimbly reversed direction and matched pace with the wagon.

Not so nimbly, Harrison kept up with her.

They slipped to the back of the wagon, trailing it closely.

"There's an alley coming up," Tori said. "Without hurrying, we'll step from behind the wagon and head straight for the alley. Are you ready?"

"Right behind you."

The alley approached at a forty-five-degree angle. Tori stuck her hands in her pockets, pulled the cap low over her eyes, and strolled toward the alley as though she didn't have a care in the world.

Harrison did exactly what she did, only he wasn't wearing a cap. Hands in pockets. No cares. He tried to match the easiness of her stride. His quivering legs fought him every step.

In a low voice he asked, "How do you know they're looking for you? Maybe they're here for some other purpose."

The alley was ten feet away.

"THERE, JAKE! LOOK THERE!"

For a second, Harrison locked eyes with Jarves's men. Even at a distance, he saw their intent. Menacing with a touch of excitement, like dogs having spotted a rabbit.

The two men plunged in after them.

"That's how I know!" Tori said, running.

Pausing to take one last look at the men chasing them, Harrison wished he hadn't. The closer they got, the uglier and meaner they appeared. And they were fast.

Harrison ran into the alley. Mouser was already at the end, rounding the corner. His head reappeared. "Use those long legs of yours, Harrison boy," he said, disappearing again.

Arms pumping, legs churning, Harrison remembered his baseball days of running to first base. He never was good at legging it out and beating the throw. If the ball didn't get through the infield, he was out. No amount of cheering by his teammates changed that. Only this time getting thrown out had more serious consequences.

He rounded the corner of the alley, glancing back as he did. Jarves's jackals were closing.

Running behind a row of businesses, dodging all manner of garbage and refuse, he caught sight of Mouser, dodging down another alley. Harrison slipped on a patch of rotten vegetables and nearly went down.

One of their pursuers, the tall one with the striped pants, wasn't as lucky. He went down. Hard. Sliding into a pile of discarded planks. The one in the vest yelled at him to get up but didn't slow to help him.

"This way, Harrison boy," Mouser urged.

He . . . *she* was halfway down the alley, holding open a door. Harrison hit the opening running.

Mouser slipped in behind him, slamming shut the door. "Follow me."

It was all Mouser. Had someone told Harrison right then that Victoria Jarves was sitting in her parlor entertaining lady friends, he would have believed it.

They were in some kind of garment warehouse. It was dark. The only available light filtered in through dirty windows ten or twelve feet above them. Using a swimming motion with his arms, Mouser made his way through row after row of coats hanging on racks. Harrison followed his example.

Behind them the door opened and slammed shut. They heard footsteps.

Harrison grabbed the back of Mouser's shirt, pulling the boy to a stop. "Let's hide under here," Harrison whispered. "They'll run right by us."

It was a good hiding place, Harrison thought. Their pursuers didn't know which row they were in, wouldn't know they'd stopped. It was dark under the racks.

"No," Mouser said. "We have to get to Five Points. We can make it, Harrison boy. Just keep those legs movin'." He shrugged free from Harrison's grip.

"We can wait them out," Harrison insisted. "Come on, it's safe."

Mouser was already on the run again. "Hide if you want, Harrison boy." There was disappointment in his eyes.

Setting his legs in motion, Harrison followed. *If Tori's not going to feel safe until she gets to Five Points, we'll get her to Five Points,* he told himself. And he meant it. He wasn't going to let either of those men put their hands on her.

A row of windows loomed ahead. A door appeared. Mouser was out the door in a heartbeat. Harrison was hot on his heels.

They emerged into another alley.

"This way."

Mouser seemed to know where he was. Harrison wasn't so sure. With all the ins and outs, turns and dodges, he'd become disoriented. Turning to follow, they approached a dead end. At the end of the alley was a fence that was taller than Harrison.

Even as a kid he'd had trouble scaling fences. His arms were too thin to haul his backside over them. Someone always had to give him a leg up. But Mouser approached the fence on a dead run, as though he could clear it with a single bound.

Reaching the fence, Mouser slid to his knees. His fingers worked a plank, knowing exactly which one to grab. The plank swung to one side, using a nail higher up as a hinge. He slipped through the opening like it was greased.

Harrison caught the board before it swung back.

"I can't make it through there!" he shouted.

"You don't have much choice, Harrison boy."

He was on his knees, aiming his head toward the opening when the factory door behind him slammed open.

Newsboy Cap leaped into the alley, looking first up the alley toward the street. Seeing nothing, he looked the other way and saw Harrison.

Harrison slid into the fence gap. He didn't get far. The top of his shoulders brought him to an abrupt and painful halt. He squirmed so they aligned with the opening and managed to squeeze them through. He was halfway through when he met resistance again. His hips.

"Give me your hands." Mouser grabbed and tried to pull him through.

Just then Harrison felt someone lay hold of his feet. Through the gap in the fence, Harrison saw a newsboy cap. Beneath it was a grin.

"Gotcha now," the man said.

Harrison's hips were wedged in the fence. A tug of war was being waged, and Harrison was the rope.

"Tori, run for it!" he shouted. "You can make it. I'll keep this one occupied."

Mouser looked at him. At the fence. Then he turned and ran, never glancing back. Within a few seconds, he disappeared around the corner of a brick building.

Harrison turned his attention to his predicament. He kicked at his pursuer, thinking he could still make it to the safe side of the fence. He got the man in the jaw with one kick, sending him sprawling backward. Harrison wiggled for all he was worth. He had to get through before—

"Wait, wait, wait!" Harrison cried.

The man recovered quickly. Now he held a knife.

Defenseless, Harrison had little choice but to surrender and hope that this was not a man who would hold the whole kick-in-the-jaw thing against him.

"I'm coming back!" Harrison yelled, lest the man think his warning was another attempt to get free.

He squirmed until he managed to free his hips. Inch by inch he worked his way back through. As he slithered in the dirt, he cast an occasional glance at the knife. It seemed content to hover over him for the moment. Apparently, they wanted to capture him, not kill him.

They'd let Jarves have the honors. Harrison raised his arms to complete the passage. He'd squirmed until the fence was up to his chin when he heard—

Clunk!

Thump.

Unseen hands grabbed his ankles and pulled. As Harrison's head cleared the fence, he saw who had hold of him.

Mouser.

Newsboy Cap lay in the dust, unconscious. On the ground beside him was a hefty piece of lumber.

"Come on, Harrison boy. We best get outta here before that other one catches up with us."

But they were too late. As Harrison struggled to his feet, the tall one with striped pants appeared at the mouth of the alley, blocking their exit.

Harrison groaned. *Not the fence again.*

"The warehouse," Mouser said quickly.

"He'll just race us to the other side," Harrison argued.

Mouser replied by grabbing his hand and pulling him toward a set of stairs. "This way!"

The pounding of their feet echoed in the cavernous building. Reaching the top landing, they followed it around the perimeter, past a deserted work area that looked like it had once been used for offices, and to the far side.

Mouser opened a window.

"Ah, no, no, Tori. I can't go out that way. I have something of a problem with heights."

"You wanna go back down and face the guy with the knife?"

Mouser didn't wait for an answer. The next thing Harrison knew, Mouser was standing on the ledge with no fear, facing the building. All he could see of the boy was from the knees down. Then, as though he were flying, his feet lifted off the sill, rose to the sky, and disappeared.

Harrison stuck his head out the window and looked up. From the roof Mouser was peering down at him.

"There's a ledge here you grab," he said. "Then you pull yourself up. Simple as pie."

Harrison peered down. The alley seemed a mile or two distant. Striped Pants ran into it from the street. He looked around, then up. When he saw them, he ran for the door. At that same instant, Harrison heard the door open and close from the other side. Newsboy Cap was back on his feet.

With a moan Harrison eased his way out the window, twisting himself so he was in a sitting position. Had he a little water and a rag, he could have cleaned the window.

There were voices below. "They're climbing onto the roof!"

Footsteps pounded the stairs.

"Come on, Harrison boy! My grandmother could do this!"

Harrison maneuvered his feet into position, rising up to full height on weak knees.

"Grab right here." Mouser guided his hand to the place. "Good. Now pull yourself up, and swing your leg over the ledge."

Do not look down, Harrison told himself. But he looked down and could easily imagine his twisted body splayed on the ground. *I told you not to look down,* he chided himself. *Don't you ever listen?*

Taking a deep breath, he pulled up with all his might and swung his leg up. His foot hit the lip and bounced back. The unexpected weight challenged his grip. He groaned and tried again. This time his foot cleared the ledge. He pulled himself up. Mouser was grabbing him by the shirt, helping him onto the roof.

"Oh, that wasn't good," Harrison said. "Not good at all." He stood on questionable legs.

A head popped out the window. "I sees 'em, Jake!"

"Where do we go from here?" Harrison looked around for a door or an exterior stairway.

"There," Mouser said, pointing.

He was pointing to a stairway, but it was attached to the building on the other side of the alley.

"You've got to be kidding!" Harrison cried. "You're kidding, right? Tell me you're kidding."

But Mouser had already backed up to make a run at it. And before Harrison knew it, the girl he was falling in love with, dressed as a boy, was sailing through the air, across the alley where he hit the landing with a thud, the side of the building stopping his momentum.

"I can't believe she did that," Harrison said more to himself than anyone.

"Come on, Harrison boy. It's not that far. I've done it dozens of times."

"There is nothing that can make me jump across this alley."

Fingers appeared on the ledge of the roof. Then a foot. Striped Pants was pulling himself up.

Harrison gazed heavenward. "O Lord, have mercy."

"Give yourself plenty of running distance," Mouser was yelling. "Whatever you do, don't hesitate. Commit to jumping, and jump!"

Harrison backed up. He made eye contact with Striped Pants, who now had an arm over the ledge and was about to make a final push. With one arm and one leg over, he paused long enough to look at Harrison and say, "You'll never make it."

Harrison peered across the alley. Mouser had moved out of the way to give him landing room.

It was now or never. Striped Pants was clearing the edge. If Harrison waited until he gained his feet, the guy might take a lunge at him or do something equally stupid.

Harrison Quincy Shaw, the boy who was afraid to swing from a rope and splash in the river, ran with everything he had for the ledge. Yet the instant his feet left the building, he knew he'd made a mistake.

It was curious what he was thinking as he hung in the air like a wingless bird. He wished Isaac and Murry were here to see him, to see what a girl was able to get him to do when they'd pleaded with him unsuccessfully to try the rope swing once, saying he'd love it. He remembered one of George Bowen's proverbs, but with a twist: *"There are moments when everything goes well . . ."* This isn't one of them.

The building rushed toward him. Too fast. In his fear that he would come up short, he never anticipated the consequences of jumping too far.

He hit the side of the building a good three feet above the stairs, and fell like a crumpled sack of potatoes onto the landing.

Mouser was instantly at his side. Only it was Tori in Mouser's clothes. "Harrison, are you all right?"

He looked up at her and, through stunned eyes, saw concerned feminine eyes staring down at him. If anything could get his heart started again, this could.

She stroked his cheek. "Say something."

"I made it." It wasn't profound, but it sounded good to him.

"You have the imprint of the bricks on the side of your face," Tori said, tracing it with her finger.

There was only one thing Harrison could think of that would make him happier than lying here and having Tori fawn over him, and that was to know she was safe. "Let's get you to Five Points."

She helped him down the stairs.

It took Harrison a good five minutes to regain his senses, but he knew enough to walk. The last they'd seen of Striped Pants, he was on top of the roof, swearing at them. Newsboy Cap was still inside the building, his head sticking out the window, adding his voice, making it a duet of curses.

They approached Five Points by way of Canal Street.

"Never thought I'd be happy to see this place," Harrison said.

They were ambling now. Harrison was very much aware that the person walking next to him was not a boy, though she still looked like one. Ever since she leaned over him, stroking his face, it was different. As though a spell had been broken. Now no matter how much she looked and acted like Mouser, Harrison saw Tori.

"I still don't like leaving you here alone," he said.

"I's been roamin' these streets long afore you ever showed up, Harrison boy," Mouser retorted.

They stood at the edge of Five Points, looking in.

"Before we go in and you show me where you're going to stay, can you do me a favor?"

"Seems like you're the one that owes me a favor for savin' your bacon back there, Harrison boy."

"Yeah. You could have made it here a lot easier if you'd gone alone," Harrison said.

"Ain't that the truth. What's the favor?"

"I know you're dressed like Mouser and all. But, could you, for just a minute or two, be Tori? It would really mean a lot to me."

Mouser peered at him suspiciously. "Why, Harrison boy? You sweet on her or somethin'?"

Harrison started to answer Mouser. Then he realized it was Tori asking the question.

"I don't think this is an appropriate discussion to be having with Mouser. A gentleman doesn't talk about a lady behind her back about anything he hasn't already discussed with her."

Mouser smiled. Only it was Tori's smile. And Tori's eyes.

"All right, Harrison," Tori said. "I'm here. Is there something you wanted to say to me?"

Just then Striped Pants and Newsboy Cap came out of nowhere. Striped Pants threw his arms around Tori, lifting her off her feet. Newsboy Cap tackled Harrison, knocking him to the ground.

Tori was screaming.

There was plenty of traffic on the street. Mostly pedestrian. When they heard the screams, they looked, then reset their eyes on their own business and moved along in businesslike fashion.

Newsboy Cap was on top of Harrison, trying to pin him to the ground. Harrison struggled, but Newsboy's arms were twice the width of his, and it was a losing battle. With Tori's legs lifted off the ground, it took little effort for Striped Pants to contain her, even though she thrashed and fought furiously.

They were so close, Harrison thought. Five Points was within sight.

He had vowed to get her there, hadn't he? No matter the cost? He renewed the fight with strength he never knew he had, surprising even Newsboy Cap.

That's when Newsboy Cap whipped out the knife and held it under Harrison's chin.

Tori was screaming, pleading with him not to hurt Harrison.

Harrison signaled his surrender.

"Smart boy," Newsboy Cap said. He started to climb off Harrison, keeping the knife at the ready lest Harrison get any ideas.

Harrison rolled over onto all fours, preparing to stand. He paused to catch his breath. Then he launched himself at Striped Pants, bowling the man over. His grip on Tori broke. She was thrown free, but like a cat, was quickly on her feet.

"Run!" Harrison cried.

She hesitated a moment, then turned and ran. An instant later she was gone, absorbed by the streets of Five Points.

Striped Pants started after her.

"Let the boy go," Newsboy Cap said. "We got what we came for."

CHAPTER 27

A couple of unnecessary fists to the stomach convinced Harrison to go peacefully with Striped Pants and Newsboy Cap.

Not surprisingly, their destination was Jarves's mansion.

Familiar walls now surrounded Harrison. He sat alone in the parlor, the scene of numerous arm-whackings for spilling tea and, of course, the infamous warm chair. He chose not to sit in that particular chair again.

A house servant guarded the doorway. Not Charles. This man had all the warmth of a cadaver. In fact, he looked like a cadaver. Bony thin. Sunken cheeks. Blue grayish tint to his skin. Even his expressions were cadaver-like; he showed no emotion. He spoke in a monotone.

Sizing up his situation, Harrison concluded he could get by his guard with little effort.

"I wouldn't try it, sir," said the house servant, as if reading Harrison's mind. "The boys are right outside. You wouldn't get far."

Harrison appreciated the warning. He'd use the back door.

"The back is equally guarded, sir," said the house servant.

How did he do that? He seemed to know exactly what Harrison was thinking. Harrison decided to test him. He thought, *Hey diddle, diddle, the cat and the fiddle—*

He waited, half expecting the house servant to add, *"The cow jumped over the moon."*

Instead, J. K. Jarves strode in. Close on his heels was a grinning Whitney Stuart III.

"Where's my daughter?" Jarves barked.

Harrison stood. He was aching to tell Jarves that Striped Pants had her in his grasp and let her get away, but that would reveal her location.

"I don't know." He could say it with conviction because it was the truth.

Jarves studied him with a long, cold stare. Whitney stood behind him, grinning, rocking on his heels, making a show of fingering his ring, the one with the amber stone. He was enjoying this.

"You think you're smart, don't you?" Jarves growled. "Using the tactics I taught you against me."

"I don't know what you're talking about," Harrison said.

"All you did was sign your own death warrant."

Harrison felt himself being fitted for a bell jar. And he still didn't know what Jarves was talking about.

"I strike at you through Bowen," Jarves said, "and you strike back through Victoria. A mistake, Mr. Shaw. A deadly mistake."

What was he talking about?

"I have to give you credit though," Jarves continued. "You surprised me. I didn't think you had it in you. You observed the situation in the mansion. Saw that I was lax in my discipline over Victoria and exploited it. You got to her. Filled her head with mystical nonsense. Addled her mind. Preyed on feminine weakness and turned her against me."

"I did no such thing."

"I blame myself." Jarves scowled. "It was the same tactic you used the first day you were here, with that coin trick. Limited imagination to use the same tactic twice though."

Harrison was beginning to understand. "Your daughter had a conversion experience. If I had something to do with that, I'll own up to it. I'm not ashamed. But I made no attempt to turn her against you."

"Have you had your way with her? Is that part of the plan? Turned her into a harlot, did you?"

Jarves was building up steam. His mask of civility was slipping. Harrison had seen it before.

"I have not touched your daughter," Harrison insisted.

"If you think you can get away with this unscathed . . ." Jarves's neck was blood red. "If you think you can take my daughter from me—" He came after Harrison with murder in his eyes.

Whitney stopped grinning and restrained him.

Harrison took a couple of steps back.

"I'll kill you," Jarves hissed. "I'll kill you. I'll kill you. But first, I'll destroy you." Jarves had regained a measure of control, though his words were delivered on a sea of rage. "I am going to impale you, Mr. Shaw. Throw you against the thorn of public opinion."

The method of the bulgy-eyed shrike.

"I'll get my daughter back," Jarves claimed. "You'll see. Your fatal mistake is underestimating her. She's a smart woman. When presented with the truth, she'll come to her senses. The flaw in your plan is that the same mind you addled to lead her astray will lead her home."

"Talk to her," Harrison urged. "She'll tell you that the decision was hers."

Jarves wasn't listening. This meeting was never intended to be an exchange of ideas.

"Then, after I've humiliated you and destroyed you, that's when I'll kill you. And nobody will care."

Harrison didn't take the threat lightly. This man had no qualms about killing him.

"Maurice!" Jarves shouted.

The cadaver stepped forward.

"Tell the boys to take Harrison back to where they found him. And tell them to give him a few reminders of his visit."

Jarves strode out, just as he'd entered, with Whitney Stuart III right behind him.

The most disturbing thing about this meeting was that it took place at all. For Jarves to come out and announce his intentions meant he was abandoning his method of operation, which was normally to lay low and strike when least expected. Unlike old Eli Hodge, whom Jarves had destroyed, Harrison doubted that after Jarves had done his worst, he'd thank the man for being a good friend.

Striped Pants and Newsboy Cap returned to escort him home.

"That's all right, boys," Harrison said. "I can find my way home."

"No, we wouldn't hear of it." Newsboy Cap smirked. "We feel a certain obligation to you."

Striped Pants thought that was funny.

They led Harrison out back.

"This time we're goin' to ride," Newsboy Cap said.

There was a wagon waiting for them.

"Only you're gonna ride in back."

Suddenly the lights went out. Struck from behind, Harrison was dimly aware of being loaded into the back of the wagon.

"Harrison boy! Wake up!"

Swimming upward, breaking the surface of consciousness, images of tired Five Points buildings slowly came into focus.

The next thing Harrison saw was Mouser. Despite the pain, he wanted to kiss her.

"Let me help ya to your feet," Mouser said.

Harrison felt his shoulders being lifted.

"You're gonna have to make some effort here, Harrison boy. I can't lift you by myself."

They were in the middle of the street. Harrison struggled to his feet, but he couldn't go far. With Mouser supporting him, he stumbled to a stairway and collapsed on the bottom step.

"This is gettin' to be a habit with you and me, Harrison boy."

"I need to talk to Tori," Harrison moaned.

Mouser peered around. She shook her head. "Ain't safe for Tori to come out right now."

"Please, it's important. We could maybe whisper."

Mouser looked around again. She leaned close to Harrison. "Where have you been? I've been worried sick about you!"

It was Tori's voice. Tori's eyes.

Harrison was so glad to see her, he nearly wept. "I made an unplanned visit to your father. He insisted."

"He's angry, isn't he?"

Harrison laughed at the understatement, but only for a second. It hurt too much.

"He's looking for you," Harrison said. "He's determined to get you back. He thinks all of this is my doing to get back at him for George Bowen."

Tori nodded. "He would think that."

"He wanted me to know that he's going to come after me. Destroy me. Humiliate me. Then he's going to kill me."

"Oh, Harrison!" A hand stroked his cheek. It was Mouser's dirty face, but it was Tori's hand, so Harrison didn't care.

"Maybe I should go back," she said. "As long as I'm with you, he'll come after me . . . and you."

"Go back and what? Renounce your faith? Besides, if you went back, I'd never be able . . ." His voice trailed off.

"Tell me," she insisted.

He looked at her. Straight into her eyes. "I'd never be able to see you again. I couldn't bear that."

A tear came to Mouser's eye.

Harrison looked away. "This is confusing. It'd be easier if you weren't dressed as a boy."

Mouser smiled, leaned forward, and kissed Harrison lightly.

That was really odd. His first kiss with Victoria Jarves, and it felt like he was kissing a boy.

"Are you afraid?" she asked.

Harrison shrugged. "I don't know. I've tried to think what I'd do in your father's place. But what's left for him to attack? I have no money. I don't have a business. He's already destroyed my career as a lawyer. I live in the basement of a church. In fact, since the lodge closed down, my whole life has been centered around the—"

Harrison bolted up. "You don't think he'd—"

"I wouldn't disregard anything when it comes to my father," Tori said.

CHAPTER 28

J. K. Jarves's lawsuit against the old North Dutch Church made headlines.

N.Y. ATTORNEY SUES CHURCH
FOR RAPING HIS DAUGHTER'S MIND

Noted attorney J. K. Jarves filed suit today against the old North Dutch Church on Fulton Street for stealing the mind of his daughter and only child. "For two decades I've raised my daughter to be a beautiful, respectable woman, a model of New York femininity. It took that church only a matter of weeks to turn her into an addled miscreant who talks to ghosts. They've ruined her. Raped her mind. And someone has to stop them before they ruin any more impressionable maidens."

At this point the normally unflappable Jarves broke down. "I just want my daughter back."

The old North Dutch Church has no comment. They're currently seeking defense counsel.

The trial is scheduled to start Tuesday, with Judge Edwin Walsh presiding.

"Are you going to do it?" Tori asked.

She was dressed as a woman, and Harrison couldn't be more grateful. Nor could he keep his eyes off her. She was a softer, kinder version of the Victoria Jarves who browbeat him at the mansion.

They walked side by side along an empty dock. The East River flowed purposefully seaward. The sun was warm. A light breeze contributed to make it a perfect day.

"I don't have much choice," Harrison said. "Every lawyer the church has approached has been scared off by your father. Your father wants me to try the case."

He wants to "impale me on the thorn of public opinion," if I remember his exact words, Harrison thought. "He also plans to use the trial as an argument to convince you that Christianity is without merit."

"He told you that?"

Harrison nodded.

"My father can be a formidable man. Are you scared now?"

Harrison sighed. "If I had any sense, I should be. But a side of me is anxious to test my skills as a lawyer. It may be the only chance I get."

"And another side of you wants to be the hero and save the old North Dutch Church."

Harrison started to object. He didn't because it was true. So he changed the subject. "Have you settled into your new place?"

Tori smiled. "It's comfortable. I have my own room. It's an old house. You have to remember I'm used to a mansion."

"Hey, you're talking to a guy who's been living for months in a basement. You'll get no sympathy from me. I'm just glad you're out of Five Points." For weeks Harrison had worried about Tori as she hid out there. But after Jarves filed his lawsuit, it seemed unlikely he would force Victoria to return home against her will. His case was stronger if it appeared she was still under the influence of those he accused of violating her. So Tori came out of hiding.

"Patricia is so much like Polly. You can tell they're sisters. And her husband is nice enough. Did I tell you he works with daguerreotypes?"

"Really? Do you think you can get him to take your picture?"

"And why would you want him to take my picture, Mr. Shaw? So you can ogle me whenever you want?"

That's exactly why he wanted a picture. Somehow saying it aloud made it seem wrong.

However, Tori wasn't offended. She was teasing. She shrugged. "He works in a studio on Broadway."

"I don't need a picture," Harrison said. "All I need are memories of today."

"Why Mr. Shaw, talk like that will turn a lady's head."

Their hands touched, felt for each other, then clasped. Had it not been for the storm clouds gathering on the horizon, it would have been a perfect day.

A week later Tori presented Harrison with a picture of herself. Dressed as Mouser. She wasn't going to do it, but when she told Polly and Patricia her idea when Polly was visiting, the sisters thought it would be hilarious fun and talked her into it.

J. K. Jarves pushed for an early trial date and got it, giving the inexperienced defense lawyer little time to prepare. Harrison immediately replied with a request for a continuance to give him time to prepare. Not surprisingly, his request was denied. With little recourse he squeezed every second out of the days allotted him. He ate little, slept less, and read so much his eyes felt like they were tied in knots.

"You'll do fine," Tori said as they climbed the courthouse steps.

She walked close beside him, which meant more to Harrison than he could tell her right now. If he tried, he'd probably break down in tears. He was so tired. Had he one more day to prepare, he'd spend it sleeping.

He wondered if Tori really thought he'd do fine. She knew full well her father's reputation. What chance did Harrison really have?

"I'll be praying for you," she told him as they entered the building.

A media crowd had gathered. Spotting Harrison, they swarmed him. He smiled and waved them off. He didn't want to answer their questions. But it didn't stop them from asking them.

"How do you feel going head-to-head against your former mentor, the best-known lawyer in New York?"

"Any young law student would kill to be J. K. Jarves's intern. Why did you resign?"

"What is your relationship with J. K. Jarves today?'

"Did you seduce J. K. Jarves's daughter?"

"Miss Jarves, what is your relationship with Harrison Shaw?"

Linking arms, Harrison and Tori pressed through the media storm and into the courtroom. Most courtrooms Harrison had been in were surprisingly small. This was the largest courtroom he had ever seen. He wouldn't have been surprised if Jarves had requested it. What better place than a large stage to try his case before the whole world?

They'd arrived early. At present the room was mostly empty—a person here, a couple there, people wanting seats to a trial that promised plenty of entertaining moments. Harrison wanted to get a feel for the room and prepare himself mentally for his opening statement.

He turned to Tori. They'd reached the railing that separated the litigants from the spectators. She could accompany him no farther.

She spoke first. "Let me talk to my father. If I offer to return home, maybe he'll drop the case."

This was the second time she had made this offer. Was it an offer to sacrifice herself for the greater good, or was she afraid Harrison couldn't win the trial against her father? Then again, who was he kidding? No one expected him to win the trial. Not even the defendants.

"Do you really think your father will back down now?" he said. "He'd never let me see you again."

Tori lowered her eyes. "At least you'd have my picture."

Harrison grinned. Remembering the Mouser picture made him realize how beautiful she looked in a dress. He loved even more being this close to her.

"I'll sit over here." She turned to enter a row of chairs, then suddenly swung around and kissed Harrison on the lips.

It was the worst—and most wonderful—thing she could have done. It sent his head spinning. His eyes watered. He became emotional. Of all the distractions that could have befallen him, this one was on the top of the list. The last thing he wanted to do right now was think about a trial.

Did she realize what kind of power she had over him? That was the problem. He was pretty sure she did.

Harrison staggered through the gate into the arena section of the courtroom as Tori took a seat. As passages go, it was a minor passage. The simple swinging of a gate. Yet for Harrison it was a step that shut him off from the rest of the world. As Tori's kiss faded and the reality of where he was set in, he felt more alone than he had ever felt.

This, too, was J. K. Jarves's doing. Once he'd officially agreed to take the case, the first thing Harrison did was seek the help of experienced lawyers. Nobody would talk to him. Either they feared Jarves, or they thought it was a case that couldn't be won. Some openly admitted as much. Others quoted outrageous consultant fees—five and six times the going rate—knowing that neither Harrison nor the defendants could afford them. By isolating the novice attorney from the legal community, Jarves scored a significant blow.

That was just the beginning of Jarves's strategy. Two messages hammered Harrison repeatedly throughout the pretrial period: One, that J. K. Jarves practiced what he taught—think outside the courtroom. And two, that Harrison was dealing with a powerful man.

Evidence of Jarves's power was demonstrated at two key pretrial events—the appointment of a judge and the selection of the jury.

Presiding over the case was Judge Edwin Walsh, or as Harrison first knew him, Sideburns. The judge had never liked Harrison, and he made no attempt to disguise his displeasure during the interview process. The fact that he served as one of Jarves's advisors in the selection of an intern indicated that the judge and Jarves had an established relationship, the nature and depth of which Harrison could only speculate. Regardless, Harrison feared such a connection would put him at a disadvantage in the court.

His fears were realized during jury selection. Judge Walsh raised a questioning eyebrow and grunted whenever Harrison used a challenge to remove a prospective juror. Jarves never used a challenge. He didn't need to.

The jury pool consisted of men who couldn't have been better suited to Jarves's case had they been handpicked, which they probably had. Of course, he had no way of proving it, but it was obvious Jarves had influenced the selection of the pool from which the jurors were drawn. Whenever Harrison dismissed a potential juror, an even worse candidate took the man's place. During one of these unfortunate setbacks, Harrison caught Jarves and the judge snickering over his misfortune.

Harrison quickly ran out of juror challenges. He had no choice but to accept the jury as it was.

The resulting jury consisted of men Harrison categorized as reprobates, drunks, womanizers, and atheists. Of the twelve, only two men seemed to have enough sense to get in out of the rain. This, too, according to Jarves's teaching: select two leaders and pack the rest of the jury with sheep. Harrison could almost hear them bleating.

Having been overmatched during the pretrial, Harrison felt things promised to get even more difficult as the trial got underway.

He removed his papers from a satchel and organized them atop the defense table, very much aware that the whispers behind him in the gallery were directed at him.

"David's here; Goliath can't be far behind."

The comment came from behind him. Harrison turned to see Jeremiah Lanphier. They'd talked openly about the odds against them. With Jeremiah was Herbert Zasser, a church elder. He was a friendly sort, in a stiff way. Good natured. A tailor by profession. He'd been an elder for over a quarter of a century and knew just about everything there was to know about the church.

As Harrison was greeting his clients, the real show burst through the back doors. J. K. Jarves, followed by Whitney Stuart III and a half dozen consulting attorneys, was surrounded by the clamor of reporters all shouting questions even as Jarves was answering one.

Jarves spoke in a loud voice, finishing a question that had been asked outside in the hallway. "No animosity. Like the early colonials, I'm merely protecting my homestead from the attack of hostile forces."

Then Jarves saw his daughter. He went to her straightaway, embracing her as though she'd been missing for years. Harrison had never seen such a display of affection from the man. From the expression on Tori's face, neither had she. It was a convincing show. The reporters were loving it. They scratched on their pads furiously.

The reunion lasted nearly two minutes, during which time Jarves and Tori huddled with their heads together and whispered back and forth. Harrison would have liked to have heard what was said between them.

Then the Jarves's entourage moved toward the front of the courtroom. He and Whitney sat at the prosecutor's table, while the consulting attorneys lined up in the row of chairs behind them.

Jarves never once looked at Harrison. Whitney looked—and grinned wickedly. They both removed papers from satchels and arranged them on the prosecutor's desk. Whitney removed one extra item, something that didn't seem appropriate for a court of law. The item was meant for one purpose only: to intimidate Harrison Shaw. Whitney set a bell jar atop the prosecutor's table. From beneath a restored glass dome, the familiar bulgy-eyed shrike glared tauntingly at Harrison.

The bailiff appeared and told everyone to stand.

The jury filed in, followed by Judge Walsh.

Seated next to Harrison, Jeremiah Lanphier reached over and gave him a reassuring squeeze.

Jeremiah's hand was ice cold.

CHAPTER 29

J. K. Jarves rose to present his opening statement.

"Gentlemen of the jury, we are here because a grievous wrong has been committed. An innocent young woman has fallen prey to an insidious, lurking evil that masquerades as a saving light."

Several of the jurors wrinkled their foreheads at the word *insidious,* including Juror 7, one of the prosecution's leaders. The choice of the word was deliberate. Jarves used it because it sounded evil.

"Let me explain. If a man were to stand on a seaside bluff and shine a powerful lamp out to sea, deliberately deceiving ships so that they flung themselves onto rocky shoals and perished, we would be outraged. We would seek out the wretch and punish him. We would hold him accountable for the deaths of those men and the loss of property.

"Should our outrage be any less when men deliberately and maliciously hold up what appears to be a friendly light, only to discover it's a light that casts men and women against rocky shoals that ruin their minds and torture their souls? That is what these men have done."

He pointed an accusing finger at the defendants.

"They have not destroyed property, nor have they taken a physical life. They have done far worse! They have preyed on innocent minds, leaving their victims alive, but tortured and riddled with guilt and remorse. While their victims continue to breathe, they are hideously enslaved to guilt and delusion. I ask you, gentlemen, who has committed the greater crime? The man on the bluff, or these men who freely walk the streets, raping the minds of innocent Americans?"

Jarves paused. He walked to the front of the prosecutor's table and turned the bell jar so that the shrike was staring at Harrison.

"One of their victims is my daughter," Jarves said. "And at some point during this trial, the thought may enter your mind that this is a personal vendetta."

He stared at the floor for a long moment.

"I'll answer that question upfront. Yes. Yes! YES, this is personal! When a man who has lost his wife has but one daughter, and that daughter is the sun and moon and stars of his existence, and that innocent young woman, who has harmed no one, is viciously stalked, mentally raped, and morally ruined, it's personal. Ask any father who loves his daughter that question, and you'll get but one answer. How much more personal does it get?"

Jarves steadied himself on the corner of the table, appearing to compose himself. "Gentlemen," he continued, "I intend to demonstrate to you that this is not simply a matter of my daughter. That this is not a crime against a single life but against *all humanity*. I intend to demonstrate to your satisfaction that these men are part of a much larger conspiracy. A conspiracy that has gripped not only this nation, but peoples the world over. That it is an evil conspiracy developed for one reason and one reason only: to subjugate and control industrious, hard-working people. Men just like you, gentlemen! Of what evil conspiracy am I speaking?"

He let the question hang in the air.

"Gentlemen of the jury, I intend to prove to you, and to the world, that Christianity is a subversive fraud. That it is harmful to a civilized society. That it is so insidious, millions of men and women will fall victim to it, just like my daughter. That unless we stop it here and now, it will be the ruination of America."

Jarves held a crusader's pose just long enough to get the idea across. Then he sat down at the prosecutor's table.

"Defense," Judge Walsh called.

Harrison didn't move. The scope of Jarves's opening statement came as a surprise. Was Jarves really intending on presenting a case alleging a centuries-old conspiracy? Harrison thought he was prepared to try this case, to prove that coercion was never a factor in Tori's salvation, that she knew fully well what she was doing. But to answer Jarves's charges, Harrison would now be forced to defend all of Christianity.

Judge Walsh grunted. "Defense waives the right to an opening statement."

"No!" Harrison shouted. "I have a statement."

"Then stand and deliver it," Judge Walsh barked. "And quit wasting this court's time."

"Yes, Your Honor."

Harrison rose on rubber legs, his mind racing to rewrite his opening statement. "Gentlemen of the jury."

He wandered into the center of the arena. Just as he was beginning to speak, Juror 2 raised his hand to his chin. A gold ring with an amber stone figured prominently on his finger. Harrison turned to the prosecutor's table. Two rings just like it were on Jarves's and Whitney's hands. Behind them in the gallery, three more rings. Behind the defense, four rings. Harrison glanced at the judge, who was fingering his ring.

Everyone with rings was looking at him.

"Gentlemen," Harrison began again. "I intend to prove to your satisfaction . . . that the old North Dutch Church did nothing wrong or did in no way harm Miss Victoria Jarves. But that just the opposite did indeed occur." He took a deep breath. "Just the opposite, in that through their ministry, they helped Miss Jarves, and that she not only participated of her own free will but is grateful for their ministry."

He'd reached the end of his prepared notes, only they had sounded a lot better when he'd practiced them in the basement of the church.

"As for the large charge," he said, thinking on his feet, "this outright and . . . blatant attack on Christianity as a whole"—he wiped his forehead that had sprouted several fountains—"it's, well, it's ridiculous . . . um, without foundation. And, well, it's . . . it's just not true."

He felt he needed to say more, but nothing was coming to him. "I guess that's about it, for now."

He wandered back to the defense table. As he passed in front of the prosecutor's table, he could hear Jarves whispering to Whitney, "After that eloquent display, we might as well throw in the towel here and now."

Whitney laughed.

J. K. Jarves's first witness was a professor of philosophy at Harvard, Dr. Everett T. Chase. It became clear that Jarves's line of argument would be from general to specific, first presenting his case against Christianity before getting to the specifics regarding Victoria, thus catching Harrison off guard and unprepared.

Harrison rearranged the papers in front of him, trying not to appear as shaken as he felt. He'd wanted the spotlight. He'd wanted to see what kind of a lawyer he'd make. Now he was finding out it was much easier to imagine being a lawyer than it was being one.

"Dr. Chase," Jarves said, "you are a professor of philosophy at Harvard University, is that correct?"

"Yes."

Chase overflowed the witness chair. He was a big man with gently arching shoulders and an oversized head to fit his body. He had a full beard and mustache, white with streaks of gray, and he licked his lips every time before he spoke.

"Dr. Chase, if you don't mind, give us your credentials."

Chase readjusted himself in his seat, eager to tell a captive audience about his many degrees, which included philosophy, theology, ancient languages, and medieval history.

"Impressive, Dr. Chase," Jarves said, nodding. "And how long have you been teaching at Harvard?"

A hand went to Dr. Chase's chin as he thought. The hand had a gold ring on it with an amber stone. "Twenty-two . . . twenty-three years."

"And during that time have you studied Christianity?"

Chase chuckled as though it was ridiculous that anyone would even ask such a question. "I'm one of the foremost authorities on the subject in America and on the continent."

"I see. Dr. Chase, have you been published on this subject?"

"Yes."

"Have you lectured on it?"

"Yes."

"Tell us, Dr. Chase. What have you discovered?"

This is what Chase had come for, and he was itching to get started. He licked his lips twice, for good measure.

"The Christian institution as we know it has been formulated over the centuries as a tool by powerful and wealthy men to subjugate the masses. Prior to this time, uprisings were common, and men of power needed large standing armies to protect themselves and maintain control. Christianity proved a godsend to them, so to speak." He laughed at his own joke.

"Now there was a way to keep the masses in their place with fewer armies. They promoted the Christian faith only because it taught the common man that humility and meekness were virtues. Christianity taught that a man should be content with what he has and not desire wealth. It went so far as to convince the masses that wealth was a curse, and a man with wealth would almost assuredly not go to heaven. In this way the wealthy and powerful were able to subdue and control millions of people simply by getting them to embrace poverty willingly in hopes that they would be wealthy after they died. Quite a feat, wouldn't you say?"

"Dr. Chase, would you say—"

"One more thing," Chase interrupted. "This is the telling point. If the nobles and the wealthy truly believed these teachings, wouldn't they do what Jesus requested of them and give all they have to the poor?" He scoffed. "I have studied history throughout the ages, and I'm here to tell you, the great men of wealth and power did not get that way by being meek and humble."

"And so you're saying, Dr. Chase, that the history of Christianity is a history of conquest and control over others."

"Most certainly! For example, when emperor Henry IV challenged Pope Gregory VII over lay investiture, the pope wielded his spiritual power by excommunicating him, threatening him with eternal damnation, forcing the secular emperor to stand outside the pope's castle garbed as a penitent, barefoot in the snow, begging his forgiveness for three days. It's from this event we get our phrase 'Going to Canossa.' It demonstrates quite clearly Christianity's historic role of using a spiritual bludgeon to control even kings."

"Thank you, Doctor."

"The church increased its power and prestige greatly from that and similar events."

Like many professors, once the flow of information was started, it was next to impossible to shut it off. But Harrison knew Jarves had established his point. He didn't want to bore the jurors with a history lecture.

"Continuing on, Dr. Chase . . . some may argue that your example, as chilling as it is, happened so long ago—"

"AD 1077," Chase stated. "Actually, the catalyst for the event occurred in 1075, when—"

"Thank you, Doctor. But can you cite any instances of a predatory and manipulative church since the time of the Reformation, possibly within our own country?"

"Most certainly. Arguably the most blatant example of this would be our nation's penchant for revival."

Jarves acted surprised. "Really? Certainly you're not referring to the kind of revival that is currently making headlines?"

"I most certainly am," Chase said.

"Interesting. Can you give us an example?"

Harrison grimaced. This was obviously a carefully scripted performance. Asking a college professor to give an example for one of his theories is like saying "sic 'em" to a dog.

"Revivalists believe that God pours out His grace in supernatural ways and has done so throughout history. They cite Old and New Testament examples as proof. However, since their examples are rooted in fable, these expected outpourings never occur. So they create them. They eagerly solicit, publish, and distribute conversion narratives without any scholarly investigation to determine whether or not they're factual. The target of these narratives is the individual, who infers that he, too, can experience a supernatural visitation from God."

"But how do you account for such great numbers of these converts, Dr. Chase?"

Chase grinned like a rogue. "The numbers are largely exaggerated. A meeting of barely a hundred becomes five hundred. And not only are the numbers exaggerated; so, too, are the stories. A woman who suffered mild depression all of a sudden becomes a demon-possessed mother who was on the verge of killing her seven children until God intervened. I have a quote from one revivalist who said, 'The object of our measures is to gain attention. You must have something new.' By the time these reports reach the papers, they've become the greatest outpouring of the Spirit of God since Pentecost."

"And so you believe these stories we've been reading in the paper are largely inventions, is that correct, Dr. Chase?"

"Without a doubt."

"But Dr. Chase, when I was a child, I was taught that our nation has been supernaturally blessed by God on more than one occasion—during the Great Awakening of the 1740s, led by spiritual giants such as George Whitefield and Jonathan Edwards; the Yale Revivals of the 1790s; and the Second Great Awakening, which featured the dynamic preaching of Charles Finney. Are you telling me that what I was taught was a lie?"

"Can anything good come from Yale?" the Harvard professor quipped. He eyed the jury for appreciative grins. There were none, so he continued. "The preachers you mention used time-honored techniques and strategies to fabricate the appearance of a spiritual outpouring of God. Charisma. Drama. Novelty. Publications such as broadsheets, pamphlets, and newspapers. Give me a handful of spellbinding preachers, an adequate budget for publications, and I could convince America that her shores have been visited by magical leprechauns on holiday from Ireland."

That got the laugh the professor was seeking.

"The point being," the professor concluded, "that standard methods of persuasion and promotion are the lifeblood of these so-called manifestations of God."

"Why now, Dr. Chase? Why would these mind manipulators portray 1858 as an acceptable year of the Lord, one fraught with an outpouring of supernatural grace?"

"Simple. By definition, revival follows decline. Last year our nation suffered a catastrophic economic upheaval, which sent the populace reeling. Desperate men reach out for anything in an effort to make sense of it all. They'll grab at anything that gives them hope. Enter church leaders, licking their chops, seeing an opportunity to profit from widespread suffering."

"One last question, Dr. Chase. Are these revival tendencies harmful?"

"Let me answer that with a question. What happens to those who desperately want to believe in a spiritual outpouring from God? What happens when they pray with all sincerity, but never experience the kind of blessing they're hearing about in sermons and testimonies and newspapers?

"I'll tell you. I have in my files the report of a man, the father of a revival preacher, who was desperate for revival. He was consumed with guilt for his sin—that part of the preaching was effective. Yet he could find no comfort. For him there was no supernatural outpouring of forgiveness and grace. His thoughts turned to self-violence. Strong temptations to cut his own throat because he could no longer stand the mental and emotional anguish."

"What happened to him?" Jarves asked.

Chase didn't respond immediately. He stared vacantly at the floor, impacted by his own story. "He eventually took his own life. But it's what happened afterward that is most shocking."

"Tell us."

"The man's son, the preacher, with little apparent remorse, used his father's suicide to frighten people to get on the revival bandwagon, telling them that they needed to pray harder, work harder, give more because Satan was at work among them and he was gaining the upper hand."

"Thank you, Dr. Chase. No further questions." J. K. Jarves sat down.

When Harrison wasn't immediately out of his seat to cross-examine the witness, Judge Walsh said haughtily, "It's your turn, Mr. Shaw. Or didn't they teach you that at Washburn School of Law in Brooklyn?"

The gallery laughed. The jurors stared at him, sizing him up for the fight.

Harrison pushed back his chair. For some reason, the memory of a prior humiliating incident chose this moment to flash in his mind. Actually, it was a double humiliation. The night before a geography exam, instead of studying for the test, Harrison entered a checkers tournament. He was the reigning checkers king at the lodge. Everyone was cheering for him. The pride of the lodge regulars was at stake. As it turned out, not only did Harrison get soundly whupped in the tournament by a visiting sailor from Cambridge, but the next day in school he gloriously failed the geography exam. The exam was oral. Not only did Harrison fail it, he did so standing in front of the entire class.

The humiliation of letting others down and of being unprepared was the memory that chose to revisit Harrison as he approached the witness stand. "Dr. Chase . . ." *Where to begin? Attack the man's credentials? What was to attack?*

He'd paused long enough that Dr. Chase said, "Yes?"

"Dr. Chase, did you say one of your degrees was in theology?"

"Yes."

"Only one?"

"I beg your pardon?"

"I mean, are you an ordained minister?"

"No."

"And yet you still feel qualified to speak on matters of the spirit?"

"Ordination is a piece of paper given to men who are not intelligent enough to earn a real degree," Dr. Chase replied.

The courtroom laughed. The judge in particular liked that one.

"Well, Doctor. I've done a little studying on my own. In the matter of history. Enough to know that history is largely an interpretation of events. Given that fact, are you willing to concede that, among scholars, there are those who would disagree with your conclusions?"

"Yes, there are."

Harrison was surprised by the admission. He'd expected a fight. "You're willing to stipulate that?"

"I'm willing to stipulate they're ignoramuses." The professor then launched into a long-winded account providing the specific details upon which he'd based his conclusions, further establishing his credibility.

Harrison tried to interrupt, but the professor continued to ramble. An appeal to the judge prompted a shrug and the mouthed words, "You asked him."

When the professor was finally played out, the only other question Harrison could think to ask was, "Professor, you're not a Christian, are you?"

"Have I succumbed to the lies and myths perpetrated by a spurious movement that has sustained itself by subjugating weak-minded people for centuries? No, I have not," Dr. Chase said defiantly.

The remainder of the day was no better. Jarves introduced two more professors, both with impressive academic credentials—one from Oxford—who built upon the foundation Dr. Chase had laid. Harrison was no more successful cross-examining them than he had been with Dr. Chase.

By the time court was dismissed for the day, Harrison felt like he'd been mugged. Only this beating was worse than the ones he'd taken at Five Points. There he was the only one who suffered. Here his beating threatened the existence of the church and belief in God Himself.

CHAPTER 30

Every major New York City newspaper printed J. K. Jarves's questioning of Dr. Chase verbatim, followed by a one-line summary comment of the rebuttal: "Defense attorney Harrison Shaw was ineffectual in refuting Dr. Chase's expert testimony."

Three days of similar testimony followed as Jarves built his case that Christianity was not only the ruin of his daughter but would be the ruin of civilization as well.

During the weekend break, the newspapers carried editorials questioning Christianity's future in America. In a quote, J. K. Jarves suggested that the nation would be better off by returning to a philosophy based on ancient Greek tradition. He claimed the writings of Plato and Aristotle had just as much influence on the founding of our country as did the Bible.

The article quoting Jarves bumped from the page an article written by T. E. Campbell that interviewed pastors and Christian professors who refuted Dr. Chase's interpretation of history.

The nation's pulpits added their voice with sermons that seemed to fall into one of two categories. Many preachers saw the trial as evidence Christ would soon return. Some portrayed J. K. Jarves as the Antichrist, the beast of Revelation. Those not predicting the end of the world portrayed the trial as evidence of a sin-sick society. They placed the plight of the nation directly on the shoulders of Christians who did not take sin seriously, who didn't pray, tithe, or witness.

The following week, attendance at prayer meetings in the city was half what it had been. Reports from other states also reported declines. At best, the effect of the trial was dampening the spirit of revival; at worst, it was causing a nation to question its spiritual roots.

A good number of the faithful began gathering outside the courthouse to pray for Harrison, that God would give him wisdom and a ready tongue to speak the truth.

While Harrison was appreciative of their support, to him the fervency of their prayers indicated a lack of confidence in his abilities.

"Things will turn around once you present a defense," Tori said.

They sat next to each other at the Astor Library in the shadow of a mountain of books. When not in court, Harrison had been spending every spare minute studying, searching for a weakness in Jarves's argument and for a way to win over a hostile jury.

"Put me on the stand," Tori said.

"We agreed we'd do that only as a last resort," Harrison replied.

"I'm not afraid of facing my father in court."

"I know you're not."

"I can tell the jury in my own words that I was not coerced."

"Let's see how they respond to my defense first."

"I can also tell them what I've seen as a reporter. About Polly and Ethan, and the saloon revival."

"And get yourself fired from the newspaper? Mayfair's already reluctant to take any more of your articles. He says he's disappointed in you. Says you've lost your edge."

"Lost my edge?" Tori shouted, drawing stares from other library patrons. "Lost my edge? My last article was a solid piece of writing. Controversial. Goes against the current tide."

"He called it traditional. The publisher wants to play up this dawn-of-a-new-nation slant. Mayfair said they printed the revival stories reluctantly, only because the revival was controversial at the time. He says there's a new controversy now."

Tori grumbled something unintelligible.

"He says if you stumble across an ax murderer, to write it up. He'll print that." Harrison rubbed tired eyes and returned to his book.

Tori was out of her chair. She circled the table a few times. "I need to walk. Let's get some fresh air."

"I need to read this."

"A walk will do you good."

"Don't have the time. You go."

"By myself? Walk the dangerous streets of New York City by myself?"

Harrison chuckled. He looked at her and couldn't believe he'd turned down an invitation to spend time alone with Victoria Jarves. But he had to prepare for tomorrow morning. It was his first day to present a defense.

But this was Victoria Jarves!

"I really have to read this," he said again.

Tori returned to her seat. She put her hand on his arm. "You're pushing yourself too hard. Even heroes have to take a break now and then."

Her touch still sent shivers through him.

"Walk with me," she pleaded.

He smiled at her apologetically.

"You realize you're putting too much pressure on yourself, don't you?"

Something snapped inside him. All the hours of study, exhaustion, and frustration at his own inadequacy were taking their toll. "Oh am I? Am I really? Strange, I was under the mistaken idea that I was the sole defense counsel in this case. That if I don't win, the old North Dutch Church could be forced out of existence. That the repercussions of this trial could very well bring a halt to the current revival. And, if your father has his way, a complete reevaluation of the role of Christianity in our nation. For all we know, I may be the only one who can prevent the collapse of Christianity in America!"

"Harrison—"

There was empathy in Tori's eyes, but no empathy could fix what Harrison was up against. He couldn't stop his words. Or the anger he felt growing inside.

"That's not so much to worry about, is it? Just a little thing. Sure, I'm putting too much pressure on myself. Let's go out for a walk. While we're at it, let's go to a party! Stay up all night. I can send a note to Judge Walsh in the morning saying I don't feel well enough to come to court and defend the future of Christianity!"

Tori studied him for a long moment, then got up. When she spoke, it was slow and deliberate. "If you're the savior of the world, then I guess that makes me Satan for trying to lure you away, doesn't it? Good night, Saint Shaw."

She turned and walked away.

Harrison was instantly repentant. "Tori . . . come back. Tori! I'm sorry. I . . ."

She swung around. "If you had any brains at all, you'd put me on the stand."

Then she was gone.

The next day, as Harrison entered the courthouse, Whitney Stuart III approached him.

"Mr. Jarves would like to have a word with you."

The way he said it, it was more of a summons than a request. Harrison looked past Whitney. Jarves was nowhere in sight.

"The cloakroom," Whitney said.

He led; Harrison followed. Jarves was waiting for them.

"If you're thinking of settling," Harrison said. "I'm willing to talk."

Jarves did not smile. He took two steps toward Harrison. Two and a half steps more and he'd be inside Harrison's skin.

"Keep my daughter off the witness stand," Jarves warned.

He didn't wait for a reply. He moved past Harrison to the door that Whitney was guarding. Before leaving he turned. "Put her on the stand, and you'll face the direst of consequences."

Had anyone else threatened Harrison with those same words, he would have taken the threat to mean a club to the back of the head, or possibly a knife in the gut. But given Jarves's collection of insects and birds, the threat had a more creative and chilling element to it.

The prosecution's final witness was a disgruntled former minister who railed against what he termed "the criminal abuses of evangelical Christianity." With a dark palette, he painted a picture of anguished souls racked by guilt and inferiority.

"Are you referring to yourself?" Jarves asked.

"For one."

"How many others are there?"

The cleric shook his head. "Sadly, most people suffer in silence. That's why I've taken to seeking them out and offering them counsel."

"So you counsel people who are victims of Christianity?"

"That's correct."

"And how many have you counseled?"

"I currently have seven clients. Possibly close to thirty over the years. But it's only the tip of the iceberg. I estimate that for every person who seeks help, there are at least twenty-five who don't. And I live in a small town."

"Let me ask you this. If a father were to come to you and tell you that his daughter has fallen prey to these wicked and cruel forces, would you be able to help her?"

"First she would have to come of her own free will. Even then, sad to say, I can never restore them fully. It's like losing a leg. You may be able to learn to function without it, but you'll never be whole again."

"So your advice to this father—a father who loves his daughter more than life itself—would be?"

The cleric shook his head sadly. "I wouldn't offer him hope."

Harrison opened his defense by putting his own experts on the stand to refute Dr. Everett T. Chase's interpretation of history. He had them enumerate at length the benefits of Christianity. However, when he attempted to have them postulate what the world might have been like without Christianity, Jarves objected. It was speculation, he claimed. Judge Walsh sustained the objection.

During the expert testimony, Harrison kept an eye on Jurors 2 and 7, the men Jarves selected to lead the jury to a verdict that would favor the prosecution. They sat stone-faced, at times appearing bored. It didn't help that during the testimony Judge Walsh laboriously peeled an orange and ate it. At one point, more jurors were watching the judge peel the orange than were listening to the Yale professor on the witness stand.

As for the testimony itself, Harrison was dissatisfied. He felt it came off weak and defensive, sounding like the mother of a known trouble-maker insisting her son was a good boy, contrary to all evidence.

The first day of defense ended without any visible progress. To make matters worse, as Harrison left the courthouse, he was assaulted by a hostile crowd of church members, accusing him of failing to defend Christ adequately, calling for him to step aside and let someone better qualified defend the church.

The only bright point in the day came when he saw Tori standing at a distance, waiting for him.

"I'm sorry about last night," he said.

"Me too."

They hurried away from the courthouse, neither of them speaking until they'd lost the last of the protestors. They found themselves in the park.

It was early evening, and the sun had yet to set. The air smelled invigoratingly fresh after their being shut up in a courthouse all day.

"How's Jeremiah doing?" Tori asked.

"He tries to put on a brave face."

"I think it went well today. The testimony."

"Too bad they don't allow women on the jury."

"They allow women on the witness stand."

Harrison stopped walking. "Please don't start."

He'd decided not to tell her about Jarves's threat. What did it matter? His defense plan had not changed. The risk of putting her on the stand was too great.

They walked a short distance, then he said, "Right about now, I'd trade all this for garden gloves and an etiquette lesson in the parlor."

Tori laughed. "You'd willingly put yourself under the scrutiny of that old shrew?"

Harrison looked at her. It amazed him how much she had changed. She was right. This wasn't the same woman who had whacked him in the parlor. If ever there was proof of a changed nature through Christ, it was Victoria Jarves.

She belonged on the witness stand. Exhibit A. But he wasn't going to do it. And not because of the threats. He didn't want to subject her to the scrutiny, for one. But there was another reason. He didn't want to give Jarves a chance to confront her directly. The courtroom was his territory. He had the advantage. And deep down, Harrison was afraid that somehow Jarves would manage to convince Tori that her salvation experience had been a mistake.

"I think you're keeping something from me," Tori said.

"Oh?" Could she tell what he was thinking?

"I think, secretly, you liked my tea lessons."

Harrison laughed. Relieved.

"Here's a question for you." Tori's eyes glistened impishly. "Which is worse? A bad day in court, or having to sit through Mrs. Pierre Belmont's rendition of the national anthem?"

Harrison laughed. Red boots and shooting flames came to mind.

Their laughter died after a dozen steps. They walked in silence.

"Polly had her baby," Tori said. "A girl."

"Ah, so that's what good news sounds like! She's staying with her sister?"

"For a month. Ethan said it's the only way he can keep her from doing her chores while she recovers. Tell you one thing though. The presence of a baby adds some interesting sounds and smells to a house."

They walked a few steps.

"Anyway, we were talking this morning—"

"We?"

"Not the baby, silly. Patricia, Polly, and I."

"Ah! You were talking—"

Tori paused. "Don't take this the wrong way."

Harrison set his jaw.

"Anyway, we were thinking," Tori continued, "maybe we're going about this trial the wrong way."

More advice. More well-meaning criticism. *Well, stand in line,* Harrison thought. *There's a whole host of people who think they can do a better job than I can.*

Her words hit him hard. Partly because it was Tori and Polly, whom he'd come to respect. Harrison knew the old adage: those closest to you can hurt you the most. And this criticism hit him hard also, because he was already badly bruised from the daily pummeling of self-doubt, the newspaper accounts, and now supporters turning on him on the court-house steps.

"So three women are evaluating my trial strategy?" he said.

"We were just talking."

"Just talking. Remind me. Of the three, how many of you have law degrees?"

"You're hurt."

"Hurt? Why would I be hurt? Just because the whole world thinks I'm doing a lousy job. Just because three women have nothing better to do than sit around a kitchen table and think of ways I can improve my performance in court? Why would you think I'd be hurt by that?"

Tori cocked her head. Now she was hurt. "Why are you acting like a baby?"

"You tell me. You, Polly, and Patricia know all about babies now, which coincidently makes you experts in the law. So enlighten me. What do the women of Patricia's kitchen think I should do to pull my bacon out of the judicial fire?"

Tori folded her arms. "Let's change the subject."

"No, I want to know. Maybe I missed something studying all those years at law school. Maybe I was asleep on the day the professor taught us how to redeem a hopeless situation."

Her lips tightened. "I don't like you when you're like this."

"When I'm like what? Belligerent? Or a loser?"

Tori walked away from him.

He sighed. The only friendly face he'd seen all day was walking away from him. "Tori, wait."

He'd gone too far. He knew it and regretted it instantly. He ran to catch up with her.

She kept walking.

"Tori . . ." He caught her arm and turned her around. "Listen. I'm sorry. I'm out of my mind. Please, don't go."

Guarded sympathy lined her face. "I'm only trying to help."

"I know. I know! And I don't mean to be like this." He shrugged helplessly. "I know you don't like me when I'm like this. *I* don't like me when I'm like this."

She placed a hand on his arm and smiled weakly. "You are out of your mind, aren't you?"

The next thing Harrison knew, he had his arms around her and was clinging to her for his life. In public. With other people watching. And he didn't care. At the moment he didn't care if she cared. He needed to hold her. Maybe it was all those years of never having parents to hug. Years of stored up need. All he knew was that he had Victoria Jarves in his arms, and he didn't want to let go. *Ever.* Maybe it was his imagination, but the longer he hugged her, the more it seemed their hearts began to beat in synchronous rhythm. He'd never experienced anything like it.

"Harrison?" She squirmed. "People are looking."

Reluctantly he let her go.

They stood facing each other. Neither moving. Not hugging, but closer than men and women stand who are just friends.

Then the moment was gone. They began walking again. For several minutes they didn't talk.

"You said the three of you were talking," Harrison prompted.

"I'm sorry, I shouldn't have presumed."

"I want to know."

"Really?"

"Please." This time he did.

"Well . . ." She was still hesitant. She had a right to be. "We were talking about praying for you and spiritual warfare, and all of a sudden I thought, *We're going about this all wrong.* While this is a court battle, the larger issue is a spiritual battle, isn't it?"

Harrison thought about it. "I suppose."

"And if it is indeed a spiritual battle, then it only makes sense that we should be fighting with spiritual weapons."

Harrison pondered what she'd said. Hope—something he hadn't felt since the beginning of the trial—began to rise in him. *Maybe there is a chance after all for us to win this case.*

She went on eagerly. "It makes sense, doesn't it? I was thinking . . ."

Harrison's heart began to beat faster as legal arguments ran through his mind. He held up a hand. "No, I think you have something there, Tori. I may be able to use that! Spiritual weapons. God is Spirit. I can use that."

And just at that moment, as if ordained by God himself, the sun burst from behind the clouds, bathing Tori and Harrison in a warm, golden light.

The next day, Harrison walked to the court building with a decidedly faster and happier stride. He had a plan. Once in court, Harrison called Herbert Zasser to the stand. He led the church elder step by step through the history of the old North Dutch Church, its founding, its relationship to its neighbors, its established place in the community. Harrison wanted the jurors to see that the church wasn't the evil Jarves described.

Surprisingly, when it was Jarves's turn, he went easy on the elder. About the only questions he focused on had to do with the church's operating budget. *Could it be this easy?* Harrison wondered.

Next, Harrison called to the witness stand Jeremiah Lanphier. He had Jeremiah describe how he went from being a businessman to being hired by the church to canvass the surrounding neighborhood, inviting people to attend worship services. He also had Jeremiah describe how the first prayer meeting in the upper room was not well attended, then how the numbers started growing when God began answering prayers in some rather extraordinary ways. Harrison went to great lengths to emphasize how people's lives were changed. Murderers repented. Thieves restored what they had stolen. Alcoholics gave up drinking. Families were reunited.

Harrison was gratified to see the intense gazes of the jury. They leaned forward, seemingly riveted by the stories of life change.

And then it was Jarves's turn to cross-examine. He attacked poor Jeremiah mercilessly. And while Jeremiah handled himself with grace, the prosecutor portrayed the church as a subversive organization funded by a significant base of financial supporters—the numbers he'd gotten from Zasser. Jarves claimed it was all a self-promoting attempt to manipulate an even larger population into giving the organization their money by pledging a portion of their income for the rest of their lives. He further insisted that these people were deliberately deceived into thinking that's what God would want them to do.

"But it's not enough for them to think they're earning God's favor through obedience, is it, Mr. Lanphier?" Jarves challenged.

"I don't know to what you are referring."

"Don't you? Tell me. What is the teaching of the church regarding the fate of persons who do not alter their lives to church expectations?"

"It's not up to the person to—"

"What is the fate of the unrepentant miser, Mr. Lanphier? Is it not the same as the profligate, the murderer, the whore?"

"If you're talking about—"

"Tell me, Mr. Lanphier, what is the church teaching about the fate of the unrepentant sinner, even the least of sinners? What is the fate of the man who perishes in sin?"

"Hell," Lanphier stated simply.

The day ended with Jarves's tirade over the injustice of eternal damnation for all sinners, no matter how minor their sin.

Despite Jarves's theatrics, for the first time since the trial began, Harrison was elated. At last the defense had made some headway! He could see the same joy, the same excitement in Victoria's face as she waited for him outside the courtroom.

The next morning showed even greater progress. Harrison called to the stand Matt Brennan, owner of the saloon on Pearl Street. Brennan was to be the first in a series of defense witnesses who could testify to the positive change in the lives of people who had experienced revival. Harrison had heard these stories before, and he knew they couldn't help but make an impact on the jury.

Testimony began under the shadow of J. K. Jarves's absence. When called upon to explain the prosecutor's tardiness, Whitney Stuart III claimed to have no knowledge as to why Jarves wasn't in court.

Judge Walsh ordered the proceedings to continue.

"Mr. Brennan, in your own words, tell us what you witnessed on the night in question."

"It happened over several nights," Brennan said.

"Begin with the first night."

"At first I thought they was drunk."

"They?"

"Tom Branson, Pete Whittaker, Ludlow Green—some of my regulars. I mean, they was hootin' it up loud enough to raise the dead. Only the strange part about it was, they hadn't drunk anythin' yet! I mean, these men are usually good for—"

The courtroom door banged open.

Heads swiveled.

Assisted into the courtroom was J. K. Jarves, his suit covered with dirt and torn at the knee. His arm was draped over a bearded man who was wearing the apron of a blacksmith.

"What's this?" Judge Walsh barked.

The blacksmith spoke. "We found him like this behind the stable. He was all beat up. We wanted to call a doctor, but he insisted we bring him here."

"The man speaks the truth," Jarves said.

They were nearly to the railing now. Jarves's knee was bloody. There was also blood at the corner of his mouth. He held a handkerchief over a wound on his forehead.

"This good man brought me here at my insistence," Jarves explained.

"Who did this to you?" Walsh asked.

Jarves steadied himself against the railing. "There were five of them. They fell upon me at the blacksmith's. My carriage has a wheel that needs repair. I was dropping it off on the way to court."

"Can you identify them?" asked the judge.

"Never seen them before. They said they were concerned citizens. Wanted to persuade me to drop this case. When I told them I had no intention of being bullied, they added fists and boots to their persuasion tactics."

"When we found him, we thought he was dead," the blacksmith said.

"They thought they'd killed me," Jarves added. "It was the only way I could stop the beating. Once they thought I was dead, they knelt over me and . . ."

"And what?" Walsh asked.

"Said a prayer."

"What?"

"They said a prayer, Your Honor. They offered my soul to God so that He could consign it to hell."

The judge fumed. "We'll dismiss for two hours to give you time to clean up, unless you feel you need longer."

"No, Your Honor. If it's all the same to you, I'd prefer to continue on. I feel I'm up to it."

The judge squinted as he mentally debated the request. "Until the noon hour. We'll take a long lunch."

"Thank you, Your Honor," Jarves said.

The blacksmith helped him to his seat. A concerned Whitney Stuart and several consulting attorneys huddled around Jarves. All eyes in the jury box were on him.

"Continue your questioning, Mr. Shaw," said the judge.

"Your Honor . . ."

"Continue!"

For all the good it did, Brennan could have given his testimony personally to Harrison. No one else heard it. Their attention was at the prosecutor's table, where Jarves leaned heavily on the table, appearing as if he would pass out at any moment.

Following the lunch break, Jarves returned in clean clothes with a bandage on his head. He walked with a stiff leg.

Concluding his questioning, Harrison turned his witness over to the prosecution.

Wincing, Jarves stood. It took him awhile to hobble to the witness stand. "Mr. Brennan, you described some rather unusual things."

"Yes sir."

"The way you described the men in your saloon last night, one would get the impression they'd had too much to drink."

"That's what I thought at first. But then, I hadn't served them anything. And they kept praisin' God."

"They mentioned God," Jarves said. "Is it unusual for the name of God to be used in your establishment, Mr. Brennan?"

"No sir. It's used all the time. Mostly in curses."

The jury laughed.

Jarves turned his head as though the laughter hurt him.

"Are you all right, Mr. Jarves?" the judge asked.

Jarves held a hand up to his bandage. "Yes, Your Honor. Just give me a moment."

The courtroom waited while Jarves fought back pain.

"Mr. Brennan," he said at last, "is yours the only establishment in New York City that serves alcohol?"

Brennan laughed. "No sir."

"So it's conceivable that the men were indeed drunk and that they'd got themselves liquored up before entering your establishment? Possibly even getting hold of some bad liquor?"

"These men have been comin' to my place for—"

"Is it conceivable, Mr. Brennan?"

"Yeah, I guess it's conceivable."

"Tell me, Mr. Brennan, how's business?"

"Not so good."

"That surprises me," Jarves said. "You have a good location. You've established a clientele over the years. I take it business hasn't always been bad?"

"No sir, I've had some mighty good years."

"When did business start declining?"

"It started going down followin' that revival thing."

"People stopped coming after that?"

"No, they come. The place is packed. They just don't buy drinks."

"People go to a saloon and don't buy drinks? What do they do there?"

"They pray."

"Isn't that what a church is for?"

Brennan chuckled. "Exactly! I tell them the church don't sell liquor, and I don't sell prayers."

Jarves pondered this. "Mr. Shaw has gone to great lengths to prove to us that the church is a good neighbor. But a good neighbor doesn't drive another neighbor out of business, do they?"

"They're drivin' me outta business."

At the end of the day, Harrison stopped at the prosecution's table.

Jarves's back was to him. He was talking to Whitney, so it was Whitney who first saw Harrison. The intern greeted him with a sneer.

Jarves turned.

"I just wanted to see how you were doing," Harrison said, pointing at the head bandage. "And to let you know that kind of act is totally reprehensible. I hope the men who did this to you are brought to justice."

"Sort of like the crusades, wouldn't you say, Mr. Shaw? Holy mayhem in the name of God."

"What those men did to you is inexcusable." Harrison shook his head in regret.

Out of the corner of his eye, he could see Tori approaching down the center aisle.

Jarves pulled Harrison aside. He put his hands on Harrison's shoulders in a fatherly way and leaned close to him. "Think outside the court-room, Mr. Shaw."

"I can't believe my father would have himself beat up just to win a case," Tori said later.

"He so much as admitted it to me. Boasted is more like it. Besides, this isn't just a court case to him. He doesn't just want the jury's sympathy; he wants *your* sympathy."

And he got it, Harrison thought. He could see it in her eyes.

"Are you going to put me on the witness stand?"

"Tomorrow I call Dr. Thaddeus Welles to the stand. He's a theologian from William and Mary. You said this was a spiritual battle, remember? I'm going to use the attributes of God to convince the jury that God is holy, despite the fact that His children act in unholy ways at times. I intend to convince them of the goodness of God and that He only wants the best for His creation, and that His best is nothing less than salvation."

"You're not going to put me on the stand, are you?" she asked.

Harrison looked her in the eyes. "No."

"Why not?"

"I have my reasons."

"Fine."

She turned and left him. This time there was no calling her back.

CHAPTER 31

After establishing Dr. Thaddeus Welles's academic credentials, Harrison began his line of questioning.

"Dr. Welles, would you agree that a person's desires, motives, attitudes, and actions are influenced by their perception of God?"

Welles was an average-size man, with two-tone gray hair combed to the side. He had a square face, kindly eyes, and a complexion that flushed as he spoke. Not from nervousness, for he spoke with ease and authority. But the coloring didn't help his credibility with the jurors.

"I would say yours is an accurate statement," Welles replied.

Harrison looked to the back of the courtroom. His attention was divided. Tori was not in the gallery. She hadn't missed a day of the trial until now. He wondered if she was ill . . . or still angry with him.

"Dr. Welles," Harrison said, "since our perception of God is so vital, perhaps you can help us out here. Describe for us, if you will, the character of God."

"God's attributes?" Welles clarified. "Well, first of all, God is all-powerful; there is no task too big for Him. He never tires, gets frustrated, or discouraged. God is omnipresent; He is everywhere. He is not restricted to being in one location at a time. God is omniscient; He knows everything. He is the source of all knowledge, understanding, and wisdom. God is sovereign, which means there is no higher authority in the universe. God is holy; His character is perfect in every way."

Harrison checked the jurors for their reaction. Already three or four had stopped listening. Juror 2 yawned; Juror 7 was cleaning his fingernails.

Welles had fallen into lecture mode. "God is absolute truth; whatever He says is absolutely right. God is righteous; His standards are perfect, and His laws are a reflection of that standard. God is just, which means He will always treat us fairly. God is love, which means He is unconditionally committed to our well-being. God is merciful; He forgives us our sins when we sincerely confess them to Him."

Judge Walsh took out an orange and began to peel it. At the prosecutor's table, Whitney Stuart appeared to be asleep, his head propped up by his arm.

"God is faithful," Welles continued. "We can trust Him to always keep His promises. God never changes; He will never be stronger or weaker, His knowledge will not increase or diminish. God does not have mood swings. Our future is secure because of the unchangeable nature of God. And God is personal. We can have intimate fellowship with Him."

Harrison scanned the courtroom. Tori still had not arrived.

One of the jurors snored so loud he woke himself.

J. K. Jarves sat at the prosecutor's table, head bandaged, and surveyed the jury with a pleased look on his face.

Dr. Welles wasn't finished. "God's attributes form the basis upon which our relationship with Him is based. For example: Because God is all-powerful, He can help us with anything. Because He is ever-present, He is always with us. Because He knows everything, we can go to Him with all our questions and concerns. Because God is sovereign, we joyfully submit to His will. Because He is holy, we devote ourselves to Him in purity, worship, and service. Because He is the absolute truth, we believe what He says and live accordingly. Because God is righteous, we live by His standards. Because He is just, we can be assured He will always treat us fairly. Because He is love, we know He is unconditionally committed to our well-being. Because He is merciful, we take comfort in knowing our sins are forgiven. Because He is faithful, we know we can trust Him to keep His promises. Because He never changes, we know our future is secure. And because God is personal, we can have a direct intimate relationship with Him."

And so it went all morning. Harrison considered cutting Welles short, but this was the crux of his case. He felt that if he could get the jury to see the true nature of God, they would realize that His church could never be an evil predator, and that believers, like Tori, were not victims.

It was a failing effort. Several times Harrison cleared his throat or raised his voice to ask for a clarification, for no other reason than to wake sleeping jurors. No matter what he tried, it did no good.

The jurors' eyes were glazed over.

The judge peeled his orange.

Whitney slept.

And Jarves grinned.

Harrison was losing this case. Although he had done everything he could think of—including presenting numerous witnesses with life-changing testimonies—he was failing. The old North Dutch Church would be found criminally liable, portrayed as a predator of innocent souls. All churches would suffer from the resulting publicity. Christianity—no, God Himself—was depending on Harrison, just as George Bowen had, and he was letting Him down.

When court recessed for lunch, Harrison went to find Tori.

Patricia's house was a small white clapboard structure with a Southern-style porch. Harrison took the steps two at a time and knocked.

From the courthouse to here, he'd fought two internal demons. Concern over Tori's unexpected absence in the courtroom gnawed at him, while anxiety over what he'd come to ask her ate at his insides.

Footsteps could be heard on the other side of the door. It opened, swinging inward.

Polly greeted him with a comfortable smile, as though it was just an ordinary day. Didn't she know that, just a couple of miles away, the fate of Christianity was hanging in the balance?

She was holding her sleeping baby. "Harrison! Isn't there court today?"

"We've recessed for lunch."

Polly's face brightened with realization. "You haven't seen my new baby, have you?" She turned the infant his direction to give him a better look. "Would you like to hold her?"

Harrison was quick to beg off.

"Her name's Emily." Mother smiled down at the infant. Just from the way she gazed at her daughter, Harrison could tell Polly was a good mother.

"I'm looking for Tori," Harrison said. "Is she here?"

"She's busy," Polly replied, quickly, curtly. It was obvious the question was anticipated.

"It's important that I see her."

"Sorry. She's in the midst of a prayer meeting."

Harrison felt his ire rise. "It'll only take a second."

"Harrison, she's praying!"

Victoria Jarves praying. A miracle in itself. That wasn't lost on Harrison, but he was desperate. He stepped forward, forcing Polly to step backward. He closed the door behind him.

"Please tell her I'm here, and I need to speak with her. I'll wait." His tone was firm, insistent.

Polly's expression lost all its geniality. "If you insist," she said. "Wait here."

From his vantage point next to a flight of stairs, Harrison could see down the hallway and a portion of the parlor. Two women he didn't recognize were seated on straight-backed chairs. Their heads were bowed. Their eyes closed. Someone unseen could be heard praying.

A few moments later, Tori appeared. Alone.

"I need to speak with you," Harrison asked.

"Now isn't a good time," Tori said in a whisper. "Can it wait?"

Polly appeared behind her. A reinforcement.

"Let's step outside," Harrison said. He led Tori onto the porch and closed the front door.

"How's the trial going?" Tori asked. She didn't appear to be angry.

"You weren't in the courtroom. I looked for you."

"I had things to do."

"It's just that you've always been there. And after last night, I thought maybe . . ."

She smiled sweetly. "I'm not angry at you. I was last night, but I got over it. I didn't come to court today because there were some things we had to do today."

"*We* as in you and Polly and Patricia?" he asked, his voice rising.

"What's wrong, Harrison?"

Harrison looked away. His emotions were spirited horses on the verge of getting out of control. It took him a moment to rein them in.

"The trial isn't going well," he said. "I thought . . . well, it doesn't matter what I thought. The jurors are falling asleep, and I've run out of options."

"I'm sorry to hear that."

Harrison was hoping she'd take the hint and offer one more time to go on to the witness stand. She didn't. He saw the old Victoria standing in front of him. She was making this difficult for him on purpose. She was delighting in his pain, making him admit he was wrong, and forcing him to beg for her help. A side of him didn't want to give her that satisfaction. But desperation was going to win out over ego.

"I'll probably finish up with my witness this afternoon." He swallowed hard. The next words would be difficult to get out. "And I'd like . . . I'd like . . . well, remember when I said I'd only put you on the witness stand as a last resort? Well, I've reached that place. The last resort. I'd like you to come back to court with me. I'll put you on the witness stand."

To Harrison's relief Tori smiled. She cupped his cheek with her hand. It was warm. Tender.

"Oh, Harrison . . . ," she said. "No."

CHAPTER 32

Harrison walked back to the courthouse alone. Angrier than he'd ever been in his life. Spite. She was doing this to him out of spite. There was no other reason for it. Hadn't she hounded him to put her on the witness stand? She'd begged him! And now that he agreed, now that he needed her . . . what was she thinking? Didn't she realize what was at stake here? This trial was bigger than both of them.

It was over. Without her testimony he didn't have a chance of winning this case. She was his last hope.

Fresh images of George Bowen flashed in his mind. The expression on his face when the jury delivered their verdict. The shock. The crush of defeat. Even separated by time—which was supposed to heal all wounds—it hurt. And now it was going to happen again. Just like he'd let George Bowen down, he'd let Jeremiah Lanphier and the old North Dutch Church down. Who would come to the prayer meetings after Jarves succeeded in portraying them to the world as dens of predators?

Harrison's anger was making it difficult for him to think clearly. His mind was reeling.

He could force Tori to appear in court. He could have the judge slap her with a summons. The downside would be that his key witness would be a hostile witness. But that was better than no witness at all, wasn't it?

Why is she doing this to me?

Harrison's day got worse when he reached the courthouse. Whitney was waiting for him on the steps.

"Cloakroom," Harrison said, anticipating what was coming next.

"He wants to talk to you," Whitney affirmed.

An impatient J. K. Jarves pounced as Harrison entered the cloakroom. "Where have you been? It's almost time to start."

"What do you want?" Harrison asked.

"Where's Victoria? She wasn't in court today."

"She has other business to attend to."

Jarves looked at him suspiciously. "What are you up to?"

Harrison turned to leave.

Jarves grabbed his arm with a crushing mantis grip. "Don't put my daughter on that witness stand."

The irony of his request was not lost on Harrison. "I assure you I will not be putting your daughter on the witness stand," he replied.

Jarves searched Harrison's eyes. He must have believed Harrison was telling the truth, because he loosened his grip. "One more item of business," Jarves said. "I want her in court for my closing argument. If you can't get her here, I will."

Harrison believed him. First, that Jarves was capable of finding Tori. It would be foolish for Harrison to think he didn't know where Tori was staying. And second, that he was capable of getting her into court, even against her wishes.

Jarves pressed his point. "Well? Will she be here?"

"She'll be here. I'll see to it."

"Once this trial is over, and I've nailed your hide to the wall, I want your word you'll never see my daughter again."

"And why would I agree to that?"

Jarves was ready for him. "It's the price for your life. You never see her again, you live. The day you see her will be your last."

Leaving me forever impaled on the thorn of public opinion as the man whose failure led to the demise of Christianity in America.

"Do we understand each other?" Jarves threatened.

Harrison shook free. He grabbed the older attorney's arm, reversing their roles. "We're not finished. If you fail to get a conviction, you leave her alone. You let her live her life."

A murderous glare gave way to a grin and a laugh. "You have my word." Jarves turned to leave.

Harrison stopped him. "I'm not done. You fail to get a conviction, and you give your blessing to our marriage."

It was the first point Harrison scored since the beginning of the trial. Jarves never saw it coming. Whitney's mouth hung open, much like it did the night of the internship announcement when he learned he wasn't J. K. Jarves's choice.

Jarves laughed. "She'd never have you."

"Then you have nothing to lose."

"You have my word," an amused Jarves said. He left the cloakroom laughing.

Dr. Welles, professor at William and Mary, returned to the stand as the afternoon session began. J. K. Jarves approached him.

"Dr. Welles, I want to thank you for that inspiring lecture on the attributes of God this morning. Truly riveting."

Harrison stood to object.

A shake of Judge Walsh's head indicated it would do him no good.

Harrison sat back down.

"Dr. Welles," Jarves asked, "are you the final authority on God in America?"

"Heavens, no," Welles answered.

"Interesting choice of words, Doctor. By your response I assume there are other qualified academics in America who are equally capable of bringing testimony to this court."

"Yes, there are."

"Not only at William and Mary, but at Harvard and Yale and Princeton."

"Yes."

"Now correct me if I'm wrong, Dr. Welles, but among these men of academic standing, don't some of them believe that we have this wonderful God—the one you so eloquently described—and that He created the world, fashioning its natural laws according to His infinite wisdom; then, He set the world in motion to operate within the laws of His creation; after which He separated Himself from it, choosing not to interfere with His creation. Are there academics who believe what I've just described?"

"They're called deists."

"Ah, yes. Deists. Now these are learned men who hold academic positions at our colleges and universities. Is that correct, Dr. Welles?"

"Yes, they do."

"Thank you for your honesty, Dr. Welles. I know that wasn't easy for you. Another question. I'm fascinated by one of the characteristics of God you mentioned. I believe it was the last one. God is personal?"

"Yes. God is personal; therefore we can have a direct intimate relationship with Him."

Jarves chuckled. "Our deist friends would disagree with you, wouldn't they?"

"Yes, they would."

"But the way you described God, Dr. Welles, makes Him sound very much like a person. I'm getting this image in my mind of a gray-bearded man sitting in the clouds looking down on His creation."

Welles chuckled. "A common misconception. While God has characteristics of personhood—after all, we're created in His image—He is not flesh and blood. He is Spirit."

"You mean he's a ghost?"

Another chuckle. "An unfortunate translation. While the Bible refers to Him as the Holy Ghost, because of the spooky, graveyard images that come to mind, it's better to think of Him as Spirit."

Jarves appeared enlightened. "So the fact that my daughter has been talking to ghosts should be of no concern to me?"

"If she's praying to God the Holy Spirit, you have no need for concern. Our God is a benevolent God."

"A benevolent Spirit, you say? Unlike the evil spirits we read about in the Bible?"

"Demonic spirits," Dr. Welles clarified.

"Aren't those the ones that invade a person's life and drive him insane?"

"That's correct."

"But God is not like them. He's a benevolent Spirit. He would never invade a person's physical being."

Welles cocked his head. "Actually, at the point of salvation, the Holy Spirit enters our lives to guide and comfort us."

"You're saying my daughter has been invaded by a foreign intelligence? That it has control over her body?"

"If your daughter has been saved, the Spirit of Christ has entered her, but He doesn't control her speech and actions in the way a malevolent demon would."

"But she calls him Lord and Master."

"It's a willing submission to God as her Savior."

Jarves didn't appear to be satisfied. "Let me ask you this, Dr. Welles: do you speak to this Spirit?"

"In prayer, yes."

"And He speaks to you?"

"Not audibly, but yes."

"Not audibly? He's mute?" Jarves suppressed a grin.

"God is capable of communicating in any number of ways—at times audibly, but from what I've read, only on rare occasions."

"But He's capable of it?"

"Yes."

"So you speak to Him?"

"Yes."

"And my daughter speaks to Him. That makes two. Are there others?"

Dr. Welles appeared to tire of this line of questioning. "We speak to God when we pray for salvation. Whenever Christians pray, they're speaking to God."

"Can I speak to Him?"

"You can."

"And He'll hear me?"

"Yes."

"Will He respond?"

"He's capable of responding."

"Let me see if I understand correctly, Dr. Welles. God is a person who intervenes in this world even to the point of possessing human beings. This person has the ability to hear us when we speak to Him and to respond in ways we can understand. Is this correct?"

"Essentially, that's correct."

Jarves grinned. "It seems to me that we can settle this matter very easily, once and for all. For if what you say is true, Dr. Welles, it occurs to me that we've been talking to the wrong person. No offense, Doctor, but why talk to an expert on God when we can talk to God Himself?"

Jarves approached the bench. "Your Honor, I think we can get to the truth of this matter rather simply."

He paused. Longer than was necessary. Long enough to ensure that he had everyone's attention.

Harrison fidgeted. He recognized the show-stopping tactic. Typical Jarves. He had something up his sleeve. A worm of doom wriggled in Harrison's belly.

Jarves said, "Your Honor, I request that a bench subpoena be issued for the person of the Holy Spirit. I have some questions I want to ask Him."

Harrison was out of his chair. "Your Honor, I object!"

"On what grounds?" the judge asked.

Harrison was struck by Judge Walsh's lack of surprise at the request. He had known beforehand it was coming. Possibly even had a part in coming up with the tactic.

Harrison stammered. "The Holy Spirit is a spirit. How would the court serve Him?"

"According to expert testimony," Jarves argued—he stared at Harrison—"testimony you yourself provided in your defense—God is a person who can communicate. He is everywhere present, so He is here now. Therefore, if this court verbally issues a summons for Him to take the stand, by your own expert's testimony, can we not rest assured that God will be aware of the summons and, as a person of free will, choose for Himself whether He will or will not appear? How does that differ from any other witness?"

Harrison was caught flat footed. He needed to respond but without discrediting his own witness. "Your Honor—"

"Your Honor," Jarves interrupted, "it is my contention that the church has fabricated the existence of an invisible God with unlimited powers for the sole purpose of exploiting and profiting from weaker minds who would succumb to such nonsense. If they are so certain of what they teach—that God is indeed a person with the ability to communicate— why would they object to having the Holy Spirit testify on His behalf? I'll tell you why. Because there is no such thing as a Holy Spirit! The issuance of a subpoena will force them once and for all to produce this so-called God of theirs.

"According to their own testimony, this spirit has possessed my daughter. I contend the possession is against her will. My request strikes to the heart of the matter at hand. Had any other personage—say, a madman, or a stalker—taken control of her against her will, would not that person be sought and, if necessary, forced to appear in court to answer for himself? If such were the case, you would not question whether or not a subpoena is warranted. By the defense's own admission, the Holy Spirit is a person. I request—no, I *demand* you subpoena this person to appear in court."

Judge Edwin Walsh looked to Harrison for a response.

"Your Honor, this is ridiculous," Harrison cried. "We don't tell God what to do; He tells us what to do. The prosecution is attempting to turn this court of law into a sideshow worthy of P. T. Barnum. To demand the Almighty God submit Himself to a human court of law is not only ludicrous, it's blasphemous!"

Judge Walsh made a pretense of weighing Harrison's objection. Fingering his amber ring, he said, "I'll admit the request is unusual, but I'm going to grant it."

"Your Honor!" Harrison objected.

The judge continued. "You have only yourself to blame, Mr. Shaw. Once you introduced into the records that God is a person, you opened the door for Him to be called as a witness since His involvement lies at the heart of this trial."

"But Your Honor . . ."

Walsh looked at Jarves. "You're certain you want to do this?"

"If God is who the defense claims He is," Jarves replied, "I doubt it will prove to be a hardship on Him. He's local."

Judge Walsh nodded. "Very well. I hereby issue a bench subpoena to the person of the Holy Spirit to appear in this court first thing Monday morning."

The sound of his gavel made it official.

CHAPTER 33

꙳

It came as no surprise to Harrison that Jarves's theatrics made the newspapers.

GOD SUMMONED TO TESTIFY

It's not every day that a New York judge subpoenas God to testify in court. Yet that's precisely what happened Friday in Judge Edwin Walsh's courtroom during a trial that is now being dubbed State of New York v. The Holy Spirit.

The subpoena was requested by prosecuting attorney J. K. Jarves following the testimony of defense expert Dr. Thaddeus Welles, professor of theology at William and Mary College. Under oath the professor described God the Holy Spirit as a person with the ability to communicate. Jarves then requested that the Holy Spirit be called to court to testify regarding His role in the salvation of the prosecuting attorney's daughter. Over defense objections Judge Walsh issued the subpoena.

While at first glance this appears to be a showmanship ploy worthy of P. T. Barnum, Jarves insists the matter cuts to the heart of his case. "I intend to prove once and for all that church leaders have been duping the populace for centuries. They hide behind an invisible God, claim to speak for Him, and frighten people into doing their will with threats of eternal damnation. Well, I say, let God speak for Himself. That's not asking too much of God, is it? But come Monday morning, when God doesn't appear, I think everyone will see that the world in general, and Americans specifically, have been hoodwinked by the greatest fraud in the history of the world. And that fraud has a name: Christianity."

The sun was setting.

Harrison and Tori sat in rocking chairs on Patricia's porch. Harrison's rocker hadn't rocked for thirty minutes. They'd had a full day to mull over J. K. Jarves's courtroom antics.

"Patricia says nearly every available room in New York is rented out," Tori said. "People from Boston, Philadelphia, New Orleans, even from Europe are here. All of them want to see what's going to happen Monday."

Harrison was startled. "Europe? That's impossible!"

Tori shrugged. "I didn't say they sailed in overnight. They were already in America. The trial attracted them to New York, that's all. You have to hand it to Father. He got his big audience. He thrives on it."

"That's just what I want to hear," Harrison said with sarcasm.

He felt drained. Sitting here alone with Tori was the first quiet moment he'd had since Judge Walsh issued the subpoena, but it was far from peaceful. He'd tried to find moments of solitude to think by hiding out in the church basement. The church elders found him. Naturally, they were anxious as to what he planned to do. Only Harrison didn't know what he was going to do. Within minutes the basement was jammed with pastors, theologians, lawyers—now they offer to help him!—and well-meaning members of the church, all telling him what he ought to do.

The church elders were angry with him for letting the focus of the trial shift into a referendum on Christianity. They gave him a long list of scriptures to read Monday morning regarding the existence of God and the role of the Holy Spirit. Harrison tried to explain to them that as a lawyer he had to present an argument based on law and legal precedent. They weren't listening.

"What are you going to do?" Tori asked.

"I haven't decided." He turned to her. "Unless I can convince you to take the stand."

Tori reached over and touched his arm. "Don't ask me to do that, Harrison."

She was asking the impossible. He was at the end of his rope. "You have to testify! It's our only hope. Look, if it's because you're still angry with me, I've apologized a hundred times! Just tell me what to do, and I'll do it."

She smiled. It wasn't forced. And there was not even a hint of anger in her eyes. "You don't need my testimony to win this case."

Harrison bit back a retort. He hadn't thought about winning this case since the second or third day. The best he could hope for now would be a hung jury.

A plain-dressed woman approached the house. She was alone. She wore white gloves, a simple hat, and walked with her eyes lowered. She didn't notice anyone was on the porch until she set her foot on the steps. The presence of Harrison and Tori gave her a start.

"Emma!" Tori greeted her. "Are those new shoes? Everyone's inside. Tell them to start without me. I'll be in momentarily."

The woman smiled and disappeared through the door.

"You're abandoning me?" Harrison said.

"Prayer meeting."

"Another one?"

Tori smiled. "Are you implying there's such a thing as too much prayer, Harrison?"

He thought of his promise to Jarves. His time with Tori was growing short. "I was just hoping we could spend the evening together. Talk of things other than the trial."

"I'd like that." She stood. "But we'll have time for that after the trial. Polly read from the Bible this morning from a passage that spoke of seasons. This is the season for prayer, Harrison. Our time will come soon enough." She bent low and kissed him on the cheek.

"Your father wants you in court to hear his closing statement."

A shadow passed over Tori's face. "I may be busy then."

"He was most insistent. If you don't show up, he'll send someone to fetch you."

Tori looked at the horizon and sighed. "All right, tell him I'll be there. Now, if you'll excuse me."

Harrison caught her hand. "Do you really have to go?"

She glanced at their hands, clasped together, then at the door. "I really need to be in there."

"Can't they pray without you just one night?"

Tori lifted Harrison's hand to her lips and kissed it. "You taught me to trust in God, Harrison. He won't let us down."

The Sunday before the Holy Spirit's scheduled appearance in court was torture for Harrison. How often had he found solace in worship? Strength and resolve from a sermon? How often had he walked among friends, brothers and sisters in Christ, and come away refreshed?

But not this Sunday. This Sunday was no day of rest for him.

While he shook one or two encouraging hands, his reception was mostly silent, angry stares from a distance. As for the sermon, it was obviously inspired by the events of the trial. The pastor's thesis was: God will not be judged in human courts; mankind will be judged by God.

Tori wasn't available Sunday afternoon. She spent the afternoon praying with her women's group.

PROOF

Harrison escaped by walking the streets of the city. Needing a place where no one would recognize him, he wandered into Five Points. A part of him was hoping he'd run into a band of Fly Boys. At least with them he had a fighting chance.

Events of the past few days tumbled in his mind. Certainly there were things he could have done better. Things he'd do differently given the chance. But would they have made a difference in the outcome? The deck had been stacked against him at the outset with the selection of the judge and the selection of the jury. From the first day, Harrison had been knocked off balance, and he had yet to recover. Even the few successes he'd had during the trial paled now.

But all that aside, what hurt him the most was Tori's unwillingness to testify. Surely she understood what was at stake. Had Jarves gotten to her? In a way he hoped so, because if she hadn't succumbed to his intimidation, she was choosing her father over him. And that hurt. Deeply. It was a wound from which Harrison doubted he could ever recover.

CHAPTER 34

Monday morning dawned hot, promising to be the first scorcher of summer. To get to the courthouse, Harrison had to wade through a crowd that had already gathered on the steps. The instant he was recognized, he was caught in the undertow of a wave of reporters.

Questions were fired at him simultaneously from every direction. Harrison put his head down and bulldogged his way into the courthouse. They wanted to know what he was going to do, and he couldn't tell them.

He couldn't tell them because he didn't know.

The courtroom gallery was packed and overflowing. People lined the walls. They jammed the doorways ten deep, hoping to see something.

By the time Harrison arrived, the prosecution was already at their table and ready to proceed. Papers were laid out. The shrike under glass was strategically placed so that every time Harrison glanced up from his seat, he'd see a pair of murderous eyes staring at him.

At the defense table, Jeremiah Lanphier and Herbert Zasser were waiting for him. Zasser leaned toward him the moment he sat down. "Did you bring the selection of Scripture passages? Are you prepared to read them?"

Yes and no. Only before Harrison could answer, the court was called into session.

Judge Walsh took his seat and looked around. He didn't appear to be impressed with the crowd in his courtroom. "Let's get on with it."

He instructed the bailiff to summon the Holy Spirit to the witness stand.

The bailiff, a barrel-chested man with a large, drooping mustache, stepped forward. He began to issue the summons, then stopped. He turned to the judge. "Is Holy His first name, or is it a title?"

A wave of laughter swept through the gallery.

The judge banged them into silence. "Just get on with it," he told the bailiff.

In a clear voice, loud enough that it could be heard in the hall, the bailiff said, "The state of New York summons the Holy Spirit to the stand."

He waited, looking for someone to come forward like any other witness.

When no one came, he repeated himself. "The Holy Spirit."

In the gallery, necks craned at every movement.

"The court summons the Holy Spirit," the bailiff said a third time.

After a few moments, he looked to the judge for instructions.

Harrison was on his feet. "Your Honor. The Holy Spirit is as His name implies. He's a spirit. And while He may be invisible, believe me, He is here. Futhermore—"

The judge eyed the witness stand. "Is He there?"

"Your Honor, the Holy Spirit is everywhere at once," Harrison said.

"All right, Mr. Shaw, if you say so." To the bailiff: "Swear Him in."

The bailiff stared at the empty witness chair. The expression on his face got a laugh from the jury. Unlike when Harrison's other witnesses were on the stand, the jurors were awake, alert, and leaning forward to see what was going to happen next. Jurors 2 and 7 shared a common expression—a thin line for a mouth, curled up at the corner in amusement.

The bailiff spoke to the empty chair, challenging the invisible Spirit to tell the truth. He waited for a verbal response and got none. "Should I do it again?" he asked the judge.

The judge looked at Harrison. "He's your witness, Mr. Shaw. Did He agree to tell the truth?"

Harrison stood. "Your Honor, God *is* tr—"

Jarves was on his feet. "Your Honor, I object. The purpose of calling this witness is to give Him the chance to speak for Himself. If you allow the defense counsel to speak for His witness, it defeats the purpose of the subpoena."

"Sustained," the judge said.

Jarves continued, "If I may make a suggestion, Your Honor. If indeed the Holy Spirit is here, I suggest we proceed with the trial."

This appeared reasonable to the judge. "Your witness, Mr. Shaw."

Already on his feet, Harrison adjusted his suit coat. He looked at the witness stand, then over at the prosecutor's table. Jarves sat back, facing straight forward as though this was any other day in court. Whitney and the shrike, however, were looking at Harrison. They were both laughing at him.

"I have no questions for this witness, Your Honor." Harrison sat down.

Zasser leaned over Jeremiah and spoke in a loud whisper, "Read the Scripture passages! Read the Scripture passages!"

"Very well," the judge said. "Mr. Jarves, your witness."

J. K. Jarves pushed his chair back, buttoned his coat, and approached the witness stand.

"Mr. Spirit," he began.

In Patricia's parlor fifteen women, including the hostess, her sister Polly, and Tori, were bowed in prayer. One by one the women prayed, some with tears. When they completed the circle, they began again.

Tori glanced up at the mantel clock. The trial would have begun by now. She closed her eyes and silently prayed for Harrison.

"Mr. Spirit," Jarves said, addressing the empty witness chair, "You have been summoned here today to set the record straight. There are a lot people claiming to know You. Claiming to know what You think. Claiming to speak on Your behalf. Oddly enough, they are not always in accord. So, naturally, there is confusion. Your presence here today will help clarify a great many things. Tell me, Mr. Spirit, exactly what is Your role in this world?"

Jarves waited for an answer. When an answer was not forthcoming, he eyed Harrison, then the witness chair again.

"Don't be shy," Jarves said to the chair. "You can speak freely here."

He waited. After several seconds he stuck out his hand and waved it back and forth over the witness chair as though he were feeling for something.

The jurors and gallery laughed.

"Just checking," he said to the judge. To Harrison, "Are you sure your witness showed up?"

"Your Honor," Harrison complained.

But Jarves wasn't finished.

"If not in Your own defense, Mr. Spirit," he thundered, "speak to us for Harrison's sake."

The prosecutor ambled over to the defense table. He stood next to Harrison as he addressed the witness. "Here's a young man who has spoken well of You. Nobly defended You. He has stuck his professional neck out on Your behalf, insisting that You are personal and benevolent, that You care for those who worship You."

Jarves approached the witness stand. "Well, Mr. Spirit, if You care anything for this young man, now is the time to speak up and prove to the world that he is justified in putting his faith in You."

Harrison was on his feet. "I object, Your Honor! The prosecuting attorney is making a mockery of these proceedings."

"I'm not finished questioning this witness!" Jarves thundered.

"Objection overruled," said the judge. "You'll get your turn, Mr. Shaw."

Jarves continued. "Tell me, Mr. Spirit, exactly what is Your relationship to my daughter? Have You indeed possessed her? Are You controlling her now? If she were to ask You to leave, would You? Or are You possessing her against her will?"

"Your Honor . . . ," Harrison pleaded.

"Did You trick her into inviting You to possess her? Did she do it out of fear? Or did You seduce her? Exactly how free is my daughter's mind now that You've taken over her body? Is she able to think for herself, or is she under Your complete control?"

"Your Honor!" Harrison shouted, now furious.

"Mr. Jarves," the judge cautioned, though he clearly didn't know how far to let this performance go.

"One more question, Your Honor," Jarves said.

The judge nodded his assent.

"I'll make a deal with You, Mr. Spirit," Jarves said. "If You speak one word, one audible word so that this jury and this court can know without doubt that You exist, I'll drop this lawsuit here and now. I'll withdraw all charges. Not only that, I'll freely give my daughter into Your care and never bother You again."

"Objection, Your Honor," Harrison cried.

"I'll allow it," said the judge.

"Mr. Spirit, if You love my daughter, if You care for Harrison Shaw and the defendants, if You indeed are the Lord over all creation, speak one word so that everyone can know You exist! One word. That's all I'm asking. One word!"

Jarves waited for a response.

The jurors waited.

PROOF

The gallery hushed.

The judge cocked his head so that his good ear was pointed in the direction of the witness seat.

The room was silent.

"Just as I thought," Jarves said. "I'm done with this witness, Your Honor."

He returned to his seat.

CHAPTER 35

Summary arguments began that afternoon. Harrison sent a messenger to inform Tori.

J. K. Jarves surveyed the gallery for her. Once he saw her, he began. "Gentlemen of the jury, it's been a wild ride, hasn't it?"

He got the laugh he was looking for. Jarves spoke to the jurors like they were old friends, which of course, they never could be outside of the courtroom.

"We began this trial with my telling you this case was personal. That hasn't changed. The future of my family is at stake. You also heard one expert witness tell me that I had little or no hope of ever getting my daughter back the way she was, regardless of the outcome of this trial."

He paused, turning his back on the jury for a minute. His head hung as he appeared to struggle to maintain control over his emotions.

"You may wonder why you didn't hear from my daughter directly. I'll tell you. Partly, it's a matter of pain. Painful for her, painful for me. But it's also a matter of shame. I would not want you to see what she's become, how thoroughly she has been seduced by this insidious doctrine. I only wish you could have seen her before, as she once was. Eyes sparkling with intelligence. A beautiful lady with a fiery spirit. Not like she is now. Disobedient. Rebellious. The fire in her eyes is gone, gentlemen. It breaks a father's heart."

Again he turned his back and took a moment.

"But it isn't too late for your daughters, your sons. It isn't too late for thousands of innocent young men and women. It isn't too late for America. The fate of the nation is in your hands now. If America is to be saved, you're going to have to do it. You're going to have to speak out with a unified voice and say, 'Enough! We've been duped long enough. We've been deceived, hoodwinked, berated, beaten down, and taken advantage of long enough!'"

He pointed at the defense table.

"These men are stealing the minds of America! Enslaving them with ancient fears and superstitions. They look harmless enough, don't they? What gives them their power? The momentum of a lie. It is the larger conspiracy that empowers them. Fifteen hundred years of abuse has conditioned us to believe what they're telling us is true!

"You're intelligent men. During this trial you've heard Dr. Welles confirm the position of respected academicians who refute the idea that God involves Himself in human affairs; that while He is the Creator, He has chosen to distance Himself from His creation, content to let it run its course by natural law. Knowing that, you must ask yourselves, 'Who then are these people speaking for? They claim to speak for God. But God is not here! So who are they speaking for?' I'll tell you. They speak for themselves! Hiding behind a cloak of an absent Almighty God, they speak in His name to convince people to do things that profit them! And so doing, they are continuing to perpetrate the greatest fraud in the history of the world!

"You have heard testimony of how unscrupulous men of wealth and power have promoted to the masses the values of meekness and humility and turning the other cheek. For what reason? To control them. Did the leaders themselves believe these values?" Jarves scoffed. "Had they followed the teachings of the church and given all they had to the poor so they might lay up for themselves treasure in heaven, they would no longer have been the rich and powerful.

"Coming closer to our own time, you have heard how revivalists systematically prime the revival pump with predictions of impending doom as signs of God's disfavor. Then, when natural disaster strikes, such as storms and earthquakes and even the recent financial market fluctuation, the revivalists prey on the hurt and downtrodden, using a combination of promotion, drama, and charismatic preaching. Then, to bolster their own importance, they fabricate manifestations of God through fanciful exaggerations of events that are no more miraculous than the dawn of another day.

"You have also heard expert testimony about how such reckless manipulation of ordinary events can lead to self-violence and self-loathing by those who commit even the most minor of sins. The smallest indiscretions. For in their scheme, even the littlest white lie told to keep from hurting someone's feelings warrants a heavenly verdict of punishment for an eternity in the fires of hell. They claim to speak for a just God! Is this justice? Is society better off for their efforts, or is it worse off? You have heard how many cower in fear of eternal torment, and in doing so suffer mental anguish of such proportion that they either surrender their wills to the church leaders or live their lives in quiet desperation as though under a powerful curse. For some the only relief is to kill themselves.

"This is the torture the defendants have visited on my daughter. How many others will suffer her fate unless we stop them?"

During his summation, Jarves didn't mention the personal attack. However, at one point he touched his wound as though it was causing him pain. The act communicated his message clearly enough.

He continued, "The most compelling testimony, however, was the testimony that you did not hear. Let me ask you this: If your son was being maligned, accused of something that was untrue, and that son came to you and said, 'Father, would you speak a word on my behalf? A word from you, and the accusation will go away.' Which of you would turn your back on him? A single word! What kind of man would refuse to utter a single word if it would rescue his child from a malicious accusation?

"Gentlemen of the jury, it's not as though we asked God to do something He is incapable of doing; He's omnipotent, isn't He? It's not as though we asked Him a question He couldn't answer; He's omniscient, isn't He? It's not as though we made it difficult for Him, or inconvenient; He's omnipresent, isn't He? Are we to believe God didn't speak because, for some unknown reason, He's angry? He's all-loving, isn't He?

"A single word! A single word, gentlemen! We asked God to do something a two-year-old can do! Something a dying man can do with his last breath! Did He do it? I didn't hear anything. Did you?" He turned to the gallery. "Did you?" To the defense table. "Did you?"

Jarves walked to the front of the jury box, looking first into the eyes of Juror 2, then Juror 7, then scanning the rest of the jurors. "Gentlemen of the jury, what are we to conclude?"

He paused for several seconds.

In a soft voice, he said, "I'll tell you."

He paused again.

Then, with a voice that was clear, strong, ringing with authority, he said, "God did not answer, because He is not here!"

Leaning forward on the jurors' railing, in all earnestness, Jarves said, "Gentlemen of the jury, I'm asking you to do a courageous thing. I'm asking you to sound a clarion call that will be heard across the nation, to raise a voice that will be heard around the world! We have had enough of this Holy Spirit nonsense! We have had enough of men's claiming to speak for God! It's time to put an end to the deception! It's time to take the power and the wealth and the guilt out of the hands of those who would use them as clubs to bludgeon us into submission. It's time for us to silence the lips of those who continue to weave a story about a God who involves Himself in earthly affairs. It's time for us to live the truth, as the real God, the Creator, intended us to—as masters of creation, using our own resources, our own intellects, our own vision to create a nation, yea a world, that no longer cowers before petty men hiding behind a God-mask.

"Gentlemen of the jury, you have it in your power to set our nation on a courageous new path. Do not be afraid of the men sitting behind the defense table or the organization they represent. With one voice, strike a blow that will silence them forever and set men free. How? By doing what God would not do. All it will take is for you to utter a single word—guilty. Guilty! GUILTY!"

As Jarves delivered his summation, Harrison watched with interest. In particular, he kept his eyes on Jarves's key selections, Jurors 2 and 7.

Jarves had them.

Everything Harrison had heard about J. K. Jarves's reputation was true. The man knew how to win in court. Behind the scenes he was devious, immoral, and unethical—which would account for his impressive string of victories—but in court he was polished, eloquent, and brilliant.

J. K. Jarves was better in reality than Harrison was in his own imagination.

The result was evident and—for Harrison and the defendants—damning. The jurors were sitting up, alert, with their chests out, their chins thrust forward, eager to get into the deliberation room and do exactly what Jarves had asked them to do.

Harrison resisted turning toward the gallery. He was curious about Tori's reaction to her father's summation speech. Even now he fought the urge to turn around.

"Mr. Shaw?" Judge Walsh prodded. "If you have something to say, now would be a good time."

The courtroom tittered at the rebuke.

Harrison stood. Out of the corner of his eye, he could see a beaming Whitney congratulate his mentor as Jarves returned to the prosecutor's table.

Another movement caught his eye. A movement in the gallery. Tori was standing. Harrison watched as she slipped out of the back row, then made her way out of the courtroom. She disappeared through the throng congregating at the doorway. She left the courtroom without looking back.

"Mr. Shaw?" There was a note of exasperation in the judge's voice.

Why would she leave now? Why would she walk out just when he was about to make his summation?

"Mr. Shaw!"

"Yes, Your Honor," Harrison said.

He approached the jurors' box. Halfway there, he turned back.

He'd left his notes on the table.

The courtroom rustled with impatience.

"Sorry, Your Honor," Harrison said.

He approached the jurors' box again.

"Gentlemen of the jury . . ." His voice cracked. He cleared his throat and began again. "Gentlemen of the jury." He paused. Pointing to the defendants, he said, "You need not fear these men. Nor should you fear what they represent. The prosecution would have you believe that for eighteen hundred and fifty-eight years mankind has been living a lie. Think about that. Eighteen hundred and fifty-eight years. Forgive me, gentlemen of the jury, but I find it difficult to accept that mankind is so stupid, they'd be making the same mistake for eighteen hundred and fifty-eight years!"

He paused for laughter. There was none.

"Doubtless, you yourselves have been nurtured by truths that the prosecution contends are lies. Our country was founded on these truths. And I'm not just talking about 1776 and our founding fathers. Long before then, in the early 1630s, godly men and women fled the oppression of England to come to our shores that they might establish a city upon a hill, a reference to an American Jerusalem. In other words, they wanted to create a country based on godly, biblical principles, and they did."

Harrison delivered the lines as he'd practiced, talking to the jurors directly, without having to refer to his notes. He kept his gaze moving from juror to juror, until he reached Juror 2. Their eyes locked. The man raised a hand to his jaw as though in thought, flashing an amber ring. It disrupted Harrison's thoughts. He forgot what came next.

He glanced down at his notes and couldn't find his place.

1776 . . . founding fathers . . .

American Jerusalem . . .

Did he say that aloud?

Mr. Jarves . . . , the prosecutor, may have lost a daughter, that's true. But he lost her to truth and goodness and salvation. She has not disgraced her father, neither does she dishonor him. She merely disagrees with him. For she has found comfort in the Christian faith, as so many have. And her only wish is that someday her father might know the truth as she knows it."

He tried to look up from his notes but was afraid to. Having lost his place once, he didn't want to do it again. So he read.

"Do you really want to be known throughout history as the men who led America away from her spiritual roots? Do you really want to be known as the men who were responsible for plunging our nation into godless paganism? Surely not.

"The defendants are not monsters. Do they look power hungry to you? These men are not wealthy despots as Mr. Jarves would have you believe. No! These are good men. Men of the church. Men of faith. Will you condemn them for that?"

Harrison looked up.

He was done. His summation had seemed a lot longer when he practiced it, and a lot more persuasive. He felt like he needed to say more. He wanted to say more. But what?

Coming up with nothing new or inspiring, he repeated his last line.

"Will you condemn them for that?"

CHAPTER 36

The second-guessing began the minute the jurors left the courtroom to deliberate. Harrison wished he had it to do all over again. The opening argument, the witnesses, the summation, everything. He felt as though he didn't do half the things he'd learned in law school.

The faces of the jurors haunted him. As he stood there after his summation, he took one last look at them, polling their faces. They appeared bored, unimpressed, unmoved by his argument. Jarves had challenged them to be Americans, bold individualists who were unafraid to take a stand against a horrible injustice. What had he challenged them to do? Believe the Bible lessons they learned in church. To keep things just the way they are. To stick to the familiar.

He sighed. There was nothing he could do about it now.

Jeremiah Lanphier patted him on the back and said he'd done his best.

Zasser growled, "You didn't read the Scripture passages we gave you." He stalked out.

Outside the courthouse a crush of reporters was eager for his thoughts.

He told them, "It's in the hands of the jury now."

What else was there to say?

The crowd of church members who had gathered to pray for him looked like they were attending the funeral of Christianity.

Harrison had but a single thought on his mind. He wanted to see Tori.

"Tori isn't entertaining guests right now," Patricia informed him.

"Does she know the jury is deliberating?"

"She knows."

"If I could just see her for a few moments," Harrison said. "Would you tell her that for me?"

Patricia grimaced sympathetically. "I already did. Now is not a good time, Harrison. Perhaps later."

Harrison heard footsteps behind him. He turned.

A middle-aged woman, plump around the middle, started up the porch steps. On the second step, she faltered. Holding out a hand, she said, "Would you mind?"

Harrison helped her up the steps. She thanked him.

"They're in the parlor, Lydia," Patricia said to the woman, stepping aside to let the woman in the house.

Harrison watched as a woman entered where he'd been denied entrance.

Patricia closed the door.

With nowhere else to go, Harrison returned to the church basement. It was a mess. Books and papers were strewn everywhere. He hadn't cleaned it since the start of the trial.

The room was different now. Everything had changed since this morning. Harrison closed a book that was of no further use to him. He doubted it ever would be again. It was a book on law. All that remained was for him to appear one final time and witness the outcome. And thus would end his legal career.

He cleared his cot, tossing books and papers aside. He'd sort through them later. Right now he wanted to lie down, even though it was midafternoon.

He was tired.

Harrison must have drifted asleep, because a banging on his door wakened him.

"Jury's back!"

By the time he got up and opened the door, the messenger was gone.

Harrison checked his watch. He hadn't slept long. Just a couple of minutes. His heart sank. The jury had deliberated only an hour.

That couldn't be good.

Word of a verdict spread like a New York fire. By the time Harrison reached the courthouse, the throng was so dense, the deepest he could penetrate was three steps.

Two policemen appeared. "We're here to escort you," one of them said.

With two uniformed officers plowing a path for him, Harrison made his way into the courtroom. Jeremiah and Zasser were already seated at the table. The prosecution table was empty.

Zasser grabbed Harrison's sleeve. "It's only been an hour. Is that good?"

"It's hard to tell," Harrison replied.

"I was talking with an attorney," Zasser said, "a member of the church—he specializes in corporate law—and he said he thought there was still time to get the Scripture verses read so they're part of the transcript. All you have to do—"

A commotion announced the arrival of J. K. Jarves, who also had a police escort. A wide-eyed Whitney Stuart III followed on his heels.

With Zasser still holding on to one sleeve, Jarves grabbed Harrison's other arm. He leaned close to Harrison's ear. "After today I don't want to catch you anywhere near my daughter. Don't test me on this."

Judge Walsh entered the courtroom. He frowned at the empty jurors' chairs.

"Where are they?" he bellowed at the bailiff.

Without answering, the bailiff exited the courtroom.

The judge pounded his gavel. Three sharp raps. He spoke to the gallery. "Be advised you are in this courtroom at my discretion," he said loud enough to be heard above the din. "There will be no outbursts, and you will conduct yourselves with decorum. Do I make myself clear?"

Harrison craned his neck. There was no sign of Tori. He wasn't surprised, though he had mixed feelings about it. She was probably staying away for his sake. Not attending in a way lessened his shame when he lost the case.

When court adjourned, he'd go see her.

With Zasser still rambling on about the list of Scripture verses, Harrison sat back in his chair, oblivious to the elder, struck by the realization that when he saw Tori next, it would be for the last time.

Could the day get any blacker than this? The loss of this trial weighed heavily upon him, but it was nothing compared to the thought that after today he would never again set eyes on Victoria Jarves. It was a devastating realization. In how many ways had he loved this woman?

As a friend, when she was Mouser.

He'd been infatuated with Katie.

Attracted in an infuriating way to Victoria Jarves.

But he loved Tori.

The thought of losing her was overwhelming.

"What do you mean they're not ready?" Judge Walsh shouted.

The bailiff whispered something in the judge's ear.

"You told me they'd reached a verdict!" the judge shouted.

"They had!" the bailiff insisted.

"Get them in here!"

Once again the bailiff left the room.

Five minutes passed.

Ten.

Judge Walsh grew angrier by the minute. His jaw worked back and forth, as though he were chewing a cud. He ordered another bailiff to find the first bailiff.

Another five minutes passed.

Then both bailiffs reappeared. Without the jury. A note was handed to the judge.

Judge Walsh read it. "Of all the . . . this is the . . . get them in here!"

The bailiff leaned forward again to whisper.

Judge Walsh waved him off. "Say it aloud so counsel can hear you. I don't want to have to explain it to them later."

The bailiff glanced nervously at Jarves before answering. "They locked the door. They won't let us in. They won't come out."

"Then how did you get this note?" the judge asked.

"They slipped it under the door."

"This is preposterous!" the judge shouted. "Counsel. In my chambers." To the bailiff: "Bring the foreman to my chambers. No excuses!"

Harrison pushed his chair back.

"What's going on?" Lanphier asked.

"I don't know," Harrison replied.

"Take this with you," Zasser said, thrusting a paper at him. "It's the Scripture passages."

Harrison took the page. Stuffing it into his pocket, he followed Jarves out the jurors' door, down a hallway, and into the judge's chambers.

The room looked like he'd expect a judge's chambers to look. Shelves lined with books. A desk overflowing with papers. A hat rack in the corner where a spare robe hung.

Judge Walsh fell into his chair behind the desk. Jarves and Harrison stood in front of the desk.

"Do either of you know anything about this?" Walsh demanded, rubbing his hand across his forehead, as if he had a headache.

Jarves shook his head and spread his arms.

"No, Your Honor," Harrison said.

The three men held their places for several minutes, not looking at each other.

The door opened. The bailiff appeared.

"He won't come out," the court officer announced.

Judge Walsh rolled his eyes in exasperation. He pushed himself out of his chair. "What room are they in?" He stormed out of the room, leaving Jarves and Harrison alone in his chambers.

It was the first time they had been alone in a room since the day Harrison resigned and Jarves threw the bell jar with the shrike at him.

"Jury tampering, Harrison?" Jarves taunted. "The last gasp of a desperate man."

Harrison started to reply that he hadn't done anything wrong, then thought better of it. He didn't owe Jarves an explanation.

"If I find you've tampered with the jury, I'll come after you. You know that, don't you?" Jarves warned. "You may gain a new hearing, but the results will be the same. And then I'll see to it that you get put away for good, possibly in the same cell I put your friend George Bowen in."

The voice of a cursing man preceded Judge Edwin Walsh's entrance into the room. He fell into his chair, his unfocused eyes darting back and forth in thought. "You're certain neither of you knows anything about this?"

"No sir."

"No, Your Honor."

The judge shook his head in disgust. "They informed the bailiff they'd come to a verdict. Then, while we were getting the word out, they took to deliberating again."

"After they'd arrived at a verdict? Why?" Jarves asked.

The judge stared at him as though he didn't want to say, but he did anyway. "New evidence."

"New evidence?" Jarves cried. "What new evidence? From what source? Tampering! What else could it be?"

Jarves looked at Harrison. So did the judge.

Harrison threw up his hands. "I haven't had contact with the jury, Your Honor. On my honor."

Judge Walsh didn't appear to be convinced.

The judge ordered everyone to wait in the courtroom. Unable to get the jury to unlock the door or communicate their intentions, he ordered everyone to sit tight. Should the jury report they'd arrived at a verdict, he didn't want to give them the time to reconsider again while he rounded up counsel.

For three hours counsel and the defendants waited in the courtroom, staring at each other while the gallery milled around behind them. People came and went, but the gallery remained full. Finally, at the end of the day, with a few choice curses, the judge dismissed everyone.

The next morning Harrison expected to be summoned back to the courthouse during the morning hours. He wasn't.

He went to see Tori. Patricia told him she was unavailable, that she wouldn't be available until after the trial was concluded. She didn't know that once the trial was over, Harrison would never be able to see her again.

Harrison walked the streets and found himself at the courthouse for reasons he couldn't fathom. Newspaper reporters were camped out on the courthouse steps, sitting around swapping stories. The crowds weren't there, but there were pockets of people who didn't want to wander far in case there was a verdict. One group was on their knees praying. Harrison considered joining them but didn't think they'd want to pray with the man who lost the trial of the Holy Spirit.

On the third day, the trial was reconvened. The jury announced they were ready to come out. Once again Harrison was ushered into court under police escort. Everything unfolded just as it had the previous time the jury announced they'd come to a verdict.

Lanphier and Zasser were waiting for him at the defense table. Zasser handed him another copy of the Scripture passages, just in case Harrison had forgotten to bring his copy to court.

As before, Jarves's entrance created a loud commotion. His former mentor stopped long enough to whisper a reminder threat to Harrison. At the prosecutor's table, Whitney set out the shrike and aimed it at Harrison.

Harrison craned his neck to look for Tori. She wasn't in the gallery.

Then the pattern broke. Instead of the judge appearing, the bailiff summoned counsel. The judge wanted to see them in his chambers.

The edge of Judge Walsh's fury had dulled a bit since Harrison had seen him last, but he was still testy.

"Don't tell me they've changed their minds again," Jarves said.

Judge Walsh reclined in his chair, his fingers interlaced over his belly. "The bailiff has informed me they're ready to come out. I instructed him to bring the foreman to me. I wanted to see what was going on. The foreman refused. He sent me a note signed by all twelve jurors. It said they had arrived at a unanimous decision that they would reveal in the courtroom with all of them present. It further said there would be no negotiating their stance. That's where we stand."

"No negotiating their stance? What does that mean? Who do they think they are?" Jarves shouted. "So you're saying we have a renegade jury?"

"I'm not saying anything," the judge replied. "Merely telling you where we are. What's your pleasure, gentlemen?"

"Declare a mistrial," Jarves insisted.

"Premature," Harrison replied, arguing against a mistrial for no other reason than Jarves wanted one. "On what grounds? For contempt? Possibly. But not a mistrial. Let's find out what's going on, then make a decision."

Personally, Harrison was divided over his own advice. A mistrial would give him a second chance at the trial—assuming the defendants retained him as counsel—but the thought of living through these last few weeks again was not an attractive prospect. The best part about a mistrial meant he'd be able to see Tori again. A part of him hoped the judge would rule in favor of Jarves.

"I agree with Mr. Shaw," the judge said. "Let's see what they have to say."

Figures, Harrison thought. It was the first time Judge Walsh had sided with him, and it could possibly keep him from Tori and hasten his own demise.

The judge stood, signaling the end of the meeting. Counsel returned to the courtroom. A few minutes later, the judge entered the courtroom. Then, as before, they waited for the jury.

Two minutes passed.

Then three.

Judge Walsh grew angrier by the second. He barked at a bailiff to bring the jury into the courtroom even if he had to break down the door.

Just then the door opened and the jurors appeared. They filed into the courtroom.

To the man, they found their seats without making eye contact with anyone. Harrison had been taught that such behavior was often a sign the jury had reached a guilty verdict. In such cases, jurors tended to not want to look at the condemned party until the sentence was read.

Yet there was something else about them. Something different. Harrison couldn't put his finger on it.

Finally, everything was in order. The jurors were seated. The gallery hushed. Harrison took a deep breath and prepared himself for the expected verdict.

Judge Walsh said, "Mister Foreman, has the jury reached a verdict?"

Juror 2, who served as the foreman, stood. "We've reached a decision, Your Honor."

"A verdict," the judge corrected him.

The foreman winced and scratched his chin, which hadn't been shaved in three days.

Something caught Harrison's eye. Juror 2's hand. He no longer wore the amber ring.

"No, Your Honor," the foreman clarified. "We've reached a *decision*."

Judge Walsh scowled. "Explain yourself!"

"Well, sir," the foreman said, "I request that I be disqualified as a juror in this case."

Harrison looked at Jarves, who was scowling at his juror.

"In fact," said the foreman, "all of us request that we be disqualified as jurors in this case."

Two rows of jurors, without exception, nodded.

"We've signed this statement, Your Honor." The foreman offered a folded sheet of paper.

The judge ignored it. "What in blazes has been going on in that room?" he thundered. "You informed the bailiff you'd reached a verdict."

"Yes, Your Honor, we did."

"Well? Render it!"

The foreman looked nervously at the other jurors, then back at the judge. "We can't, Your Honor."

"Why can't you?"

"Well, Your Honor, we changed our minds . . . or, more correctly"— he looked at the other jurors—"had them changed, wouldn't you say?"

The other jurors nodded.

"Tampering! I knew it!" Jarves shouted. He swung around to glare at Harrison.

The judge shot a glance at Harrison, too, but directed his next remarks at the bailiff.

"I want a list of every person who went into that room."

The bailiff raised his hands helplessly. "I swear, Your Honor, no one but the jurors went into that room. No written correspondence came in or out of the room."

His response did not appease the judge. He thumped the bench with his forefinger for emphasis. "I want to see every piece of paper that was in that room. I want a transcript of every word. Do you understand me?"

The bailiff knew his career was on the line. His expression was a combination of fear and anger. "Yes, Your Honor."

"Your Honor, the bailiff did nothing wrong," the foreman said. "It wasn't his fault."

The judge leaned forward, shifting his anger to the foreman. "If it wasn't his fault, then whose fault is it? You said you reached a verdict. Who changed your mind?"

Harrison fidgeted under the weight of suspicion. Even though he knew he was innocent in this matter, he felt their expectation that his name would be the next word out of the foreman's mouth. He hadn't seen this one coming. It had all the earmarks of another Jarves tactic—surprise, misdirection, and then . . . *WHAM!* A fatal blow from nowhere. Harrison knew as sure as he was sitting there he wasn't going to leave this courtroom a free man.

The foreman wasn't quick to answer. He studied his fingers. "Well, Your Honor—"

"Answer the question!" Judge Walsh bellowed. "Who influenced you to change your minds?"

"The Spirit, sir," the foreman said softly.

"The spirit? What spirit? What are you babbling about?"

"The Holy Spirit, sir."

Harrison scanned the jurors' faces. That's what was different about them! These weren't the same faces he had studied throughout the trial. They'd changed. There was a sense of wonder to them. These were the expressions of men who had seen the loaves and fish multiplied on the hillside, who saw the blind given sight and fire fall from heaven.

Jeremiah Lanphier nudged Harrison. He saw it too. They were the same expressions he'd seen at prayer meetings—a mixture of awe and joy—the expressions of men who had been humbled in an encounter with the Almighty God.

"Before I throw you all in jail for contempt," the judge barked, "you had better tell me exactly what went on in that room."

The foreman—Juror 2, who had never so much as smiled during the trial—broke out in a grin, a grin so wide it almost looked comical on him. "Thomkins—Juror 9—was the first. We had just voted and thought we had a verdict. So I informed the bailiff. That was what? One? Two days ago? Then, all of a sudden like, Thomkins collapses to his knees. We all thought he'd been struck by apoplexy or something of the sort."

The other jurors nodded, smiling at their mistaken assumption.

The foreman continued. "He was holding his belly, rocking back and forth like he was in pain. We managed to get him into a chair. He was staring up at the ceiling, and he kept mumbling something that we couldn't make out at first. Then—I think it was Smythe, Juror 4—who first understood him. He was saying, 'not worthy, not worthy,' over and over and over."

Even now Thomkins mouthed the words as the foreman spoke them.

"We were just about to send for a doctor when it hit Stoddard."

"What hit him?" the judge shouted.

"That's what I'm trying to tell you, Your Honor. The Spirit of God."

The judge threw up his hands in disgust.

"It happened to us all," the foreman insisted, close to tears himself.

"Why didn't you send for a doctor?" the judge cried.

"It wasn't a doctor we needed."

The judge looked at Jarves, who sat at the prosecutor's table with eyes as brassy as the lion knocker on his front door. They were fixed on Juror 2.

"That explains what we've been doing all this time, Your Honor," the foreman explained.

"It explains nothing! Just what have you been doing for the last three days?"

The foreman smiled at the other jurors in a warm way, as if they were family. "We've been talking, sharing, crying, rejoicing. But mostly praying. We shared something extraordinary in that room, Your Honor. At first it was like a huge boulder had been placed on us—an incredible weight that we couldn't bear. But that's the strange thing. It wasn't a physical force, wouldn't you say?" He turned to the other jurors.

"It was and it wasn't," Thomkins tried to explain.

"It was something we felt inside," the foreman said. "A black feeling that buckled our hearts, leaving us feeling helpless, leaving us feeling hopeless."

"Unworthy," Thomkins said.

"Unworthy." The word echoed from mouth to mouth among the jurors.

"That's why we signed this paper, Your Honor," the foreman said, offering it to the judge a second time.

He handed it to the bailiff, who handed it to the judge. When the judge made no effort to take it, the bailiff laid it on the bench.

"Anyway," said the foreman, "we concluded that now that we had the Spirit, we couldn't reach an impartial verdict, Your Honor, because the prosecution is flat out wrong. We know that now, without a doubt."

"Amen," one of the jurors said.

"God does exist. And He is here. We know what his daughter felt, and it's not evil. And maybe God didn't say anything on the witness stand, but He spoke loud and clear to us in that room."

The jurors laughed.

"Yeah, He did," one of them said.

Having no other recourse, Judge Walsh declared a mistrial, citing jury tampering. He ordered an immediate investigation.

A storm of reporters engulfed Harrison the moment he stepped from the courtroom. He looked past them, scanning the crowd for Tori. A sea of faces stared back at him. None of them was the face he was looking for.

"Mr. Shaw! Can you explain what happened in the courtroom today? Did you have anything to do with it?"

"No, I had nothing to do with it," Harrison said. "As for an explanation, what's to explain? You heard the foreman. I can tell you this though: what happened in the deliberation room is happening in churches and offices and theaters all across the nation. It's called revival, gentlemen. A spontaneous movement of the Spirit of God."

"Do you seriously take their story at face value?" a reporter asked.

In reply, Harrison Shaw read from Herbert Zasser's page of Scripture passages.

When pressed for more, he said, "What happened in that room is not inconsistent with the character of God as revealed in the Bible. Why do you find it so hard to believe that the God of the Old and New Testaments can't reveal Himself in power today, just as He has in the past? He hasn't retired, gentlemen—"

"What do you think the investigation into jury tampering will reveal?"

"That the jurors experienced exactly what they say they experienced."

"Was there tampering?"

Harrison stiffened. "Look at the facts. The deliberation door was locked. A bailiff was posted outside the room at all times. No one was allowed in or out." He paused for effect, a lesson he'd learned from J. K. Jarves. "Of course, there was tampering. Someone got to those men."

"What do you think Judge Walsh should do?"

Harrison smiled. "Issue a warrant for the arrest of the Holy Spirit."

When the reporters began repeating themselves, Harrison broke away. He had but a single thought. He wanted to see Tori and tell her the news.

He didn't have to go far. She was waiting for him at the edge of the crowd. When she saw him, she did something Harrison never thought he'd see Victoria Jarves do. She flew into his arms.

"I heard! I heard! Isn't it wonderful?"

It was a moment Harrison Shaw would relive a million times in the course of his life. He never thought he'd see her again. Yet here she was, in his arms, squeezing him as hard as he was squeezing her, his face wet with tears pressed against her neck, her breath warm on his ear as she spoke. Their bodies pressed against each other, and it felt natural, like they were made for each other. At that instant, Harrison knew this was how God intended them to be all along.

She pulled away. In the back of his mind, he knew they'd have to part sometime. Otherwise, how would they walk home? But knowing and accepting were two different things. He didn't want to let her go. Not so soon. Maybe in a year or two, but not now.

Her face was wet with tears. Her eyes—those brown orbs that had so captivated him when she was Katie—were alive and happy and brimming with love. They were almost his undoing. It was all Harrison could do to keep from crushing her against him again. But if he did, he knew he'd never let go.

Tori held him at arm's length. "How many?"

Her question didn't make sense. "How many what?"

"The men. The jurors."

"There were twelve of them."

But she knew a jury was composed of twelve men. What was she getting at?

"All twelve?" she shouted, covering her mouth with her hands.

A short distance away, Harrison recognized one of the women he'd seen going into Patricia's house. He watched as she ran up the courthouse steps and into the arms of a man.

Juror 7.

"You did this!" Harrison cried.

Through her tears Tori nodded. "The wives and God did this."

Harrison had told the reporters he had nothing to do with the outcome of the trial, but until this moment, he didn't know how true his statement was. From the start, he'd thought the outcome rested on him. Tori knew better. She knew they couldn't beat Jarves at his own game. She also knew they didn't have to.

Harrison felt the fool. All this time he was trying to defend God. The very idea was laughable. *God is perfectly capable of defending Himself.*

"The wives of the jurors," he said, shaking his head with awe. "You brought them together to pray for their husbands."

"Just like Polly and Patricia prayed for their husbands," Tori said.

"That's what you've been doing all this time. That's why you refused to testify."

Tori smiled. "When we realized that the battle was spiritual . . ."

"You fought it with spiritual weapons," Harrison finished.

"Mr. Shaw. A word with you."

A familiar voice came from behind Harrison. He knew he'd have to face that voice sometime. Did it have to be now? He turned to face it.

J. K. Jarves strode down the courthouse steps. He was alone.

"Victoria." Jarves greeted his daughter coolly. He evidently saw her tears and, from the expression on his face, blamed Harrison for them.

Tori intercepted her father. She embraced him. Jarves didn't seem to know what to do with such a public display of affection. He accepted her embrace awkwardly, then turned his attention to business.

"Mr. Shaw, I don't know how you got to them," Jarves said, "but believe me, when I find out how you did it—and I will find out—charges will be brought against you. I suggest you get your affairs in order, for you will soon join Bowen in prison. I promise you that."

Harrison wanted to tell Jarves he wasn't responsible for what had happened in court—that his daughter deserved the credit. But Jarves wouldn't understand, so Harrison said, "I'm confident the investigation will clear me of any wrongdoing." Then he added, "There are forces at work here more powerful than you know, Mr. Jarves."

Jarves took a long look at him. "My solace in this is that despite all your self-righteous posturing, you had to resort to my own tactics in order to save your own skin."

"I didn't tamper with the jury," Harrison said firmly.

"That's twice you've beat me at my own game, Mr. Shaw. It won't happen again."

EPILOGUE

Reporter Nellie Bly held the pink fan.

So involved was Harrison in telling his wife's story that the elderly judge had forgotten that his morning routine had been disrupted. Newspaper articles covering the events of the revival of 1857–58 were scattered atop his desk.

"As it turns out," Judge Harrison Shaw said, "Judge Walsh did us a favor by declaring a mistrial and ordering an investigation."

"He had little choice," Miss Bly said.

Harrison shook a lecturing finger at her. "And let that be a lesson to you, Miss Bly. Let man do his worst. In the end, God will use the actions of wicked men against them to bring glory to Himself."

"Did Judge Walsh issue an arrest warrant for the Holy Spirit?"

Harrison laughed. "He should have. There was enough evidence to do so. During the investigation the bailiffs proved to be men with exemplary service records. They swore no one but they had contact with the jury. As you might expect, the testimony of the jurors made all the newspapers. Tori wrote several of the articles herself.

"The investigation concluded that the jury had indeed been influenced. But by whom? All evidence pointed to the Holy Spirit. By declaring a mistrial, Judge Walsh inadvertently established in a court of law that the Holy Spirit is a person who involves Himself in human affairs."

"Was there ever another trial?" Miss Bly asked.

"No." Harrison sighed. "Jarves had other worries. A few months after the trial, a coalition of three men launched an assault against him with the intent of destroying him. He was so busy protecting his business, his reputation, and his interests, he had little time to worry about me."

"A coalition of three. Who?"

"Former interns."

"Was Whitney Stuart III one of them?"

"He was the driving force."

"Did they succeed?"

Harrison nodded. "The court battles went back and forth for a couple of years. In the end, Jarves was debarred and stripped of everything he owned. He died about a year after that."

"Why? Why would they do such a thing? He was their mentor."

"That's what predators do, Miss Bly."

"So, in a way, he trained his own assassins."

"The nature of evil, Miss Bly. The nature of evil."

Nellie Bly handed the pink fan back to the judge. She reviewed the notes on her pad. "Obviously you and Victoria married. And you have a son."

Harrison smiled. "An attorney in Washington. He specializes in constitutional law."

She pointed to the top of his roll-top desk.

"Is that a picture of your wife?"

Judge Shaw reached for the photo and handed it to her. "She gave me this after the trial. It was taken by Patricia's husband."

"The man who took the photograph of her dressed as Mouser?"

"The same."

Miss Bly studied the image of Victoria Jarves. She looked up. "Do you have the other picture?"

"Oh, it's around here somewhere," Harrison said, waving a hand over the desk. "But I'm not going to show it to you."

Nellie Bly had been gone for more than a half hour.

Harrison Shaw sat alone at his desk, still holding the picture of his wife. The pink fan lay on his lap.

He slid the photo out of its frame. There was another photograph beneath it, also of Tori. She was dressed as Mouser.

Harrison smiled at it through teary eyes.

In 1887 America was abuzz over a daring piece of investigative journalism published in the *New York World*. Nellie Bly, female reporter, had written a scathing firsthand account of the atrocities visited upon patients of the asylum on Blackwell's Island. To get the story, she infiltrated the institution disguised as a patient suffering from insanity.

That same edition of the newspaper printed the obituary of Judge Harrison Quincy Shaw. Miss Bly smiled as she read it, wondering what disguise Tori used to greet Harrison upon his arrival in heaven.

AUTHORS' NOTES

The trial described in this account is fictional, as are the major characters—Harrison Shaw, Victoria Jarves, and her father, J. K. Jarves. George Bowen, the Newsboys' Lodge, and its residents are also fictitious. However, each of these, including the outcome of the trial, are reflections of the wondrous historical events that occurred during the revival of 1857–58.

The account of the revival, including the Fulton Street prayer meeting, the newspaper headlines, and the revival events investigated by the characters of the story, are based on actual accounts.

Jeremiah Lanphier and the old North Dutch Church are historical. Five Points, likewise, is historical. Its depiction in this novel has been drawn from accounts of those who walked the streets and toured the buildings.

Nellie Bly (1867–1922) was a groundbreaking female newspaper reporter who feigned insanity to get into the asylum on Blackwell's Island. Her exposé brought about needed reforms. She became a celebrity by beating Phileas Fogg's time circling the globe. Fogg's account was the inspiration for Jules Verne's *Around the World in Eighty Days*. Miss Bly's time: 72 days, 6 hours, 11 minutes, and 14 seconds.

For more information about The Great Awakenings and this series, please go online to: www.thegreatawakenings.com.

READ THE SNEAK PREVIEW

OF THE EXCITING SECOND BOOK

IN THE

GREAT AWAKENINGS SERIES

FIRE

(1740–41)

BY

BILL BRIGHT & JACK CAVANAUGH

CHAPTER 1

"This is a mistake."

From atop Fiedler's Knob, Josiah Rush surveyed his hometown for the first time in seven years. The granite perch afforded him a sweeping view of the coastal town of Havenhill.

In the harbor below, a pair of merchant ships cozied up to each other. The smaller craft appeared bereft of activity, its masts and yardarms as bare as trees in midwinter. Next to it, the larger ship, a snow, good for coastal and short-sea trade, had apparently set anchor a short time ago. Featureless sailors scurried about the rigging, fearlessly hauling in huge canvas sheets. A rowboat waddled its way toward the ship to inspect the recent arrival.

Josiah, throat parched and bone weary, hitched up the worn, leather haversack slung over his shoulder and knocked the mud from his shoes. He stank of five days' journey.

From here the postal road made a gradual descent into the town. Noticeably absent were any cherubim and a flaming sword barring him from reentering his personal Eden.

"Would that I were so fortunate," Josiah murmured to himself. "Adam had a mere armed angel with which to contend. I have Eunice Parkhurst."

A familiar wind, moist, tangy, and smelling of spring, leaped the granite ledge. With it came memories of happier days—days of swimming and making sailboats, of flying kites and shooting marbles and exploring creeks.

Josiah winced, stung by nostalgia. He'd anticipated having these feelings, but he'd underestimated their strength. Tears of regret blurred his vision as his gaze jumped from landmark to landmark—First Church, the meetinghouse with its bell tower; the graveyard on the opposite side of the road; the village green; the schoolhouse; the gristmill; Bailey's Tavern.

Nabby's house.

Josiah's heart seized at the sight of the two-story yellow structure. His eyes felt the pangs of a seven-year hunger for just a glimpse of her as they searched the residence for movement, a door opening, the brush of a curtain.

If only his first glimpse of her could be from a distance . . . a trial run for his emotions. Maybe then he could keep himself from gawking or mumbling incoherently and generally making a fool of himself when he saw her face-to-face.

But the curtains of the yellow house were still. The doors remained shut. No movement except for two chickens pecking at the muddy ground between the house and the barn.

He would have no morsel of satisfaction today.

With a heavy sigh, Josiah lifted his eyes again to the wharf, the section of town most changed since he had seen it last. The new warehouses were twice the size of the old ones, a tribute to Philip's leadership. All that remained of the original structures was a portion of one wall, jagged, its bricks charred black with soot.

Why would they leave that portion of wall standing? A memorial to the three who died?

Josiah closed his eyes as the screams from that night echoed in his memory. Little girl screams . . .

Kathleen Usher—four years old, round brown eyes, always barefoot, the edges of her dress dirty, clutching her straw doll. She was never without that straw doll. Molly, wasn't it?

Mary Usher, Kathleen's older sister by a year. Her face so covered with freckles that some of them merged into oddly shaped brown spots. The thing Josiah remembered most about Mary was that she got scolded every Sunday because she couldn't sit still during the sermon.

The third voice of the screaming trio of that horrible night belonged to an adult male, Rev. Parkhurst. He had been the spiritual leader of Havenhill, Josiah's mentor, and the father of Nabby, the only girl Josiah had ever loved.

The townspeople had found the three bodies huddled together. Rev. Parkhurst's arms had been wrapped around the Usher girls, attempting to shield them from the fire with his own body.

A fire Josiah had started . . .

All this pain—three lives lost; his own life ruined; and a town nearly destroyed—because of one senseless, drunken, muddleheaded night! The crazy part about the entire incident was that Josiah had never been drunk before that night, nor had he taken a drink since.

One night. One lousy night.

But lousy nights, no matter how bad, could not be undone. And Josiah could no more change the events of that night than he could take back a misspoken word. That night was history. The town's. His. They would forever be linked by tragedy.

What made him think he could ever convince the town to forgive him?

"This is a mistake," Josiah said again.

He stepped away from the ridge. The postal road offered him a choice. One way descended into Havenhill; the other way led back to Boston where he wouldn't be reminded every day of his monumental sin.

"Having second thoughts?"

The voice startled him. Josiah swung around to see a man sitting tall on a horse.

"Philip! Back so soon from England?"

"The return winds were favorable."

For only the second time in seven years, Josiah gazed at his oldest and dearest friend. During their encounter in Boston a month ago,

Josiah had found it difficult to believe this was the same Philip he'd grown up with. Even now it was hard to catch glimpses of the old Philip behind all the finery and polish.

This Philip appeared sophisticated, a gentleman sitting straight-backed on an exquisite horse. The last time Josiah had seen Philip on a horse, Philip's legs had flailed uncontrollably as he tried to stay atop Deacon Cranch's old field nag that had bolted into the cornfield. Josiah had nearly split his gut laughing, until Deacon Cranch got home and saw the path that had been plowed through his cornfield.

Could the horseman in front of him—with his tailored green coat, white silk shirt and stockings, and impressive wig be this same Philip? That wig. From this distance, Josiah couldn't be certain, but Philip's wig—pulled back and tied with a black ribbon—appeared to be made of human hair. Josiah had never known anyone wealthy enough to own a wig made of anything other than horsehair or yak hair.

"You look like you're having second thoughts," Philip said again.

"It's that obvious?"

Philip dismounted. He'd changed, and it was more than just the clothes. His demeanor, the way he carried himself, was different. Deliberate. Self-assured. Gone was the youthful slouch and impish smirk.

In the old days, they were inseparable. Philip, the prankster; Josiah, the philosopher; and Johnny Mott, the muscle. Oh, the pranks they pulled! And the unforgettable summer days of roughhousing, swimming, lying on the bank next to the water without a care in the world.

"Actually, your indecision is impressive," Philip said. "A sign of maturity. Only a fool would do what you're doing without reservations."

So solemn. So businesslike. As though an unfamiliar adult spirit had taken over the body of his friend.

"You were quite honest about the situation when you approached me in Boston," Josiah replied, matching Philip's tone. "I know it won't be easy, but it's something I want to do."

"Excellent!" Philip cried, allowing himself a smile.

"I want to thank you for standing up for me," Josiah said. "I know the only reason I'm being given this chance is because of you."

Philip's smile widened into one Josiah recognized. A shudder of joy passed through him at the sight of his old friend.

Philip leaned over and said quietly, "'A friend loveth at all times, and a brother is born for adversity.' Isn't that what the Good Book says? Besides, I think everyone deserves a second chance."

"That's all I'm asking."

Philip dismounted. Leading his horse, he inclined his head toward town. "Then let's greet your parishioners, Rev. Rush."

As they walked the postal road into Havenhill, Josiah brushed his nose repeatedly.

"Something wrong?" Philip asked.

Conscious now of what he was doing, Josiah lowered his hands. "It's nothing. Just something I picked up in Boston."

The tickling sensation grew worse. It was all Josiah could do to keep his hands away from his nose. If the pattern held, he knew what was coming next, and it wasn't a sneeze.

On cue, a wave of pleasure swept over him with nausea close on its heels.

Philip stopped and cocked his head in concern. "Are you sure you're all right?"

"It'll pass. I'm fine. Really."

Two years ago, when Josiah had first begun exhibiting these symptoms, he'd mistaken them for signs of a physical ailment. He knew better now. These physical manifestations weren't physical in nature at all. They were spiritual. He also knew what they indicated, and it wasn't good. It wasn't good at all.

As they reached the edge of town, the pain in Josiah's gut doubled him over. It was a sign of what awaited him, not unlike Dante's warning at the gates of hell: "Abandon all hope, ye who enter here."

ABOUT THE AUTHORS

Bill Bright passed away in 2003, but his enduring legacy continues. He was heavily involved in the development of this series with his team from Bright Media and Jack Cavanaugh.

Known worldwide for his love of Jesus Christ and dedication to sharing the message of God's grace in everything he did, Bill Bright founded Campus Crusade for Christ International. From a small beginning in 1951, the organization he began had, in 2002, more than 25,000 full-time staff and over 553,000 trained volunteer staff in 196 countries in areas representing 99.6 percent of the world's population. What began as a campus ministry now covers almost every segment of society, with more than seventy special ministries and projects that reach out to students, inner cities, governments, prisons, families, the military, executives, musicians, athletes, and many others.

Each ministry is designed to help fulfill the Great Commission, Christ's command to carry the gospel to the entire world. The film *Jesus,* which Bright conceived and funded through Campus Crusade for Christ, is the most widely viewed film ever produced. It has been translated into more than 730 languages and viewed by more than 4.5 billion people in 234 countries, with 300 additional languages currently being translated. More than 148 million people have indicated making salvation decisions for Christ after viewing it live. Additional tens of millions are believed to have made similar decisions through television and radio versions of the *Jesus* film.

Dr. Bright held six honorary doctorate degrees: a Doctor of Laws from the Jeonbug National University of Korea, a Doctor of Divinity from John Brown University, a Doctor of Letters from Houghton University, a Doctor of Divinity from the Los Angeles Bible College and Seminary, a Doctor of Divinity from Montreat-Anderson College, and a Doctor of Laws from Pepperdine University. In 1971 he was named outstanding alumnus of his alma mater, Northeastern State University. He was listed in Who's Who in Religion and Who's Who in Community Service (England) and received numerous other recognitions. In 1973 Dr. Bright received a special award from Religious Heritage of America for his work with youth, and in 1982 received the Golden Angel Award as International Churchman of the Year.

Together with his wife, Vonette, he received the Jubilate Christian Achievement Award, 1982–1983, for outstanding leadership and dedication in furthering the gospel through the work of Campus Crusade and the Great Commission Prayer Crusade. In addition to having many other responsibilities, Bright served as chairman of the Year of the Bible Foundation, and he also chaired the National Committee for the National Year of the Bible in 1983, with President Ronald Reagan serving as honorary chairman. When Bright was named the 1996 recipient of the one-million-dollar Templeton Prize for Progress in Religion, he dedicated all of the proceeds of the award toward training Christians internationally in the spiritual benefits of fasting and prayer, and for the fulfillment of the Great Commission. Bright was also inducted into the Oklahoma Hall of Fame in November 1996.

In the last two years of his life, Bright received the first Lifetime Achievement Award from his alma mater, Northeastern State University. He was also a corecipient, with his wife, of the Lifetime Inspiration

Award from Religious Heritage of America Foundation. In addition, he received the Lifetime Achievement Award from both the National Association of Evangelicals and the Evangelical Christian Publishers Association, which also bestowed on him the Chairman's Award. He was inducted into the National Religious Broadcasters Hall of Fame in 2002. Dr. Bright authored more than one hundred books and booklets, as well as thousands of articles and pamphlets that have been distributed by the millions in most major languages.

Bill Bright celebrated being married to Vonette Zachary Bright for fifty-four years. They have two married sons, Zac and Brad, who are both actively involved in ministry today, and four grandchildren.

 **Jack Cavanaugh** is an award-winning, full-time author who has published sixteen books to date, mostly historical fiction. His eight-volume American Family Portrait series spans the history of our nation from the arrival of the Puritans to the Vietnam War. He has also written novels about South Africa, the English versions of the Bible, and German Christians who resisted Hitler. He has published with Victor/Chariot-Victor, Moody, Zondervan, Bethany House, and Fleming H. Revell. His books have been translated into six languages.

The Puritans was a Gold Medallion finalist in 1995. It received the San Diego Book Award for Best Historical in 1994, and the Best Book of the Year Award in 1995 by the San Diego Christian Writers' Guild.

The Patriots won the San Diego Christian Writers' Guild Best Fiction award in 1996.

Glimpses of Truth was a Christy Award finalist in International Fiction in 2000.

While Mortals Sleep won the Christy Award for International Fiction in 2002; the Gold Medal in *ForeWord* magazine's Book of the

Year contest in 2001; and the Excellence in Media's Silver Angel Award in 2002.

His Watchful Eye was a Christy Award winner in International Fiction in 2003.

Beyond the Sacred Page was a Christy Award finalist in Historical Fiction in 2004.

Jack has been writing full-time since 1993. A student of the novel for nearly a quarter of a century, he takes his craft seriously, continuing to study and teach at Christian writers' conferences. He is the former pastor of three Southern Baptist churches in San Diego county. He draws upon his theological background for the spiritual elements of his books. Jack has three grown children. He and his wife live in Southern California.

Enjoyment Guarantee

If you are not totally satisfied with this book, simply return it to us along with your receipt, a statement of what you didn't like about the book, and your name and address within 60 days of purchase to Howard Publishing, 3117 North 7th Street, West Monroe, LA 71291-2227, and we will gladly reimburse you for the cost of the book.